I0831146

A mere step to his left awaited a certain meticulously polished lever. Directly behind this revered handle a brass plate, also agleam from the habitual attributes of Brasso and elbow grease, told one who might care to read the poignant red-lettered notice: **Warning! Do not activate this lever!**

If the main engines' lubrication tank levels became too low, a limit switch would trigger off loud bells and flashing red lights to inform the engineer on watch that irrefutable disaster would visit his engineroom unless he corrected those levels promptly. If one was too slow to react, a safety mechanism instantly closed the main steam stop valves thus immobilizing the engines. It was hoped by the ship's designers that such a desperate action would prevent damage to critical turbine and gear transmission bearings.

This then was the lever Charlie was totally focussed on. With a savage shove he threw it over and all hell broke loose!

Also by Francis Kerr Young

A Novel
Hang on a Second!

Children's Stories
The Paperweight
Wing-Ding!

Poetry
The Legend of the Mary Celeste and Other Poems

Short Stories
Round About Christmas and Other Roundabout Stories

TSTS *Queen of Dalriada*

CRUISE SHIP

FRANCIS KERR YOUNG

Cruise Ship

ISBN 978-0-9813447-0-6

Jacket design by author

Pict Line Badge on jacket by:
S.M. Bass & Co Manchester Ltd
Manchester, England

Contents

With the exception of the historical figures of the Rt. Hon. Harold MacMillan, former Prime Minister of Britain, his wife Lady Dorothy, all other characters in this novel are fictitious and any names that may seem to relate to real persons are purely coincidental

To my dear niece,
Jacqueline
who sailed in my wake
And
In loving memory
of her parents,
my beloved sister, Isabelle,
and her husband, Archie

Piet Line

FOREWORD

Two years after WWII ended and most of the troops had sailed home, the surviving great passenger liners finally got their interiors refurbished before returning to normal service. Europe saw much rebuilding during the next decade but many sought a new life in another country, usually in the New World or in Antipodes: a lucrative time for the merchant marine. With the advent of the Sizzling Sixties the business of transporting humanity by sea had deteriorated alarmingly as travelling by air became vogue. One could now cross the Atlantic much cheaper and in less than eight hours.

Up until this time cruising to exotic ports was expensive and only the affluent could afford it. In Britain holiday camps had become popular because the working man could take his family away for a week or two on the cheap or on Higher Purchase, the forerunner of those little plastic cards. To combat this state of affairs some shipping companies considered: why not take the holiday camp business to sea - short sea cruises at economical prices?

The Scottish shipping firm, Pict Line, ushered in this innovative idea with parsimonious endeavour. With little modification their ancient Atlantic passenger liner, RMS *Queen of Dalriada*, was designated to sail on three short cruises during the winter festive season out of the Port of New York to The Bahamas. In spite of the lack of proper air conditioning, outdoor swimming pools and a cruise director to manage the acutely limited entertainment on board, the enterprise was declared a success. So much so that the liner was to embark on a second cruise out of Southampton to Lisbon, Portugal, Las Palmas on Gran Canaria and Funchal in the Madeira Islands.

The voyage goes well, if one can discount a bomb threat and a hit man stalking his victim, until the vessel departs from Funchal when an entity from Earth's distant past imbues a young Scottish engineer's mind.

The consciousness of this Sasquatch is displeased by the way Man has mismanaged our world. But our globe's environment in January 1962 is too cold for the creature to set things to right - both with nature and the human race. Sixty years must pass before it will rise like a phoenix out of Saline Bay in the Bailiwick of Guernsey when a former engineroom rating recalls certain happenings on that ill-fated voyage.

Public room layouts and descriptions in this novel are drawn from personal recollections during the period 1963-64 when the author served as an engineer officer on air conditioning, steering gear and general hotel service aboard the RMS *Queen Mary*.

The British class system was still very much apparent during that period of time, especially among the Cunarders. An insight to life aboard ship for the lowly engineroom ratings is revealed as the story unfolds. These men lived in a Spartan environment: badly cooked food, fresh fruit once a week and poor facilities for washing and laundry. Off watch hours were filled by reading, games of cribbage or euchre, or a pint from the crew bar on the Pig Deck. These men came from all walks of life. Many a judge offered minor criminal offenders a choice between prison and the sea. Wayward youths usually embraced a maritime adventure in lieu of Borstal. Avoiding National Service (draft) also helped to swell the Merchant Navy ranks.

A life on the ocean wave built character and what kind of characters those folk developed into had to be witnessed to be believed. Many of their escapades were unusually funny but more likely to be sad. Homosexuality, mainly among the stewards and catering staff was blatantly rife and was still considered a criminal offence.

Francis Kerr Young
Hamilton, Ontario 2009

Pict Line

Pict Line

CHAPTER ONE

Guernsey, Channel Islands

Sunday, January 21st, 2022

The skimmer slowed and hovered about a metre above the sea floor like an orange manta ray. The metal detector sensed a small object buried in the grey ooze directly below him. Eric Guilbert confirmed its location on his global positioning system wrist monitor and slipped off his skimmer to drift down onto the silt. A cloud of nasty brown sediment angrily blossomed at this rude intrusion to la mer's smooth bottom. Using the exhaust of his Gill the diver hosed away cloying ocean debris to reveal a tin can that had once hosted an oak-smoked quartet of Messrs. John West's gastronomic kippers back in 2007. With a sigh he retrieved this cast off specimen of human garbage and shoved it into the net bag dangling from his diving belt before uniting with his skimmer to reconnoiter the next grid.

"False alarm," he said into his microphone embedded in a partition of his Gill's helmet.

The Gill was just that - a gill. This unique device had superseded the aqualung many years back. A minute electric pump pushed water through a series of artificial setae, bristles or hair-like filaments that captured air in the same manner a fish does and then delivered it to the diver's helmet. An auxiliary system scrubbed carbon dioxide from subsequent exhalations before reintroducing refurbished air to the breathing system. The battery powering the unit was automatically topped up from the skimmer's main electrical system. The versatile skimmer was a flat, elliptical platform that was propelled and steered by water jets actuated from an ion powered delivery pump. The hydrocraft sailed just as easily upon the surface as it could glide in ocean depths. Solar cells covered its upper exterior so that the main battery could be recharged when the marine vehicle was either on the surface or simply lying idle on the beach. Eric referred to his Global Positioning System before searching another grid.

An elderly gentleman sat in a wheelchair, his head lolled to one side. An attractive woman leaned over him and tenderly wiped away the drool trickling down his chin. Seated at a nearby table Gerrard Renouf sadly shook his head and mused, 'To think that a man with such vitality should have to suffer the last days of his life as a vegetable. Even so, in spite of the fellow's brain injury he appeared to be about twenty years younger than he is.'

Renouf sighed. Next month he would be eighty-three, two years older than his one-time shipmate.

The invalid's ward was approaching her fortieth year. She had brown hair augmented with locks of ripening chestnut. Enhanced by glistening, yet sad tawny-green eyes, her girlish cheeks accented an oval face of dusky gold. Gilt hoops dangled from the lobes of her small round ears. 'Cor, trust Mister King to latch onto such a loving and caring wife,' thought Renouf.

The pub's terraced patio began to thrive as late morning customers sought vacant tables. An elderly gentleman with the white, grizzled beard of a typical mariner jauntily worked his way between and around the canopied tables. He stopped to gaze down at his disabled friend before hugging the fellow's wife. "Hello Jessica," he said, kissing her cheek.

"Hi Jake," she replied in the same Canadian twang. "How are things in Hamilton?"

"Oh, so-so," he answered, adding: "They're talking about fixing up the Lister Building on James North again. Weather wise, it's a little bit cooler and a darned sight more humid. How's Gus doing?"

"Still the same," she replied. "The injury from his fall hasn't improved and the specialist tells me that the surgeons keep insisting that it is too dangerous to operate. In the meantime he continues to have the symptoms of Alzheimer's disease, which as we all know was cured a few years back."

"So what actually happened?" inquired the visitor.

"The cliff walks along the south coast have always been his passion," she replied. "But eighteen months ago the silly old beggar decided to climb down the rugged bluff to the beach on Fermain Bay instead of sailing round the easy way by boat. His body is still healthy and robust for it hasn't deteriorated in any way." She went on. "Sometimes his eyes will seem to focus on some distant object and every once in a while his fingers will tap in time to a piece of music."

"I'm sure sorry to hear that there has been so little progress," consoled Jake. Bracing himself on the terrace rail he reached over the table and proffered a bony hand to Renouf. "Hello Gerry, you're looking well."

Gerry grinned shyly, his ancient cheeks crinkled as he smiled. "Hello Chief, it's been a long time. I'm glad that my letter has brought you to Guernsey."

Jacques White, Ex-Chief Engineer of the RMS *Queen of Dalriada* II, shrugged readily. "I'm retired now Gerry - have been for the past eighteen years or so. The same as you I suspect. A few million miles of wake have flowed since you were my lead hand aboard the QD2." His hand withdrew from the firm grip and he sat down opposite his former rating. "Please call me Jake."

Gerry shook his head. "Old habits die hard, Chief," he said and nodded toward his shipmate in the wheelchair. "He'll always be Mister King to me."

A pretty young waitress sidled up.

"A pint of your local beer sweetheart," requested Jake.

"Monica, give him a pint of Randle's best bitter on me," smiled Gerry.

"So do you English still drink warm beer?" grinned the newcomer.

"Mister White, I'll thank you not to call me English," he censured the newcomer with a smile. "Nearly a thousand years ago the Channel Islands were part of Normandy's domain. In 1066 William, Duke of that province, invaded England and took over the place. So theoretically England is a colony of Guernsey and Jersey."

He wiped some sweat off his brow and took a swig of beer. "The beer is served cold here but if you don't sup it up fast enough in this heat then it's your hard luck!"

"Thanks for the history lesson," White said dryly. His brew arrived with a coating of condensate frosting the glass. His first sip left a moustache of creamy foam, which required a freshly ironed handkerchief to dab the yeasty residue from his thin lips. "Mmm - not bad."

He craned his head up at his shipmate's wife. "But it's not as good as the beer in the old *Witness Box* - eh Jessica?"

She smiled back and bent over to sponge saliva from her husband's face. The low vee of her summer frock sagged open to reveal a tattooed *Jessica* just above her right breast.

"Have you named the other one yet?" Jake teased.

"That's none of your business Mister White!" snapped Jessica, although her eyes sparkled with humour. "How's Francesca?"

White shook his head dolefully. "Ok, I guess. We were divorced seven years ago."

"What is *The Witness Box*, Chief?" Gerry inquired, changing the subject.

"It used to be a little bar attached to the *Budapest Restaurant* in Hamilton, Ontario. Back in 2007 it became a Chinese eating-house for vegans. It was just a stone's throw away from Jackson on John Street South," explained White. "The pub got its name from the old courthouse that lay diagonally across the street."

"Jessica used to serve beer in the pub. Gus here came over for a visit so me and the wife put him up for two weeks. Francesca was a third generation Italian from Stoney Creek and loved her garden. She noticed that some of her prize blooms were starting to disappear with alarming regularity. After a week or so I caught him . . ." he thumbed at Angus. "Giving flowers to the female staff in *The Witness Box*.

"Let's see if I can recall some of their names: There was a Swiss lady called Claudette who could yodel better than Roy Rogers. There were two Jessicas, one with a tattooed boob. I forget the names of the other girls." His brow furrowed in thought. "Except little Debbie tended bar on weekends. She was a feisty fifty-year-old shortstop with rusty hair. It was a lively place with interesting females; good beer, Hungarian grub, of course, and the patrons were very friendly too.

"Anyhow it was Gus who had been nickin' the flowers. He said that they piqued the curiosity of the girls by bringing a different variety each day. The sly old bugger was getting hugs and kisses as well as prompt service."

Angus' private grin went unobserved.

"Have things changed much over the past dozen years?" asked Jessica.

White reflected for a moment before answering. "Yes, it has changed very significantly - no thanks to the ever-bickering, bumbling buffoons who run city council."

The lovely lady's face fairly radiated. "Still hemming and hawing over important decisions, no doubt?"

The rhetorical question received a dry 'You got that right' from Jake. Jessica went on:

"The last time I was back in Hamilton they couldn't make up their minds on whether to resurface City Hall with the original marble, limestone, glass or concrete. What did they finally do if anything?"

White shook his head and grinned. They covered it with concrete slabs. They talked about turning the front into a greenhouse but as usual all the councillors except the mayor got cold feet and kiboshed it. A few years went by and the concrete began to deteriorate and you'll never guess what they did. He reached out for his glass of beer. "D'you remember Randle Reef?" He watched Jessica nod as he took a sip. "Well, a guy from St. Kitts had this idea of recycling the toxic wastes after it was dredged out the bay. He mixed some stuff into it, poured into slabs and baked them in a special kiln. The slabs cooled into a hard creamy material with feathery streaks of brown through them. So now our illustrious City Hall is completely clad with aesthetic crap."

"Quite an ironic tale Mister White," observed Gerry. His eyes squeezed shut suddenly and for a moment his face tightened as if in pain.

"Are you all right Gerry?" asked a concerned Jake, touching his old shipmate's arm.

A weak grin lit up the old fellow's countenance. "Just a little twinge, Mister White. Probably the bacon I had for breakfast was a bit too greasy." But to himself he thought, 'Damn bloody cancer!'

"Are you sure that you're all right Gerry?" asked Jessica.

"Sure, I'm sure Mrs. King," he said for the pain had gone, for now. "Tell us a bit more about Hamilton, Mister White.

"Not much to tell really," said Jake.

"What about the steel plants?" Jessica inquired. "Are they still puffing out red and black dust?"

"Oh dear me no!" exclaimed Jake. "The steel mills are long gone. Pollution and environmental edicts drove 'em out of the city years ago. You can walk or cycle round the entire bay now. There are fine restaurants and gardens everywhere. The water is as pure as it was during Brock's and MacNab's time. Hamilton thrives as a big tourist industry now.

"There are lots of marinas too. They widened the Burlington Canal to allow cruise ships in from the Great Lakes. And it was mostly her influential citizens that made it work."

With both elbows lodged on the white pine rail Jake squinted seawards across Saline Bay. Right in front of the terrace was a parched strip of ground infested with pale yellow salt hay and desiccated wild flowers. Land snails held clustered conventions on the stems of sturdier weeds. Beyond this strip of tired terrain the coastal road raced the western sea wall to draw in a dead heat at Pleinmont on the southwest corner of Guernsey.

Jake motioned toward a stir of activity. “What in the hell’s going on over there?”

A guy operating a portable remote control console was staring skywards and a girl was dabbing face powder on another fellow’s face. “Good morning ladies and gentlemen! I’m Bill Hanson.” The *Guernsey Press* reporter cheerily announced eying the camglider. “Sixty years ago today RMS *Queen of Dalriada* the First ran up on that beach yonder.”

The camglider dutifully obeyed the stabbing digit to focus on the expanse of Saline Bay on the northwest coast of Guernsey. It slowly panned south across a low rocky causeway into Cobo Bay before crossing northerly along the horizon to rest on the rugged promontory of Grande Rocques. The lens crept south again to zoom among the sun worshipers who languished on dun-coloured sand under a hazy UV sun. Some of the women were topless, quite oblivious to the stares of lusty males and the lingering Cyclops ogling from a hundred meters away. It was not quite eleven o’clock on that January morning yet the temperature was already 26° C and climbing steadily.

Slowly the picture diminished and the camera once again lavished its reverence upon the commentator’s buoyant countenance. “I have here in front of me Mister Gerrard Renouf, a crew member who was aboard the vessel when she beached all those many years ago.”

The camera dipped to hone in on Gerry’s wizened face. He’d donned an antiquated set of wirerimmed specs and studiously peering into a copy of the local ‘newspaper’, a broadsheet which was entirely different from the one he had known in his youth. A thin opaque sheet displayed ever-changing plasma pictures, both in script and audio. It was thirty-five centimetres wide by forty-two long and could be rolled up like the newspapers of yesteryear yet this state-of-the-art edition never crinkled. Images from global occurrences kept the reader acquainted with current events.

The owner of that frosted countenance smiled shyly up at the inquisitive camglider. The worthy’s rheumy eyes lit up when half-a-litre of Randall’s best bitter slid into the screen’s foreground. He reached out and picked up the free beer. With a wide grin he toasted the donor, the commentator and the camera lens.

“Now Mr. Renouf, can you tell our readers the reason why you picked this particular day to sit here on the patio of the *Wayside Cheer Tavern*?”

The camglider soared above the multicoloured canopies that shaded the gaily-covered tables to show viewers the white walled establishment. It pirouetted gracefully and bowed to the panoramic crag of Grande Rocques. *Grande Rocques Hotel* and Soif Beach peeked in from the right side of the picture. Still restless, this scout-in-the-sky crept stealthily along the roof of the *Wayside Cheer Hotel* stalking two felines. A black cat and a yellow cat both spat an arched back confrontation as they had since time immemorial.

The old fellow slipped off his specs, took a sip of beer and wiped away the creamy lather with the back of his hand. “I usually pop in here for a pint or two because this place is my local.”

Unperturbed, the newscaster patiently rephrased the question. “But this *is* a special day. Isn’t it, Mister Renouf?”

The old man reflected for a moment. “There isn’t much to tell really,” he growled, peeved and yet simultaneously pleased at the unexpected attention. “We were returning after a cruise to Madeira. I was out on the after end of A Deck with Mister King here . . ."

Hanson became aware of King's condition. He nudged the camglider's operator and shook his head. Drawn from the newspaper's archives black and white scenes of the stricken vessel flit across Renouf's broadsheet. The camera focussed on Jake White.

"Nah-nah," chided Gerry. "Chief White wasn't on that trip." He rubbed the grey stubble on his chin, recollecting his thoughts. "It was just a regular cruise, y'know. Nothing special, other than it was a forerunner of modern day cruises."

He went on, his manner filled with pride. "The old *Dally* was a graceful old lady but her air-conditioning was too ancient for pampering passengers in warm weather. Back then winter temperatures in Lisbon, Las Palmas and Madeira were in the low seventies. Our decrepit a/c system could handle a few degrees above that but there was a limit. 'Course, everything is measured in centigrade now . . ."

He tailed off.

"Thank you Mister Renouf," said the interviewer. "But did the poor air-conditioning have anything to do with the ship running aground?"

Gerry took another sip. "Maybe - maybe not," he replied uncertainly. He put down his pint pot. "Although it was just a normal trip, the crew as well as the passengers all had a great time. Hang on a second though - there was one curious incident shortly after we left Southampton. But other than that everything was just hunky-dory - that is - until we left Funchal. That's in Madeira, y'know."

The commentator hid his exasperation. "Yes, we know. Can you tell our readers just what happened after the ship sailed from Funchal?"

"Difficult to say really," Gerry's reply was noncommittal. "A lot of minor things."

"Can you name one?"

"I suppose I could." More beer was sipped. "Take Mister King's accent for instance."

"Yes?"

"Well, his accent was something else," answered Gerry. "Normally his rough Scotch dialect could scour scale off a boiler but towards the end of the trip he periodically acted and talked a bit strange. I can't describe it exactly . . ." His voice tapered off again.

"Do you suppose that he might have had something to do with the ship steaming up on that beach Mister Renouf?" prompted Hanson.

"Dunno. I mean he was on deck with me - so how could he?" Gerry screwed up his face trying to unearth that distant memory from sixty years long past. "I can remember a few moments before we struck Mister King's voice deepened and he sounded like one of them upper class fellers from Eton or some place like that."

He took a deep slug of beer and sighed. "Getting pretty muggy," he opined. "Just like the old *Dally*'s jenny rooms in her heyday. Yeah, that was really weird y'know. This Scotchman usually yabbered in haggis jargon then suddenly he switches to Laurence Olivier at the drop of a hat."

"Who?"

"He was a big movie star when I was a young man."

"Oh! Well now, tell us what happened," persisted Hanson.

"We'd been told that we were nearing Guernsey so him and me went out onto the starboard side of A Deck aft to have a butcher's. The West Coast slid up ever so clearly because we were passing quite close. About three miles or so I'd say."

"Three miles?"

"About five ks maybe. Well anyhow . . ." The glass upended and the remaining dregs of beer surged down old Renouf's throat. "It was early morning but the coast could be seen quite clearly in the twilight. And it was cool - not like the weather we've been getting for the past ten years or so."

He dabbed his brow with a serviette to substantiate his statement. “Suddenly the ship veered to starboard and there we were, steaming at twenty-odd knots towards that there seawall.” He jabbed a gnarled thumb at the massive stone construction. Hanson hesitated and impatiently waited for him to proceed. Moments passed then it came to him that Renouf’s attention was totally absorbed with the startling reality that his beer glass was filled with emptiness. White stifled a grin. Gerry’s eyes riveted on the reporter’s for a second before reverting their gaze on the still empty pint pot. The hint was taken and presently a replenished glass materialized in the old man’s hand and the interview progressed anew.

A fresh layer of foam was licked away from the thin lips before he proceeded anew. “The next thing we knew was that the ship was shuddering like a dog shiting razor blades.”

Hanson slowly shook his head in censure.

“Oops! Sorry, pardon my French,” apologized Gerry. “The main engines were going full astern. The water under her counter was boiling like mad and stirring up mud and silt so that the bay out there became the exact same colour of sh - chocolate milk!”

Another sip.

“At that very instant my mind seemed to have gone blank. The next thing I recall was that I was sprawled flat out on the bloody deck and the ship had stopped. Somebody told me later that some of the passengers throughout the ship had all went arse - sorry - over teakettle. The tide was out y’see, like now, which was a good thing really because we got back off again with the flood and her main engines. But we weren’t goin’ nowhere without tugs.”

“Why not?”

“Because there are more bloody rocks sticking up out there than there are seeds on a sesame bun,” Gerry told him. “How we got as far as we did without hitting one I’ll never know.”

White interjected. "Gerry, what do you mean the tide's out? I walked along there just a few minutes ago and the water is only a few meters from the sea wall."

"Back in the sixties one had to cross about half a mile of sand before reaching the water at low tide," Gerry recalled. "But now, the sea has risen quite a bit from them days, what with the melting of the Arctic and Antarctic ice caps."

"Yeah," agreed Jake. "I should've realized that from the many ports that I've visited."

With a do you mind? glare at White the reporter resumed his interview. "Was there any damage to the ship's keel?"

"Nah. We went right into KG Five dry dock when we got back to Southampton. Bit o' scratched paint and a few creels of barnacles, that's all." He reconsidered for a moment. "Oh yeah, our starboard prop got dinged on a rock almost as soon as we backed off the beach. And that led to . . ." He tailed off. "but that's a story for another day."

"The Board of Trade's inquiry couldn't pinpoint the reason for the unexpected change in course. I don't suppose you have any ideas, do you?"

The old man gazed out across Saline Bay before looking the reporter straight in the eye. "No, I don't suppose I do."

With the commercial break the reporter called it a day. He wanted to report on a convention of arms dealers over at the Old Government House Hotel. The offshore banking facilities in Guernsey still attracted affluent characters from the seamy side of life.

"So what are you holding back Gerry?"

"Not a helluva lot Mister White," replied Gerry. He gestured at Angus. "Mister King here is the one with all the answers and he's not talking."

A distant bleep sounded.

"Yes Eric?" queried Gerry, touching what White thought was an old-fashioned hearing aid.

"I've found one Papa Gerry. Should I bring it in?"

"No Eric," answered Gerry. "The other one shouldn't be too far away. I'll wait here at the tavern until you bring 'em both in."

"What was all that about?" asked White.

Gerry grinned.

"Mrs. King, move Mister King closer to the table and take a seat. I'm going to tell a story about your husband."

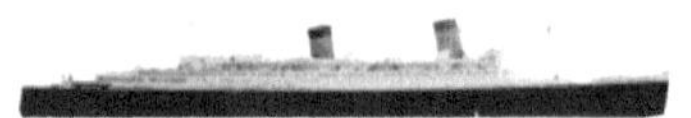

CHAPTER TWO

Southampton, England

Monday afternoon, October 30th, 1961

The harbinger of winter arrived in the shape of a dusting of snow swirling in front of Bernie Sneddon's office window. The dozen-or-so cars in his scrap yard apathetically waited on the surgical removal of their mechanical organs. Sooner or later those parts would be deployed to resuscitate some of their more fortunate brethren. It's a living, he thought, ruthlessly stubbing out a Capstan Full Strength cigarette into the hub nut that once secured an MG's front left wheel.

An actor, he brooded, that's what I should've been his memory recalling that time when his English teacher urged him to stand in front of the class and recite Mark Anthony's Friends, Romans and Countrymen speech from the Bard's *Julius Caesar*. The day before all the senior students in his school had trooped down to the local cinema to watch *Julius Caesar*, a film that starred Marlon Brando. After the show Bernie had mimicked Brando almost perfectly in class. Mrs. Frame was so delighted that she put his name down for a rôle in the Christmas play. From then on the teacher had taken him under his wing and introduced him to a character actor who freelanced in the film industry.

Nine months of tutelage later the city newspaper did an article on the local theatre adding that the company was seeking local talent for its upcoming play, Oliver Twist. Bernie was accepted and cast as the Artful Dodger. All went well during rehearsals but on opening night he stepped out onto the boards and froze. In spite of all attempts to overcome his stage fright Sneddon's acting career was doomed.

After his thespian career vanished like a puff of smoke he began stealing semi-valuable metals from the various yards which abounded in the Southampton - Portsmouth vicinity. Time after time he'd come within a hair's breadth of being nabbed by the local constabulary. All too often shady scrap dealers had given him a mere pittance for the risks that he'd taken.

The snow was getting heavier. The has-been-that-never-was let out a sigh as the present came flooding back. Business had been slow lately. Not only was it slow but bankruptcy was an itchy palm whilst rubbing forefinger and thumb.

Another memory came to the fore as his mind went back that night in the King George V graving dock area, which was not far from where this office stood in Millbrook. One of the Cunard Queens had slipped into the dry dock for her winter layup. A trailer load of cupra nickel tubes was waiting to replace leaky ones in a couple of main condensers in the vessel's enginerooms. Sneddon sat in the stolen rig's cab while Morris Greene blatantly flashed forged documents at the dock gate. The security guard was more concerned about getting back into his heated bothy than perusing papers in a chilly winter's night.

"Told you it would be easy," Mo'd said, double-declutching into second gear. Squinting through the windscreen where wipers scoured away snowflakes he carefully maneuvered the rig towards the ship.

The whole area was dimly lit because some of the low powered bulbs in the tall light standards were out. The ship's superstructure and upper deck was only partially lit. Only a dozen or so portholes emitted light. The truck eased passed the vessel until the tarpaulin-covered trailer laden with the cupra nickel tubes came into sight. Bernie's crony drove right up to the dock's edge and was beginning to back the rig into position when another security guard suddenly appeared to hail him. Greene leapt down from the cab with phony papers.

Mo was a short stocky fellow who was prone to violence. He had grown up the hard way, toughened by a life on tramp steamers and hostile waterfronts. Sneddon had heard that some fifteen years before in Galveston, some stevedore had gypped Greene in a card game and it was rumoured that he'd killed the guy. Whether the story was true or not one ever knew for sure but Greene never went back to Texas again. Bernie believed this tale because he'd once witnessed an example of Mo losing his cool after being short changed in a pub. The guy had gone ballistic over a mere ninepence.

Like a wraith Bernie slipped down from the other side of the cab. In the distance a ship's foghorn moaned over the darkened waters of the River Test from the Town Quay. Although the guard was an old man just trying to supplement his pension, he nevertheless was determined to do his duty. The penumbra of his torch beam flit over the first page. "'Ere!" he declared. "These . . ."

That was as far as he got before Greene nudged him into the dock. "Hope you can swim old timer!" he called softly.

"That's strange," Bernie mused aloud.

"Wot?"

"No splash."

The two thieves peered down into the inky blackness before surveying the ship's length. Three gangways were down but no one was in sight. The ship's security guards were probably hovering somewhere in the vicinity of the shell doors seeking warmth. There was just enough light to show that the dock had been pumped dry. About fifty feet below them a broken body lay somewhere upon the shadowed concrete.

"Let's switch trailers and get to hell out of here," hissed Mo.

By the time the old sentinel's body was found the cupra nickel had been sold and well on the way to a German shipyard. Sneddon's cut went to the down payment for his present business. Not long after Mo Greene went to prison for aggravated assault in another robbery.

The scrap merchant was a rogue as well as an accessory to the murder that still hung over his head like the sword of Damocles. Yet his conscience never bothered him. Although he'd kept his nose clean as far as the law was concerned, stolen copper and brass or the occasional sheet of lead ripped from a church roof sometimes passed through his hands.

He straightened his slim tie in a windowpane's reflection and glanced down at his off-the-peg suit. It was made from some brown material with a faded check. Pretty good really, he opined, but one of those days when and if business picked up he'd get fitted out with one those Savile Row jobs or perhaps an Armani suit. Then reality defecated on his dream.

Sneddon lit up another Capstan Full Strength and let smoke trickle from his thin lips. His face was gaunt and sallow with worry. The curly sandy locks that once made him attractive to the opposite sex were long gone and a rapidly receding hairline had taken their place. He was almost six feet tall with a permanent stoop and his cheap suit was anything but snug on his lean frame. He was practically living on cigarettes instead of taking wholesome food. Presently his fist went to his lips as he bowed over hacking and coughing, yet no phlegm came up.

A chic red car slid to halt in the front of his office and his wife got out. A few minutes later after pecking him on the cheek Denise brushed a persistent snowflake from her ermine coat. "I've got a bit of good news Bernie."

"Oh aye?" he said, flopping down into the worn black leather chair behind his desk. He glanced at her reflectively. She was forty-four, five years older than him and went to a gym daily to keep her svelte figure trim. "What's that then, love?"

"How do you fancy going on an ocean cruise?"

"Things are a bit slow here right now," he replied. "Cash flow is barely trickling in - hardly enough to go on one of your cheap holidays."

Denise Sneddon was not the stereotyped ‘dumb’ blonde. She was smart, shrewd and well acquainted with all the ins and outs of the travel business. She had worked very hard, hard enough to earn her present position of managing director of Tranquil Moments Travel Agency. Her station often enabled her take advantage of valuable discounts. The female’s behaviour tended to be forceful for she spoke with an authoritative air that daunted her male confederates in the business. In the presence of clients however her manner became all smile and smarm.

His wife’s features were virtually unadorned with makeup. Intelligent blue eyes rarely missed a detail and she always was sharply dressed. Her attire though, was quite manly for she wore a charcoal-grey pant suit with pin stripes. A slim red tie complimented her frilly satin blouse of washed-out pink.

“Don’t worry about the expense,” replied Denise. She went on to explain: “I did pretty well with some promotional ideas for the Pict Line cruises out of New York City. Their flagship sails during the first week of December. I’ve learned that their booming sales are partly due to my input. They’re working out great here too. So far five hundred tickets have been sold for their British cruise early in the New Year. That’s the one we’ll be on. If you want to go that is,” she added.

Bernie hesitated.

The other night Mavis, a buxom waitress in the *Lord Louis*, had been quite receptive to his charms. Or more likely the brass she thought I had, he reflected. Still - any port in a storm. This bossy bitch standing in front of him hadn’t put out for quite a while now. She always complained of being too tired after a hard day at the office. What about the hard I get in this office?

“How long is this cruise?” he asked.

Denise leaned across the desk towards him. “Ten days. Ten days of peace and relaxation and maybe we can have a second honeymoon as well.”

Ten days and nights with Mavis would be a bit of all right too, envisioned Bernie, a leer lurking behind his eyes. “A little bird told me that there might be a big business contract heading my way early in January.”

The lie came easily as he reached out and laid a hand on hers. “Just give me a couple of days or so Denise, to see if it pans out.”

“All right Bernie.” She shrugged. “Don’t wait too long. I’ll be going on this cruise one way or the other.”

That Saturday while tossing her jacket carelessly onto the bed Denise let out a loud moan. “God! I’m absolutely spent.” She kicked off her shoes and dropped a thick paper wallet on the dressing table. “I’m going to soak in a warm bath for about an hour,” she announced, closing the bedroom door behind her.

Bernie was lolling across the bed checking the racing results on the evening paper. He stretched over for the wallet and dumped out its contents on the counterpane. A steamship ticket bearing the name, Mrs. Denise Sneddon accompanied a host of colourful brochures. He opened a pamphlet that advertised the advantages of sailing at economical rates aboard some cruise liner called the RMS *Queen of Dalriada.*

Twenty-one public rooms it lauded, beginning with a first class restaurant of nearly seventy-five hundred square feet. The vessel had two swimming pools, spacious lounges, smoking rooms, dancing salons, two other restaurants, cocktail bars, libraries, and children’s playrooms as well as a theatre that held over three hundred people. Here was the opportunity for the man-in-the-street and his missus to go on a luxury cruise for a price that his pay packet could handle. This included duty-free cigarettes, liquor, French perfumes, and a host of other commodities that were still rare in the drawn-out aftermath of World War Two.

The vessel’s dimensions of seven hundred and sixty-one feet long with a beam of eighty-six feet and a gross weight of fifty-one thousand, five hundred and seventy-three tons, two funnels wide enough to drive trains through, and a hefty anchor and rudder were quite irrelevant to Sneddon. He picked up another brochure. Glossy pictures of Lisbon, Portugal; Las Palmas in the Canary Isles and Funchal in Madeira leapt out at him, as did vistas of endless beaches and subtropical verdant glory. Finally a document bearing the legend, Travel Insurance fell open. A superbly watermarked letter was unfolded. He scrutinized the fine print and stopped when the sum of £125,000 blazoned back at him. "Shit!" he exclaimed. His jaw dropped as he read on. "*Holy shit*!" he gasped. "Double indemnity!"

He diligently perused the vessel's itinerary, his mind fleetingly contemplating a convenient time and place where his wife might meet her demise - only on the off chance, of course. Bernie carefully put all the paraphernalia back into the wallet. He lay back on the bed and stared at the ceiling. "I wonder what Mo Greene is doing now?"

They noshed on cold pork pies and scotch eggs in a little pub behind the Southern Echo's offices. Their lunch was supplemented with Watney's Red Barrel beer, *The Spa*'s best selling bitter. The tavern was a popular place with office workers from the newspaper during lunch period. Seagoing engineers often frequented this establishment too. These gentlemen were readily identified by their well-rumpled suits which were out for their in-harbour airing having spent much of their life squirreled away in suitcases or musty wardrobes.

Greene had lost a few pounds doing porridge, the colloquialism for being a guest in one of her Majesty's Prisons. He was currently earning his keep as a bookie's runner, an illicit occupation in the years before future politicians would legislate a decree to abet such enterprise and thus benefit the national coffers. He was leery of accepting Bernie's proposition.

It was true that he needed cash but was £5,000 worth the risk of being caught? In low murmurs and consistently glancing about for possible eavesdroppers the pair casually discussed the termination of a human being's life. When Sneddon upped the ante by half as much again, the old lag began to wonder just how far this guy would go to get rid of his missus.

Another pint later Sneddon's offer had grown to £10,000. He was getting desperate. Still Mo hung back. "Look Mo," said Bernie, his voice almost pleading. "I'm going to level with you. Denise has taken out an insurance policy for £30,000. You will be getting almost one-third of it."

"Half," said Mo, carefully setting down his glass. "I want half. It's me who's taking the risk so why shouldn't I get an equal share?"

"Get real Mo,' entreated Bernie, his tone worthy of snitch in the TV show, *Murder Bag*. "I have to come across with some money to pay for your trip. First Class I might add. If I give you half, I'll lose out."

Greene ruminated on this latest fact as he helped himself to a wedge of pork pie. "Twelve thousand, five hundred quid then - plus the price of the cruise."

Bernie stared at him hard and long. The actor in him successfully masked his relief for he was willing to go as high as £100,000. "You drive a hard bargain Mo," his voice heavily laced with chagrin. They would've shook hands to seal the bargain but both knew that neither of them were gentlemen. Honour among thieves or any other kind of crook exists only in literature.

"So," ventured Greene. "When do you want it done?"

"I don't know yet," replied Bernie. "We'll just have to play it by ear."

"Why don't I knock her on head during some dark night and drop her over the side?"

"No!" Bernie vehemently protested. His eyes searched the pub for any patron who might be listening. "I think the law says that seven years has to pass before a missing person is declared dead. I don't want to wait that long for my money. And I'll bet you don't either."

"So do want me to nudge her over a cliff or off some castle wall?" Mo asked. "Maybe she could fall in front of a bus."

"No-no Mo," rhymed Bernie. "I don't want to be around when it happens. The rozzers usually suspect the surviving spouse first. Don't do nothing until I give you the word," he emphasized. A thought entered his head. "And another thing - we don't know each other on board or in port. Don't come up to me for a light. Don't talk to me about the weather. Don't talk to me about nothing. Zip! Understand?"

"So when . . . ?"

"I'll let you know," said Bernie, cutting him off. He rose suddenly and dropped half-a-dozen fivers on the varnished tabletop. "I'll see you in the *Horse and Groom* around this time two weeks from today. I'll have your boat ticket and some spending money for you by then."

Walking towards his 1949 Vauxhall Wyvern, Sneddon wondered how much it was worth. Not much he reckoned since it only cost him three hundred and fifty quid when it was brand-new. No, he'd have to cozen up to Denise to get enough money to help her into the next world.

CHAPTER THREE

Glasgow

Monday morning, December 4th, 1961

The canteen looks busier than usual this morning, observed Nan Barrie as the tea urn oozed a cloying black liquid into her cup. She took the still warm seat that a student recently vacated and planted her bulky briefcase on the floor. Seated on the opposite side of the table behind a copy of last night's Glasgow *Evening Citizen* was Brian Dickie, a fellow colleague. He was packing a yolk-dipped wedge of toast into his mouth. Having digested a news snippet he turned a page, quarter folded the newspaper and propped it up against an HP sauce bottle. The brown square-shaped bottle stoically asserted itself in its new endeavour. With his hands now free he enthusiastically waged war on his platter of bacon, egg, sausage and fried bread, slashing and stabbing into the fry-up.

Dickie's eyes shifted to a level slightly above the tabloid. They absorbed a longish oval face which was completely devoid of makeup. The thin unsmiling lips were seldom adorned with lipstick. A few crows' feet etched the outer edges of iron-grey eyes that exuded intelligence. A wisp of sandy hair escaped from the severely combed-back whole, a self-crafted coif that had been fiery-red only two-and-a-half decades ago.

"Hi Agnes," he mumbled.

When the eyes shot back daggers and her thin nostrils flared Dickie smirked, knowing full well how she hated her given name. His attention reverted to a mugging in Renfield Street. Nan dropped a saccharine tablet into the so-called tea and stirred furiously for a second or two then stopped. 'Bugger!'

she swore under her breath. She was much more angry with herself than this wee niggler. Normally she would've shrugged his gibe off, if only by just considering the source. 'Maybe I'm starting to go through the change or maybe I just need a holiday.' She glowered at the pale-green newspaper in front of her until her eyes centred on a photograph of a ship. Nan reached over and relieved the sauce bottle of its burden.

"Hey!" protested Dickie, making a futile grab for the journal.

Nan clutched the paper to her sparsely-filled cashmere sweater. "It's very bad manners to read at the table!" she retaliated shrilly. The pitch of her voice was a passable imitation of Alastair Sim's Miss Fritton caricature of St. Trinian fame. "What kind of example are you setting before these impressionable students?" she asked, her arm motioning to the now-interested alumni. Some faculty members were grinning too. With a bowed beet-red face Dickie gave up his griping to pay meticulous attention to some bacon rind removal surgery. Extraordinarily pleased with herself at getting even with the 'wee nyaff' for the Agnes remark Nan began to peruse the cruise ship advertisement.

"Ah-hem." Dickie cleared his throat.

"Yes?"

"How come it's ok for you to read at the table?"

The paper waved airily in front of him. "I'm only having a cuppa, you silly wee man you."

PICT LINE BEGINS CHEAP CRUISES paraded a headline bylined by the *Citizen*'s travel expert, Mairie Kaye. Directly beneath the article was a photograph of the RMS *Queen of Dalriada* berthed alongside Southampton's Ocean Terminal. The column went on to enlighten the reader of the vastness and the opulence of the ocean liner. The itinerary of the next three cruises between New York City and The Bahamas followed. Nan closed her eyes and sighed. The columnist went on to say that on the morrow, tickets would be on sale for a ten-day cruise starting early in the New Year. The renowned vessel's ports-of-call would be Lisbon, Portugal; Las Palmas, Gran Canaria, and Funchal, Madeira before returning to Southampton. Tourist or Economy Class prices began at £155.

She sipped her tea and grimaced, the bitter taste bringing her back to the truth. 'Some hopes,' she thought. Propping the paper back against the sauce bottle, this time upside down, Nan grabbed her briefcase and made her way to the anthropology lab.

The two undergraduates already seated in the lab chorused, "Good morning Miss Barrie."

"Good morning," reciprocated Nan and dumped her burden on the badly scratched mahogany desk in front of the blackboard.

Other students filed in chatting and giggling, some relating their weekend experiences. While the class was settling down at their work stations, their mentor was hauling a sheath of foolscap folders from her briefcase. The paleoanthropologist waited for silence and presently a pair of eyes met hers. She pinned that individual's attention momentarily before moving onto the next subject, the chatter dwindled to nothing as her vision had panned across the room. The folders dropped heavily onto the desk, their corresponding thud was a statement.

"For the past two months we've been discussing the Late Cretaceous period in the Mesozoic era. These essays demonstrate that some of you have a good grasp on the subject although spelling and grammar leaves a lot to be desired. After I've passed them out and you've checked your marks we'll go onto the Maastrichtian stage and touch on palaeozoology. We'll discuss how the climate influenced the flora and fauna."

When the class ended Nan decided that rather than go to the cafeteria she'd take a jaunt along to Helen's Bakery which was noted for its tearoom. The day was unusually bright for that time of the year so it was a pleasant walk to Sauchiehall Street. On the way she purchased a *Daily Record* from a paperboy. The tearoom was relatively quiet considering that it was lunchtime. The aroma of fresh baked pies, sausage rolls, and bridies assailed her nostrils the minute she entered the shop. Even so she decided to settle for a pot of tea, a potato scone, and a crumpet. She opened the tabloid and browsed through the pages. Another Pict Line advertisement caught her eye and for a moment a glimpse of sun-drenched decks flooded her imagination.

"Thinking about going on a cruise Nan?"

She glanced up and back at Maggie MacDowell who was peering over her shoulder.

"I wish."

Maggie claimed on the chair opposite. The women had known each other for many years and in Nan's eyes her friend had everything going for her. The brunette with the bubble-cut was what women across The Pond called a Size Ten - ten years younger and ten inches shorter. She had a clear complexion, large brown eyes, a perky turned-up nose, rose bud lips and was still single. Maggie had often said that she had to beat off admirers with a stick. An' had a' her back teeth tae, a Scottish vernacular for being very smart. She had a Bachelor of Science honour degree in geology and one in chemistry. For the past couple of years she'd been studying the brand-new field of volcanology.

"Can I have a wee keek at your paper for a second?" Maggie asked, reaching over. An advertisement drew her curiosity. "Aye," she said, in a soft pleasing tone. "Just as I thought."

Nan retrieved the paper. "Thought what?"

"I think that's the boat that we're trying to come back home on - providing the cabins are not all taken, of course."

Nan ogled the advert before staring incredulously into her friend's face. "Coming back from where?"

A waitress came by to take the newcomer's order.

"São Vicente."

"I beg your pardon?"

"Oh sorry, I was talking to my companion." She glanced over the array of baked goods displayed in the glass counter. "Ooh! Those bridies smell just smashin'. I'll have one with a pot of tea, crumpet and a wee slice of sultana cake."

When the girl went away Nan asked: "Where's that?"

"Madeira."

Maggie slapped her paper. "You're going on this cruise?"

Her companion scrunched up her shoulders and placed her arms akimbo in an exaggerated shrug. "No-o," she drawled before explaining. "Y'see, I'm going to do some research on the volcanic caves there. I've been invited by the *Instituto Nacional de Meteorologia e Geofisica* of Madeira to do some studies there." The Portuguese pronunciation navigated haphazardly through a Scottish lilt.

"An' wha micht they be when they're at hame, hen?" asked Nan, laying on the Glasgow twang with a vengeance.

"The National Institute of Weather and Geology - I think," revealed her friend. "They are investigating a lot of the Micronesia island groups, including the archipelagos of Madeira, the Canaries, Salvajes, Azores and Cape Verde. All of them were created from volcanic upheavals.

"So when are you going?"

"A week tomorrow," said Maggie. "I'll be flying from Heathrow to Lisbon and then getting a boat to Funchal. The Institute hinted that if there any cabins available on that liner," she gestured at the *Record*. "I'll be aboard it with bells on."

"Lucky bitch!"

"Aye - maybe so but I bet that I'll have to earn it spelunking through all those volcanic caves."

They chatted for a while before journeying back to the university under threatening rain clouds. It drizzled all that afternoon without letup.

When classes ended Nan cowered under an old black brolly and made her way to the nearest tram stop. After a short shoogley ride across the River Clyde she got off near Govan Cross where she had a flat.

Just before climbing the single flight of stairs to her lodgings Ella, her landlady, came rushing out excitedly flapping an envelope. “It’s for you Nan!” she cried. “It’s for yoo-u!”

“What is?” sighed Nan, loosening a damp head scarf.

“Littlewoods!” Ella shrieked. “Ye’ve won! Ye’ve won!”

Nan took the envelope without too much enthusiasm. About eighteen months ago she had her hopes dashed upon thinking that she’d won the soccer pool big time but it had been only a few shillings. This was probably just another ten bob. She opened the envelope and pulled out a cheque, her bottom sagged down onto the carpeted stair.

“How much is it?” squeaked Ella.

In silence Nan held up the check.

“Fower thoosan’ one hundred an’ eighteen pounds, three shillings an’ a tanner!” whispered Ella in awe. “Whit are ye gaun tae dae wi’ it?”

Still flabbergasted her lodger reclaimed her bounty, stared at it, and just shook her head. “I don’t know. It’ll take me a wee while to get over the shock.”

Nan stood up and slowly climbed the stairs. She switched on her room lights and closed the tired curtains to shield out a dismal Glaswegian night. She dropped the cheque on her dressing table, flopped down onto a padded stool, and looked into the mirror. She saw the pale drawn countenance of a lonely woman who would be fifty the following month. She was nearly a stone overweight though it didn’t show too much because of her height. At five foot eleven she always had to look down at the men in her life. It was a sad fact of life that most Glaswegians were short-arsed Scots.

She had been making ends meet since her second husband had tried to climb a tree in his Rover over Balloch way. A woman had been in the car with him. Nan didn't go to the funerals but not long after bills came pouring it. That was almost a decade ago and it took her seven of those years to get back in the black. He had been a car salesman and a bit of a fly man.

With Jimmy, her first husband, life had been marvellous. He'd made good money as a firsthand melter in Clyde Iron until an open hearth furnace charger laid its scrap box on top of him. She remarried two years later to Davie, the spiv. He was good in bed but then look at all the practice he'd had.

Nan scrutinized the cheque again. £4,118 - 3s - 6d.

'Tomorrow at lunchtime,' she promised herself. 'I'll nip into the bank and deposit this cheque. Next Saturday I'll book up on that cruise ship and get away from this miserable *dreich* weather for a wee while. I wonder how much First Class is? Och, what the hell - let's go for broke. I'll watch my diet starting from now until after Christmas then go out and get some nice gowns and frocks.'

Her reflection smiled and made her seem not so dull and drab. She pushed up her slightly sagging breasts. 'I'll need to get a bra to perk these up and perhaps I'll latch onto a nice sailorman - an officer maybe.' This induced another train of thought. 'Might as well shoot the works and go to a high class beauty salon before sailing day.'

Now that she was in a better frame of mind Nan went into her tiny kitchen. She selected a can of Frey Bentos stew from her pantry. A potato unwillingly shed its peel in the dingy sink while being serenaded to the hummed version of Petula Clark's hit, *Sailor*.

Her kitchen window was unusually large and faced south. Originally the sink had been located in front of the window but shortly after she moved in it was shifted and re-piped adjacent to the gas stove. The pantry and dish cupboards were mounted above them. The kitchen walls and ceiling were done over in matte white to enhance the available light.

The renovation left her with just enough space to erect an easel. She had painted ever since she was a child and was quite accomplished in water colour. For the past five years she had experimented in oils and gradually got the hang of it. The short Scottish winter nights only allowed her to work for about a couple of hours a day except for weekends. Even then a bright sunny day was a rarity. Still, the long summer days helped to make up for the difference.

The canvas that was presently set up on the easel was half-finished oil depicting a small mammal called *Repenomamus giganticus* from the Cretaceous period in the Mesozoic era. Although it looked something like a shrew, it was reckoned to have been about the size and weight of a husky. The creature was supposedly carnivorous and wasn't likely to turn down a meal in the shape of a small dinosaur. Six weeks had lapsed since Nan had last daubed on the painting.

During her unimaginative repast she mulled over her upcoming cruise and resolved to take a sketch pad and charcoal to catch any memorable scenes. 'A box of water colour paints wouldn't go wrong either,' she thought, but hoped to meet someone nice who'd make a nice romantic attachment to her hobby.

CHAPTER FOUR

Learning the ropes

1615 Thursday, 11th January 1962

The Senior Second Engineer of the four-to-eight watch was going over his roster. Some of the engineers under his control were familiar to him. Others would bear scrutiny. John MacKay was responsible for the machinery spaces as well as the personnel who manned the early morning and late afternoon watches. It could be a daunting task at times. His duty was to patrol the boiler and engine rooms to oversee, give advice, and generally make his presence known to the watchkeepers. His continual migration from fore to aft and back again earned him the title, 'walking' second.

The ship's power train began at the forward end of the vessel in the Water Softening Plant located directly aft of the holds. As the name implied the area consisted of pumps and special units to condition water for the boilers. A large zinc-topped sideboard served as a laboratory and sported a host of beakers, pipettes and burettes as well as chemicals in glass receptacles. This was the Water Softening Engineer's domain but since he only worked the eight-to-twelve watches the fuel-oil engineer was supposed to keep an eye on it during the off watches. A freshwater and a saltwater calorifier and an oil separator occupied the level above the lab.

Aft of the WSP was Number One Boiler Room, a huge watertight compartment that held three fifty-ton scotch boilers which supplied steam to the trio of turbo generators in the Hotel Service Generator Room. MacKay recognised Charlie Benson as a responsible engineer who could be trusted to look after 1BR on this watch. Next door was the HSGR itself which was run by Martin Lowe, a Scouser, as Liverpudlians are often termed. Although he had passed the examination for his second's ticket in steam Lowe was just a junior third on the stepladder of attrition. As the term suggests, electricity produced in the HS generator room powered lights, air-conditioning fans and compressors and a multitude of other tasks to fulfil the needs and whims of passengers.

Still moving aft into 2BR watchkeeper Taffy Morgan, a tubby jovial Welshman, kept a suspicious eye on six twelve-ton Yarrow watertube boilers. Taff was well known to the senior second, having served under him for quite a few trips. These units acted in tandem with half-a-dozen identical ones in 3BR to power the great turbines in the engineroom and four turbogenerators that screamed out their hearts in the Main Generator Room.

Fifer Dick Currie, a senior third engineer, stood his watch in the MGR. The walking second often stopped to have a discourse upon the merits of Arbroath FC as compared to Raith Rovers.

3BR followed where a tall handsome engineer with black curly hair and a tanned complexion stood watch. Will Keyes hailed from the Maryhill district in Glasgow. His given name, Wilberforce, was a millstone around his neck and he took great pains trying to keep it secret from his comrades. MacKay knew him to be a competent engineer.

The engineroom was comprised of two main engines, each driven by four turbines which in turn were linked to a massive gearbox. A twenty-seven-inch diameter shaft emerged from each of those gearboxes to pass through their individual main thrust bearing and into the tunnel as the shaft alley was called. After passing through three watertight compartments and the stern glands, the shafts spun the ship's propellers that drove her through the briny at substantial speeds.

On this watch the engineroom was manned by three engineers, a junior second, a senior fifth and a junior sixth.

Termed the platform second Bob Christie was a morose man in his late thirties. From the shadow of black bushy eyebrows intense eyes of obsidian glowered through horn-rimmed glasses. Black Bob was the nickname he'd earned from the junior engineers on board for his perpetual foul mood. MacKay never had any problems with the man since he ran his engineroom efficiently. The senior second was not familiar with the engineroom's junior but trusted associates had informed him that Terry Baker knew his onions as far as steam was concerned.

This bad tempered platform second was Baker's cross to bear for the duration of the voyage. Terry's responsibilities were all the pumps and associated machinery in the engineroom, the tunnel and whatever else the devious Christie might dream up.

But luckily for him a scapegoat called Peter Deery became a target for Black Bob's venom. Assigned 'floater' for the trip Deery was destined for some of the hottest and dirtiest tasks in the machinery spaces. Already his short squat stature and Irish dialect had him dubbed The Leprechaun in a department that was rife with nicknames. The Irishman was a soft-spoken individual with wire rimmed glasses perched on a pug nose. His close-cropped hair was steel-grey which made him appear to be in his fifties, an unusual age for such a junior position.

This then along with a handful of ratings was the staff that came under John MacKay's jurisdiction. The walking second clamped his watch list to a clipboard and hung it on a bulkhead peg. He seized another clipboard holding the typed itinerary for the upcoming voyage. Sea watches had just begun and he was double-checking Pete Eaton's report regarding the newly loaded bunker C. Pete, who was burdened with the sobriquet Steamboat, was the fuel-oil engineer on this watch.

Angus King vacated the engineroom elevator into the working alleyway on C Deck. He had turned to for his watch in the engineroom but he'd since been relieved by Baker. Terry passed on the information that the walking second desired his presence immediately in his office. He knocked on the scuffed vanished door, which bore the brass plate legend, Senior Second Engineer.

He went in.

In a broad Scottish accent he said, "Ye wanted tae see me Mister MacKay?" The surname MacKay was pronounced in the proper Scots way: mac Kye.

The senior engineer was a big man in his early sixties. He had broad shoulders and hands like shovels. "A-ye," he said, elongating the word like elastic as denizens of Arbroath are wont to do. He peered over his spectacles at the clipboard hanging on the bulkhead. "It seems that your talents are in demand elsewhere than in our engineroom. Do you ken anything about air-conditioning?"

The junior shook his head.

"That's ok then," nodded MacKay. "You knew bugger all about the turbines and boilers when you started with us last trip. But you're an expert on them now - right?"

The youth did learn a lot on his first trip to sea and also learned to keep his mouth shut in front of his betters.

"Never mind," the second went on: "You've proved that your head's screwed on the right way so you should be ok. Do you know where the a/c office is?"

King shook his head.

"It's on A Deck, port side. You go . . ." MacKay reached for the phone. "Never mind, on a vessel as big as this one you'll probably get lost. Hello?"

His gruff voice assumed a silky courteous air for Rona, the Hertfordshire telephonist. "Yes my dear, would you please put me through to air-conditioning? Thanks. Hello?" The authoritative tone resumed. "MacKay here, send somebody down to my office to pick up one of your staff. No, not in a wee while. Bloody right now!"

It seemed like hardly any time had passed at all when a timid knock could be heard through the door. "Come!" MacKay bellowed.

The door opened and a slim young man with tousled raven hair peeped in. He was rigged in clean denims. His sky-blue eyes cautiously roamed around the walking second's inner sanctum before settling on the young engineer.

Sunday afternoon, January 21st
Gerry recalls:

This was the first time Mister King and me met. He was dressed in typical engineer attire, a white fresh-laundered boilersuit that bore the usual faded blotches of dirt, oil and grease. A black peaked cap was perched on a swath of unruly ginger hair. He had grey eyes and baby-fat cheeks. He was about the same height as me which was five foot eight inches in old measure. Like me he was slim and quite wiry.

"Hello," I said. "My name's Gerry Renouf and I'm one of the a/c greasers on this watch."

Mister King grinned and stuck out his hand. I took it and noticed the frown on the walking second's face. The old British class system still had a long way to go before equality would become the norm. On board that ship and many others like her officers were not supposed to fraternize with ratings.

"C'mon Mister King," I said hastily. "Let's go up to the a/c office and find out what's happening."

I turned on heel and sped forrard at a good clip. I nipped up a wide ladder leading to the first class galley. I could hear Mister King clumping up after me.

Stainless steel tables, vats, tureens and assorted cuisine machinery stood all agleam and patiently waiting for chefs, bakers and other galley staff who at that moment were beginning to trickle in. Before long a hubbub of activity would descend on the area readying food for the imminent arrival of passengers. I darted up another ladder that led to a pantry on B Deck. I could've taken one of the elevators that interconnected all the pantries all the way up to Sun Deck but I was on a roll and scampered up a third ladder to A Deck. A door led us from the pantry into that deck's port passageway. I surmised Mister King to be a smoker for the upward jaunt had him gasping slightly. His eyes took in the corridor's polished oak and elm panelled decor that seemed to stretch for miles and miles.

"Have you been here before?" I asked.

"As a matter o' fact Ah have," he replied with a lecherous smirk but didn't elaborate. His heavy Scotch accent was so atrocious that I wondered how on earth he would be able to communicate with the passengers.

I could only guess that he probably had his leg across a piece of crumpet on his previous trip. Them engineers had certain liberties that we ratings could only dream of. Anyway A17 fan room was but a few steps aft from that particular pantry. I eased its door open and ushered him in.

The fan room was typical of all the other a/c units on board. The only difference was that this one had a desk, a telephone and four grey-painted steel chairs. Don Travers, the senior a/c engineer-of-the-watch, was seated at the badly scuffed desk with the phone to his ear. My oppo, Jack Purcell, momentarily looked up from a girlie picture that graced an old *Reveille* before resuming his deliberation.

Mister Travers slapped down the receiver. He was at least three inches taller than me and sort of burly. His sandy hair was receding although he was just in his early thirties. Pale-blue eyes emanated intelligence from a squarish bronzed countenance. He hailed from Inverness. A lot of the old *Dally*'s engineers were Jocks although his vernacular hadn't that distinctive burr which encumbered many of his countrymen. In fact he was soft spoken and civil. He always asked a person to perform a task as if it was a personal favour to him. "Archie's on his way down."

He glanced up at the newcomer and stuck out his hand. "Gus King, isn't it? I'm Don Travers. I'm the ringmaster on this watch."

"Pleased tae meet ye Don," replied Mister King. "Whit's the score here?"

"Archie MacAdam, our new Hotel Service Engineer, will line you up when he gets here," he was told.

"Wee Archie?" echoed Mister King, somewhat disconcerted. "Whit happened tae Uncle Milty?"

Mister Claus Milton had been our HSE on the previous trip.

"He went ashore with a broken wrist," replied Mister Travers. "I gather that you are acquainted with our new boss."

"Och aye," declared Mister King. "Last trip him an' me -"

The door swung ajar, and as the *Reveille* hastily slid into the desk's top drawer, a runt of a man dressed in a black patrol suit entered. He was accompanied by another engineer attired in a white boilersuit. Twin solid gold bars on the former's epaulettes denoted his rank: Third Engineer Officer. Mister Travers was a fifth engineer and the other two were sixths. I suppose Mister MacAdam must've been in his early forties at that time. With a scowl on his shrivelled apricot face, his brown eyes sought discrepancies in the fan room before settling on Mister Travers like a pair of hazelnuts.

"The Boat Train'll be here in aboot twa 'oors," the HSE announced harshly. His garbled dialect was worse than Mister King's. He sounded like a demented haggis crunching bottles of Scotch. "Ah want a' the fans runnin' at hauf speed an' the thermotank steam cracked open jist a wee totty hair."

He thumbed a leathery fist over his shoulder at Mister McBride, the four-to-eight steering gear engineer. "MacBride here'll gie ye a haun' since he's goat bugger-all else tae dae until Trial o' Engines ramorra mornin'."

Roughly translated: All the a/c fans are to be started and set on half speed. The thermotank control valve to be opened just a touch so that steam will be admitted to heat fan-blown air destined for the passengers' cabins. Mister MacBride was at liberty to help out until the main engines were tested during the following morning.

He stood closer to Mister King and eyed him up and down as if he'd tumbled from a manure cart. "The joab wid gang faster if a'boady kent whit tae dae."

Mister King just shrugged offhandedly. It wasn't his fault that he was ignorant of three hundred or so fan room locations. The HSE reopened the desk's top drawer and frowned when he saw the Reveille. He lifted it up and removed three T-shaped keys, each with a square socket for operating the steam valves on the Carrier thermotanks. He issued them to me, Jack, and Mister MacBride before demanding that we get our arses in gear.

Off we went.

MacAdam rolled up the *Reveille* and stuffed it in his back pocket. "Don, you stey here an' man the phone an' Ah'll show oor new guy here the ropes."

From the back of the drawer he withdrew a sling psychrometer and a pocket-sized white Formica log board, colloquially known as the 'slate'. Vertical and horizontal lines had been etched on it. Scratched along the top were the words: Room | Dry | Wet. The left column listed all twenty-one public rooms aboard the ship beginning with first class followed by cabin class and finally tourist class.

"Yase this tae record a' the wet and dry bulb temperatures." The rapid snappy Govan brogue even troubled King's endeavour to decipher. "When ye've done that, work oot each humidity readin' by referrin' tae yon chart up there oan the bulkheid above the desk. Write a' yer readin's in the a/c logbook - neatly mind."

A massive sheet of chart paper, browned from the passing years, bore ratios between various sets of wet and dry bulb thermometer readings. When the appropriate ratio was found and multiplied by one hundred the relative humidity was determined.

"Pit this in yer pocket," prompted MacAdam, handing him the slate. "Have ye ever seen or yased a Twaddle afore?" He placed the sling psychrometer in King's hand.

It was a peculiar instrument. The curious terminology Twaddle was coined from the company that manufactured hygrometers and similar instruments. Two thermometers were fastened in parallel to a small board with a handle attached. The silk sock over the wet thermometer's bulb had to be kept damp at all times. After the board had been revolved like a football rattle for a minute or two, the temperatures were compared and logged.

"Weel, are ye gaun tae staun' here cuddlin' that thing a' day?" MacAdam snarled. "Let's go an' Ah'll show ye the public rooms that are maist critical."

The junior folded the Twaddle's handle and placed it in his back pocket. He followed MacAdam as they headed forward along the panelled corridor. Angus had no difficulty keeping up with him because the short-arsed Glaswegian was thwarted by short bandy legs. Passing the closed doors of cabins, pantries, and fan rooms, they reached A Deck Square.

Stalwart pairs of elevators stood like oblong sentries on either side of the square. Barclays Bank was situated aft of the left set of lifts. To their right a magnificent companionway rose to a landing where it straddled into twin stairways that led to Main Deck. The staircase bulkheads were panelled with vertical courses of oak nut with a horizontal band of chestnut. The lower part or dado was enhanced with elm burr. The steps and stairwell sported elaborate designs of mixed woods. Angus was to ascertain later that these designs were consistent themes on every companionway all the way up through R, B, A, Main, and Promenade Decks.

Beyond this elegant staircase they could see the mail and baggage room which was situated directly aft of the starboard lifts. Amidships between the elevators lay the purser's office. MacAdam stepped into the port inboard elevator. When the doors closed he pressed the button for R Deck. Angus would have preferred skipping down the ornate companionways through B Deck to R Deck but instead he had to play 'follow the leader'.

They stepped out into an enormous foyer. The engineers strode across the short blue pile of carpeted deck to a pair of bronzed rococo doors. Within, the great expanse of the main restaurant lay in front of them its stillness and grandeur as impressive as that of a cathedral. The highly polished parquet deck was almost square with sides of eighty-six feet, the width of the ship amidships. Huge square ports or windows were dark because night had fallen although some reflected the odd dockyard light. Enormous columns rose to the lofty deckhead. This restaurant catered to both First Class and Cabin Class passengers.

Like ghosts white-jacketed stewards flitted silently about the great room placing fresh laundered linen on myriad tables. On the far bulkhead a map of the North Atlantic Ocean displayed the east and west courses of the vessel when she was sailing on her regular Southampton-New York run. A tiny clockwork ship was stuck in the mid-Atlantic, a testament to the days when it plotted the daily run before its mechanical demise.

"Ye've been here afore, have ye no'?" asked the HSE.

"Aye," admitted Angus with a gloomy sigh. "Ah've been in this place afore."

"Aye," repeated MacAdam, with a leer. "Ah heard aboot yer wee run in wi' the skipper last trip. In front o' a' the bluidy passengers tae."

He tittered like a school lassie.

"Weel, whit happened was . . ."

The HSE cut him off. "Ah ken whit happened. A' Ah'm sayin' is - jist dinnae get up tae ony shenanigans while Ah'm runnin' this show. Ah dinnae need ony mair clowns."

Angus was well aware that his escapade had gone round the ship and no doubt the story was embellished with each telling. Through no fault of his own he'd been ordered into this room while lunch was being served to the captain and his passengers. It had been most unfortunate that his boilersuit had been saturated beforehand with a fire retardant that smelled like bovine ordure.

"Onywey," said the HSE. "This is no' gettin' oan wi' the joab. Is that sock oan the wet bulb damp?"

The Twaddle was hauled out, its handle unshipped and the thermometer's base felt for moisture. He nodded.

"Weel then, gie yer swinger a wee twirl an' we'll see whit's happenin' in here."

The dry thermometer reading was 60^{0} Fahrenheit and the wet registered fifty-eight.

"Aye, that'll be a' richt when the thermotank's steam is turned oan," opined MacAdam. "The dewpint will dry up a wee bitty. Noo then," he said. "The folk in here eat aboot the same time as us. That is - frae aboot seven tae aboot hauf nine - mornin' an' nicht.

"Dinnae bother aboot lunch because ye'll no' be oan watch then. Jist efter seven ye'll take a readin' richt here, ane in the middle, an' anither yin aboot twenty feet this side o' yon fancy doors leadin' tae the galleys. Ok?"

The junior nodded and they meandered about the restaurant. The HSE told him that the tourist class restaurant was aft of the galleys hence the name R Deck.

"Noo, it's awfy important tae keep a close eye oan on the humidity because the airconditionin' system in this place is quite unique. Ye see, it serves the First Class Main Lounge richt above oor heids there, the ballroom aft o' it, an' the Lang Gallery tae."

The HSE glared into King's eyes as if to weld this germane wisdom to his brain. He walked forward on the starboard side to another pair of doors, the mates to the port entry doors.

Back in the foyer MacAdam pointed forward to a revolving door and told his junior that it led to the First Class Swimming Pool and Turkish Baths. Another elevator took them to Promenade Deck where an arcade of fashionable shops surrounded the main stairway. Other shops branched away along short parquet aisles. Easy chairs and small tables were staggered here and there for passengers to sit and window-shop among sheer opulence.

Still proceeding forward they passed the First Class Library on their left, an Austin Reed shop on their right, and some smaller public rooms. A pair of swing doors unselfishly granted audience to the Observation Bar and Lounge.

An immense half-moon cocktail bar expansively surveyed a plush lounge, which in turn was encompassed by large square windows. At sea on a clear day a splendid view of the fo'c'sle head charging towards a blue horizon would be enjoyed by first class passengers. But right now the dimly lit foremast was etched against the distant Town Quay and the blackness of night.

"Richt," resumed the HSE. "Jist like us engineers, some passengers like their plonk afore dinnertime so dae a swing in here aboot this time every day. An' dinnae accept ony booze either." He waited in vain for a nod or shake of denial before setting off to a second set of swing doors. Shoving his way through he said, "A'richt then, we'll gang alang tae the Hielan' Grill."

They passed the First Class Drawing and Children's Playing Rooms and went out on deck. Here the Prom Deck was enclosed from the elements by what seemed like a few furlongs of vast glass windows. Nearing midships they ascended a companionway to the Boat Deck. Boat Deck and Sun Deck were perhaps synonymous to each other. Lifeboat davits were located on the former which was exposed to the weather. The latter could be accessed by climbing a few steps to the various entrances to the First Class suites forward, the engineers' quarters midships and by Number 21 Lifeboat, or the Highland Grill further aft. Energetic passengers often jogged off a heavy meal by circumnavigating the slightly higher Sun Deck at Boat Deck level.

They ascended the Highland Grill's after entrance steps. Within was a very special room indeed for the notably affluent voyagers who wished to have their meal apart from the other passengers. Luncheon and dinner was served here and after ten o'clock in the evening the Grill metamorphosed into the Gloaming Nightclub so patrons could dance the night away while imbibing on elaborate drinks from the cocktail bar. Here lay opulence indeed. How does one begin to describe such grandeur?

The immense windows surveying the games area on the after deck were reflecting shards of light from Hythe, which is located across the Rivers Test and Itchen estuaries. At sea guests would soak up the superb vista of the propellers' wakes, boiling twins of green and cream churning right to the distant horizon.

Like the crows of Ponfeigh that fly backwards to see where they've been, mused Angus.

This room was devoid of the usual wood panelling. Instead paintings of white-face clowns, tumblers, startling animals, coloured hoops and balloons, captured scenes from circuses and pantomimes. Gilt and silvered colonnades emulated the style of the ceiling where psychedelic lights were controlled by entertainers from a microphone stand on the dais.

The carpet was jet black and small square tables, mostly set for couples, encompassed the dance floor, a cross-grain sycamore parquetry inlaid with thistle-shaped motifs. The nine by seven-yard floor was a step below the level of the carpet and bordered with lines of other pleasing woods such as mahogany, ironwood, and quince. They approached the rococo type railing that divided the dancing well from the rest of the room's raised portion.

Quite a fancy fence, King thought, his fingers resting lightly on this balustrade of silvery-bronze and glass. The supports of this ornate guardrail were fitted with permanent lights. When the nightclub was in full swing other lights on the handrail's lower section were devised to flash ever-changing colours. A baby grand piano set off the low stage and would accompany performing artists and small musical combos.

Silently the two engineers strolled through this à la carte restaurant and glanced out onto the deck games area beyond. Beyond the ship's stern a dark sullen Southampton Water brooded in the reflection of hazy sodium lights.

"Richt," said MacAdam. "This place is yased for lunch an' dinner. Get in here wi' yer swinger afore hauf seven. Efter ten o'clock at nicht it becomes a nightclub an' a wee den o' iniquity. Still that pairt o' it will no' affect ye too much unless some o' them are drinkin' until crow piss." He headed toward the exit. "Come oan an' Ah'll show ye whaur the Freon compressors are for coolin' doon this joint."

On the way back to A17 fan room the HSE told Angus of a blueprint in the a/c office that marked the locations of the other public rooms. Travers, MacBride, Gerry and Jack were just finishing coffee when they came in.

"There's some coffee for you two," said Don. "It could be a mite cool now."

MacAdam shook his head and glanced at his watch. "No' for me," he said. "Ah'm awa for my dinner."

Twisting the door handle he imparted some last words to Angus. "By the wey laddie, here are some important rules while in the company of passengers." He let go of the door knob and held out his left hand with outspread fingers. He grasped his pinky. "Frae noo oan, ye'll be turnin' tae in best bib an' tucker." The ring finger was clasped. "Nae smokin' in front o' the passengers." The third finger was next. "Ayeways be polite an' helpful tae the passengers - nae matter how much snazz they gie ye." The index finger. "Nae pickin' yer nose in front o' them or scratchin yer arse either." And finally the thumb. "An' definitely - Ah say definitely - nae chattin' up the young things." The HSE's hand closed into a tight fist which wavered under Angus' nose. "Or else," he threatened and left.

Don grinned. "New guys always get this job because their Number Ones are brand-spanking new. I hope that you've got plenty of clean shirts. You'll need one for every watch. Otherwise you'll be dhobiing every other day - right Teddy?"

Teddy agreed and gave Angus a tip. "The valet service is just a couple of doors down from here. If you give the guy three half-crowns he'll sponge and iron your uni."

"Thanks Teddy," replied Angus and took a sip of coffee. Making a face he put the cup back down.

"Here," offered Teddy. "Since there's nothing for us to do for the rest of the watch, why don't you come down the tiller flat with me? Les, my greaser, has always got a pot of something brewing."

Angus looked at Don in askance. "It's fine with me," he assented easily.

Off they went, tripping down the pantry stairs to C Deck into the working alleyway then aft to another flight of stairs, which rose back up to R Deck. Just like the working alleyway, this deck area was painted a glossy burnt red. The port shell doors were agape. A conveyor belt was delivering trunks, suitcases, and other luggage almost as fast as crewmembers could load them onto flatbed trolleys. The baggage would be distributed to cabin sections where stewards made sure they reached their owners. At sea this area metamorphosed into the Pig and Whistle, the vernacular for the crew's bar. Behind it lay the entrance to the steering gear compartment.

It had been a long and tedious journey from Glasgow Central Station. A taxi had taken Nan from Euston Station directly to Waterloo Station where she had barely time for a cup of tea before the boat train's departure. Surely a dining car would be attached. One was, although the quaint English fare of bite-sized, wafer-thin slices of brown bread with cucumber fillings failed to titillate her. Gammon-filled sandwiches and a cup of hot sweet tea helped to stave off hunger. At every place setting an illustrated brochure enlightened the would-be voyagers to certain interesting facts about the RMS *Queen of Dalriada.*

The boat train wended its way through the dockyards and stopped outside an immense building called Ocean Terminal. Porters seemed to materialise from everywhere. Baggage from the train's guard van was steadily being unloaded onto the railway platform.

The acrid stink of smoke and steam assailed her nostrils as Nan alighted from the boat train. She cautiously followed the hustle-bustle of travellers into the building. Officials directed them to elevators which went to the upper floor where two luxurious reception halls were located. One was a little more Spartan than the other, intimation that the British class system was still alive and well. In the First Class-Cabin Class Hall, sofas like island atolls offered plush comfort to the soon-to be voyagers. Later Nan was to discover that the Main Hall aboard ship would present similar vacilities such as a bank, a flower shop, a writing room and other indulgences useful to the well-heeled traveler.

A cup of tea at the refreshment buffet was a welcome respite after having her travel and health documents had cursory checked. Not long afterwards she and other passengers were politely ushered to open doors on the opposite side of the building.

Speared by a gangway, a wall of night pierced by regimental lines of manmade stars loomed up against the chilly sky. Here, looking along the length of the ship its physical dimensions took on new meaning. The twin blacktopped orange funnels were dimly illuminated above an off-white superstructure. Seven hundred and sixty-one feet long with a beam of eighty-odd feet the little book had revealed. Then as now the fifty-one thousand, five hundred and seventy-three tons had escaped Nan's comprehension. Below her, other gangways rose from the dockside to stab the ship's side.

On R Deck Square an assistant purser checked Nan's name on his clipboard. Fervently hoping that a hot bath awaited her, she docilely tailed a steward to her stateroom on Main Deck.

Angus and Teddy clumped noisily down a spiral ladder to the tiller flat far below. At bottom Les Doran was craning his head upwards to see who the interlopers were. "Hello Les, is there any coffee left?" Teddy asked.

Doran grunted, picked up a grey plastic carafe and shook it. This was one of the ice-water thermos flasks that could be found in any passenger's and officer's cabin. With another grunt he poured some coffee into a clean cup. Teddy took it from him and gave it to Angus. "Sugar's over there, Gus," he said, pointing to a wooden bench. "No cream I'm afraid." He introduced the new a/c engineer to the greaser.

Les was a husky man with broad shoulders. He was tidily garbed in clean, well-worn blue denims. His rolled-up sleeves exposed well-formed biceps. Appearing to be in his early forties he had thin blonde wavy hair and piercing light-grey eyes that had a tendency to stare off into space.

Angus dropped a couple of sugar cubes into the cup and stirred the coffee with a teaspoon that sported a Blackpool crest. He took a sip and his cheeks puckered unintentionally. Strong, but least it was hot. "Thanks Les," he said.

Les scowled. He withdrew a clean wiper from his back pocket and unnecessarily rubbed a gleaming brass gauge. Like the pressure gauge, everything else in the tiller flat was spotless. One could see that hard work and pride kept the area immaculate.

"So then Teddy, how's aboot showin' me the ropes in here."

"Ok. First of all, there are three steering wheels on the bridge, two manual and one automatic. When the wheel in operation is turned, say to port, a gear mechanism inside the telemotor activates a rack and pinion, which causes a piston to move. This piston displaces a mixture of water and glycerin through a copper pipe along the entire length of the ship right to here. He placed his hand on a valve handwheel that was part of a manifold of twelve others. If the quartermaster turns the helm to starboard the fluid is, of course, directed down another pipe. A hand touched an adjacent valve.

"Three wheels - six valves," said Angus. "Whit's the ither eight for?"

"The power trains of all Pict Line ships are designed to the Royal Navy standards," replied Teddy. "Last trip when you were in 2BR you might have noticed that two of the boiler steam discharges are piped along one side of the ship to the engineroom. The other four steam headers from the same boiler room run along the opposite side. In 3BR the reverse takes place. The theory is that if a torpedo, heaven forbid, hit one side of the ship and knocked out the steam flow, valves would be changed over to that one boiler room could still create enough power to drive the ship, pumps and lights. It's the same with steering - pipes along both sides of the ship."

Teddy moved over to a pedestal that supported a matched pair of small hydraulic pumps which were driven by two electric motors. "These Sperry-Rand servos are rotary-piston hydraulic pumps. The minuscule energy from a touch on the wheel acts through a system which amplifies and directs the power of these pumps to that great lever that links those three big black ones over there." MacBride pointed to a trio of Denny-Brown rotary hydraulic pumps which emulated the servo pumps more than a thousand fold.

"Now come over here Gus." Teddy directed.

He went up two steps and went along to the rudder post that was harnessed to a great yoke. The yoke formed the crossbar of an aitch. Four huge hydraulic rams were this aitch's legs. To turn the rudder, pressure was introduced to a pair of rams that were diagonally opposed to each other. This not only turned the rudder but allowed the other two rams to empty, draining their oil back to tank. Naturally the reverse happened so that the rudder would turn in the opposite direction.

MacBride led his new shipmate over to a switchboard on the port side of the tiller flat. "Really only one hydraulic pump is needed to operate the rudder. To be on the safe side, one drive motor is powered from the Hotel Service Generator Room, the other from the Main Generator Room. It's unlikely to have an electrical failure in both jenny rooms or so I've been told."

Angus nodded, his mind absorbing this new wealth of information. He glanced over to the starboard side at Les who was seated on a bench that ran parallel to the ship's side. The rating seemed to be in another world for he was staring off into space.

"Is he ok?"

Teddy gave him a sad smile. "Les is as normal as any other guy who's been torpedoed twice."

"Nae shit?"

"Yeah, he was torpedoed in a tramp steamer in the Pacific during the war. A Jap cargo ship picked him up and it in turn was torpedoed not long after by a Yank sub. Another Jap ship picked him up and he spent the rest of the war in a POW camp about twenty miles away from Hiroshima.

"Christ!" swore Angus, suitably awed.

"Yeah," repeated Teddy. "He's told me some awful war stories down here when I'm on sea watches with him. Thank God I'm on steady days after we clear port. When those big pumps start moaning and the rush of water from the props swishes against the hull, it can get pretty eerie down here at night I can tell you."

They ambled back to the starboard side. An enormous ship's wheel with a binnacle in front of it stood between the servos and the main hydraulic pumps. “Did this come aff the Flyin’ Dutchman?” Angus joked. He grabbed a couple of the spoke handles and turned the highly polished dark mahogany wheel.

“Hardly,” said Teddy, pointing to a machined steel pin chained to a bracket. “If both servo motors fail, they can be disconnected allowing that pin to be inserted into that hole.” He directed King’s attention to a clevis. “That connects the wheel mechanism to the main pump linkage. The bridge sends down one of their drivers in one hellova hurry and the ship is steered from here. That’s the bridge phone there.”

Someone clumping down the spiral ladder drew their attention. It was Jimmy Evans, Teddy’s relief. “Hey Gus,” he said. “Dan MacTaggart’s is looking all over for you.”

“Ok thanks Jimmy,” replied Angus. “Ah’ll see ye in the mess Teddy.” And he scampered up the corkscrewed stairway out of sight.

CHAPTER FIVE

Sailing Day

0335 Friday 12th January, 1962

Some of the watchkeeping engineers gazed up from their corned beef sarnies at Angus as he strolled into the mess. Only one trip old and freshly brushed his new Number Ones positively stood out against his bleary-eyed colleagues' patrol suits that had endured abuse from sloppy table manners and the onslaught of oil and grease from the machinery spaces. Removing his peaked cap, which was adorned with a blinding white cover from beneath his arm, he carefully rested it on the linen tablecloth before assuming a chair. A few mumbled remarks chewed back and forth before settling down to the humdrum conversation that only can be appreciated by marine engineers who have lived through countless early morning hours with eyelids partially gummed up from sleep.

Angus filled a cup with hot black liquid from a sterling silver coffeepot. The cream looked fresh enough to blend with his beverage now sweetened by two cubes of Redpath sugar. He stirred his Java and peered across the table to where Don Travers sat. Don absorbed his junior's appearance and puckered his lips in approval. "You're just liable to be ravished by sunup."

Gerry and Jack were already on duty when the engineers turned to in A17 fan room. Angus relieved Dave Hedges and Don took over from Kevin Cunningham. They reported a quiet watch. Gerry went out to fetch some coffee from a neighbouring pantry. When he returned Angus declined this refreshment because he was keen to get started. A cursory glance at the slate imparted that Dave had failed to erase the pencilled readings. Not realizing that the log had been flogged he decided to leave them so that he could compare his findings from the previous watch. Don advised him to begin at the top and go through each public room deck by deck. "When you get back down to this level, drop by for some cocoa."

Armed with his swinger and boundless enthusiasm Angus set off aft heading for Sun Deck and the Highland Grill. It was closed. He made his way down to Promenade Deck and went into the Tourist Class Lounge. He knew little about décor or any aspect of room design but this place looked all right to him. It was reminiscent of the Motherwell Football Club where he had gone once with his Aunt Ina and Uncle Ben. The room was empty but he took a reading anyway and pencilled in his results on the slate. He went forward to the Tourist Class Smoking Room and repeated his procedure. The Cabin Class Smoking Room was next. Right away he noticed that a lot of thought and expense had gone into the comforts of cabin class passengers than the previous public rooms.

Pot plants with cascading ferns and variegated spider plants dangled from the deckhead of the Starboard Garden Lounge like verdant chandeliers. Here, cabin class passengers could imbibe at the Naiad Bar while enjoying an ocean view.

Now he entered a room with which he was familiar: The Port Garden Lounge. Angus had signed on the ship right there at that particular glass-topped table with legs of scrolled wrought iron; one of the dozen or so that abounded amongst the varied vegetation. Large windowpanes on the seaboard side gave the room a plush greenhouse atmosphere. The room was, of course, for first class passengers and a mere hint of luxuriance that he was to witness as his rounds progressed.

The elegant Long Gallery was the young engineer's real introduction to the environment of the elite. It was followed by the First Class Cinema, the First Class Main Lounge, and the First Class port and starboard Writing Rooms. He proceeded along the port side of the Main Hall, checked the First Class Library before progressing to the Observation Lounge. It was strange, Angus thought, he had yet to see another living being. It was if he was in a ghost ship. The sound of a vacuum cleaner droning in the First Class Children's Playroom changed that line of reasoning. He peeked in to see a steward at work. He investigated the First Class Drawing Room before going down to Main Deck.

The engineer ambled down a long, long carpeted corridor, its walls panelled in various shades and varieties of wood. He passed countless First Class staterooms and cabins on his way aft to the Cabin Class Main Lounge. Not quite as plush as First Class the room still had certain panache in King's estimation. The motif here was Iberian but it might as well have been Siberian for Angus' ignorance in art and design was rapidly becoming very evident. The Cabin Class Library and Writing Room received a cursory check as did the Cabin Class Children's Playroom.

The Tourist Class Main Lounge on A Deck was directly below the Cabin Class Main Lounge. Checking his watch he realized that half the watch had gone already. Once more he plodded forward to A17 fan room. Don was doing his rounds down below. Jack was out on a call and the cocoa was cold.

"Never mind Mister King," Gerry mollified him. "I'll fetch you a fresh cup of coffee from the pantry."

Breathing his thanks Angus sat down. Gerry was barely out the door when the phone rang. "Eh - air conditioning," he said cautiously.

"One of my passengers is complaining that his cabin is too cold," replied a voice. "He's in B31."

"Aye ok. Ah'll hae somebody fix that right away."

"Oh Christ, not another bloody Jock!" A voice exclaimed before the phone went dead.

Angus relayed the message to Gerry when he came back with a carafe of coffee. The rating left immediately to answer the call. King lit up a cigarette and a cloud of smoke floated to the deckhead. Presently he began to record his readings in the logbook. Jack came in, shook the carafe, and filled a mug.

"Find everything all right, Mister King?" he asked.

"Aye," replied Angus. "If Ah just follow the list oan the slate, everythin' falls intae place."

They chatted for a while until Don came back. "Hi Gus, how's it going?"

"Just fine Don. Ah'm mair than hauf done."

A few early birds were beginning to drift into the main restaurant for breakfast as Angus was doing his rounds. He discovered that this dining room accommodated both first class and cabin class passengers. Journeying aft through the galleys he checked out the Tourist Class Restaurant before calling it a day. He was well aware that some public rooms had been missed but a better effort would be made during his next watch.

0830

King hurriedly changed into his civvies and headed for the engineers' mess which was situated on the port side of the engineers' lower quarters. Bob Christie was waddling on flip-flops along from the showers kilted in a white rough towel when he ran into Angus. "Fancy a game of chess after breakfast?" he asked.

It might've been said in certain quarters, particularly in the engineers', that the four-to-eight platform second had very few friends. This was not true. In actual fact he had none - until the previous trip that is. Angus King had been assigned 'floater' at the beginning of that voyage and had suffered the indignities Christie was wont to inflict on brand-new juniors. However during a drunken conversation in the Big Apple at the Merchant Navy and Airline Officers' Club the platform second learned that his new junior was a competent chess player. From then on Angus could do no wrong.

"Sorry Bob," said Angus. "But Ah need to get some white shirts an' toiletry stuff afore we sail."

Christie brandished a bar of soap in one hand, a blue and white flat tin in the other and had a loofah tucked under his arm. He waved the tin at his friend. "Can you get me a couple of tins of Johnson's Baby Powder? This is my last tin and it's almost empty."

Angus always used men's talcum to help keep his skin dry and cut down on sweat rashes in the engineroom. "Ah'm surprised that ye use baby powder," he said.

"It's better'n rubbing Vim on your balls," returned Christie.

A guffaw surged from his shipmate. "Ah'll bet it is. Ok Bob, Ah'll pick some up for ye."

At a pinch this dining room could seat about forty engineer and electrical officers but that rarely happened because there was always a watch on duty below. Two rows of tables ran fore and aft. Four people could be seated at each of the tables running along the seaboard side. Usually the senior watchkeepers dominated that side. Inboard tables were set for six juniors.

Breakfast for the four-to-eight watch began at 08:40 and ended at 09:20. Only about half the watch were in the mess: Bob Christie, the platform second, his two engineroom juniors Terry Baker and Peter Deery. Three stokehold engineers sat at a window table. They were Charlie Benson, Taffy Morgan, and Wilberforce Keyes, who steamed 1 BR, 2 BR and 3 BR respectively. Angus walked to an inboard table where Pete Eaton, the fuel-oil engineer, sat with Don Travers and Teddy McBride.

"Going ashore?" asked Pete who had earned his soubriquet, Steamboat on the previous trip.

"Aye," replied Angus, reaching for a menu. "Ah'm gaun tae get some shirts, toothpaste, Brylcreem, an' stuff."

"Will you pick up some French letters for me?" Teddy blithely asked.

Keyes, whose excellent hearing overheard the question from the opposite side of the mess leered, “That’s regular size Gus. Not the donkey size for yourself!”

This brought a general cackle that turned King’s ears quite red. His generous physical endowment had been discovered on the previous cruise and even yet some of the distaff crew members were known to be making subtle enquiries. “Ach, ye’re just jealous Wheelkey.”

“Damn right,” acknowledged Keyes, whose nickname was derived from the engineers’ friend, a curiously hooked but indispensable tool which was used for opening and closing valves. “You’ve got more to spare that me and Taffy here have together.”

“You speak for yourself boyo!” protested the tubby Welsh engineer through a mouthful of Canadian back bacon. “My missus says that more than a handful’s a waste, see you.”

With that Angus wiped his lips with his linen table napkin, stood up and exited the mess. He went back to his cabin and donned his gabardine coat, tucking his yellow scarf inside.

Although the air was nippy on the dockside with abundant patches of hoar frost, he judged that brisk stroll would do him good. Passing a taxi rank he strode energetically along the mile-long jaunt to the dockyard gate. From there he made a beeline to Marks and Spencers to purchase his shirts. On the way back he went into a chemist’s shop just off Canute Road. A few toiletry items including Christie’s baby powder and two packets of Durex contraceptives for Teddy MacBride went into his shopping bag.

An ironmonger’s shop window drew his interest. After browsing over a display of tools he went inside. Tools and gadgets always had a fascination for him so that he felt like a kid in a sweetie shop. He considered a slim penlight would be more of an asset to him in his new job than the bulky Brightstar flashlight that he’d bought in New York City. A pocket sized multiple screwdriver might prove useful too. An adjustable wrench less than six-inches long piqued his interest. Its jaws opened to nine-sixteenths of an inch, wide enough to accommodate the head of three-eighths bolt. Even so Angus doubted the strength of the cheap drop-forged steel. Still, it might prove handy for the hex-headed self-tapping screws that flourished on the ship's air conditioning duct work. Half-a-dozen spare AAA batteries completed his needs.

Heading back to the ship, he came upon a newsagent and tobacconist shop. This avid reader couldn't give that a miss. A book carousel drew him like a moth to a flame and he was soon rewarded with *The Carpetbaggers* by Harold Robbins, *Fear is the Key* by Alistair MacLean, and a work penned by Harry Patterson: *The Thousand Faces of Night*. That very morning's *Daily Express* went into his shopping bag too. On his way back to the ship he bumped into Will Keyes outside the Nag's Head.

The fourth engineer was a jovial fellow with a ready wit. "Fancy a beer?"

"Aye sure," replied Angus.

They went into the pub and sat at a window table. "Two pints of best bitter luv," Wheelkey hailed the girl behind the bar. Angus bought the second round. The engineers talked about the upcoming trip and meantime beer was immersing them into a state of well-being. A long harsh blast shattered their euphoria. A mild vibration on the cigarette-damaged tabletop increased effervescence in their brew. Alarmed, they stared into one another's eyes. A blast from the *Queen of Dalriada*'s foghorn was unmistakable.

"I thought we were sailing at one," said Wheelkey.

"So did Ah," concurred Angus.

The fourth hastily drained his glass. "She's calling for tugs!"

He stood erect and slammed his pint pot on the table. His companion gathered up his merchandise and headed for the door. "Aren't you going to finish that?" asked Keyes, pointing his shipmate's glass which was still three-quarters full.

"We dinnae hae time."

Keyes downed the beer in one swallow and rushed out.

A ten-minute run brought them in sight of their ship when succeeding blasts emitted from the liner's other two whistles.

"*Holy shit*!" swore Wheelkey. He came to a gasping halt and bent over, his hands on his knees. The cold morning air condensed his exhalations emulating the clouds of steam ballooning from all three ship's whistles.

Angus halted too and through puffs and wheezes asked, "Whit's up?"

"Trial . . . of . . . bloody . . . Engines!" replied Keyes, gasping through heaves from his swirling beer-filled stomach. "Engines, rudder, whistles - everything is tested two hours prior to sailing."

"Och aye - right," remembered Angus, whose breathing had gone back to normal. "Ah guess we panicked a wee bit."

Keyes stood up straight and the redness faded from his face. "Let's get back on board and get some kip."

Nan consumed a light breakfast in the main restaurant. The sumptuous food on the first class menu was tempting but she had no desire to grow out of her brand-new outfits on this cruise. She'd settled for a grapefruit half, a soft-boiled egg, a slice of toasted whole-wheat bread and a pot of Earl Grey tea.

Although the Main Hall shops would be closed until the vessel sailed she spent some time window-shopping. Their wares included Gerrards jewellery, antique silver, colourful Jacqmar scarves by Arnold Lever, unique Finigan handbags embroidered by the Royal School of Needlework and a host of other products that might titillate affluent passengers.

Like fellow voyagers she marvelled at the décor of the first class public rooms. Frivolous notes were scribbled to friends on letter-postcards that bore a picture of the ship. A notice on a letterbox assured the mailer that any letters posted within would go ashore on the pilot boat.

It was much chillier than expected when she went for an exploratory jaunt along the enclosed Promenade Deck but her sealskin coat kept her warm. At intervals, a balmy flow of warm air could be felt coming from somewhere. Looking down through one of the huge windows the scrambling and jostling of people on the dock appeared to be getting more frantic as sailing time neared. She could hear the muted clatter of gangways being withdrawn from open shell doors. The glass panes in the Prom Deck windows shimmered in response to the bass A resonance from the whistle on the after funnel.

Far aft of Nan out on the open section of Prom Deck, Bernie and Denise Sneddon were peering over the port rail. A watery sun was trying to break through ominous grey clouds. Across the basin Bernie studied the small community of Hythe. He could remember relieving a couple of their church roofs of their lead sheeting. It had been a wild rainy night and he had to stop the lorry once or twice in the New Forest to shift some tree branches off the road.

The after whistle blew suddenly and startled Denise into grabbing Bernie's arm. Her husband patted her gloved hand soothingly. The answering toot of a tugboat heading towards the cruise ship drew his attention. His eyes panned from the after docking bridge, across the tidal water and took in the vista of Southampton Water before settling on a figure on the deck above.

Bundled up in a camel haired coat the squat frame of Mo Greene could be observed on the Boat Deck. He took the stogie from his mouth and cast it overboard. Their eyes met. Mo lifted his homburg in mock salute and walked away.

Sunday, January 21st 2022
Gerry recalls:

The blasts from our ship's whistle awakened me. I rose and washed the sleep from my eyes. I considered having a shave but dropped that idea. I would have a five o'clock shadow by the time my afternoon watch came around. I wanted to keep my cushy number in air conditioning. The rules were simple; clean cut, clean shaven, clean clothes and a clean mouth.

I'd worked on a couple of other ships and knew the ropes before coming aboard the *Dally*. Here, I was assigned to the engineroom, sometimes known as the black gang. Newcomers always got the dirtiest jobs and I wasn't any different. Engineers are quick to pick out a rating with a mechanical aptitude. Before too long I was promoted away from the dreary humdrum job of fireman-trimmer and became bilgediver. This position wasn't much cleaner but it did have the advantage of roaming through all the machinery spaces and few engineers would ever bother me. Part of my duties was fetching coffee, tea, or cocoa for the watchkeepers.

On one particular trip Mister Claus Milton, who was the third engineer in the Hotel Service Generator Room, turned to five minutes late and was half sozzled. Other than booze he hadn't anything in his stomach. As I was pouring his beginning-of-the-watch coffee I suggested that he should get some grub inside him before the walking second came through. Blearily he asked where he could get grub at that time in the morning. I went topside and brought him a pint of piping hot Scotch broth from our mess. By the time the third had ravenously devoured his second helping he did his Oliver Twist and asked for more. When he was reasonably sober the man couldn't thank me enough and he promised me if the time came he'd see me right.

A few trips later, Mister Milton was made the ship's Hotel Service Engineer. This job entailed many duties that affected the welfare of the passengers and crew. Among them were air conditioning, galleys, deck machinery, lifeboats, watertight doors, the steering gear and the emergency generator. He made a point of asking the leading hand for me. And that's how I got the job.

Anyway I could feel the ship shuddering as I dressed. I figured that since it was shortly after one o'clock and the vessel was underway the Pig and Whistle might be open. I grabbed my pint pot, fork, knife and spoon and made my way after along the working alleyway. Yes, I know one doesn't need eating utensils for drinking beer. These items were issued to ratings when they came on board. If broken, lost, or stolen the replacement was charged against the rating's wages when he paid off at the end of the trip. Consequently their pint pots and utensils went wherever they did.

The bar was closed because the Pig Deck, which was really a section of R Deck, was still littered with baggage because of some mix-up. I proceeded aft up another companionway to B Deck past the Emergency Generator Room on the port side, and up yet another ladder to A Deck. Out on the open deck seamen were tidying up after the big stern hawsers had been stowed away. It was bloody cold that afternoon but then I was only wearing my jeans and a denim shirt with rolled-up sleeves. I wandered back inside and made a beeline for the firemen's mess.

That day was Friday - Fish'n'Chip Day. It's funny how the Church of Rome can cater a menu the world over for Protestants and Catholics alike. Our cook for that trip wasn't one of the greatest. It was normal for a rating from the engine gang to be assigned cook for the trip. He usually remained in that position if he was any good. If not, another victim was nominated. The shanghaied cook's culinary attributes or lack thereof mattered not one whit to the leading hand. With his contacts in the main galley he fared better than most.

It's difficult to screw up fish and chips but this guy did. The chips were crisper and much darker than Smith's potato crisps. Me and my messmates reckoned that it was the weight of the batter that kept the haddock from flopping off the plate. And the mushy peas well - they were as hard as ball bearings. I really felt sorry for the rest of my mates. Jack and me would be ok because cabin stewards were famous for keeping their unlocked pantries well-stocked with goodies for themselves and their passengers' whimsical tastes.

Although the Pig and Whistle was closed to the crew and the haute couture shops on Main and Promenade Decks remained inaccessible to the regular passengers until the ship cast off, the Highland Grill was busy serving lunch to society's elite - those who booked that illustrious restaurant weeks in advance. Elegant tableware and flatware quivered on Irish linen table covers as the ship's engines rumbled full astern. Claude Debussy's *La Mer* rippled softly from the baby grand piano on the dais.

There was more cutlery surrounding their tented napkins than sojourned in Denise's kitchen drawer, surmised Bernie as he gazed down upon their windowed table set for two. A kilted waiter glided alongside and gracefully offered them a menu each. He hinted that an aperitif might be pleasant while they perused the luncheon fare. Bernie glanced at his wife with raised eyebrows. When Denise nodded, Bernie reached for a folded blue and white card performing sentry duty over a bouquet of sweet violets nestling in a tiny cup of Waterford crystal in the middle of the table.

Unfolding the three sections the card became almost letter size. The right and centre portions announced Cocktails Liqueurs Cigars Cigarettes and at the bottom of the lists was an embossed Pict Line logo. The left side lauded beer, lager and stout lists including prices in British and US currency. Ales such as Worthington, Bass, Whitbread, Strong Scotch beer and McEwans were listed at 1/6 or one shilling and sixpence or 25 cents US a bottle. Guinness and Whitbread stout fetched the same price per bottle as did Carlsberg, Tuborg and Heineken bottles of lager. American ale and beer were thrupence (4 cents more) while lager on draught was 9d per half pint.

Handmade Havana cigars ranged from 1/9 to 4/6 or 27 to 68 cents each. The list went to other types of cigars, blended tobaccos, and cigarettes. Flipping the card over revealed three other columns of alcoholic refreshment: Liqueurs, Cocktails and Mixed Drinks respectively. The most expensive drink was Martell Extra, which was guaranteed more than seventy years old Bernie noted and the price of one glass was 4/6 or 68 cents. He settled for a bottle of Worthington ale and Denise had an Amer Picon with soda water.

While Ocean Terminal and Hythe merged into the afternoon mist, crab flake cocktail was served. The crowds that once aligned the after Prom Deck railings now had dwindled to a few. A strident blast from the forward funnel was the cruise ship's sonorous farewell to Southampton.

The Sneddons ordered Russian salad but skipped out on those mysterious unknowns, *hor d'oeuvres*. This course was followed by Consomme *Cheveux d'Anges*, which surprisingly turned out to be some kind of chicken soup. The scrap dealer promptly reached for his dessert spoon, dipped it into the soup and blew noisily before consuming it. A basket of warm rolls embalmed in scarlet cloth like hot water bottles was placed at his side. He lifted the basket and gestured to Denise who shook her head. Bernie extricated a dinner roll from its cosy nest and cruelly eviscerated it with his fish knife, a tool he considered too blunt to slice even soft butter.

When the soup was finished the waiter removed the plate, the soup and dessert spoon and the fish knife. He replaced the latter two utensils in their respective places with diplomatic nonchalance. Denise didn't have any trouble with the flatware placing. She simply applied common sense and worked from outer settings inward.

The sommelier sidled near when he ascertained that the couple had ordered. Bernie had chosen Poached Fresh Haddock with egg sauce and Denise had selected Grilled Red Snapper with Lime Butter. They settled on a half litre of

Chateau Rayne Vigneau Sauternes 1ere *Grand Cru Classe.* The only thing they knew about vintners' products was that white wine went with fish and red went with red meat. This 1955 wine was only six years old. The sommelier gracefully poured a sample of wine into Bernie's glass. Sneddon's face fell with chagrin at the stingy amount. However, it was hastily slurped back sans the swirl, clarity, colour, and bouquet tests. He puckered his lips and held out his glass to be topped up. "Give her some too," he commanded. "I'm beginning to enjoy myself dear."

Denise had one glass and Bernie drained the bottle. A hazy view of the oil refineries at Fawley slipped past on the liner's right and directly opposite across Southampton Water lay the village of Hamble Le Rice. There was so much to choose from the next three entrees, one was a continental speciality, a grill, and a joint. Denise decided on the continental speciality. It consisted of a veal cutlet fried in butter then swirled in the pan with sherry followed by an addition of mushrooms and cream. When thickened, this concoction was dubbed *Escalope de Veau, Plaza*. A baked Idaho potato and braised lettuce accompanied this dish.

Bernie, a meat and potatoes man since way back, ordered the grill which happened to be a Minute Steak, *au beurre* and Lamb Kidneys, *Paloise* - whatever that was. It turned out to be sauce nurtured from shallots and myriad condiments. It was only natural for him to ask for mashed spuds, Creamed-Purée according to the menu and the good old standby Brussels sprouts. The sommelier materialized again. This time a 1953 Hungarian *Tokaji Aszu* was offered as well as a 1959 Bordeaux, *Chateau Citran*. The latter was selected after Bernie's mental eeny, meeny, miney, moe. Denise had one glass and Bernie drained the bottle.

Calshot slipped away almost as fast as Bernie's apple pie with vanilla ice cream. Denise threw caution to the wind and indulged in *Gâteaux Etoile*. The couple was so completely stuffed they declined the extensive cheeseboard with accompanying biscuits. They felt that a cuppa would be a well-deserving treat to complete the outstanding meal. The ship drifted to a stop while a pot of Oolong tea was served.

Presently a tremor could be detected from the engineroom far below them and the curious ninety-two foot steel cylindrical structure known as Nab Tower glided astern and lost in a smirr of grey foggy rain, a sign that their voyage had really begun.

A one-ringer catering officer attired in highland garb jauntily approached their table to ask them if they enjoyed their luncheon. When the pair beamed their hearty approval, a chit book materialized in the young officer hand. He scribbled something on a page and asked, "Suite?"

"Y'know," replied Bernie, feeling no pain because of the wine, adjusted his trouser band. "I might just have room for one of those Hot Lancashire Eccles Cakes."

"Yes sir," said the officer. "I'll see that you get one right away but I meant your suite or stateroom number."

"Oh!" uttered Bernie. "Er - Sun 15."

"Thank you sir," replied the young man, laying the chit book down on the table. "If you'd be so kind as to initial below."

Bernie's eyes focused on a small list: Luncheon for two - £2, one bottle of ale - 1/6, one glass Amer Picon - 2/6, one half litre white wine - 7/6, one half litre red wine - 7/6. The total was a blurry £2-19 shillings - less than ten dollars to a Yank. Sneddon initialled his BS with a flourish and the catering officer roamed off to another table.

Denise was feeling a little tipsy when she stood up. Bernie, although a bit woozy, was more used to drink. He took her arm and they left by the after door. Out on deck the moist sea air blew away some of the cobwebs and both resolved to watch the drinks and calories at future meals.

Sunday afternoon, January 21st
Gerry recalls:

Jack and me were doing quite well at the euchre game when the watch was called. We were up two bob which meant a couple of extra pints at the end of our watch. As usual we turned to about five minutes early for the four-to-eight. Mister King was taking over from Mister Dave Hedges. I relieved Eddie Buchanan and Jack saw off Marty Wilton, his twelve-to-four oppo. Mister Travers showed up right on the button which teed off Mister Kevin Cunningham.

As the senior watchkeeper he had the most information to hand over so it cut into his beer time. Mister Travers was feeling a little under the weather. HM Customs had allowed the bar to open when the ship cast off. At sea, afternoon bar hours were usually noon until one-thirty p.m. The confused baggage situation had screwed up our liquid recreation but the engineers and other officers enjoyed the privileges of rank. That, combined with an admirable lunch, led to a most enduring watch.

On the other hand he'd brought each of us a sizeable Jaffa orange from the constantly replenished fruit bowl in the engineers' mess. At that time Board of Trade rules stated that ratings must have at least one piece of fresh fruit per week - a rule that the Pict Line and most shipping companies strictly adhered to. Upon learning this many engineers got into the habit of stuffing bananas, pears, apples, oranges or grapes into their patrol suit pockets for their lesser fortunate workmates below decks.

As time went by Mister King got into the same habit and soon Jack and me became pretty well off as far as fresh fruit was concerned. In fact at times I'd trade some fruit for a pint of beer or some ciggies. Jack didn't smoke.

It was during the watch change over that we felt the ship slow down and the engine vibrations faded away. Presently she began to work up to full revs. Mister Travers asked Mister

King to go out on deck and get the temperature before starting his rounds. I recall that it was around 46° Fahrenheit or thereabouts.

"Look Gus," said Mister Travers. "I'd like you to check the outside air temperature every hour. The skipper will be asking for more revs to get into warm weather ASAP." He faced to me and Jack to say, "That'll probably happen later on in the watch. Both of you will probably be zooming around like blue-arsed flies shutting off the steam on the thermotanks."

The engineers went off on their rounds. The phone rang. "Air conditioning," I answered.

"Could you ask Mister King to fill up the Cabin Class Swimming Pool please?" requested a feminine voice.

"You should phone the direct line to the engineroom Miss," I replied.

"Just give Mister King the message please," persisted the voice.

"Yes Ma'am. I'll tell him when he gets back from his rounds." I hung up and pointed a revolving finger to my temple. "That broad is nuts."

About three-quarters later Mister Travers returned. Jack was out on a call. I relayed the message about Mister King. My boss leered and said that it wasn't the pool Daphne wanted filled up.

At this point in his yarn Gerry threw Jessica a shy glance. "Maybe I shouldn't be telling Mrs. King this part of my tale."

Jake chortled. "Don't worry about that Gerry. Jessica knows how sailors are."

Still embarrassed Gerry went on:

Even though there were only two of us in that fan room Mister Travers crouched forward and in a conspiratorial whisper said, "This is only Mister King's second trip to sea and already he's a fuckin' legend!"

He slid open the desk drawer and hauled out a rarely used wheelkey because it was too big in our type of work. It was more suitable for opening or closing one of the enormous valves for the main condenser recirculating system.

Wielding the hefty drop-forged steel shank for emphasis his voice lowered even more so that I could hardly hear him over the drone of the fans.

"I've heard that he's got a dick bigger than this bloody thing. There's a rumour going round the engineers' quarters that every female knows about it and that they're - well, some of them are - anxious to catch sight of it or even get their hands on it."

"No shite?" I remarked, momentarily forgetting that I was speaking to an officer.

"No shite," he repeated. "And he doesn't go hunting for 'em either. They come to him so to speak. He's a magnet for women who are ten, twenty or even thirty years older than he is. I've heard too, that there's very little foreplay involved. It's as if he's an automaton and screws on command."

I must admit that I was sceptical about all of this. We come across all kinds of characters at sea and some yarns have to be taken with a grain of salt. About an hour or so later Mister King dropped in for smoko. He reported no change on the outside air temperature. He offered his pack to Mister Travers and Jack but they were non-smokers. I was glad to accept a Senior Service from him. Ten minutes later Mister King resumed his rounds.

As far as I can recall little else happened for the rest of that watch. In fact it might have been the smoothest one of the whole trip.

CHAPTER SIX

The Bomb

2110

Platform second Bob Christie encountered Angus outside the mess. "Fancy a game of chess?"

King hesitated for a moment, his innards contemplating their onerous task ahead - digesting a superb meal. "Aye, sure Bob. Ah'll gie ye a game."

They retired to the second's cabin where chessmen had been set up ready to do battle. The cabin was a bit larger than King's but the furniture was much the same; a single bunk with a red and white chintz counterpane, two easy chairs, one coffeetable resting on a reddish-orange rug, a combination tall boy and desk, a wardrobe, a wash hand basin and mirror. Black Bob was in his Doctor Jekyll mood as he ushered his junior into an easy chair. He dashed liberal splashes of Laphroaig into two whisky glasses and gave one to his friend.

"*Slainthe Mhath*!" toasted Angus and took a sip of the Islay single malt whisky.

"*Slainthe*!" mumbled Christie, taking a seat on the opposite side of the chessboard. He held out two clenched fists.

King tapped one and was rewarded with a white pawn. An hour later he checkmated Christie and yawned.

"If you think that I'm that easy," snarled the second. "Let's play another game."

"Ah didnae yawn because Ah beat ye Bob," rebutted Angus. "Ah yawned because Ah'm bluidy tired."

Christie grudgingly accepted this answer and looked at his watch. "Right. Same time - same place - tomorrow night. And I'll have my revenge."

0320 Saturday

"Wake up Mister King!" urged Harry Jeffries, the engineroom storekeeper. The flick of a switch erupted the engineer's cabin into a blaze of light.

"Huh?" grunted Angus, his pupils shrinking to pinpoints. "Oh - aye - right. Thanks."

He clambered down from his bunk and padded across to his sink. The mirror reflected a bleary face adorned with fine reddish fuzz. Had he been standing engineroom watches this growth would've been left until daylight. Instead he shaved and dressed into his best blues. He combed his hair, retrieved his peaked cap and headed for the mess.

It was noticeably warmer, a fact that his messmates were harping on about because the engineroom and stokehold temperatures would be considerably higher. The salami and mustard sandwiches with unappetizing wings of air-dried bread slices poised for flight didn't help either. Dick Currie, the main jenny room engineer, said the tea tasted like bilge water. His companions refrained from taking him up on this challenge not having personally sampled that debatable medium that eddied with such wild abandon in the lower confines of the ship.

Gerry recalls:

Boy! - was Eddie and Marty pleased to see Jack and me when we relieved them. They were panting like greyhounds after a ten-mile run. Sweat was running off them as they flapped their shirts trying to get cool. Mister Cunningham, he wasn't much better. He'd spent the previous hour jousting with the Fozzie on the main jenny room's mezzanine. Positively glowing in his doeskin uniform, Mister Hedges was dabbing his brow with a soggy handkerchief.

"Three hours ago the outside air temperature jumped up fifteen bloody degrees - just like that," related Mister Hedges, trying to snap his damp fingers. "The phone started to ring off the blasted hook. Marty and Eddie were running around shutting the steam off the thermotanks."

He accepted a smoke from Mister King.

"Ta," he said, blowing a blue cloud into the confines of A17 fan room.

"Not long after, the outside air temperature went up another five degrees. I scooted out and began to speed up the a/c fans on this deck. He gestured at Eddie and Marty with his Senior Service. "When these two got back, they had to go out again and boot up the speed on all the fans. God! What a watch."

Our two oppos got up to leave. "Hoi!" growled Mister Hedges. "Tuck them shirts back in. The passengers don't want to see a couple of tow rags like you wandering around in the middle of the night."

"I think everything has settled down now Don," said Mister Cunningham. "Just make sure that the old Fozzie is running hot and normal by seven o'clock. We don't want our cargo all hot and sweaty while they nosh on their breakfast of eggs 'n' bacon 'n' devilled kidneys."

After the twelve-to-four personnel left we enjoyed a coffee before the engineers went on their rounds. The phone rang. It was a complaint about a lack of air flow in a stateroom on Main Deck.

"A fan motor's probably kicked out," surmised Mister Travers. His finger traced the fan room layout for that deck. "M3 fan room I think. See to that - will you Gerry?"

"Sure thing Mister Travers," I said, rising to open the door.

"Ah'll walk alang wi' ye," declared Mister King.

We went up the pantry ladder and exited on the port side. M3 was situated up forward in a cross alleyway. We reached it just in time to see the door of M3 fan room swing open and witness a steward leaving. He had a furtive expression on his swarthy face. About the same height as us, he had a much leaner frame. His hands were dark with long sensitive fingers. The man had greasy raven hair, pointy ears, and a mere slit for a mouth. His dark brown eyes flickered from side to side as if considering flight.

"Whit were ye daein' in there?" Mister King demanded.

No answer.

"Dae ye no' ken fan rooms are aff limits tae everybody but engineering personnel?"

The guy shrugged.

"Weel, dinnae dae it again," he censured. "Bugger aff!"

The man spun on heel and walked aft a few paces.

"Here!" uttered Mister King. "Have Ah no' seen ye somewhere afore?"

The steward shook his head.

"Hmm," said the engineer, unconvinced. He turned to me. "We'd better check oot that fan room afore there are any mair complaints." He placed a hand on the door knob. "Here!" he repeated and glanced back at the nervous steward. "Och, Ah mind noo! Ye were in the Albany Hotel just the ither night there. Ye wanted me tae get ye oan board this ship. Whit hae ye been up tae?"

The guy shot around a corner and out of sight. I ran to the starboard alleyway and looked all the way aft but he'd gone.

A quick survey inside the fan room revealed that all the fans were running at eighty percent speed. "Ah'd better go roond tae the stateroom an' find oot if everything's ok."

I watched him stroll a few paces forward and stop to talk to a big stocky guy in a dark suit.

Angus cocked his head past this fellow to read the stateroom number on the panelled door.

"What do you want?" growled this tough-looking sentinel.

"Ah would like tae see if everythin's ok in here," replied Angus. "Ah'm the air conditioning engineer an' Ah'm checkin' oot a complaint frae this stateroom."

A pair of dark eyes glowered down at him reflectively. One long rap followed by three short was a signal for someone within to open the door. A small bald-headed man eased the door open.

"Air conditioning engineer," said the bruiser.

"Come in please," welcomed the little guy.

Angus stepped into a small anteroom. "Whit seems tae be the problem?"

"I'll take you through and show you," whispered the gentleman.

"Ok," replied Angus. "Hey, whit's wi' the bodyguard?"

"He's a Special Branch police officer," the man enlightened him. "Four of them are required to guard my employer: one constable for each shift with a Detective-Inspector in charge. Now follow me, please."

They entered a plush sitting room. A gentleman garbed in a russet terrycloth robe remained ramrod stiff as he glared down at the intruder. His face was very familiar. He had soulful hound dog eyes with an expression to match. His thick bushy walrus moustache complimented his brushed-back grey hair. The engineer's eyes widened in recognition. He was none other than the Right Honourable Harold MacMillan, Prime Minister of Britain!

The flunky explained the reason for the engineer's presence. Acknowledging him with a curt nod the PM sat down on a comfortable easy chair. Directly opposite a grey-haired woman who was sound asleep on a sofa. Lady Dorothy was taking the complete cruise. The PM was only journeying as far as Lisbon. No doubt he had a high level meeting somewhere on the Iberian Penisular.

Angus was so shocked with this sudden meeting that he failed to appreciate the splendor of the suite. Elegant handmade rugs were scattered on plush Wilton carpet. The hardwood furniture was inlaid with rare wood, gold and silver veneers. The embroidered curtains, designed to cover the spacious windows, were agape so that fresh sea air wafted through the open portholes. The PM singled out some documents from a coffeetable and flicked his head at his flunky hinting him to get on with it.

The valet ushered Angus into a bedroom where there appeared to be two of everything; two beds, two chairs, two dressing tables, two windows and a walk-in closet, all made from the best of materials. Above the beds were the inoperative louvres.

"That one's stuck in the off position," said the flunky, pointing. "And there isn't any air coming out the other one. The Prime Minister and Lady Dorothy are having trouble sleeping."

Angus eased one of the beds to the side and he reached up to move the louvre. It was stiff. The Punkah louvre was a sphere of white plastic-type material which was fitted to a spherical socket. It could be swivelled in any direction just like an eyeball. A three-inch hole passed through the center of the sphere allowing the passage of hot or cool air from the duct work. This louvre was positioned at maximum elevation which effectively shut off the airflow. In any other position, air could be directed in any direction. A large plastic ring nut kept the louvre assembly securely fastened to the bulkhead. Simply backing off this nut about an eighth of a turn eased the stiffness, permitting smooth operation.

Sliding the bed back into position the engineer focussed his attention on the other louvre. This bed too, had to be moved so that he could reach the vent. The Punkah oscillated easily enough and yet air failed to flow through it. He stood on a chair to investigate the problem. Angus took out his penlight to see inside. Something was restricting the flow of air. It appeared to be some sort of object bundled in rags and too big for the cylindrical vent. He made an effort to remove the Punkah assembly but the retaining ring nut was seized solid. He would need a leather mallet to loosen it.

King shined his light into the duct and searched around the package. Regimented lines of screw tips indicated some sort of inspection plate. Maybe the obstruction could be removed from inside the fan room. He replaced the furniture and with tongue in cheek, the engineer informed the valet that all would be well in a jiffy. The diplomat barely looked up from a document as the engineer passed through muttering profuse apologies.

Gerry recalls:

When Mister King came out of the stateroom, he was very excited. "Ye'll never guess who was in there!" he exclaimed. "The bluidy Prime Minister!"

"No shit?" I said. "What now?"

"Let's go back intae yon fan room. There's somethin' blockin' one o' the damn louvres."

When we reentered that fan room, Mister King wended his way past fan units toward the bulkhead that abutted the stateroom's bed chamber. He pointed at a section of ductwork where an inspection plate was secured by a dozen self-tapping screws. A tiny screwdriver popped into his hand and reaching up said, "Ah dinnae ken if this wee tottie screwdriver is strong enough tae loosen these screws but . . . Ah!"

The screw turned effortlessly. Before long the plate was off and he was exploring the opening. He withdrew a clump of rags which was roughly the size of a cigarette carton. He handed it to me. "Damn it!" he swore, brushing dust from his sleeve. "What dae ye think it is Gerry?"

I removed the rags. It certainly seemed to be a carton of cigarettes wrapped in brown paper. I turned the parcel over in my hands. "I think it is somebody's stash."

"Whit dae ye mean - stash?"

"Well, when we go into lay-up for six weeks or so a lot of the guys hide a supply of duty-free smokes from the customs." I went on. "Sometimes a guy might be laid off as soon as we dock and his smokes are left hidden for ages. About six months ago we took down some ceiling tiles and discovered a carton of Woodbines. They were too dry to smoke because they'd been up there for God knows how many years."

"Ah'll just put this plate oan wi' a couple o' screws for noo," said Mister King. "Yon guy's a cop oot in the passageway an' we dinnae want him tae come in here an' investigate. Stuff that parcel doon your shirt an' we'll gang tae anither fan room an' open it."

He checked with the valet to make sure that everything was shipshape before we left. On the way down to A Deck we decided that the less people who knew about this the better. Since Mister Travers and Jack didn't smoke we planned to split the stash and take our share back to our cabins immediately.

In A9 fan room Mister King tore off the paper wrapping to reveal a cardboard box. He lifted the lid. Inside was a smaller cardboard box at one end. The remaining space was filled with some soft ochre compound. Touching it left fingerprints. We thought that it was some kind of plasticine. Lifting the lid of the smaller box revealed batteries, wires and a stopwatch, all wrapped in clear plastic. The watch had six minutes and forty-eight seconds to run.

For a single brief second our eyes met.

Mister King's eyes bulged as I suppose did mine.

"Jeez-us! We'd better shove it oot the nearest porthole!"

"No!" I whooped. "It might explode and blow a hole in the ship's side! Over the arse end is the best place for it."

"Then we'd better get bluidy movin'!" snapped Mister King. "Open that effin' fan room door!"

Thus in the wee hours of the morning of Saturday, the 13th of January 1962, an engineer and a engineroom rating ran helter-skelter along an A Deck passageway. I led the way through a door that took us out onto the open deck. Mister King rushed out down onto B Deck past winches and bollards with me right behind him. Reaching the ship's rail, he tossed the bomb far out into the boiling wake.

Both of us hung on the railing gasping in relief. The sea was relatively calm proving that the Bay of Biscay was in an unusually good mood. The night was warm and the ship was steaming through low rollers blanketed by a low-lying film of sea smoke which billowed around the vessel and only to close in again as it passed.

Quite suddenly, a distant thud could be felt and a mushroom of violent raging power eradicated the wake. A geyser of water shot up into the air punching a hole in the mist. The sound of the explosion was masked by its depth and by the chattering rigging and other fastenings. The falling spray was soon swallowed by the wake's turbulence. It was just then it occurred to me that I hadn't been obligated to run aft with Mister King. I suppose that it is just human nature when one rises to meet a crisis.

In spite of hands shaking like leaves in a tempest, we managed to light up our cigarettes. After our smoke, Mister King tossed his dog end to the wind. "We'd better get that inspection plate fastened oan properly afore the vibration knocks the damned thing aff again."

"What about the bomb?" I asked.

"Whit aboot it?"

"Well, aren't you - we - going to report it?"

"Who'd believe us?"

"That steward might try to assassinate the PM again."

Mister King looked me right in the eye, his face swathed in concentration. "Aye Gerry, ye're right. At the end o' the watch Ah'll tell oor boss, Mister MacAdam. He can field it tae the Chief Engineer. Noo, come oan an' we'll secure yon plate then go back tae oor office for a coffee."

We had just reached M3 fan room when who should come out its door but the steward we'd confronted earlier. Mister King grabbed him by his shirt front and shoved him back inside the fan room. "Ah suppose ye're back tae see why the bomb didnae go aff."

"Excuse plis?" the steward squeaked.

Mister King glanced over the guy's shoulder at the inspection plate dangling on one screw. He extracted his screwdriver from his pocket and gave it to me. "Gerry, hae a quick keek in there in case this bastard has planted anither bomb. If everythin' ok screw that bluidy plate oan fast afore yon cop comes in an' accuses us o' conspiracy." He hauled the steward closer to him so that their noses were all but touching. "Right noo Abdul or whitever your name is - whit's your game?"

"My name's not Abdul," the steward told him and drawing himself up proudly, said, "It is Kimotho ibn Kalil."

"Whitever," Mister King grunted, not impressed. "How come ye want to blaw up oor Prime Minister?"

"He murdered my family," was the simple answer.

"Och, c'mo-oan!" he scoffed, his brogue thickening with disbelief. "Ye're haverin' man!"

"Not havering - true!"

I gave the screwdriver back to Mister King. "The plate is secured now and all the screws are tight."

"That's fine Gerry. Thanks!" He pocketed the tool. "Right noo, how come ye're tryin' tae murder the PM?"

"You know about Mau-Mau?"

"Just whit Ah've read in the newspapers," replied Angus. "It started aboot ten years ago when a bunch o' darkies cut up some white settlers in Kenya. The British government called it an emergency an' sent in the sodjers. How come ye're involved with them? Ye dinnae look like a darkie."

"My mother was a Kikuyu lady and my father was a Saudi," explained the steward. "And my skin is lighter than what you call a darkie." He pronounced the latter word with venom.

"Aye - weel," said Mister King. "Maybe ye'd better explain why ye wanted to blast Harold MacMillan an' his missus awa' tae hell - sayin' nothin' aboot all the ither passengers and the bluidy ship besides."

"Let go of me plis," begged the assassin. "And I will tell you why I did this bad thing."

By this time, I think that Mister King's fingers were stiff and cramped anyway for he stretched and massaged them after releasing the culprit.

"Yes it is true," conceded the steward. "Some of the rebels did commit atrocities towards the white people." His dark-brown eyes flit slowly from side to side to meet ours. "But many of the British soldiers could not differentiate the few rebels from the many law-abiding natives. Some villages were completely destroyed and most of the females were raped and shot. Men were often tortured before they were shot."

"Ah dinnae believe that!" chided Mister King. "There was nothin' in the papers aboot it. Did *you* read anythin' aboot that, Gerry?"

I just shook my head.

"Even so," continued the steward. "Complaints to higher authority in Nairobi were ignored. One day they came to my village and tied me up. I witnessed the rape and murder my wife. Native troops slashed my kids to death with pangas."

"Och man, is that no' awfy?" said Mister King glancing grimly at me.

He had turned quite pale and I suppose that I must've too, because my stomach felt queasy. But that was nothing compared to what was to come next.

"So how did ye get awa' unharmed?" Mister King asked.

The man loosened his belt. "I didn't get away unharmed."

His trousers dropped to his ankles and he slid down his boxer shorts. His genitals were completely gone, only an obscene scar remained. No penis - no testicles - nothing!

"Oh jeez!" exclaimed Mister King.

I all but barfed.

Kimotho ibn Kalil, I think that was his name, pulled up his shorts and trousers and made himself presentable again. "So Mister Officer, what are you going to do now?"

"So why dae want tae blow up the PM?" countered Mister King. "Could ye no' go efter the sodjers that done it?"

"He was Foreign Minister at the time and must be held accountable," was the logical reply.

"Aye - weel," began Mister King. "A' this politics is beyond me. Blawin' him up alang with the ship will no' get your weddin' tackle back . . . Nor your puir wife an' bairns either."

"What are you going to do?" asked the steward.

"Ah dinnae ken. What dae ye think, Gerry?"

God! What a mess, I thought. Here's an officer asking a rating for advice on a subject which neither of us knew anything about. "Do you have any more explosives on board?" I asked.

The guy shook his head. "All I could afford was the cheap stuff," he replied. "Where is it anyway?"

"We chucked it ower the arse end," replied Mister King. "An' as for bein' cheap stuff, it made a fair-sized bang considerin' that ye didnae buy it frae Brock's!"

"Have you any more?" I repeated.

The man shook his head.

"Nae guns, knives, hand grenades or whitever?"

"No."

"I think we should hand ye ower tae the Chief MA," Mister King said finally.

"Look, Mister King," I said. "If you do that we're both going to get snarled up in all kinds of shit."

"Whit dae ye mean Gerry?"

I took a deep breath. "We'll probably have give statements to the cops. Go to court and whatever else the authorities can dream up." I thought for a moment. "Don't you think that this fellow's been punished enough?"

Mister King pondered for a moment. "Ah think that he should dae a stint in the slammer."

"Can you imagine what the convicts will do him?"

"What dae ye mean?" the Scot repeated.

I knew that he was at least a couple of years younger than me but for an officer, he was pretty naive as far as life was concerned. "He's as close to being a woman as anyone I've seen. Can you imagine what tough criminals will do to him?"

"Dae ye really think that they would hurt him?"

Mister King was a really nice guy but at that time he was greener than grass.

"Oh, they'll just love him in Strangeways," I said sarcastically. "And I really mean love. In fact, his arse will be a busy two-way street."

The penny dropped. His eyes left the felon's and into mine before reverting back on our prisoner. "We'll be in Lisbon by nine tonight. If we let ye go, will ye go ashore an' stay there?"

The steward's body sagged with relief as the tension of the situation eased. "Thank you, sir. You never hear of me again."

"Ah should hope no'," replied Mister King vehemently. He stepped back and allowed the fellow to leave. Turning to me he said, "We'll just follow him doon tae his cabin an' make sure that he's tellin' the truth."

The cabin down in D Deck was billeted for four but nobody was home when we went in. Nothing sinister was found when we examined his meagre kit. "The minute we dock Ah'll be at the crew gangway tae make sure that ye leave this ship," Mister King warned him.

Subdued the steward nodded and promised that he'd seek work elsewhere.

"An' dinnae go back to Britain either," he was warned.

Outside the cabin the engineer signed with relief. "Ah could dae wi' a fag an' a coffee right noo."

Nan wasn't quite sure what the proper attire should be for breakfast in the main restaurant. She decided on one of the print frocks that she'd bought only a few days before in Marks and Sparks. A good night's rest combined with warm sea air whetted her appetite. No sooner had she sat down at a table when a waiter was at her side with a menu. He lifted a glass ewer of iced water from the array of silver containers in the middle of the table and filled her glass. Like the silver flatware, the butter dish, cream jug, and bowls of sugar, jam and marmalade, all were embossed with the company logo - a lion rampant, clutching a thistle.

The basket of fresh-made morning rolls looked inviting. The waiter filled her glass and tarried while she scanned the profusion of choices. Calories floated before her eyes. Obviously the Chef considered that his Portuguese Omelet with linguica, onions, peppers and *Queijo da Serra* cheese would compliment the ship's impending visit to Lisbon. The egg dish appealed to her for it conjured up a promise for that evening. She ordered half a grapefruit and some apple juice.

While she waited her eyes took in the opulence of a room which could seat over eight hundred people at one time. The colour scheme of the great room gave the impression of autumn. Great columns, veneered in Brazilian peroba and interlaced with silvery-bronze reeds rose majestically to the high ceiling which was tinged with pink. Lower down, soffits adjoined lighting troughs that were veneered in Mazur birch. The surrounding paneling was set off with horizontal bands of the same Amazonian wood as the lofty columns. The names of the various exotic woods were quite unknown to Nan, as were the squared patterns of russet and buff of unique linoleum called Korkoid that had been laid diagonally to cover the vast floor. The window curtains emulated the autumnal theme of the restaurant.

Passengers gradually filtered in, some choosing to sit nearby while others went into private dining saloons that took up three of the restaurant's corners. The fourth corner, forward on the starboard side, was a cocktail lounge.

A pink grapefruit half, centred on a gilt-ringed plate sporting the Pict Line crest, was gently placed in front of her. "Would you prefer coffee or tea, ma'am?"

"Tea please," replied Nan, unfolding a linen napkin that was naturally embroidered with the thistle-toting king of beasts.

A small salver carrying a burnished silver teapot filled with boiling water, a quantity of tiny sachets of dried tea, a teaspoon, and a tea strainer was placed near her. She charged the teapot with two orange pekoe teabags and left it for a few moments to mass.

Angus entered the restaurant. He stopped near Nan's table and birled his sling psychrometer. Pencilling his findings on his slate he noticed that the lady in front of him was bending to the side to retrieve something from her handbag. In doing, so her napkin dropped on her other side to the deck. He stooped to pick it up. "Ye drapped your hankie, ma'am."

Peering into those steel-grey eyes gave Nan a bit of a stir. When King drew up to his full height his fresh rosy cheeks made her aware of their age gap. Still, she was on holiday after all and there was something about this young ship's officer that attracted her.

"What part of Scotland are you from?" she enquired.

"Carluke, ma'am."

"Oh, Carluke steak!"

Angus grinned self-consciously. R&W Scott, the makers of world famous jams and marmalades, had their factory, orchards and soft fruit fields in and around his hometown. It was common for non-residents of that little community to use this derisive term for a sandwich filled with jam or jelly. She had an Anniesland accent that tended be over polite in the ears of coarser spoken Scots.

He recalled his Auntie Ina's attitude whenever she heard that vernacular. "Sh-eye-t!" she would say rather than the more common word for feces - shite!

From his point of view Angus guessed that was in her early forties. Her shoulder length hair was almost the same colour as his. Her eyes, sans crowsfeet, had a dark greyer hue than the engineer's. She had a longish oval face with a fresh complexion with lips bearing a hint of pink lipstick. The expensive treatment in that beauty salon in distant Renfield Street had hewn some years from her normal appearance.

She in turn saw a handsome young officer in his early twenties. Early was right because Angus was only twenty-one years of age. Had she saw him barely a month ago at the beginning of his first trip, green as the sward on Glasgow Green, she would've recognized him for what he really was. However, the burden of responsibility thrust on his slim shoulders during that first trip had matured him considerably. Confidence exuded from his bearing and the colour of his red hair didn't come out of a bottle either.

"Aye weel, there are worse things in this world than makin' jam." A waiter neared with an omelet on a hot plate. "Noo if ye'll excuse me ma'am, Ah'll continue wi' my duties."

He made his way to the centre of the restaurant and took another swing which precipitated curious stares from the diners. Nan beckoned him and returned to her side.

"I was very rude to you a few minutes ago," she apologized, laying her fork on her plate. "Can you please forgive me Mister eh . . . ?"

"King ma'am," replied Angus, a finger touching the skip of his cap. "Angus King, at your service."

"Nan Barrie," she replied, holding out a fair hand with neatly manicured fingers.

"Please tae meet ye Miss Barrie," replied Angus, gently taking her hand. The two-ringed catering officer setting course in his direction reminded him that engineers were not allowed to, or not allowed to get caught, fraternizing with female passengers. Mumbling a few words about urgent duties he beat a hasty retreat.

The senior a/c engineer had his feet up on the desk when King returned to A17 fan room. Angus filled in the log book. Jack came back from a call and had brought back a couple of issues of the ship's daily newspaper from the printers' shop.

As usual, the news was found wanting. The ship's radio snatched world news headlines and little else from the ether and passed them along to the printers' shop. The rest of the broadsheet's space was filled by snippets about traveling and fashion, curious facts combined with anecdotes and jokes motivated its name: The Pict-Wit Papers.

"Here," said Don. "Did you know that Supermac is sailing with us? He is accompanying his wife, Lady Dorothy, as far as Lisbon. From there he is going on alone to parts unknown. I wonder what cabin he's in?"

Angus and Gerry looked at each other in silence and a few minutes later the watch changed over.

CHAPTER SEVEN

Lisbon at night

2110 Saturday

A tender was pulling alongside when Angus peered over the starboard rail on Boat Deck. He'd rushed through dinner to be in time to witness the thwarted assassin Kimotho ibn Kalil over the ship's side. The engineer made his way forward and entered an elevator on Sun Deck. Excited passengers milled around R Deck Square waiting to board the tender. Angus edged his way through the throng and came upon a familiar face.

"Betty - I mean Detective-Sergeant Stevenson!"

Betty Stevenson's chartreuse eyes darted around the square before she acknowledged him. "Hello Angus." She smiled. She would've liked to have kissed him but she was on duty so they held hands briefly. "It's Detective-Inspector now."

"Congratulations!" beamed Angus. "Ye deserve tae be promoted after solvin' yon murder case last trip." He frowned. "But Ah didnae ken that ye were aboard."

The DI wore a grey-linen suit with a simple white-satin blouse. The low-heeled shoes that matched with her suit made her at least two inches taller than her former lover. Her slightly elongated face was framed by wavy chestnut hair with bangs. On the previous voyage, which also happened to be the engineer's first trip, romance had developed during a murder investigation. Angus had been a big help to her in more ways than one.

Stevenson noticed a flurry of activity as the British Prime Minister appeared when an elevator door opened. He and his wife were escorted by two officers from Special Branch.

"Sorry I can't stay and talk Angus. I've been seconded to guard the PM while he's out of the UK."

She gave him a quick peck on the cheek and moved toward the entourage. They passed through the shell door out of sight.

A door opened behind him. Gerry Renouf, Jack Purcell and two firemen-trimmers drew to his side. They had come up the ladder from the working alleyway on C Deck. Gerry touched the engineer's arm and gestured his eyes towards Kimotho ibn Kalil who was edging his way through the crowd toward the shell doors.

The Chief Steward confronted him and pointed to the doors that had allowed the engineroom ratings entry. His eyes nearly fell out his head when he realized part of the black gang had the audacity to mingle with his passengers. He nudged the steward ahead of him until he reached Angus.

"What are those people doing here?" the boss steward all but gibbered, his fingers flapping about as if he was manipulating a marionette's strings.

Angus shrugged and looked at Gerry.

"We're going ashore, Mister King," replied the rating. "The lead hand said that we could take shore leave as long as we were back in time for watch. Sober," he added.

"Not on the passenger tender, you're not," countered the Chief Steward through clenched teeth. "Look, there's another tender coming alongside by the Pig Deck shell doors. You can go on that after it has been unloaded. It's carrying fresh fruit and vegetables. The quicker it's unloaded, the quicker you can go ashore - if you get my drift." He nodded at the steward. "You can go with 'em."

Gerry recalls:

An hour after we sighted the Tagus River the liner had steamed up its estuary to come within a mile of Lisbon. As it happened the ship was too big to go alongside so we dropped the hook in the river. Me and Jack and two other guys had showered and changed, ready for a run ashore. We'd been to the crew purser's office earlier. Each of us exchanged five hard-earned quid for four hundred escudos. All of us figured that would be more than enough to insure a good time in the Portuguese capital. There was a convenient ladder near our mess on the working alleyway that took us up to R Deck.

Right away we noticed Mister King chatting up a woman in a grey suit. She looked a bit of all right but too old for my taste. She must've been about forty or fifty years old. She soon disappeared after some bigwigs left the ship. I could see that Mau-Mau chappie hovering among the passengers so I touched Mister King's sleeve to bring his attention to him. Just then the Chief Steward came out of his office on the port side to jar the Mau-Mau. That three-ringer steward would've shit himself if had he known that he was badgering a mad bomber.

"Oh-oh!" warned Jack.

The three-ringer was heading our way.

The next thing we knew was that we were slugging crates of fruit and veg. up the ship's steep side ladder and the Mau-Mau was helping us. The lead hand came on the scene and commandeered a few boozers from the Pig and Whistle to help. It didn't take too long to unload the tender and we were soon on our way. Mind you, an awful lot of oranges didn't quite make it to the fruit locker.

Our transport dropped us at a stone pier which was part of a massive square hosting a gigantic archway at its far end. On either side of this portal ornate buildings of stone and brick appeared to be part of a palace or government offices maybe. There was an enormous statue of an armored man on a horse. He could've been Don Quixote. It was difficult so see everything properly because after all, it was night time. Even though lights encompassed the square the shadows were disorienting. I last saw our would-be assassin merge into the gloom carrying a small dark grip.

Meandering through the lofty portals we ignored the street beyond. It appeared to be totally pedestrian for it vaunted all the glittering signs of being a tourist trap. Instead we followed Teach, one of the fireman-trimmers from 2BR. His sidekick and helpmate, Tinker, was an old toothless fellow who existed on the cusp of senility. Teach was reputed to find cheap women and cheap booze at the drop of a hat. Sure enough it wasn't long before a couple of tarts latched onto him like remoras onto a shark.

Like a pair of tugs they nudged him into a nearby bar. The rest of us followed in line astern. The establishment was old and dimly lit. Fishnets drooped from adze-hued beams blackened from centuries of tobacco smoke. Paired oars with curious blades and looms were part of the décor. We berthed a table and a seedy waiter slunk up to take our order. He couldn't speak English and our Portuguese was nonexistent. Or so I thought.

"*Quatro cerveja por favor*," saidTeach, pronouncing the words with obvious experience.

When four bottles of beer duly arrived, we complimented Teach and asked where he'd learned to speak Portuguese. Two feminine hands exploring his thighs so distracted him that he couldn't enlighten us.

Perhaps at this point I should tell you a little bit about Teach. He was about six feet tall and as lean as a beanpole. What hair that remained on his balding head was strawberry-blonde. He lurched rather than walked, his shoulders hunched in a permanent stoop. He had been at sea for countless years. Scuttlebutt had it that he'd once taught sixth form schoolgirls. He had left the school under a cloud and joined the Merchant Navy. Gossip had it that he'd molested one of the girls. One rumour said that he'd been caught shagging the school's gym teacher. But nobody really knew the truth and Teach wasn't a fellow to volunteer information about himself. The bottle of vino that he'd ordered for the girls was consumed with gusto.

Each of the whores captivated an arm and navigated him upstairs leaving us to be entertained by Tinker while waiting for Teach's return.

Tinker must have been about sixty years old. Even so, his curly raven hair was utterly devoid of grey, a feature that normally marks the passing years of men and women. He had obsidian eyes, like little chips of the coal that he'd shoveled all those years ago on coal burners. A rumour said that one of the ship's engineers once said that he resembled a tiny wee tinker. The name stuck and he was called Tinker ever since.

I wondered if his family originated on Guernsey for he had the pointed ears of a pixie. I grew up on the island indoctrinated by stories about those mythical beings. The old folk maintained that in their distant past faeries interbred with the local populace. Looking at Tinker I could well believe those yarns for he had the face of an imp with a mere slit for a mouth. His skin had yellowed like parchment, his nose like wrinkled vellum.

Tinker was short and skinny and somewhat of a legend aboard the *Dally*. The *Titanic* was reputed to be his first ship but he'd missed it because his mother had locked him away in his room on sailing day. To pass the time waiting for Teach, Jack asked Tinker to tell us about his life on the old coal burning ships . . .

There was a balmy breeze on the Boat Deck. The lights of Lisbon were twinkling all along the shoreline and up the higher reaches of what Nan supposed was the Alfama. She had skimmed through one of the Lisbon brochures which had been provided for all passengers. The great city had the promise of allure, romance, and maybe even adventure. The first tender was already heading for shore and taxis were jockeying into position to pick up its passengers. Looking directly down over the ship's rail a second boat was supplying the vessel with fresh produce. A third tender was steering towards the liner. Nelson Riddle's romantic tune *Lisboa Antigua* rippled from a Boat Deck tannoy, a wile to get voyagers in the mood.

As of yet Nan hadn't communicated with any shipboard acquaintances unless one counted the young engineer who recorded the temperature readings in the main restaurant. She had always been a bit of a loner. Her few friends had proven to be trusted and reliable. Having spent all her life in Glasgow, Nan thought nothing of experiencing the nightlife of another major city and now to her, at least, money certainly wasn't an object.

She was attired in a green gingham dress with a matching cardigan for the excursion ashore. There were three queues at the purser's office on A Deck as passengers converted pounds sterling into escudos. The thick wad of Portuguese bills was too much for her purse so she placed the smaller denominations in her new handbag. She went down the steep ladder to board the tender.

On shore a bevy of taxidrivers lanquished near their cabs. Many of them conversed by using a smattering of English. Nan chatted to three of them before one would relent and say that he could make his cab available to her for that evening and the following day. Naturally some hard bargaining took place before a price was deemed agreeable to both parties.

The cab whisked off around an enormous stone-flagged square which Duarte, her new guide, said was *Praça do Comérci*o or Commerce Square. Duarte prattled on about how the square was sometimes called *Terreiro do Paço*, or Palace Square, after the Ribeira Palace which was destroyed in the great earthquake of 1755. Driving up a thoroughfare called *Rua Aurea* the cabdriver airily gestured to his left or right to demonstrate his local knowledge. He flitted past historical edifices and other points of interest until eventually his vehicle eased into an area called the Alfama, the oldest district in Lisbon.

Here restaurants, bars, and nightclubs abounded. Duarte slid to a halt and turned in his seat to face Nan. Dark brown eyes sparkled with amusement from a swarthy countenance, his slim aquiline nose seemingly supported by a greying pencil-thin moustache. His silvery hairline was an exaggerated monk's tonsure.

"Senhorita has already dined aboard her great ship?"

Nan, anticipating an opportunity to try Portuguese cuisine, had only consumed a light salad and some consomme soup for dinner. She shook her head and held out her hand. "I'd love to taste some of the local fare, Duarte." She'd learned his name from the ID card dangling on the cab mirror. "My name's Nan Barrie."

With old worldly charm Duarte brushed her hand with her moustache before exiting his cab. His small wiry frame nimbly rounded the vehicle to open the door. He escorted her to the door of a nightclub with an unpronounceable name. Inside a smoke-filled candle-lit room he introduced the manager. "Jorge, this is my good friend Senhorita Barrie. Please take good care of her." He gazed up at Nan's face. "I will be back in one hour and take you to another place if you wish. *Até a vista*!"

She was led to a small table that had an outstanding view of the dias where a female vocalist, accompanied by a twelve-string guitar sang *fado*, the haunting music of Portugal. A glass of rich red wine began her evening in old Lisbon.

"How come you're still in your uni?"

Will Keyes castigated Angus when he returned to his cabin. Wheelkey was in his civvies as were the other occupants of his cabin swilling back King's beer with wild abandon. "Aren't you going ashore?"

"Ah'd somethin' else tae dae," replied a downcast Angus. He quickly changed into his suit and refilled the coat hanger with his uniform. The fresh case of Tennents lager that

Barnes, the steward, had deposited in his cabin just before the bar had closed that evening was rapidly disappearing down the throats of his colleagues, Will Keyes, Taffy Morgan, Larry Treen, Don Travers and Pete Eaton.

Since it was such a nice evening the six engineers decided that a pleasant stroll was in order when they debarked from the tender. Larry Treen speculated aloud that the enormous equestrian statue might be of El Cid. Taffy just scoffed at the Englishman's ignorance. The towering archway echoed their footsteps as they came upon *Rua Augusta*, or Victoria Street. Here lay a hive of commerce; shops, flower peddlers, cafés, and all manner of entrepreneurs.

But the engineers preferred keeping their newly acquired escudos in their pockets for less savoury fare, sex and booze. They were passing along a great boulevard when Wheelkey flagged down a taxi. The cabdriver was reluctant to cram six foreign crewmembers into his vehicle until a fifty escudo note was flaunted before his eyes.

Morris Greene watched the tender leave from shore from the Boat Deck. He remained in the shadows beneath the starboard wing of the bridge. He was bored almost to distraction. Bernie hadn't contacted him as yet. He'd done absolutely nothing during the first part of the voyage except, perhaps having the occasional drink in the Observation Lounge. He stayed away from the Highland Grill where he knew the Sneddon couple preferred to dine. The ship's cinema and libraries held little interest for him. He deliberated about tailing them when they went ashore in the morning.

The engineers tumbled from the taxi into a bustling, brightly-lit street. Neon signs flashing psychedelic messages in the Portuguese vernacular lured the unwary to enter within and sample their forbidden delights. Wheelkey was never one to ponder on multiple choices. He simply strode through the open doorway of the closest bar and like an herd of sheep the others flocked in behind him. They were quickly ushered to a vacant table.

Steamboat, a.k.a. Pete Eaton with a display of exhuberance, thought he'd demonstrated his fluency in the Portuguese language. He held up his right palm with outspread fingers and a single digit on his left hand.

"*Seis pintas de cerveja, por favor*!"

The waiter beamed his respect to this foreigner who could speak his language confidently before scurrying away. Five engineers gaped at their shipmate in amazement. "I didn't know that you spoke Portuguese," said Wheelkey.

"I didn't just study engineering in Mushland y'know," boasted Steamboat. "Residing in a magnificent seaport like Southampton encourages us Mushers to communicate with visitors from abroad."

Quite unknown to his colleagues as of yet, Eaton had been making overtures to a comely stewardess at the beginning of the trip. Teresa had spent her childhood in Sao Paulo, Brazil, before coming to Britain. From her Steamboat had learned among more intimate techniques, basic Portuguese, very basic. During his romantic hours he'd learned the word for beer, the amount that one might order - up to a limit of ten. He also learned where he might get rid of the beer's residue.

A round each later when the company had raised just about enough steam to 'warm through' Angus had to ask Steamboat to interpret his expanding need to the waiter. With pride the fuel-oil engineer beckoned their server and asked, "*Onde fica a casa de banho*?"

The fellow pointed the way to ecstatic relief.

Nan was thoroughly enjoying the food and atmosphere of the nightclub. Duarte had dropped by to see if she wanted to go elsewhere but she declined. A group of men came in laughing and joking. Through the gloom of blue smoke she judged that they were British from the style of their suits. She surmised that they might be some of the liner's crew out for a night on the town. One of them got up and threaded his way between patrons heading supposedly for the men's washroom. It was that young air conditioning engineer.

As Angus strolled jauntily back to his table, his peripheral vision picked up a flutter of white. His eyes heeded the distraction. A handkerchief waving like a flag of surrender on the raised naked arm belonged to that woman in the main restaurant. What's her name? Barrie, aye that was it: Nan Barrie. He changed course and headed away from his mates.

"Where's Gus?" Keyes asked a beer later. "It's his shout."

"He hasn't come back from the shitter yet," replied Larry Treen. "Maybe he's puking his guts up."

"Huh!" grunted Wheelkey unfeelingly. "Some guys will do anything to dodge their round."

"Isn't that him over there?"

Heads craned to follow Don Trevor's pointing digit.

"Ooh!" pouted Taffy Morgan. "That's a bit of all right, the lucky bugger!"

"She's quite a dish," opined Don.

"Must be fifty if she's a day," sneered Wheelkey.

"That wouldn't stop you getting into her knickers, see you!" retorted Taff.

"Damned right!" Keyes agreed. "I wonder how these old broads know? I mean, it's not like he's sloping arms with a bazooka, is it?"

"He could though, boyo!"

"Yeah," Wheelkey sullenly agreed, then wistfully: "Man, if I could just borrow his first six inches for the night."

"You'd have seven and-a-half inches then, see you!" Taffy quipped. "And you still wouldn't have a woman."

Taking a deep swig Steamboat slammed his glass down on the tabletop. "That sounds like a hand-on job to me."

Just then a woman who'd seen better days took Angus' vacated seat and whispered something in the fuel-oil engineer's ear all the while stroking between his legs.

"*No hablan español*" protested Steamboat, shoving the wanton's questing fingers away.

The woman stood up and let go a stream of invective before storming away.

"What did she say Pete?" asked Larry.

Wheelkey chimed in before Steamboat could answer. "Well, considering he told her in Spanish that he didn't speak Dago, a sort of loose translation would be: This is Portugal, you dumb bastard!"

Just then Angus approached their table with Nan in tow. "Ah'll see ye later guys," he said. "This lady here is one o' our passengers an' she's offered me a run in her taxi back tae the ship. Cheerio for noo."

"*Hoi*!" countered Keyes. "You haven't paid for your round."

"Oh aye Ah but Ah did," replied Angus. "When you lot helped yourselves tae the beer back in my cabin. Ta-ta!"

Glumly his colleagues watched him leave.

Wheelkey ruefully shook his head. "Sailors are reputed to have a woman in every port. That guy picks them up in port and sails off with them!"

The tender was easing away from the great stone pier just as their taxi arrived. Duarte adroitly nipped out and opened the door for his senhorita benefactor. He accepted a fold of escudo notes and promised to be back for the same duty at nine-thirty the following morning. When the cab had zipped away Angus glumly looked for the second tender. There wasn't one. It would be at least three-quarters of an hour before the other lighter came alongside again. He turned his left wrist towards the nearest light source: the moon. It was in the first quarter. God! He'd be lucky to get two hours sleep before Jeffries called the watch.

"Do you want to go for a walk Angus?" asked Nan, taking his arm and steered him towards the great equestrian that dominated Commerce Square.

Like a barge being shoved by a tug Angus gave way. From Nan's point of view romance was in the air. The black velvet night was strewn with diamonds with the moon's lower cusp trying to scoop them up. Out on the Tagus or *Rio Teja* as it was known here, the *Queen of Dalriada* was captivated on fluid ebony and glittering like a jewel box under strobe lights. The meagre twinkling lights from the tender declared that it still hadn't reached the liner. *Deja vu*, was the term flitting through the young engineer's mind as he pondered his first capitulation to a matronly female.

He was behind the lower science annex in Carluke Higher Grade playground when the school bully accosted him for his dinner money. Angus had resisted but Mugs Mitchell was too big and too strong. While he lay bruised and bleeding on the tarmac, the fourteen-year-old schoolboy wondered how some measure of revenge might be inflicted on Mugs. There were only two days left until the school closed for the summer, so going to the headmaster was futile. Besides Mugs was fifteen now and quitting the school forever. He'd a job lined up with a local grocer.

When classes finished for the day Angus went home by way of Hozier Street. At the bottom of the hill he noticed Mitchell leaving a council house with a couple of his cronies. He stood by the fence that edged Mitchell's home. A woman was working around some rose bushes wielding a set of secateurs to deadhead some blooms. The bottom corners of her pinny had been lifted to form a basket for the withered flower heads. Presently she noticed Angus. The tired blooms were relegated to a galvanized pail.

"Whit in ever happened tae yer face laddie?" she asked, her voice soft with compassion. She was a pleasant woman with long auburn hair interspersed with more than a few filaments of grey. Crow's feet were prominent at her brown eyes. Other lines too etched the passage of years on her face which hadn't saw makeup since last Friday's game of Housey-Housey in the old Windsor Cinema.

"Mugs Mitchell gied me a toberin'," was the sullen reply.

"My laddie did that?" she all but screeched. "Wait till Ah get a haud o' him! Ah'll gie whit's fur."

The gate creaked ajar and she ushered Angus along the path into the house. Sitting him down at her kitchen table she soaked a clean cloth in tepid water and proceeded to bathe his bruises. A styptic pencil appeared in her hand. The teenager flinched from this new treatment. Mrs. Mitchell held his head against her left breast. "Be still laddie!"

In spite of a slight stinging above his eye Angus had found his situation quite pleasant - sensuous even. "Staun' up an' take aff yer shirt, laddie!" Mrs. Mitchell commanded. The teenager complied. "Oh my!" exclaimed the woman. "Ye've goat scratches an' bruises a' ower!"

The youth's torso welcomed the soothing administrations of Germoline. "Take aff yer troosers laddie! It's likely that yer bum an' legs need treatment tae."

A reluctant Angus blushed and bowed his head.

"Come oan laddie. Ah dinnae hae a' day." She quickly unbuckled his belt. "Ye dinnae hae onythin' that Ah haven't seen afore." Those words would soon serve as an apéritif before *L'Entré Andouille Ecossé*. The lad's trousers were at his ankles before he knew what was happening. "Here laddie, dae ye no' wear ony underwear?" Mrs. Mitchell's eyes bulged and she repeated, "Oh my!"

She put a hand inside her bra and hauled out a white breast, its nipple beige and bold. "Have ye ever seen onythin' like this laddie?"

Angus had, but only in the saucy magazine, *Lilliput*, and they were in black and white and partially covered. The real thing live in Cinemascope and Technicolor was significantly better. Mrs. Mitchell's sudden unveiling achieved the desired effect. Alarmed he shot a glance at the back door.

"Och, dinnae fash yersel' laddie," consoled the housewife. "My boy is awa' doon the Waygateshaw Braes. He'll no' be back until dark o'clock an' my man's oan backshift ower at the Castlehill pit. We've goat the hoose tae oorsel's." She grabbed the now erect penis and whispered, "Oh my!" for the third time.

From that far-off experience, mere seven years before, Angus grew to be philosophical about sexual relations with women much older than him. Why he was attracted to them was unknown but just an interlude to be pleasantly accepted. The term 'cougar' was still decades in the future. And it was, after all was said and done, a pretty unusual way of getting even with a school bully.

Even though she was wearing a cardigan Nan was trembling as if from the merest murmuring zephyr from the Tagus. Always the gentleman Angus slipped off his jacket and it placed around her shoulders. Appreciating this gesture Nan reciprocated by kissing him full on the lips. Her hands flit across his chest, loosened his tie, and ventured inside. But they didn't stop there - his zipper was next.

"Christ!" thought Angus. "She's opened my ballop!"

In the shadow of the great plinth which supported Gerry's reckoning of Don Quixote and Larry Treen's El Cid was in fact, King José. While this illustrious monarch's steed was aggressively trampling writhing stone snakes Nan had another serpent in her hand. Far from squirming this soon-to-be spitting cobra was stiffening into life.

Fired with passion the paleoanthropologist had lifted the hem of her dress, eased a panty leg to one side and began rubbing her flustered lover's turgid member up and down the cleft between her legs. Angus was of the opinion that his glans was being scoured against a coarse Brillo pad. Presently he took hold of the situation, so to speak, and came about the prime objective.

Gerry recalls:

Tinker eyed up the fresh pint of beer and took a sip. Since he didn't have any teeth to place his tongue against, his th's came out as tees. He drew his sleeve across those thin lips of his and went into his story, dropping and adding his aitches in the wrong places as his tale unfolded.

"You young fellers 'ave got it so heasy t'ese days," he wheezed like a magpie lodged in a drainpipe. "In my day we shovelled coal. Na t'at were 'ard work. If you was lucky, an' t'e ship docked at a large seaport, a bloody great crane loaded t'e coal into t'e bunkers. Great big scoops shifted a couple o' tons at a time. If not, t'en the 'ole bleedin' crew, hincludin' t'e bleedin' hofficers would be shovellin' bings o' coal into baskets an' t'en 'eavin' t'e bleedin' baskets up t'e ship's gangway. T'at went on day an' niaght until all t'e bleedin' bunkers was full. We'd wash an' scrub for 'ars until all t'at grime 'ad gone. In my case, it didn't make any difference because I were shovellin' all t'e time. Besides my skin is bran, like a nut."

Sunday afternoon January 21st, 2022

Jake laughed at Gerry's passable imitation of Tinker for he had known the little fireman too. But the dialect was somewhat enigmatic to Jessica and it showed on her beautiful countenance. Gerry found the exercise had a numbing effect on his tongue so that he tended to spit from time to time. However, he struggled on with that distant recollection in his normal voice, purposely continuing to screw up the grammar:

"My job at sea were simple," said the little man between sips of beer. "Although it were very hard work. I were assigned to a particular boiler an' told to keep it stoked. This meant that I'd shovel coal from a bunker into a wheelbarrow, wheel it to the furnace face, an' dump it onto the footplates. The fireman would then stoke the fire, spreadin' the coal evenly across the furnace fire bars. The engineer would tell me to use the port or starboard bunker every so often. This meant that the ship were kept trimmed all the time. The best burnin' coal were Welsh coal. It burned hotter, an' made less flame, an' didn't make as much smoke as Scotch or Newcastle coal.

"The fire bars was usually about six feet long an' the furnaces was about three feet wide. If the boiler had four furnaces it would burn about twelve tons a day. Them smart 'uns among us right now who can cipher, will figure out that I used to shovel two tons every watch if the furnaces only 'ad natural draft. I'd to shovel twice as much if they 'ad forced draught air.

"An' don't forget, when you burns coal you makes ashes. The fireman were constantly breakin' up clinkers an' scoopin' ash from under the fire grate. Of course he'd joke that energy were wasted wheelin' empty wheelbarrows about. So I'd to shovel all them ashes into my wheelbarrow, wheel 'em to the ash hopper so that the ejector could dump the ashes over the bleedin' side. Then I'd load my wheelbarrow up with coal again. Per'aps some day one of them nuclear submarines will go down to the bottom o' the sea an' find thousands o' ridges o' ashes that has been dumped from thousands of ships' boilers. Most o' the boilers had firetubes back then. This meant that the flue gases was piped through the water to heat it. As you've probably guessed, the reverse happens in watertube boilers.

"Since we weren't allowed to leave the stokehold while on watch, we had to piss in the bilge. If we needed a shit we'd do it in our shovels an' feed it into the fire. I bet the owners got a few extra miles for free with all that brown fuel. Us trimmers would wear out a shovel in less than two trips. They was always shiny - like chrome - they was. In fact, every once in a while, we'd swipe some bacon, eggs, sausage, an' maybe some mashed spuds from the galley when the cook weren't lookin'. We'd use our shovels to 'ave a fry-up when our engineer were off havin' smoko.

"The boilers I fed was massive but then they had to be - to steam those giant up-and-down engines. Some had triple-expansion cylinders while others had quadruple expansion cylinders. Turbines was comin' into fashion then, especially on the fast passenger liners.

"As I said before life were hard on a steamer. Our watches were the same as now, four hours on with eight hours off. Eight-to-twelve, twelve-to-four, an' four-to-eight: mornin' an' bleedin' night. Our off hours haven't changed much since then. We spent 'em eatin', sleepin', an' readin' for thems that can. Snakes 'n' ladders an' ludo ain't played these days but I still see card games goin' on. Some old hands, them that sailed on ships that had both sail an' steam, scrimshawed.

"You might know that in the old days whalebone, ivory, an' hardwood was the main materials for carvin'. Well, there weren't much of that stuff on these great liners but we did have plenty of coal. So that's what they did: they carved little animals, birds, an' the like, out o' coal. But them skills are all long gone now. Most of you young fellers just hang around in the Pig an' Whistle swillin' beer nowadays."

His little tongue popped out to lick his lips and he took another sip of beer, quite oblivious to the fact that he was doing the same thing.

"On the whole, grub weren't all that bad unless we had a very bad cook who didn't know what he were doin' half of the time. Much like today. For instance, a lot of 'em don't know that dried peas have to be soaked for about six or eight hours before cookin'. I mean peas are musical enough at the best of times but if they're still hard, men'll fart like cannon fire. An' considerin' bein' bunked together four or six at a time in one cabin like now, it's sheer hell - as you all know. Especially if a feller has ate onions or garlic for supper.

"Still, after shovellin' coal all watch, a cully like me got pretty hungry an' so I kept on shovellin' grub into my mouth so fast that I couldn't hardly taste it anyhows."

Teach came back exhausted and with a silly grin on his face. Tinker's nostalgic tale fell by the wayside as his shipmate related the highlights of his recent exploit. We finished our beer and headed back to the ship.

We'd been told that there was only one tender in operation. That meant we'd to board by the shell doors on R Deck Square - not a pleasant prospect since most officers with the exception of our engineers considered the engine staff lower than dirt. The area fairly bustled with tired passengers who'd apparently enjoyed their evening ashore.

We waited until all of them boarded the *Dally*. Among the last to step onto the boarding ladder pontoon was Mister King who was escorting a lady. She seemed old enough to be his mother. Her face was flushed and her chestnut hair was dishevelled. The cape she bore about her shoulders was remarkably like Mister King's suit jacket. He sure looked absolutely shattered, his hair tousled and shaggy like an orangutang's.

With her leading the way up the steps, I could see that both her nylons were laddered from knees to knickers. At the open shell door the woman gave the jacket back to my engineer and tried to kiss him. Mister King took her firmly by the lower arm and shook her hand as a master-at-arms glared on. Like us the engineers were not allowed to truck with female passengers. On board the woman went straight to an elevator whereas Mister King made a beeline for the door that would take him down to the working alleyway. We edged round the duty MA and followed the engineer.

CHAPTER EIGHT

A day in Lisbon

Sunday 0320

"It's time to go on watch, Mister King," called Jeffries, and with the merest flick of his forefinger the darkened cabin blossomed into blinding light.

The Scot's eyes opened wide then closed immediately, shunning out the unwelcome incandescent irritant. "Aye. Ok," he mumbled. It was followed seconds later with an uncharitable "Thanks!"

How much sleep had he had? Two hours? Less? He groaned and dragged his fragile body down from his bunk. He yawned and stretched his arms expansively before charging his washbasin with warm water. He washed his face and sponged down his torso. A smooth shave made him feel better and he climbed into his Number Ones.

Entering the mess revealed the same depressing tabloid as the previous morning watch and the watch before that into perpetuity. A dozen bleary-eyed engineers and electricians were hunched over their respective tables contemplating the usual wingéd sandwiches that had been stuffed with tongue, spam, cheese, or corned beef. Angus sidled in beside Will Keyes and lifted the stiffening lid from a corned beef sarnie. Wheelkey watched him plop a generous dollop of HP sauce onto the meat.

"Get your end away?"

Angus closed the lid and took a bite. He raised his hand, palm down with outstretched fingers, and rocked them from side to side.

"Lucky bastard!"

Taffy, sitting opposite, reached for the coffee pot and topped up his cup. He gave the a/c engineer a questioning glance. King blinked yes and received a measure of diluted bunker C.

"I suppose that you're going to shag her during this next watch?" opined Wheelkey.

Shaking his head in reply, he finished his sarnie. A gulp of coffee made him grimace. "See you guys at breakfast."

The watch went by quietly enough. All the public rooms were quite empty when King made his rounds. Even the eerie creaking of panelling in the corridors had ceased because the ship was serenely swinging on her anchor in the middle of the Tagus. About six o'clock, pantries could be heard stirring as stewards prepared for their awakening charges.

Shortly after seven he ambled into the main restaurant. Nan was sitting at her usual table wearing a floral summer dress. She looked as fresh as the printed daisy adornment on her white linen frock.

"Hello Angus," she whispered throatily.

The engineer's eyes panned across the room before answering. The place was devoid of authority. "Hello Nan," he replied. "Ye look like a picture sittin' there."

"I did get a bit more sleep than you," she smiled, buttering a tawny wedge of toast. "Your eyes are slightly bloodshot."

"Ye should've seen 'em at hauf three this mornin'. They were practically hemorrhagin' then!"

"Oh! I'm sorry that I kept you up so late!"

"Och, that's ok Nan," shrugged Angus, and with a leer added: "It was worth it."

"Did you have plans for today?"

"Ah'll probably go ashore wi' some o' my pals," surmised the engineer, his eyes darting this way and that in search of imminent authority.

"Would you like to see Lisbon with me?" Nan asked. "I've rented a taxi for the day and you're likely to see a lot more of the place than walking around with your friends."

"Aye," agreed Angus and under his breath. "An' stay sober as weel."

"What was that?"

"Nothin'. Aye - ok. If memory serves yon taxi's pickin' ye up at nine-thirty?"

"That's right," replied Nan. "Can you make it by then?"

Hodgkins, the fourth mate, materialized by the galley doors. "Aye sure," Angus said hurriedly, taking another swing. "Ah'll need tae go noo. See ye." Jotting down his readings he speedily left by the forward doors.

Relieved on time Angus welcomed the quick shower, changed into his civvies, and went into the messroom. Taffy, Wheelkey, and Steamboat wore their John Collier and Fifty Shilling Tailor suits too. "Are you going ashore with us, Gus?" asked Keyes, sprinkling a dash of Worcester sauce into his tomato juice.

"Sorry lads," apologized Angus. "Ah've got a date."

"Don't tell me you're going to go out with that old broad again," mocked Wheelkey, jealousy lacing his tone. "She's old enough to be your mother."

"Aye, weel - maybe so," Angus reluctantly agreed. "A' the right bits still work though."

"Probably like throwing a salami up the Bargate," pitched in Steamboat, waving his fork-impaled breakfast sausage to emphasize his rude comment.

"Possibly to us guys," admitted Wheelkey. "But Gus has got a cylinder rod that doesn't need gland packing!"

Taffy gave King a slow wink. "One size fits all, eh boyo?"

Angus blushed, all the while taking meticulous care to spread a dollop of R & W Scott's lime marmalade on his toast. He hung around until the bantering became too much and excused himself. Just before he reached for the exit door handle Wheelkey started whistling L. Casucci's '*Handsome Gigolo*' much to the merriment of the more senior officers, who recalled the tune from the early thirties.

His paramour was already on the tender when he boarded. She was toting a black leather cylindrical tube. “Can Ah carry that pipe thing for ye Nan?” the engineer volunteered.

“Yes, thank you Angus,” she replied, holding it out by its leather strap.

The cylinder weighed about eight pounds. “Whit is it?”

Nan just smiled and said, “You’ll find out.”

Among the horde of beeping taxis Duarte was trying to attract their attention by leaping up and down, performing jumping jacks at the designated rendezvous. The couple embarked and off they went on a whirlwind tour of Lisbon. Passing little yellow tram cars, green and white double-decker buses and other busy traffic Duarte motored through the beautiful city. They visited Baroque churches with towering turrets, sprouting spires and glowering gargoyles. One of them was the magnificent Lisbon Cathedral which was built by an Englishman some eight hundred years before. The season was unfortunate as far as public gardens went. Deciduous trees were still leafless although their boles and branches seemed to emit a haze of green, a promise of early spring. Lawns were bright emerald with new grass.

Casa dos Dicos, or the House of Spikes, was an unusual abode faced with diamond-shaped stones. It was here that they decided to have lunch because many cafés and restaurants abounded in the area.

Lisbon Castle was next on Duarte’s agenda. The cab driver’s spiel about that ancient edifice was obviously well-practiced. It seemed that back in 1147 Portugal’s first king, Afonso Henriques, captured it from the Moors. The fortress was badly damaged during the great earthquake of 1755. Still, eighteen towers and many long walls remained intact and it was to those keeps that the couple was headed.

The Sneddons were sightseeing too but with a more expensive itinerary. Constantly referring to a map in a guidebook Denise sent their taxidriver away after being dropped off at some place of interest. After using up the best part of a spool of film she would tell her husband to flag down another cab. Stoically Bernie complied with her demands.

It had been the same routine as the previous evening, thought Bernie. She had this bee in her bonnet about creating a pictorial travel brochure for her company. Twenty-odd restaurants and nightclubs saw copious notes being collected along with myriad snaps of their interiors and attractive and tasty Portuguese dishes.

Mo Greene had taken a leaf from Nan Barrie's book and hired a cab for the morning. At every stop he watched the couple from a distance. If an opportunity arose, he'd pay off the cabby to further investigate.

The view from the ramparts of *Castelo de São Jorge* was an exhilarating sight. A panorama of the great city sprawled before them. Off in the distance RMS *Queen of Dalriada* was facing upriver, held from drifting by her huge anchors. Quite suddenly a plume of black smoke billowed from the after end of the forward funnel. Scooped up by the wind it drifted west down the river towards Belém, which was close to where the foundations of the new suspension bridge where being laid.

"Oh-oh!" said her escort. "Jimmy the Pariah is in for it."

"I beg your pardon?"

"Och, just a wee inside joke," smiled Angus. "Jim Parry is on watch in 2BR. One o' his boilers has got a dirty burner so he'd better find it afore Slack Jack - sorry - Jack Williamson finds it. Mister Williamson is the walkin' second oan the twelve-tae-four watch."

"I won't ask what a walking second is," said Nan, flipping open the lid of the cylinder that still dangled on Angus' left shoulder. Carefully, she extracted an expandable frame of some kind. When locked in position it turned out to be an artist's easel. Coiled around the inner circumference of the tube were blank sheets of drawing paper. Nan slid one out and spread it across her easel. Clips from her handbag were positioned at the edges to hold the paper flat.

"That's quite a gadget ye've got there," said her companion, impressed. "So - where dae ye keep your paint supplies an' brushes?"

In answer her handbag yielded up an aluminum tube containing charcoal sticks and soft graphite pencils.

"Very clever," smiled Angus. "But Ah thought your forté was dinosaurs an' cavemen an' such like."

"It is," replied Nan, peering out over the city and the Tagus beyond. "I usually flesh out fossilized bones, insects and flora indentations for the university. But I like to keep my hand in doing other work." Selecting a piece of charcoal, she made deft lines across the blank paper. "I've already done some scenes of the Boat Deck."

Intrigued her companion watched the succeeding strokes quickly form into a recognizable picture of the scene below them. "That really is quite amazin'," he whispered in awe. "Ye're very talented Nan."

"Thank you Angus," she replied graciously. She removed the clips allowing the paper's springy memory to roll itself up. Adroitly she tightened further before slipping it back into the black tube. "Let's move up onto that tower there," she said, and lifted the easel.

The easel was set up at a convenient spot and a fresh sheet was locked in place. "Angus, stand by that buttress and stare out as if you were Vasco da Gama." Her paramour posed and Nan's charcoal tip danced across the paper.

More tourists could be heard climbing the stone steps. Bernie and Denise Sneddon came into view. They hesitated when they saw Nan and Angus. Not wanting to intrude they turned to go back downstairs.

"No," called Nan. "Don't go. I'll be finished soon. You two are from the ship, aren't you?"

"Yes, we are," admitted the newcomer. "Bernie Sneddon - and this is Denise, my wife." The couple took up a position only a few feet from Angus.

Nan continued to sketch.

Presently another footfall echoed from the steps. Mo Greene came into view to nod his acknowledgment before moving to the east wall.

Nan wiped her hands on a damp tissue. "I'm finished Angus."

The engineer moved to her side and placed his arm round her waist. His likeness on paper was remarkable. She had even sketched the Sneddons into the scene. "That's bluidy marvellous, Nan!" He glanced at his wristwatch and frowned. "Ah'll need tae go soon Nan. Ah'm due tae relieve Dave Hedges in an hour's time. Ah hope yon taxidriver o' yours is standin' by handy."

"He will be Angus," he was assured. They packed up and saying goodbye to the Sneddons, went downstairs.

In the meantime Greene had edged his way around the tower walls until he was directly behind Denise who was leaning over the parapet. Raising both hands he glanced at the woman's husband. Bernie stared into Mo's eyes for a few seconds then shook his head ever so slightly.

"Look love!" declared Denise, turning.

Greene quickly lowered his arms and the moment was lost. Nodding to the couple he went below.

What an idiot! Bernie thought. Didn't Mo realize that there would be an inquiry if he'd pushed her over? And in Portugal yet. Now there are two possible witnesses to come forward if there is a police investigation when we finally do get rid of Denise. He moved to his wife's side and lovingly put his arm around her. "What is it dear?"

She pointed off over to top of the Alfama's houses with burnt red terra cotta roofs and blinding white walls into the distance. "Look," she repeated. "Over there we can see . . ."

Duarte dropped Angus off at the tenders' berth. With a parting kiss Nan set off for the Tagus ferry destined for Belém. The engineer was back on board the liner in plenty of time for tea.

It was nearly five o'clock when Angus peeked into the synagogue or scroll room located on B Deck forward. It was empty. The strains of young voices singing a Gang Show melody drew him into the Tourist Class Children's Playroom. He was surprised to see about eight or ten Life Boys belting out the Boy Scouts' favorite theme. The lads were all dressed in short trousers and wearing their lanyard adorned navy-blue Guernsey sweaters that were bedecked with shiny brass life rings encircling a fouled anchor. The chorus stopped suddenly when the engineer appeared in the room.

"Can I help you?" The elderly gentleman who was conducting the choir with an HB pencil turned to Angus.

"Oh no," replied King hurriedly. "Ah'm sorry that Ah've disturbed ye. Ah'm just daein' my checks." He lifted his swinger as proof. "Ah'll come back later."

"Please don't go," exhorted the man before introducing himself. "My name is Ed Ordowich. I was delegated by the Lanarkshire EU Church Committee to oversee these lads on this trip." He elaborated. "Every one of those youngsters earned a sea voyage by being the best of the best in all the EU kirks in Lanarkshire. I'm really a Captain of the Boys Brigade in Hamilton.

"That's quite a responsibility ye've taken oan," stated Angus. "I was surprised tae hear your laddies singin' the opposition's song."

"We don't look at the Boy Scouts as opposition," asserted Ordowich. "Any organization that keeps young folk off the streets and on the straight and narrow is a blessing in my book."

"Ye soond like ye ken whit ye're talkin' aboot."

"I should - I'm a retired judge!"

"Oh!" Angus eyed the old chap. 'He must be eighty if he's a day,' he mused.

The passage of years had bent his thin frame into a permanent stoop or perhaps it was the burden he'd carried during his sojourn on the Bench. Nevertheless, he carried a humorous glint in his pale blue eyes and his manner was most congenial.

"Eh - Ordowich . . ." Angus mused. "That's a mid-European name, isn't it?"

"Polish, actually. I flew fighters for Britain when the war started."

The engineer stared at him doubtfully. "Eh, were ye no' kind o' auld tae be a Spitfire pilot?"

Ordowich laughed and slapped his knee. "The Great War, young fellow. I flew SE 5a's and Sopwith Camels. In fact, I hold the record for flying five thousand feet below sea level."

The disbelief on King's face made him chortle again.

"Maybe I'll tell you about it sometime," he said. "But in the meantime I have to give these lads a bible lesson since they missed Sunday School by being ashore all day."

Angus glanced at his wristwatch and brightened. He could spare a few minutes. "If ye like, Ah could tell these laddies a biblical story that my grandfaither was fond o' relatin'."

"That would be splendid!" He faced his troop. "How about it you men, how would you like Mister King to tell you a story from the Bible?"

Immediately the boys voiced their agreement. Ordowich toddled over to a lounge chair and slowly eased his ancient frame onto it. The boys formed a partial circle in front of the engineer and squatted comfortably on the deck. "Aye, weel this story began a very long time ago in the Bible," and he began his grandfather's version of a tale from the Book of Samuel I:

It was a time when the Israelites were haein' anither rammie wi' the Philistines. Ye see, there was this place called Glen Elah that had a wee bit o' a stream or burn runnin' through it. Baith armies were camped opposite one anither oan the slopes o' the glen. Every day they would hae a wee bit o' a fight but it never came tae anythin.

One day the gaffer o' the Philistines hailed a challenge across the burn at the king o' the Israelites. "Hey Saul," he shouted. "Since we're no' gettin' anywhere wi' this war, howsaboot baith o' us puttin' up a champion each tae get a result: Winner take a'."

Saul rubbed his beard an' thocht aboot it afore answerin'. "Ah'll tell ye whit," he yells back. "Ah'll ask my lads if ony o' them would like tae hae a crack at your guy. Where is he, by the way?"

The Philistine gaffer pointed tae a squad o' sodjers standin' directly behind him. "See the big guy in the back row?"

Saul gawked an' spluttered, "Dae ye mean yon fella that's heid an' shoulders above a' the rest?"

"Aye, that's him. That's my lad from Gath."

"Weel, like Ah said," replied Saul. "Ah'll put it tae my lads but Ah cannae promise anythin'."

Saul commanded a' his captains tae find volunteers interested in fightin' the Philistine but there were wasnae any takers. Finally Saul's Sennachie had a word in his ear. "Sire," he said. "Ah might just hae the very lad for ye."

One wee boy from Wishaw shot his hand upward as if trying to reach the deckhead.

"Aye laddie?"

"Please Mistur, whit's a Sennachie?"

The engineer gazed at the freckle-faced wee fellow. "Usually it's a clan chief but in this case he's King Saul's top advisor. Noo if Ah can continue the story . . ."

"Oh aye, who might that be?" Saul asked his counsellor.

The Sennachie, a big hairy-faced soul, gestured tae a burly sodjer playin' beds wi' some o' the squaddies' daughters.

"Och no," objected Saul. "Yon's Big Geordie Fife. A'body kens he just a big saftie."

"Aye," admitted the Sennachie. "But when he gets his dander up, there's nae stoppin' him. Mind ye, he's quite useless at the Highland Games. He's thrown awa' mair cabers an' lost mair hammers than we can keep up wi'."

"Izthatafact?" remarked Saul, his interest renewed. "So how dae we get his dander up?"

"When he gets a bevy inside him, he goes daft. He'll clear oot a bar room in nae time."

"Ok," agreed Saul. "Let's gie him some o' yon stuff in the wee keg that the Phoenicians brought from beyond the Pillars o' Hercules. Whit's it called again?"

"Laphroaig," replied the Sennachie, lickin' his lips with anticipation.

"Whit's Laphroaig?" piped up a wee tousle-heided boy frae Hamilton.

"It's one of my Papa's medicines," replied another Life Boy knowingly.

"Och aye," agreed the freckle-faced lad standin' at his side. "My Papa keeps his in a medicine cabinet next tae the TV."

"A' his medicines come frae Speyside," announced the third kid and warming up, began to recite from memory: "The Balvenie, The Macallen, Talisker . . ."

"Ahem, that's quite enough thank ye, laddie," grunted Angus, bringing his repertoire to halt.

"Cardhu, Glen Morangie," intoned a fourth kid.

"And there is even one called Sheep Dip!" supplemented a fifth adolescent.

"Dae want tae hear this story or no'?" Angus asked, his voice taking on a slight edge. 'An' this bunch are suppose tae come from a religious background,' he muttered to himself. Then aloud, he went on with his tale:

"Aye weel, ye can forget aboot guzzlin' doon my single malt," Saul told his Sennachie. "Ye're next task is tae get Geordie whitshisface a guid bevy inside him. Just get him steamin' mind, no' too full that he's nae guid tae us by fallin' doon drunk."

"Aye Your Grace," said the Sennachie, crestfallen

So afore long, Big Geordie was ready tae take oan the hale Philistine army. "Where is this champion that Ah'm supposed tae fight?" Geordie bellowed.

Saul scanned the enemy array an' pointed. "That's him ower there," he told Geordie. "The big yin in the second row o' yon squad ower there."

"He's a big guy, a' right," conceded Geordie. "His heid an' shoulders tower above his pals. But that's a' right, Ah'll soon hack him doon tae my size."

He gave his sword a practice swing.

"Hey, hey!" protested his king. "Take it easy wi' that thing. Ye nearly wheecht my arm aff!"

Saul screamed across the glen tae the Philistine gaffer as Geordie began swaggerin' doon the brae. Weel, it wasnae quite a swagger, it was mair like a whisky barrel bobbin' alang oan coiled springs.

"Whit's up noo?" The Philistines' gaffer roared back.

"Our man's comin' doon tae hae a better look at your guy," answered Saul.

"Oh, is he?" came the reply. The Philistine gaffer spun aroond an' hollered up the ither brae: "Hey Goliath, stand up!"

As Goliath came tae his full height, the rest o' his squad jostled aboot, a' tryin' tae get the benefit of the sudden shade frae the boilin' hot sun. Geordie went gey, gey grey an' started tae run back up the brae towards Saul.

"Here, where are ye gaun'?"

Geordie, quite sober noo, replied: "Ah'm gaun hame. Ye're no' payin' me enough for this job!" An' he ran awa'.

The Sennachie strode ower tae Saul an' shook his heid.

"Aye, things are lookin' grim noo," moaned Saul.

"Aye, they aren't hauf," agreed the Sennachie. "A' yon guid Laphroaig wasted!"

Frae ahent one o' the soldiers' marquee tents they heard the shrill voice of a young person beratin' somebody. The two men stepped ower some guy ropes an' had a wee keek aroond a flap o' canvas tae see what was gaun on.

"They saw a wee laddie with hair as red as mine," Angus removed his peaked cap to show off his ginger locks. "He was giein' three big soldiers a telling aff. Like a lot o' red-heided folk he had a temper tae match once he got his dander up. This laddie was aboot hauf-a-heid taller than yoursel'." He gestured to the kid from Wishaw before going on. "An' he was madder than a bear with a burnt backside."

"Here, here," admonished Saul, movin' intae sight. "Whit's gaun oan?"

"Och Mister, Ah'm just giein' my big brothers a row," answered the wee boy.

"Is it the custom in your faimily tae gie your elders, an' your betters - Ah might add - a severe tongue lashin'?" asked Saul. "An' by the way, ye'll address me as Sire, or your Grace."

"Are ye one o' the High Heid Yins?" the wee laddie asked.

"Aye," replied Saul. "Ah *am* the High Heid Yin. Ah'm King Saul. Noo, ye can tell me who in the blazes *you* are!"

"My name's Davie," responded the wee boy. "My faither sent me up tae the front just tae feed yon three lazy beggars there."

"Enough o' that!" commanded Saul. "Ye'll no' speak aboot my sodjers like that. Tell me, how come ye're mad at them?"

"Ah've been wheelin' this heavy barrow up steep braes an' doon rugged crags a' day in this heat. It's loaded doon wi' stuff that Mither made for they brithers o' mine, Eliah, Abinadab, an' Shammah." Wee Davie explained. "Ah've got tattie scones, shortbreid, oatcakes, bannocks, an' the like.

Ah've brought some o' my Faither's cheeses for their sergeants. An' here Ah find them lollin' aboot as if they were on Saltcoats Beach durin' a Sunday School trip."

"Dae ye hae ony rolls filled with pressed corned beef an' beetroot wi' ye, Davie?" asked Eliah, lickin' the growth o' hair aroond his mooth.

"No, Ah dinnae!" snapped Davie. "Ah've just got some dry breid for ye an' strong cheese for your captains . . . Who dae ye think ye are, anyway - Rebus?"

Eliah shook his heid glumly an' slumped doon on a hummock o' dry grass.

"Aye," went on Davie, "That's ye at your best - layin' aboot like a store dog. Ye should fightin' a' that rabble ower there!" he exclaimed, his finger jabbin' at the opposite hillside.

His brothers said nothin', starin' shamefaced at the ground.

"Here laddie, Ah'll need tae hae a word with your faither aboot your lack o' manners," censured Saul. "Whit's his name, by the way?"

"Jesse," replied wee Davie.

"Jesse whit?" prompted the Sennachie.

"Jesse - Your Grace," came the sullen reply.

"That's better," said Saul. "Is he no' yon big tall fella from Ziklag?"

"No Sire," said wee Davie, shakin' his heid. "My Da's a big man a' right but he stays in Bethlehem."

"Och, that big Jesse!" Saul beamed with recollection. "Aye, Ah ken him fine. Weel noo young man, ye're an awfy bad mannered wee boy an' Ah'll be tellin' yer Da next time Ah see him."

"Ah'm sorry, Yer Grace," apologized Davie. "But ye ken, this war should've been ower an' done with a while ago."

"What dae ye ken aboot wagin' war?" bellowed the Sennachie. "Ye're just a bairn."

"Just a bairn!" echoed Davie. "Ah'll let ye ken that Ah've killed twa bears in my time an' countless jackals that were after my Da's goats an' sheep." He glared back at the Sennachie afore continuin': "Dae ye see this?" he demanded, grabbin' at his sporran. He carried it on the right side o' his belt just the same as a pipeband snare drummer does. This is made frae the skin o' a lion that Ah slew just afore Ne'erday. Ah'm man enough for ony battle."

"So how come ye're so tough?" asked Saul.

"Because Ah've got the power o' The Lord in my arm," boasted wee Davie.

"Who telt ye that?" Saul asked.

"Sammy," replied wee Davie.

"Sammy Dreep?" guffawed the Sennachie.

"No. Sammy, the prophet, when he anointed me."

'So-o,' thought Saul.'This wee scunner must be gettin' lined up tae take ower my job. Weel, we'll soon see aboot this.' "A wee hard man, are ye?' Saul scoffed aloud. "Dae ye see yon lump o' a Philistine ower there?"

Wee Davie nodded.

"Dae ye think that ye could beat him?"

"Maybe," said Davie, hesitantly. "Ah'll hae a go at him if ye want."

"Here-here, Your Grace," protested the Sennachie. "Surely ye no' gaun to send this wee plooky-faced nyaff tae fight Goliath? Man, that's like puttin' Carluke Rovers up against the 'Gers!"

"Aye weel, Ah've got my reasons," Saul told the Sennachie. He thought for a minute an' wondered how he could handicap the wee lad even further frae winnin'. "Ye ken, it wouldnae dae tae send wee Davie oot against yon big hulk athoot the proper weapons. Sennachie, awa' ower tae my tent an' fetch my special armour - ye ken - the *heavy* sword, the *heavy* shield, an' the *heavy* spear."

The Sennachie came back presently with the king's own armaments. He handed the great spear tae wee Davie. The wee laddie nearly fell ower with the weight o' it.

"Here," protested Davie. "The burn's no' that wide that Ah hae tae pole-vault it!"

"That's no' a vaulting pole," the Sennachie said. "Ye chuck at him. Point the sharp end at him first afore ye throw it."

"Chuck it?" squeaked wee Davie. "Ah can barely lift it, never mind chuck it. It stays here," he said determinedly. "Alang wi' a' yon ither scrap metal."

"Scrap metal?" says Saul, quite flabbergasted. "Ah'll let ye ken that Ah paid guid gold for the forgin' an' fancywork." 'Still,' he thought with some appeasement, 'When Goliath slays him Ah'll get tae keep all yon nice armour tae myself.' "Och weel, hae it your ain way, aff ye go . . . Guid luck," the king said as an afterthought.

Wee Davie started tae tramp doon the brae towards the burn. He was still teed aff at his brithers, the King, an' the Israelite army in general. "Ye're a' just a bunch o' lobby dossers!" he called back at them.

By the time the wee laddie got doon tae the burn, he had a thirst that would put shame tae a camel. An' it was guid water tae, wi' a tinge o' red oan the bottom stanes. This meant that it was iron water."

He stopped and spoke to the Life Boy from Wishaw. "Ye'll likely ken that's the stuff that they make Irn Bru from since Barr's produce it in your hametoun."

The story continued:

Onyway after he'd wiped his mooth, he noticed that the burn wended its way near a strand o' white pebbles. He splashed ower tae it an' picked oot five smooth roond stones . . .

The cool water frae the stream had refreshed Davie. His temper had eased so that he didnae feel so crabbit ony mair. He sclimbed up the ither side o' the bankin' an' strolled easily up the wee bit o' a slope tae where yon big lump called Goliath was standin'.

Noo Goliath, who'd killed a hundred men, was called Goliath the One Hundred. His squaddies also called him

Goliath the Hun for short. He leaned easily oan his spear an' watched wee Davie approach.

"Vot are you dooink here mein kinder?" he boomed.

Wee Davie sized up his opponent afore replyin'. Goliath's long black hair an' a big bushy beard an' moustache covered maist o' his sunburnt face. His eyes were like twa bits o' polished coal. The giant had a big hooked nose that ye could open beer cans wi', an' his broken teeth were as yellow as custard. Goliath's heid was encased in a massive brass helmet with a pair o' steer's horns stickin' oot it. It was bigger than Davie's mother's jeely pan. His long shaggy cloak was the skin o' a musk ox an' his arms an' legs bulged wi' muscles like Desperate Dan's. His sandals resembled twa auld coracles.

"Ah'm here tae kill ye," wee Davie stated simply.

"Ho! Ho! Ho!" laughed the giant. "This is a choke?"

"Ho! Ho! Ho! yourself Santa Claus," responded wee Davie. "This is nae joke."

"You com to keel me, vee poy?" Goliath jabbed his thumb against his polished breastplate, a piece o' armour that may have begun life as the end bell o' a steam drum on a Yarrow boiler. "After today, they vil call me Goliath the Hundred-und-one-hauf!" He emphasized this remark with a clang o' his spear slappin' against his shield - which could've been the other end o' yon same steam drum. He laughed at his jest an' roared, "You do not even haf veapon."

"Is that right?" said wee Davie. He put his hand intae his sporran an' drew oot a fathom o' leather thong.

Curiously Goliath watched the laddie straighten the twists oot the leather thong. "You are goink to strangle me, liebchen?" he grinned. "How are you goink to reach mein neck, eh?"

Wee Davie didnae say anythin'. He took a wee smooth stane oot o' his sporran, placed it in the sling's sheath, an' began his windup. Up the front, ower his heid, an' doon the back, the sling was birlin' faster an' faster. Then a fraction o' a second after it passed the lowest point, Davie released the stane. Goliath never seen it comin', even though it hit him atween the eyes. Stunned, he fell doon oan the ground with a loud thud - just like the winnin' caber at last year's Cowal Games. Quickly the wee boy ran over tae Goliath an' started pullin' the giant's sword oot its scabbard.

"Oooh!" moaned Goliath. "Mein heid ist sair."

Davie, who by noo was totterin' aboot tryin' tae keep yon great big sword balanced upright above his heid, gasped: "Dinnae worry man, Ah've got the very cure for it right here."

An' afore Goliath could ask, "You haf aspirin?" wee Davie wheecht the sharp sword doon on the giant's dirty neck. The big heid rolled awa' doon the wee bit brae: Clunk-i-ty, clunk-it-y, clunk!

A loud moan could be heard from behind him as the Philistines realized that their champion had been slain. The Israelites started cheerin': "Ea - sy! Ea - sy! Ea - sy!" an' came runnin' doon through the heather afore splashin' ower the burn tae congratulate Davie.

"Dibs oan the shield," shouted a soldier.

"Yon bronze greaves are mine," shrieked another.

"Ah want his leather kilt," yelled somebody else. Soon Goliath was just layin' there in his BVD's.

"Here," protested wee Davie. "A' yon stuff should be mine. Whit will Ah take hame tae prove tae that Ah beat Goliath?"

Saul came runnin' up a' oot o' breath. "Take his heid," he gasped. "That'll make ye a fine souvenir."

So that's whit wee Davie did. He put Goliath's heid in his barrow an' wheeled it hame.

"Hey Mistur," piped up a lad from Carfin. "What did Davie dae with Goliath's heid when he got hame?"

"Och, he just put it on his mither's sideboard. An' sure enough it made a fine showpiece tae talk aboot when relations an' acquaintances came visitin'!"

The lads jumped to their feet and cheered their appreciation to the engineer. Judge Ordowich took his hand saying, “My word! That was a most unusual account of David and Goliath.” He turned to his charges. “Right men, form up two abreast and we’ll go for afternoon tea.”

Obediently they marched out of the room with Angus taking the salute.

Six o’clock rolled around with more and more happy but tired passengers embarking laden with souvenirs. Many headed straight to their cabins to bathe or shower before dinner. Gerry and Jack were kept busy speeding up a/c fans on all decks.

Angus went into the main restaurant fifteen minutes before the dinner gong sounded. Already it was half full with returning diners adding to the throng by the minute. As of yet his temperature readings were still in the acceptable range but with all the added body heat that would change. He’d better give Don a head’s up so that he could open up another nozzle on the Fozzie. He saw Nan come in and go to her usual spot. Using a circuitous route the engineer closed in on her and swung his psychrometer. “Did ye enjoy yourself at yon place - Belém - was it?”

“Yes,” replied Nan. “That place is just steeped in history. In fact, the whole city is.” As if in response to that statement the strains of *April in Portugal* oozed from hidden speakers. “Will I see you when your watch is over?”

The engineer’s eyes reconnoitered the room for suspicious authority. “Ah’m sorry Nan,” he whispered from the edge of his mouth. “Dae ye no’ mind me explainin’ tae ye last night aboot engineers fraternizin’ wi’ passengers?”

“Vaguely,” replied Nan. “But if you’re willing to take a chance right after dinner my cabin number is M21.”

Angus shook his head. “An engineer caught wanderin’ aboot passenger accommodation when he’s aff duty is just beggin’ for trouble. Besides, Ah’ll be on standby at ten o’clock.”

"What's that?"

"Ah'll be drivin' the ship doon the Tagus," replied Angus, smirking.

Nan glanced up at him in surprise. "I didn't know engineers steered the ship."

"Naw, it's nuthin' like that. Ah'll be maneuverin' one o' the main engines."

"That must be exciting," laughed Nan.

"Well, it certainly was the first time Ah did it," Angus smiled, ruefully recalling his very first experience at the manoeuvring wheels. Was that just five weeks ago? He reminisced. Boy! How green he was then. A two-ringer materialized from the after private dining saloon on the starboard side. "Cheerio just noo," he said hastily. "Ah'll probably see ye at breakfast tomorrow."

He downed a couple of pints of draught lager before going into the mess. The lobster bisque was so delicious he did an Oliver Twist and asked for more. Toni, the homosexual steward, was no beadle so the second plate of soup was served with aplomb. Still on a sea food bent Angus ordered Dover sole with croquette potatoes and mixed vegetables. There was little conversation at the table. His fellow diners were Will Keyes, Taffy Morgan, Don, Travers, and Larry Treen. All of them were consuming their food in haste because the beer in their cabins was warming and going flat. Two trays of beer had been ordered for last call since the main bar closed at nine for engineers.

Angus had just begun digging into his favorite sweet, strawberry shortcake, when his shipmates hastily excused themselves and tumbled from the mess. To complete his repast he asked for the cheese board and some coffee. King felt quite stuffed by the time he had reached his cabin.

He had barely returned to his cabin when there was a knock on the door and a wan face with black tousled hair peeked round the edge of the door. It was Walters, the eight-to-twelve storekeeper.

"Standby, Mister King."

"Ok - thanks."

With effort the engineer rose and went to the wash basin at the after end of his cabin. He splashed some cold water in his face to freshen up. He checked his appearance in the mirror above the sink before heading down below.

The great engines were panting as if they had just completed a marathon run. Steam was feathering above the 2nd Intermediate and Low Pressure Turbine glands. The portly Tony Ball, otherwise known as The Sphere, was manipulating the flow control for these glands as Angus descended the engineroom ladder. Bob Christie was leaning on a portable dias, ready to record the engine movements. Alan Lindsey, the Chief Engineer was tete-a-tete with Phillip Edwards, the First Senior Second Engineer.

Maxie Harris, holding a 1-1/16" open-ended spanner, was poised on the starting platform's starboard ladder waiting for the first engine movement. His job as feed man was to make sure that the water demand from the boilers kept up with the steam supply to the engines. At sea this chore was done automatically by the Weir Robo valve mounted on every watertube boiler when the water feed pumps' pressures were maintained at a constant 500 pounds per square-inch. But for now, each and every erratic movement had to be treated accordingly. Old Mister Parr, the eight-to-twelve platform second, was as usual, fiddling with the saline indicators for the boiler feed water.

With a passing nod to Black Bob Angus went to the starboard maneuvering wheels. Minutes later Terry Baker was in front of the port wheels. When Don Travers appeared, Christie directed him to the port wheels. Peter Deery was directed to the starboard controls beside Angus.

All the telegraph needles were on *Standby.*

Up on the bridge the quartermaster waited by the port steering wheel. Bridge boys stood alert by the telegraphs. Their green needles were at standby too. The fourth mate hung up the phone receiver and nodded to the chief officer. Out on the port wing Captain Fawcett, accompanied by the Portuguese pilot, was peering forward over the darkened deck. A voice tube relayed the phone message. The anchor watch was ready.

Floodtide kept the ambient flow of the Tagus at bay. The pilot spoke into the voice tube. "Dead slow ahead pleese," his Iberian accent carried a slight lisp. By the time he'd walked back into the wheelhouse water and silt was boiling under the great vessel's counter. Slowly she steamed up to her anchors.

"Up and down!" a distant voice announced and the clank-clank of the anchor chains were heard being hauled through water jets to the chain locker. The anchor was hove to.

"Rudder hard to port! Full astern, port engine! Full ahead, starboard engine!"

With practiced ease Angus slid the handle of the burnished brass telegraph to align it with the green needle pointing at *Full Ahead*. He gripped the great handwheel that controlled the steam to the starboard turbines and quickly eased it open until the propellor shaft speed was spinning at 100 rpm. Over on the port side Terry was simultaneously dumping great volumes of steam into his astern turbines. The roar of the accelerating engines was deafening. Lights and overhead fan deflectors vibrated madly and dust that had settled on them eons ago gently drifted down on the engineroom personnel.

The steam pressure, once at the ambient 400 psi, was dropping alarmingly as if the astern turbines were sucking steam right out of the boilers. The feed water followed suit prompting Maxie to bound down to his pumps and disappear into a cloud of steam like some genie clad in white overalls.

Presently both engines were ordered to stop. Presumably the vessel was now pointing downriver. Telegraph bells jangled again. *Dead Slow* Ahead, both engines. They were on their way to Las Palmas.

Captain Fawcett gazed longingly across the black waters and deliberated on his future. He'd less than three years to go until mandatory retirement. His mind rolled back to his youth when John Fawcett, his father, had been a freighter skipper for a Chinese Hong. He usually travelled between Hong Kong, Singapore and Macau. Sometimes he came to Lisbon but most of his trips were in the Orient. On a voyage to Darwin he'd met and married an Australian girl. The following year she died in childbirth.

The product of that union was Jamie Fawcett. Jamie was raised by Soo Li, an amah who was a second cousin once removed to John Fawcett's boss, the Hong of the Whangpoo Trading Company. His old man often took Soo Li and him away on wondrous voyages. Once he grew old enough to understand he realized that his dad was banging his amah. Nonetheless the boy learned to navigate as he absorbed the lore of the sea.

Jamie was only fourteen and studying in an English school in Hong Hong when his father's ship was lost with all hands in a typhoon. His dad's employer took him under his wing and he signed on as an apprentice on a cargo-liner. Although the First World War was raging in Europe, it barely touched the seas of the Far East. German raiders were causing alarm in certain areas but the sea was vast and none were ever sighted.

But pirates roamed the Bornean waters. Any sailing vessel that had been unfortunate enough to lose the wind was fair game to watchful Dyaks who'd paddle out from tree-choked creeks. With sumpitans or blowguns, krisses and other deadly weapons, luckless sailors met horrific and bloody ends.

On the whole, steamers chug-a-lugging along ten or more knots enjoyed a safe passage in those hazardous territories until one night a lineshaft bearing overheated. First light saw hordes of canoes paddling toward the stationary vessel. Steam hoses were hastily rigged.

It was like some exciting adventure out of *Boy's Own Paper*, reflected Fawcett, touching the tri-colored ribbon on his tunic jacket. One of the Dyaks, a fearful individual with a narrow white bone through his nose, rushed screaming along the upper deck brandishing a razor-sharp kriss. The Hong's son, who was travelling as supercargo that trip, just happened to step out of his cabin door and find himself right in the path of this rabid warrior.

At that moment Jamie was assisting the fourth engineer who was engrossed with hooking up a fire hose to a steam outlet. The apprentice grabbed the canvas tube directly behind the brass nozzle, swung it about his head, and let the attacker have it right across the bridge of his nose. The fourth gave him another one on the back his head with his wheelkey and together they heaved the stricken Dyak overboard.

Back in Kowloon a grateful Hong gave the pair one hundred Hong Kong dollars each and bestowed them with the Hong's Service Ribbon - no medal - just the ribbon which consisted of a circlet of yellow silk with an azure centre and three monogrammed letters of the honour in white. Fawcett proudly displayed this unique award on all his uniform jackets and dress tunics.

He sighed and looked aft down onto the Boat Deck where passengers were watching the glimmering lights of Lisbon fading into nothingness beyond the ebon waters of the mighty Tagus estuary. A familiar figure on stiletto heels flounced into his view. He stepped over the coaming, hurriedly thanked the pilot for his services, and ordered the First Officer to take over. He vacated the wheelhouse and scooted down the ladder after the buxom blonde.

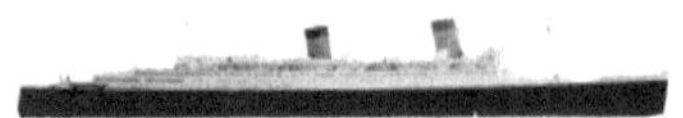

CHAPTER NINE

Morning interlude

0355 Monday

"Hi, Gus. Boy! I'm sure glad that you're on time," sighed Dave Hedges. "I can't wait to get out of this bloody ice cream suit and relax with a cold beer."

He was referring to the white uniform that all officers had to wear now that the ship was steaming into a warmer clime. The cut was similar to the casual black patrol suits engineers wore when in transit between their quarters and engineroom change area. Starched high-collared white uniforms were unwanted burdens to ships' officers. The jackets were single breasted with six brass buttons up the front. The shoulder boards denoting rank were fastened to the jacket with a brass button, which in turn was secured by a cotter pin. A white shoe lace tied inside the coat held the lower end of each epaulette. The brass split pin and the lace aglets scratched and aggravated the skin.

Wearing an undershirt helped to eliminate this annoyance but restricted air circulation to the body and made life even more unbearable. Keeping this type of uniform was hard to keep clean. So too, was each officer's white canvas shoes which had to be blancoed regularly, often twice daily.

"I'm off for a cold one," said Dave, opening the fan room door. He hesitated. "Oh, by-the-way, some bugger is screwing around with the heating, midships on D Deck."

"What dae ye mean - screwin' aroond?"

"Well, somebody keeps turning on the thermotank steam supply that feeds some of the stewardesses' cabins."

Don chipped in.

"D'you mean to tell us that some nutcase has got one of our valve keys?"

"Yep," snapped Kevin, just as Don came in to relieve him. "It started just over an hour ago. All the stewardesses are bitching like hell."

"What's happening?" asked Don.

Cunningham told him.

"Holy shit!" exclaimed Travers. "We don't need this. It's toasty enough down there on D Deck already without some practical joker's weird sense of humour."

The phone rang. "A/c." He listened for a moment before slamming the receiver down on its cradle. "Shit, the bastard's at it again!"

He jerked his head at Gerry who grabbed one of the teed square-socket keys that were utilized to adjust the steam flow into the thermotanks. Originally, back in the dawn of time when the *Queen of Dalriada* was slick and brand-new, regular handwheels were fitted to thermotank valves. Stewards and other unauthorized personnel would sneak into the fan rooms and turn the steam valves full open. Turning one of those valves open more than one quarter of a turn was the equivalent of converting a cabin into a Turkish bath. This practice was frowned upon by all concerned. Consequently all handwheels were removed and the valve stem was enclosed with a narrow pipe so that not even an adjustable spanner could be used to operate the valve. Thus, the tee-shaped square-socket wrench came into being.

Gerry recalls:

I beetled down to the starboard alleyway on D Deck. There were two fan rooms located amidships there. I went into the first one. The tank was cool and the three fans that served that section were going out full blast. I came out and made my way aft towards the other a/c room. One of its thermotanks sounded like an asthmatic hippopotamus, its sides pinking and cracking under the strain of such excessive heat. I shut off the steam and checked all the fans. They were barely ticking over. I cranked up their rheostats and left.

I'd just closed the fan room door when Daphne, the cabin class swimming pool attendant, stepped out from a cabin and accosted me. She was a stocky muscular woman and quite tall, about five foot ten maybe. Her normal wavy hair, if bleached blonde can be called normal, was lank and dank. Sweat was leaking from the pores on her round face like dewdrops on a ripening tomato. Her tight white attendant's uniform was made even tighter by a great bosom that thrust toward me like the bows of a battlecruiser. The person who'd sewn the buttons on her outfit should've been commended for such sturdy workmanship. Any antiperspirant that she might have applied was long gone, diluted by the dark salty stains under her armpits.

"Do you work on airconditioning?" She asked in a whisper that sounded like boiler's safety valve feathering. Nodding, I gulped. We stood almost nose to nose, her piss-coloured eyes threatening to strike me blind. A hint of gin hovered in the balmy atmosphere.

"Who's your engineer?"

"There's two on this watch," I answered nervously. "Mister Travers and Mister King."

"King?" she repeated, her eyes softening to the consistency of amber. "He's a Scotchman, isn't he?"

I nodded.

She stood back a step. "Tell him to get his arse down here. Me and Debbie and Devina all want to file a complaint."

I just stared at her.

"Right bloody now!" she spat.

I bolted back to the a/c office. Halfway up the pantry stairs, between B and A Decks I ran into Mister King. I blurted out the siren's message, adding how everything was ok as far as the cooling system was concerned.

"Aye - ok Gerry," he replied easily. "Ah'll go doon an' sooth some feathers. Dinnae worry aboot it. Tell Mister Travers where Ah'm heidin' for."

Jack glanced up from the exploits of Dan Dare when I entered the fan room. "What's up?" he asked.

I told him what had happened.

"*Chree-ist*!"

"Is Mister Travers still on his rounds?"

"Yeah," replied Jack. "He should be back in about five minutes. Here," he said, handing me his *Eagle*. "I'm going to take a leak. I'll bring some kye back."

"Don't forget to wash your hands first!" I reminded him.

How Tommy Wall ever managed to get through all those adventures on a bar of ice cream always amazed me. I tossed the comic book in the desk drawer just as Mister Travers came back in.

"Jack gone for some kye?" he asked, sitting by the phone. He planked his size tens on the scruffy desktop. "Any calls?"

"Only that one down on D Deck."

"Oh yeah! Is everything all right now?"

"Yes," I replied. "Except . . ."

"Except what?"

I told him about my run in with the cabin class swimming pool attendant.

Mister Travers grinned knowingly. "You're lucky that she only tore a strip off you and not your shirt. What a maneater that one is. Do you know what I saw her do last trip?"

I shook my head.

"I popped into the cabin class gym one morning to work off a few pounds on the rowing machine. There she was bench pressing and grunting like a navvy digging a canal."

Jack came in with a pot of cocoa and as he poured. Mister Travers went on with his story.

"Somehow Daphne managed to knock the weight stand away so she called me to lift the barbells off her chest. And what a chest that is! Daphne's a 40-40-40, y'know. Forty inch chest, forty-years-old with the fortitude of a nymphomaniac. He smirked at his little pun.

"Anyhow I went over to help her and grabbed those bloody barbells. Christ, I couldn't shift them! I thought a hernia would push my balls off!"

"'Put that bloody stand back in its place!' she roared. I did just that and she plunked that weight back in position just as easily as you'd place a pen on that desk." He took a sip of cocoa. "Look at me," he said. "I'm as strong as the average fellow yet she called a ninety-pound-weakling." He squinted over his cup at me and Jack. "That weight must've been fourteen or fifteen stone. Gerry, my boy, you can count your lucky stars that Daphne was in a good mood!"

I frowned, lowered my cup and hesitantly cleared my throat.

The engineer's face drew closer to mine. I could read trouble in his eyes. "What's the matter?" he asked me.

I told him about meeting Mister King on the pantry ladder and how he was going to have a chat with Daphne.

"Gerry old son," Mister Travers began solemnly. "You've just condemned a good man to a fate worse than death."

The ship riding through a slight swell, tweaked creaking protests from white-painted plywood walls on D Deck corridors with masochistic delight. Otherwise it was quiet, quiet as it should be an hour before dawn. Angus had confirmed Gerry's report that all was well in the affected fan room. Since nothing else could be done he made his way for'ard. A door opened and he glanced aft towards the sound. Daphne was wearing a pink terrycloth robe and matching slippers. She trundled right up to him to ask, "Who are you?"

"Eh, Ah'm the a/c engineer, Angus King. Ah'm just checkin' that everythin' is hunky-dory." His eyes enveloped in this formidable female. A forced-draught job as Wheelkey would've said. "Everythin' is ok, isn't it?"

"No sonny," replied Daphne. "It's stinking hot in my cabin."

Angus shrugged apologetically. "Weel, Ah'm really sorry but the fans are already gaun at high speed."

"Not in my cabin sonny. There is no air flow whatsoever," retorted Daphne assuredly and taking him by the arm said: "Come and see."

The innocent blithely stepped into her cabin. Two other women, also attired in terrycloth, waited within seated on separate bunks with a drink-laden coffeetable between them. The pair lasciviously eyed Angus up and down. On a dresser and confined in a pewter bucket, the last vestiges of melting ice cubes were cracking into oblivion. The single Punkah louvre was shut off.

When she was on duty Debbie was the First Class Swimming Pool attendant. Davina's duty was the sauna and Turkish baths. Debbie had auburn hair while Davina's was raven, otherwise they both could have been clones of Daphne.

"Yon louvres need tae be open if ye want fresh air," said Angus. "How come they're shut aff?" He eased past Debbie, on the inboard bunk. "Excuse me please."

"It's stiff," said Daphne, closing the cabin door.

Angus reached up to open the louvre. Debbie reached up to open something else. He peered down at Debbie. Her robe had slipped off leaving her topless. Daphne's terrycloth was on the carpeted deck and behind him Davina was cradling a wobbly set of dun-tipped mammaries in her hands. The engineer gulped and slid the louvre down to open it. "It's no' stiff at a'!" he croaked.

"Something is," said Debbie, with a wicked grin.

"Well?" said Daphne. "Is the rumour true?"

With her nimble fingers manipulating the young man's member toward complete turgidity, Debbie hauled out it out for all to view. "Oh yes!" she breathed as it pouted into view like a Turk's head on a straining hawser's bitter end. "And then some."

'Whit in the bluidy hell have Ah got mysel' intae here?' Angus asked himself. He shuffled back and tried to disengage Debbie's enthusiastic digits. Just then he noticed a brass thermotank key lying on the dresser top. These three bitches had set a trap for some unsuspecting victim from the a/c department. Even in his present predicament he had the gumption and fortitude to pocket it.

Debbie switched tactic and nestled the heated organ between her capacious breasts. Daphne pushed the coffeetable under the sink out of the way. She glided closer to the action. Now Debbie was working her lips over the purplish-blue glans.

"Take it easy Debbie," Daphne cautioned her colleague. "There's enough there for all." Her supple fingers encircled part of the shank that was not in use. "Ooh!" she all but squeaked. "Let's not get that pretty white uniform dirty sonny," she whispered, her tongue lapping at the young man's ear like a friendly wee dog is wont to do. Angus grinned weakly.

Her hand reluctantly moved away from his member and up his chest. Six brass buttons were relieved of their chores and his white tunic jacket retired to a coat hook. The engineer was now stripped to the waist. Kneeling down she rescued his organ from Debbie's mouth and temporarily exchanged for her own. Her manipulative fingers were dextrously loosening both laces on the canvas shoes.

Meantime Davina had knelt on the deck to get a closer look at the situation as she slipped off the shoes. Reaching up Daphne focused on his leather belt and presently the uniform trousers dipped like a flag at sunset. Davina, lifting one white stockinged foot at a time, divested the engineer of his starched flannels. The removal of his shorts revealed everything the women wanted to see - and then some.

By now all four of them were stark naked. Angus was pushed onto a bunk and held there while Daphne sat astride his narrow hips. With an ecstatic groan she directed the engorged organ inside her, and with eyes held tightly shut with concentration, began rocking back and forth. Not to be outdone Davina scrambled up in front of Daphne and pressed her cleft against the engineer's mouth, her coarse haired pudenda all but suffocating him. He'd heard of being killed by kindness but being killed by cunninglus was becoming a distinct possibility.

In the meantime Debbie had grabbed Angus's right hand and was working it up across her ample breasts and down into the forest between her thighs, quite irrespective of the designated dexterity of the engineer's arm and wrist joints. At times she came quite close to dislocating the fellow's elbow.

Gerry recalls:

Mister Travers finished his coffee and glanced at his watch. "Christ!" he swore. "It's five past six and no sign of Gus." He drummed his fingers on the desk in thought. "You two had better get back down to D Deck and find Mister King."

Jack and me headed out the door.

"And don't come back without him!"

The problematic fan room checked out ok. Lingering in the passageway we wondered what to do next. Some of the ship's female staff moved back and forth readying for a new day.

"Tell me again what Daphne said to you."

Jack listened carefully as I retold the story.

"So where is this cabin?" he asked.

I pointed to a door a few yards away.

"D'you reckon that's where she lives?"

I shrugged. "It seems likely."

"Well, let's knock on her door and find out if she's seen Mister King."

"We might wake her up," I warned.

"So what?" Jack replied. "She probably has to be up at this time anyway. She has to get down to the pool early and arrange to have it refilled for the passengers."

"I dunno," I said, for I was reluctant to cross swords with that harridan again.

Jack played a loud tattoo on the cabin door. "Nothing ventured, nothing . . ."

The door swung open and a dishevelled Daphne peered out, her eyes dreamy and her terry robe clutched to her ample bust.

"Excuse me Miss," began Jack. "But has our engineer been here?"

The door swung completely ajar and a seedy Mister King was forcibly ejected into the passageway by two other tough looking females. He was stark naked except for his white socks. One of the women had her housecoat agape and nothing underneath. She stuck the engineer's peaked cap on his tousled red hair. A bundle of white clothing and brass buttons was tossed behind him like so much dirty laundry. His canvas shoes clattered to the linoleum deck just before the door slammed shut.

Mister King's eyes were glazed, his chest was heaving like he'd just ran the four minute mile. A stream of sweat was trickling down towards the crack of his arse. There were scratches, contusions and welts all over his limbs and torso. His dick was like a Christmas stocking hanging on a mantle waiting for Santa, all rosy-red empty and limp. Jack stooped to pick up Mister King's uni.

He pointed down the alleyway. "Let's get him into that fan room right away!" he urged.

A couple of stewardesses did a double-take observing a ginger-headed nude male marching along the passageway, sandwiched between two engineroom ratings. Our engineer had become fairly lucid by the time he'd dressed. He didn't exactly relate his recent experience to us but it wasn't difficult to figure out what he'd endured.

When we left the fan room heading for the a/c office, Mister King led the way. Walking side-by-side with me and behind the engineer, Jack put a hand up to his face and whispered to me. “Boy, wait till the lads hear about this,” he sniggered, his grin splitting his cheeks like a demented Cheshire cat.

Mister King stopped dead in his tracks and did an about-turn. “Jack, have ye ever worked in 3BR durin’ the summer months?”

Jack looked shocked then he stammered, “Yeah, a year past last July. Why do you ask, Mister King?”

The boiler room in question was reputed to be the warmest of them all because some of its forced draft fan intakes came through the heated air of the Main Generator Room first. Summer stints in that stokehold were reserved for certain individuals who didn’t toe the line.

“Ah think ye get my drift,” replied the engineer.

He shifted his gaze onto me. My fingers made a buttoning motion on my lips. With a satisfactory nod he walked away.

But the saga seeped out anyway because the three women were overheard relating their exploit in a Las Palmas bistro. It appeared that Davina had lost out during that memorable morning. Daphne took advantage of the first served - first come policy but Debbie’s aggressive antics used up all their victim’s steam which left the former frustrated and angry.

A quick shower scoured off the female musk and was exchanged with a liberal application of Germolene’s aromatic balm. A quick plate o’ porridge, thought Angus, that’ll tide me ower until teatime. Ah must get some sleep.

He was the last one to enter the mess that morning. The ambient sounds of cutlery and dishes could be heard as engineers spooned and stirred, clattered and clinked their way through their morning repast. Angus headed for a busy table with one remaining place. Don was leaning over the table keeping Taffy, Steamboat, Wheelkey and Terry spellbound with some saucy story. The Leprechaun was making an exaggerated issue of buttering his toast in an effort to avoid hearing such vile verbiage.

The tale ended abruptly and incompleted as Angus berthed alongside Keyes. Reciprocal good mornings acknowledged his presence and the officers diligently applied themselves to this most pleasant meal of the day. The steward approached and Angus ordered orange juice and porridge. Everyone at the table stopped momentarily from their breakfast and stared at Angus with almost reverent respect. “Whit’s up?” he asked.

Don’s guilty expression gave him a clue.

‘The dirty rotten bastard!’ Angus swore under his breath. ‘Cannae keep his big mooth shut. Noo, it’ll be a’ ower the bluidy ship!’ His oatmeal and juice arrived. Glowering to the world in general he sprinkled salt on his cereal, added a generous splash of fresh cream, and delved into his thick cloying repast. ‘As soon as Ah finish this,’ he considered. ‘Ah’m awa’ tae my bunk for the rest o’ the day.’

How wrong he was.

“Mister King! Mister King!”

It was Walters, the eight-to-twelve storekeeper.

“Mm?”

“Emergency Drill in fifteen minutes, Mister King!”

The clamour of bells confirmed his announcement.

Angus sat up and blearily stared back at the rating. “Ok thanks - verry much,” he growled with a total lack of appreciation.

He got up and went to the mirror above his washbasin. Bloodshot eyes glared back at him. A hand explored the ruddy stubble on his chin. He filled the sink and sloshed water on his face and on his head. Dabbing himself dry on a rough towel he stared into the looking glass again. If there was any change, he couldn’t find it. His hurts felt like they were on fire so he reapplied more zinc ointment.

“Damn it,” he swore, but a lightning fast shave certainly made an improvement both cosmetically and mentally. He quickly dressed and donned his lifejacket. Grabbing his peaked cap he merged into a steady stream of engineers *en route* for the elevator.

The working alleyway on C Deck thronged with individuals attired with blue and orange carapaces. Stewards, engineroom ratings, cooks, butchers, bakers and printers were all bustling hither and thither, each heading to or standing at their assigned emergency station.

At 1100 hours sharp the watertight doors began to move. Nosing up steel ramps which usually covered their lower tracks the ribbed cast-steel doors moved slowly and relentlessly toward their mated seals. The ones closest to the main hydraulic pump located on the port mezzanine in the Main Generator Room closed first. As one door closed others perceptibly moved faster as the pump's pressure gradually built up. A warning bell clanked on each door as each gear tooth on a hydraulical rack meshed and turned its pinion.

But long before the watertight doors had closed all the off watch engineers and electricians were crowded inside the Emergency Generator Room on the port side of B Deck aft. In front of them stood the walking seconds, Big John MacKay and Slack Jack Williamson.

The whole group formed a living amphitheater around a pair of twelve-cylinder Perkins four-stroke engines that were coupled to its own generator. Beyond the engines stood an ancient switchboard with copper knife switches as thick as sandwiches.

Archie MacAdam, the HSE, tarried at the business end of the machines ready to explain their function and demonstrate how to start them. Mike Finney, the deck engineer, was stationed to one side ready to give any assistance.

"Richt noo," began Archie. "These ingins here ur Perkins internal combustion ingins. Each hae a dozen-in-line cylinders that run oan paraffin. Hooever they hiv tae be stertit oan petrol until they're hoat enough tae chinge ower." He looked at his audience. "Dae ony youse guys hae ony questions?"

Quite naturally his fellow Scots opined that so far, his explanation had been clear and concise. Welshmen, Irishmen, Scousers, Geordies, Yorkshiremen and Cornishmen had a vague indication since a few words coincided with some in their own dialect. But to engineers from the Home Counties and points south and southeast, the guttural babel might well have been in Mandarin Chinese.

There were no questions.

"Richt then," said Archie, completely satisfied that his lecture was being understood. He pointed up to a brass cock above the carburettor of the inboard engine. "Mike, wid ye kindly reach up an' turn that wee cock oan?"

The deck engineer moved in between the pair of Perkins and complied. Archie stood directly in front of a tiny console with a button, a switch, and three gauges on it.

"Ye'll notice that every cylinder has a wee petcock that's linked tae this here rod." The HSE put his left hand on a steel square rod. "Richt noo - a' yon petcocks ur open so that there's nae compression oan the cylinders when the pistons gang up an' doon." He took a breath and went on:

"The reason for this is oan the aff chance that the batteries ur run doon, the ingin can be stertit by birlin' this here haundle." He touched a hand crank at knee level. "Bit the batteries are ok since they're checked every ither day. So then, here goes."

He pressed the start button and as the engine turned over he pushed the rod over effectively closing all the petcocks. There was a bang followed by a blue flash that escaped from a pinhole in the exhaust pipe as the engine roared into life. The audience stepped back in dismay. Archie glowered at Mike and switched off the engine.

"Mike, Ah thocht Ah telt ye tae replace the spring oan yon rocker erm afore the drill."

"Sorry Mister MacAdam," said Mike. "I was going to do it yesterday but Hodgkin, the fourth mate, wanted me to work on Lifeboat No 23."

"Whit's the maitter wi' it?"

"Nothing now," Mike smiled, proudly.

"Wha's yer boss?" snapped MacAdam. "Me or some damned bridge wallah?"

"Well, theoretically the BOT is the boss as far as safety at sea is concerned."

"Weel noo Mike," said Archie. "Ah'm sure that the bluidy Board o' Trade is jist as concerned aboot this jenny as it is wi' one bluidy lifeboat."

"That's true," conceded Mike. "But personally I'd rather tootle along on a lifeboat than sinking in an illuminated ship!"

"These jennies drive the emergency bilge pump tae - dinnae forget." The HSE reverted his attention back to the engine. "Ok then, is there ony questions afore Ah restert this ingin tae make sure its generator's workin'?"

The Leprechaun put up his hand.

"Yes Mister Deery?" enquired MacAdam.

"Excuse me sor, but we had a similar engine in me last ship and we always started it boi hand."

"Is-that-a-fact?" slurred the HSE. "It must hae been a gey big ship tae hae a jenny engine this size."

"No sor," countered Deery. "Not a jenny sor. The *Liffey Belle* was powered by a big engine just like this."

This brought a gale of laughter from the onlookers.

With indignation Deery drew himself up to his full height of four foot eleven. "And Oi was the Second Engineer!"

"Is-that-a fact?" repeated the HSE. "An' is there a pint tae a' this?"

Deery craned his neck up at him. "Oi started our engine boi hand and we should start this one the same way."

MacAdam glanced at his wristwatch then eyed MacKay, who nodded. "Ah suppose we've goat time."

Groans could be heard among the throng.

The HSE ignored them and shifted the decompression rod back to its original position. "Weel then Mister, ship that crank an' gie it a birl. Gie's a shout when ye think its gaun fast enough."

Although small, Deery was a very stocky individual with muscular shoulders and he bent to his task with a will. With a flurry of pants, heaves and farts, his right hand was just a blur when he shouted, "Roight!"

The rod went over and the engine roared into life although a trio of blue and green flashes sallied from the pinhole on the exhaust pipe. The only bang came from the front of the engine. Deery withdrew the crank from its seat and handed it to MacAdam. The crankshaft was bent like a bow and its lugs were broken off. As the little man clutched his right wrist with his left hand, a ten-shilling note changed hands somewhere deep within the crowd.

One of the electricians switched over breakers and the lights dimmed to a candle-like glow when normal power was resumed. The engineers dispersed and the drill was over. A forlorn Irishman made his way to the hospital and a recently ravaged engineer gratefully sought out his bunk.

CHAPTER TEN

A run ashore in Las Palmas

Tuesday 0700

Angus was out on deck checking the outside air temperature just as the sun was rising. Less than an hour before the cruise ship had slipped into the last berth on a lengthy pier. The morning air was a balmy sixty-six degrees. Down on the concrete quay taxis were tooting and honking as they jockeyed for early bird fares. Maybe there would be one left for him when he went ashore after breakfast. But first he had to check out the temperature of the main restaurant.

Passengers on both sides of Sun Deck were either getting into or waiting for elevators. When the traffic eased off he boarded one. On Main Deck it stopped, allowing more passengers, including Nan, to enter. She was toting her portfolio and portable easel. She wore chic black and yellow beachwear under an open skirt which was also bright yellow. Her long slim legs supported on high heeled cork-soled sandals. A set of sunglasses was perched above the brim of a wide straw hat which sported a golden band of silk. He had to admit that she looked very fetching. After the lift disgorged its living burden on R Deck the engineer asked her where she was headed.

"I'm going to spend the morning touring around Gran Canaria in a taxi. Today will be a kind of busman's holiday for me. I'll be investigating the Guanches. They were a group of neolithic people who were wiped out by the Spaniards about five centuries ago.

She gestured with her portfolio. "If I discover anything worthwhile I'll do some sketches."

"That sounds very interestin' Nan," replied Angus, not too convincingly. "Ye ken, a' work an' nae play makes Jane a dull lassie."

"Do I look dull to you Angus?" teased Nan, flashing her skirt open like a sunburst that caught admiring glances from some officers loitering in the square.

"Eh - weel - no," stuttered the engineer. "Ye look braw. Ah thought dressed like that ye'd be gaun tae the beach."

"But I am Angus," confirmed Nan. "Right after lunch I'll be soaking up the sun at Las Canteras." The Spanish term came easily from her lips.

"Never heard o' it," said Angus. "Are ye no' haein' a wee bit o' breakfast first?"

"No - I'll eat ashore," responded Nan. "A good friend of mine told me about Las Canteras on the other side the city. It's a bay with a long golden beach that's usually strewn with Scandinavian hunks. What about you?"

Angus was a bit miffed at the reference or more importantly, her interest to other men. Whether he could've been up to having sex with her again was debatable since he was still sore from his harrowing orgy just twenty-four hours ago. "Ah'm no' free until eight," he replied, sullenly. "Ah'll maybe go ashore wi' some o' the engineers efter a wee bitty breakfast."

"Maybe I'll see you later then," she smiled, chucking him gently on the chin before heading for the starboard gangway.

The engineer glumly watched her debark then went about his duties.

Denise Sneddon already had the day's itinerary mapped out for herself and Bernie - and unknowingly for Mo Greene. The only difference was that Greene had to use a taxi to tail the couple in their rented car. There had been lots of opportunities for Bernie's wife to have an 'accident' but the signal never came.

Every once in a while their car would stop at some rugged volcanic landscape that the locals termed a caldera and her camera would click some snaps for posterity and a coloured travel brochure. Mo wondered if Bernie had given up on the idea of bumping her off. Still, he didn't really mind for he was getting paid expenses too. Which was just as well, because the taxi meter was sure racking up the pesetas.

On the way back from their tour they stopped in a town called Aruca, a community about seven miles west of Las Palmas. An ancient chapel's architecture became a subject for Denise's camera for within that distinctive edifice lay important paintings and sculptures. Aruca was a centre for distilling rum for the community. It was surrounded by fertile land that produced sugarcane and bananas, the main ingredients for that potent liquor. Also, various cereals and grapes as well as cocoa were among the valued commodities.

Sunburned and tired they returned to the ship for showers, high tea and a siesta. They would take a look at the city's nightlife at sundown.

Gerry recalls:

Las Palmas sits on the isthmus of a peninsula on the north coast of Gran Canaria. It has changed one hellova lot since we went alongside during that January morning back in '62. There was only one pier then. And what a pier it was! It was actually a mole pier and it must've been over a mile long. We parked at the extreme end - closest to the Atlantic Ocean. We had to, because even though our ship had roughly the same dimensions as the Cunarder, *Mauritania* II, she was much, much heavier. The city was and still is a deepwater port made to accommodate the big oil tankers that were being built bigger and bigger every month since the Suez Crises some six years before.

When my watch finished that morning I put on my bathing trunks after taking my shower. If the chance arose I'd take a swim in the ocean. I dressed into a pink sports shirt, faded but clean jeans and plimsolls. With a pair of wraparound sunglasses perched on my face I was ready to go ashore.

Jack, Teach and Tinker tagged along with me for an explorative jaunt into the city. Every damned taxi on the island must've been parked on the dockside vying for fares. None of them would give us a ride into town though. They could tell by our rig that we were crew and unlikely to tip as generously as our human cargo.

A Fyffes boat nosed its way out of the harbour, no doubt loaded with bananas destined for the UK. On our way into town we passed lots of enormous tankers, some them 100,000 tonners. Of course, that's pretty small by today's standards but they made our old *Dally* look quite puny in comparison.

Anyway, it was a pretty long walk getting to the far end of that pier and the morning sun was getting higher and warmer. When we reached a street called Juan something-or-other we followed it. The roadway was cobbled and all the buildings were glaring white but the pavements didn't have the mosaic patterns that we saw in Lisbon.

We happened upon a costermonger whose barrow was laden with fresh produce that grew in great abundance on Gran Canaria. A dilapidated donkey had its grey muzzle submerged in a feedbag. But dilapidated or not, the beast had a functional leg in each corner which satisfied the vendor. A rope fastened to the weary animal's bridle was attached to a conical weight on the cobbles, securely anchoring it against the off chance the creature might try to gallop away. The greengrocer was a very old man with skin was like dull mahogany. He wore a battered straw hat so tattered that his donkey may have been involved in its configuration.

Newly harvested potatoes, onions, and various greens made fetching displays. Here, of course, was a splendid opportunity for us to make up the dearth of fresh fruit aboard ship. And there was much to choose from too: bananas, tomatoes, sugarcane, grapes, dates, oranges, lemons, figs, apricots and peaches as well as almonds.

"Want a chunk of sugarcane to chew on, Tinker?" Teach asked the little gypsy.

Tinker shyly grinned a toothless grin. "Nah, a bunch o' those lovely bananas will do for me, Teach," replied Tinker. "You know that I don't 'ave me teeth on this trip."

"Oh yeah," said Teach. "Why don't you tell Gerry and Jack here how you came to lose your teeth?"

"Nah - nah," said Tinker, pointing to the yellow fruit while handing a ten-peseta note to the vendor. He hauled a banana from his bunch, peeled down four strips and took a bite. "Them are really good," he reported before generously proffering the bunch. "You should try one."

"Yeah - maybe later Tinker," replied Teach. "When you tell us the story of how you lost your teeth."

Jack showed some interest in some packets of flower and vegetable seeds that were stowed in a tiny rack near the driver's seat. He gestured to some fruits and soon a bunch of black grapes accompanied a peach, an orange, a few figs and dates in a brown paper bag. Jack had the same plus a handful of almonds. Testing each tomato for firmness I handed them individually to the old fellow until he had about half-a-kilo in another brown paper bag. After paying for them I took a tomato in hand, removed its husk and sniffed it.

"What's the matter Gerry?" laughed Jack. "D'you think the old geezer pissed on them or something?"

"No - nothing like that," I answered. "A couple of watches ago Mister King and I were discussing the merits of different types of tomatoes. He told me that you could tell the difference between a Clydeside tomato from one from Guernsey or the Canary Isles simply by removing the husks and sniffing the fruit. He explained that if the tomato had a minty smell then it probably originated in a Clydeside greenhouse."

"Go on mate!" gibed Teach. "He was probably pullin' your leg! That's just another version of a bucket of steam."

I didn't think so because Mister King seemed to be a genuine bloke apart from his atrocious accent. I gave them a further explanation. "Y'see at the beginning of the year tomatoes are imported from here to Britain until the ones on Guernsey came into season. I used to work in the tomato houses around St. Sampson when I was a kid. I can remember the men loading up lorries destined for St. Peter Port where they were shipped to the mainland.

"When these crops arrived in Scotland and had been on the shelves for a while, the price went down on them. When the Clydeside tomatoes came in season they were more expensive than the imported ones. The greengrocers mixed the local tomatoes with the imported ones and tried to charge full price but the smell gave them away."

Teach looked skeptical. "What does that one smell like?"

"A tomato," I replied. "If I remember I'll check it out when I go on leave."

"Well fellows," chipped in Jack. "If you're quite finished discussing *Solanum lycopersicum* . . ."

We all turned to stare at him.

"The Latin name for tomatoes - I read it on one of them seed packets," he revealed with a grin. "I'm getting thirsty. Let's see if we can find a pub in this town."

We came upon a pub called Bar International or *Internacional*, as it was spelled in Spanish, and since it had no door we naturally sauntered right in. I wasn't too keen on drinking before noon. I still hoped to get some use out of my bathing trunks figuring that there must be some beaches on this sub-tropical island. Teach, as usual, was searching for a bit of skirt. Jack wasn't bothered either way and Tinker - well, being Tinker - he just followed on.

The pub was a long narrow room, its wide marble countertop running nearly the full length of the room. A couple of customers were perched on two of the dozen-or-so high stools. It didn't take us long to find out that rum was cheaper than beer, *cerveza* as it was called there. So we all opted for a rum and coke and hopped up onto four stools that were closest to the open doorway. A fly did a u-turn and buzzed over our heads in welcome.

The bartender, a large, heavy set bloke with a black bristled moustache, was girded in an off-white apron. He turned away from a patron and clumped across the wooden floor towards us and reached down. Four glasses, each containing a small ice cube, were placed in front of us, a sliver of lime was wedged on every brim. A bottle of rum appeared in his hand as if by magic and soon a pale orange liquid was generously gurgling into our glasses.

When our host, a pleasant sloe-eyed fellow named Luis, determined that our glasses were more than half-full he set the bottle down on the bar. He withdrew a bottle of Coca-Cola from a tiny refrigerator that had the attributes of a safe rather than a cooling unit. Carefully wrapping the bottle in a clean linen napkin as if it was a magnum of Dom Pérignon he opened it and parsimoniously poured about a thimbleful of coke into every glass. He used the heel of his hand to reseal the cap on the coke bottle before returning it reverently to its place of honour inside the fridge.

The Cuba librés as the bartender called them slid down the gullet like mother's milk. We all bought a round. The drinks worked out to be about eightpence each. Feeling quite sober I put a twenty-five peseta note on the counter top and stepped off the high stool. My legs seemed to go all rubbery and it took me a few minutes to cope with that sensation. The bartender waved us adios, pleased with his one-hundred peseta income.

We meandered through the neighborhood until we came upon a street called Paseo de las Canteras. We entered one of the many cafés or bistros abounding the edge of a beautiful beach. A wooden railing enclosed a flagstone patio that accommodated thirty or so tables. Colourful parasols embellished with beer and wines logos from all over Europe shaded every table. The place wasn't too busy although I believe that I recognized a few faces from the ship.

A vista of blue water and golden sands stretched on for miles. 'This is the life for me,' I mused, eying the bikini-clad bodies that were strewn everywhere. This beach ran roughly south southwest, and beyond, a ridge of mountains rose up to the pale blue sky. I was to learn later that these peaks were volcanic.

"*Cuatro cerveza San Miguel, por favor*," Teach said to a waiter, who showed us to a table.

The man soon returned carrying a tray of four dew-coated bottles of pale beer accompanied with frosted tumblers. We poured the beer, casually sipped with collective sighs and soaked in the grandeur of azure water, saffron sands and bronzed flaxen-haired beauties.

I felt peckish and reached for a menu card from the center of the table. Solid food in my belly would help to absorb the booze. The fare was printed in Spanish. I handed it to our linguist, Teach. "I want something to eat," I said. "Translate this and see if there's something edible."

Teach scrutinized the list like an Egyptologist deciphering hieroglyphics. Much later when he was babbling drunk, I was to learn that his knowledge of the Spanish and Portuguese languages were merely enough for his essential needs: buying beer and getting rid of it in a washroom. Apparently jig-a-jig didn't count.

The word *patata* caught his eye. It looked quite similar to potato. "How do you guys fancy some spuds?"

"With what?" Jack asked.

In vain Teach searched for some clue which might ease his predicament. "Mojo," he said finally.

"What's that?" I asked.

"I think it's some kind of sauce that comes with chips," said Teach without much conviction.

"What do you think guys?" asked Jack.

"Sounds ok to me," I said.

"I hope they're mashed," Tinker voiced from vacant gums.

Teach beckoned the waiter and ordered *papas arrugadas* for four. The Islander beamed and scurried away to the kitchen. We all frowned when the dish was placed in front of us. A clutch of tiny potatoes, their wrinkled skins encrusted with salt, gazed forlornly up at us from stoneware platters.

"These are not chips," complained Jack, prodding the baby spuds round his plate.

I lowered my sunglasses to study this dubious repast. I skewered one of the golf ball-sized tubers and popped it into my mouth. It tasted salty of course but not bad. "We boiled much larger ones back home and called them potatoes-with-their-jackets-on." I stabbed another one and slid it around in the accompanying sauce. The peppery condiment accented the spuds' flavour stimulating me to delve into the meal with greater enthusiasm.

This motivated Jack and Teach to try the dish. The sides of Tinker's thin lips curled down in dismay as he watched all of us eat. "'Ere," he whimpers. "What about me then?"

"What about you Tinker?" mumbled Jack through a mouthful of spuds.

"Me teef," he whines. "I can't chew them without my teef."

Just then the waiter returned and noticing that my plate was almost empty he asks, "You like *papas arrugadas*?"

"Yes, they were very tasty." I replied. "But don't you have bigger potatoes?"

It turned out that his English was better than Teach's Spanish. Too bad we never thought to ask. "My name ees Miguel," he said. "You are from beeg sheep too?"

He gestured to other diners a few tables away.

We nodded.

"The potatoes are supposed to be small," Miguel explained. "*Papas arrugadas* ees tradeeshional dish een our Islands."

"Why are they so small Miguel," I asked.

"Smalleest *patatas* fresh from the fields are best. We wash them steel in their skeens then boil them een seawater. Then they are baked. Small *patatas* have best flavour but taste even better with Mojo, a sauce made from peppers. If you . . ." He stopped and stared down at Tinker's plate. "What's matter - you no 'ungry?"

The little fireman pointed to a cavity totally devoid of teeth. No teef," he repeated. "I can't chew them hard spuds."

"Hard?" echoed an indignant Miguel. "They melt in mouth - like what you say - meringue." He pronounced the egg white sweet with a hard gee.

He picked up Tinker's fork and speared one of the potatoes on his plate. Then pinching the pixie nose between thumb and forefinger he tilted back the old fellow's head and the spud was shoved into the gaping mouth. Tinker's jaws began chomping up and down as he masticated the delicacy. Enjoyment lit up his swarthy drawn features.

"Ah - you like?" beamed Miguel then left to serve more customers.

"So eh -" I hinted. "How did you lose your dentures Tinker?"

The little fellow popped another spud into his mouth and his narration began:

"Well, it were quite simple really. Some time ago durin' the evenin' watch I were munchin' on this here sandwich an' a bit went down the wrong way. I were coughin' an' chokin' so much that me teeth fell out of me mouth an' down into the bilge. Now, the bilge were quite full at the time I so says to my engineer that it needed pumped out. He called through for the bilgediver who came along an' started pumpin' it out. As the level were goin' down, my engineer told me it were time to blow tubes so I sent one of the young fellers up an' got him to start. All I had to do was stand at his back to make sure he were doin' it right.

"By the time I got back down, the bilge were nearly dry. I went to the spot where my teeth had popped out of my mouth an' they were nowhere to be seen. The bilgediver was just leaving the stokehold so I grabs him an' asks him to open up the mud box to see if my teeth was caught by the strainer. So we both walks round to the mud box an' there's the strainer a-layin' there on the floorplates.

"'Ere, I says, what's that doin' there?'

"The bilgediver tells me that the strainer were plugged so he opens up the box to clean the strainer an' forgot to put it back in. I asks him if he found my teeth but he says that there was just an oil wiper an' some orange peel in it. So I guess my teeth are at the bottom o' the ocean."

Tinker looked very woeful as more crewmembers filtered into the bistro's patio.

"I'm sorry to hear that Tinker," I replied. "But it isn't such an important story. After all it could happen to anybody."

"No, no," says Tinker. "That were only the start of it. At the end of trip I nicked my Missus' teeth an' sailed off with 'em! She weren't half mad when I gets back. The following trip the *Dally* got in a couple of hours early so I goes home, unlocks the door, an' calls out, 'I'm home my love.'

"She calls down from upstairs. 'Tinker? Is that you Tinker?' An' I says, 'Yes my love, it's your sweetheart home from the sea.' She shouts back down to me, 'Tinker, nip down to the corner shop an' get me a packet o' Woodbines.' So I says that I had brought a carton of duty-free Woodbines with me. 'I don't like them export ones,' she shouts back. 'They're too strong for me.' 'Funny,' I says, 'You've always smoked 'em before.' 'Well,' she shouts back. 'I've got a bit of a sore throat. Go an' get them Woodbines, right away Tinker.'

"I didn't think of it at the time but her voice sounded awfully strong, shoutin' down them stairs with a sore throat. Anyways when I got back with the Woodbines my brother, Sid, were sittin' in the kitchen havin' a cuppa with the missus. We chatted a bit until he left.

"Later that night when I went up to bed I noticed a set of teeth lyin' on the dresser. Oh, I thought, my sweetheart must have found 'em. So I put 'em in me mouth. It were great, it were, I could eat steak again.

"That next trip I must've put on about ten pounds. I were eatin' stuff that I hadn't ate or couldn't eat for years. When I got home again from that trip the missus asks me where I got the teeth. 'On the dresser,' I says. An' she says that they were Sid's teeth. I asks her why Sid's teeth were on the dresser and she says, 'He were up here to put a nail back in the wall.' 'What nail? What wall?' I asks. 'That picture we got for a weddin' present from Aunt Peggy over there,' she says. 'It fell down. Lucky it didn't break the glass though. Anyway Sid put it back up for me.'

"So I gives her Sid's teeth. It didn't dawn on me until later but why would Sid take his teeth out to hang a picture?"

He took a sip of beer, quite unaware of the rest of us trying to stifle our laughter.

"A year or two later my brother, Sid, suddenly ups an' dies. I had just got back the day before the funeral so I goes down to the local undertaker an' asks him if I could have Sid's teeth. The undertaker weren't too happy about that idea. So I says since he don't need 'em where he's goin' I can use 'em. So after a bit of an argument the undertaker finally gives me my brother's teeth.

"He had a real good send off too, did old Sid but like any funeral it rained. Standin' by the hole we looked down on that beautifully-finished coffin while the vicar were layin' it on thick about the dearly departed. That rain were drippin' down the back of me neck an' must've be givin' me a chill because I sneezed an' afore I knew it, Sid's teeth were sailin' down to join him. The hollow clump on the box made every one look down at the teeth a-layin' there among them white lilies. 'Course I tried to look innocent but when the missus gave me a hard jab with her elbow everybody knew it were me.

"When the ceremony were finished an' all the mourners rushed away to get out o' the rain I hung back. The missus tugged on my arm askin' what I was waitin' on. I says, 'I'm goin' to climb down an' get them teeth afore them pair o' grave diggers fill in the hole. 'No you're not!' she screams. 'You're not goin' to get your best suit all covered in clay.'

"So that's how I lost my teeth," Tinker told us glumly. "One set by land, an' one by sea."

"Well," I said to him. "That really is a sad story but tell us, why don't you go to a dentist and get a new set of dentures?"

"What? And get all that pink waxy stuff crammed down my throat? Not bleedin' likely. I only had that done once an' that were once too many."

We were still laughing when a scuffle started directly behind us. A table was knocked over by two guys from our ship. Some of the others were taking sides while Miguel and another man, presumably the manager or owner, were anxiously trying to bring calm to the scene.

A jeep screamed to a halt outside and four policemen toting carbines headed for the meleé. In the blink of an eye Jack, Teach and Tinker were gone - vanishing seemingly into midair. I vaulted over the railing and I hit the sand running. Following the contour of Las Canteras beach I headed for a row of red and white striped tents.

A tiny burst of sand erupted at my feet and I heard a sound like a balloon popping. Some bastard was shooting at me! I scooted past the row of tents and stepped aside, hidden from the line of fire. I crouched down and lifted the skirt of a tent. It was empty. I squirmed inside. I slipped off my shoes and socks and quickly shed my garments except for my bathing trunks. A hole was hurriedly scooped in the sand to hide my wallet. I placed my clothes on top.

Donning my cheaters and gritting my teeth I lifted the tent flap. Looking directly straight ahead I sauntered nonchalantly toward the water. Nearby a bronzed woman with mousey hair lay prone on a gaudy beach towel. Choosing a spot about a fathom away from her spot I lay down on the sand. She turned onto her stomach, facing away from me. I closed my eyes to the bright sun nearing its zenith and soaked up its soothing rays. This was the life, miles away from frost and snow.

Perhaps ten minutes had lapsed since I had lain down. The toe of a polished black boot nudged my rib cage. I opened my eyes raising my sunglasses. An upside-down swarthy face festooned with a black moustache stared down at me. His companion's boot poked me with a little more force urging me into a sitting position. Two guys in blue uniforms glared sternly at me, their carbines at the ready. An Iberian staccato erupted from the nudger's thin lips.

Without turning her head the lady next to me interrupted to pose a question in Spanish. The cop who'd been standing at my head bowed slightly and touched his peaked cap. His answer displeased her. Her riposte heightened the darkness in both faces of the *Policia Local*. The nudger's return was laced with anger and he rattled his weapon in affirmation.

The woman jumped to her feet and withdrew a wallet from a soft leather bag. She stepped over to the cop and flipped it open to flash something in their faces. Two pairs of eyes went like saucers and simultaneously they both clipped their heels snapping to attention and flourished snappy salutes. She dressed down the chastened cops like a pair of disobedient schoolboys and they trooped off, their carbines slung on their left shoulders.

She turned to me and smiled. "You are safe now Englishman," she said in a delightful lilting tone.

I gaped at her. Appearing to be in her late twenties she had a round face with high cheek bones. Her startling blue eyes twinkled with humour like sun rays bouncing off the sea. Her body was slightly stocky, her golden skin contrasting with her white bikini. She had shoulders and legs comparable to that of an Olympic swimmer, strong and powerful.

"How - how did you know I was English?" I asked.

"Your skin, Englishman," she smiled, her white teeth dazzling in the sunlight. "It is white like the belly of a fish." She gestured at the colony of sun worshipers scattered around the beach. "You stand out - as you English say - like one sore thumb." She held out a delicate soft hand. "My name is Ursula Guznishcheva. What is your name?"

I took her hand. It was delicate yet firm. "Renouf," I said. "Gérard Renouf." But it didn't come out quite as suave as Bond - James Bond.

Those large beautiful eyes grew even larger as if she was unaccustomed to error. "Ah! So you are French, not English? So why is a Frenchman working on an English ship? You are from that big ship that sailed in this morning - yes?"

"Sarnian actually," I said and seeing the blank look on her face enlightened her. "Guernsey, in the Channel Islands?"

She nodded, her face becoming melancholy. "Yes - I know," she said slowly. "My father, he worked there during the war."

"Oh?"

I'd vague memories of scuttle-helmeted soldiers strutting all over my island. Although I was very young at the time the hardship of the German occupation of the Channel Islands was still quite vivid.

"What did he do there?"

"He died," she replied, simply.

Then it dawned on me. I could recall groups of men in rags being herded by Jerries to build the great concrete gun placements all around the coast. A hammer and sickle was hand-carved from living rock in the roof of the underground hospital, a symbol of Soviet defiance. A mass grave in the Island of Alderney marks the demise of countless Russians who slaved for the Todt Organisation.

"I'm sorry," I said. "You must be, of course, Russian. But tell me," I sought to change the grim subject. "How is it that you can boss the Spanish cops around?"

She made a face and shrugged. "I work for Soviet Embassy in Madrid," she said easily, adding: "I'm here on a two week holiday. We have, how you say, certain privileges."

I'd read Ian Fleming's novel, *To Russia with Love*, on my previous trip. NKVD and KGB were still fairly fresh in my mind. Then another acronym popped to the fore. "SMERSH!" I said aloud.

Her eyes went like azure saucers and she quickly glanced around at the indifferent sunbathers. She beamed suddenly and took my hand. "Come, we swim now."

We ran down into the incoming tide. The water temperature must have been about sixty-five degrees Fahrenheit, an absolute delight compared to the chillier summer waters around Guernsey. She plunged into the light surf and swam gracefully towards the reef. With bull-like vigour I followed doing a clumsy Australian crawl. After ploughing through about twenty-five yards of very light swell I stopped and breathlessly swam on the spot. I spun around. She was nowhere in sight. Every fifth or sixth wave was higher than the rest. What seemed like a couple of minutes went by and still no Ursula.

Suddenly I felt a bump and a dragging sensation on my legs. Shark? Were there sharks around here? Ursula burst to the surface like a dolphin. She was chortling with glee and waving my swimming trunks about her head. I quickly sank and swam towards her. I was no slouch when it came to swimming underwater for I'd often dived for ormers, the famed shellfish that is considered a delicacy in the Bailiwick.

Her trunk and lower body was slowly revolving, no doubt trying to catch a glimpse of me. With a swift downward motion I had her white bikini bottom in my hand. A blurry dark triangle waited invitingly mere inches from my face. The temptation was too much. With both hands I gripped her firm buttocks and nuzzled her. Whether she gasped with delight I have no way of knowing but I assume that she did for her hands pulled my head closer. My tongue did its duty and her thighs responded in quivering appreciation. Bubbles dribbling from my lips heightened her excitement.

It was time to surface but I couldn't move. Her legs were about my shoulders and her hands clamped my swimming trunks about my ears. I tried to disengage from those tanned robust limbs but resistance had a diverse effect. It was debatable whether I would be drowned, strangled or suffocated. I tried to bite her, but on reflection, that would've probably increased her rapture. No matter how much I struggled that vicelike hold was relentless. Panic with a capital P!

I felt our bodies lifting the swell and fervently hoped that it was pushing us shoreward. We sank again when that wave had passed and my toes brushed against fine pebbles. The next high wave couldn't come soon enough for me but when it did, I was ready. Thank God for the breathing exercises I'd learned when diving for ormers. I folded my legs as we went down again. When my toes touched the lagoon bottom again I straightened my legs thrusting with all my might.

Ursula went a lovely arse-over-elbow when I broke through the surface. Upon release I got a welcome breath of air and she got a mouthful of brine. Coughing, spluttering and laughing she swam against me, her right hand manipulating me to hardness. We did it right there in the lively sea, bobbing up and down whilst bobbing in and out.

At last we retrieved and donned our swimwear. With easy relaxing strokes we reached the shore. We went into the canvas chalet and after drying each other off we did it again. We dressed and went outside where two men in charcoal-grey suits waited patiently. Both wore reflective sunglasses. Ursula introduced me to them. The tall one with the blonde close cropped hair was Pankrati. The short squat bald one was Mitva. I proffered my hand and both men disdained it as if I was holding a turd.

Stiffly, the men spun on heel and we tailed them up off the beach. We threaded our way between a couple of busy bistros to where a large black limo was parked. It was quite like a Humber Pullman but larger and had extended grills below the headlamps. The car could've been a Zil but I'm not absolutely sure. The tall guy opened a door to allow us entry. The vehicle's leather upholstery smelled new as we climbed in. Pat and Mike squeezed into jump seats directly behind the chauffeur. James Bond flit through my mind and I wondered if I was going to be kidnaped so that Ursula could have her way with me.

No such luck. Within minutes the car was cruising along the great quay past ships large and small until we reached the great bows of the *Dally*. She rolled the window right down after I got out.

"This car will be waiting right here for you at nine o'clock tonight."

With her face turned upwards she pouted her full lips. I leaned in and kissed her. The Zil did a three-point turn and headed back towards the city.

I walked toward the nearest gangway. Between it and the next one aft a line of bodies lay on the flagstones. Firemen-trimmers, greasers, stewards and other crew members were either laying out cold or sitting nursing bruises and cuts on their faces and bodies. Their clothes were messed up and torn. It looked like a disaster of some kind had taken place. What had happened?

A black paddy wagon came screeching to a halt with my answer. Its rear doors sprang open to disgorge another cargo of drunk and disorderly shipmates. Behind them two Spanish cops bounded out and flailed them with billy clubs. The driver and his mate stepped out and angrily got in some licks too. A couple of our masters-at-arms were demonstrating an acute lack of interest in preventing further injury to their fellow crew members. Eventually they calmed down the Spanish cops by means of international communication: the Esperanto of the world, duty-free smokes.

Before going on watch I went into our mess for tea. Jack had an ice cloth on a black eye. Teach was gently stroking a bump on the top of his head and Tinker was gumming a jam sandwich. At other tables various members of the black gang were nursing contusions and lacerations, each misery a reflection of their run ashore and the hazards of consuming cheap rum. I sat down beside Jack.

"What happened?"

The damp rag lowered to reveal a reddened orb oscillating in a field of royal blue, purple, and all the hues between in livid Technicolor. "I got fucked man," he moaned, ruefully.

Teach relieved Jack of the cool rag and placed it on his bump. "I got fucked as well, man!" He winced and went about his ministrations much tenderly. "What about you Gerry?"

With a dead pan face I said, "Yeah Teach, I got fucked too. Well and truly fucked!"

I grabbed a sandwich and a mug of tea and commiserated with my fellow shipmates although sexual connotations were spiriting my mind into the very near future. An MA stepped over the coaming of our messroom and pinned a sheet of paper on our notice board.

'Because of the despicable action that has brought disgrace to this vessel today,' it read. 'I hereby cancel leave to all ship's ratings for the remainder of the voyage, signed, J. Fawcett, Master.'

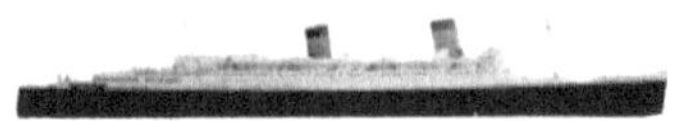

CHAPTER ELEVEN

The Owl

0910

"Well, I'm ready to hit the beach," announced Wheelkey, wiping egg yolk from his lips with a pristine white linen napkin with a PL monogram. He laid it on his side plate. "Who's coming with me?"

Depending on what dish his colleagues were consuming at the time, silver plated forks, knives and spoons were raised one at a time in assent. Keyes craned his head across to other tables and was pleased to note that most of the watchkeepers were willing to accompany him on his jaunt ashore. They were Angus King, Terry Baker, Peter Deery, Charlie Benson, Taffy Morgan, Pete Eaton and Don Travers.

All eight engineers were attired in suits à la mode John Collier and stood out like sore thumbs on the quay. Since the guise of holidaymakers was lucratively apparent, taxi drivers were hooking passengers in like tuna fish. So like the engineroom ratings hiking some half-mile ahead of them, they drudged southward towards the sunlit city of Las Palmas. They were sightseers after all and the different types and shapes of the ships docked along the great pier drew comment and professional opinion.

Some ships were new while others were practically hulks. Rust and fresh paint denoted the pride, or lack, that respective captains had in their commands. One tanker must have sailed through a terrific storm for the handrails around her bow were twisted like pretzels. The skin of her hull was down to bare steel as if it subjected to the rigor of sandblasting.

At the end of the mole the engineers traced the harbour's perimeter until their ship was directly opposite them. Turning west they chose a street that led in the general direction of Las Canteras beach. Shop windows exhibited cheap and flimsy Iberian objects d'art, mementos and other wares to lure the passing tourist within. The *Dally*'s engineers were certainly no exception. Soon they were examining hand-sized gilt caravels filigreed in full sail, pearl handled letter openers mounted with the heraldic crest of Gran Canaria, gaudy triangular pennants, made-in-Toledo? rapiers and similar bric-a-brac. Angus purchased a dainty ivory-coloured mantilla made of nylon tulle for Nan. Some of his colleagues procured inexpensive keepsakes for their sweethearts, loved ones, and in some cases, their wives.

Wheelkey sneered at his shipmates for passing over money before bargaining. To prove his point he chose a large bottle of Bacardi rum from a massive liquor display and asked its price. Three hundred pesetas was the shopkeeper's reply. Keyes shook his head and offered the fellow two hundred. The man stared hard at him before placing two glasses on his counter top. From an open bottle of local rum he splashed two fingers into each glass and toasted: "*A su salud*!"

"Cheers!" replied Wheelkey and downed the liquor. He coughed and his eyes watered. "Say, that's not bad!" He eyeballed the Spaniard. "How much for that stuff?"

The man flashed three outspread palms in rapid succession.

Wheelkey shook his head and held up ten fingers. "One hundred," he said.

The shop owner sighed and replenished the glasses. His counter offer was one-forty.

Wheelkey downed the rum. He didn't cough that time although a tear welled in an eye. "This is good stuff amigo."

The owner's face reflected his smile.

"But not good enough."

He mimed one-ten.

The Spaniard scowled and splashed one finger's width into Wheelkey's glass.

They settled on one hundred and twenty-five pesetas or fourteen shillings and eleven pence. The shopkeeper put his bargaining bottle away. But Wheelkey still wanted the bottle of Bacardi. He pointed to it in askance.

"*Trescientos*," said the owner.

"Two hundred," replied Wheelkey.

The open bottle reappeared and the ritual was repeated. Three shots later a bargain was struck and the proprietor received two hundred and fifty pesetas. Outside the shop a slightly tipsy Keyes expounded the value of bargaining in foreign lands. Meanwhile, in the backroom of the shop the owner was sorting through a sheaf of Appleton, Myers, Lamb, Captain Morgan and other notable rum labels to stick on another bottle of local plonk.

Carrying their wares in brown paper bags the engineers stumbled upon *Playa de Las Canteras* and its bounty of tanned Scandinavian talent. Some sort of commotion was going on at a bistro further along the beach. Prudently they opted for another watering hole nearer at hand. They pushed three tables together and sat down to survey the scantily clad sunworshipers. A waiter approached with a battery of menus.

"Gracias!" beamed Wheelkey before staring blankly at the list of Spanish victuals. "Eh - *Ochos cerveza, por favor*."

Keyes was quite relieved to discover that the waiter spoke English when he came back with eight beers. Questions darted back and forth regarding the cuisine and its contents. Leery of consuming octopus, squid or goat's meat the general consensus of the visitors that something safe would be in order. A sort of ploughman's lunch of bread and cheese naturally complemented with beer was more in line with the British palate. Now that the meal was ordered Wheelkey lounged back in his chair, his eyes devouring the tableau of nearly naked women.

"Aah!" sighed the Glaswegian with an air of euphoria. "Surf to seawall shags."

Paper coasters, bearing advertisements of must-be-seen island attractions, lay on the table to induce the visitors. Steamboat, seated between Angus and Taffy, drew their attention to a nightclub called *La Lechuza*. Word was passed to the others and a ripple of interest drew positive commentary. Wheelkey wasn't listening, his eyes and mind totally focussed on a certain section of the beach where a well-endowed siren was provocatively slipping down her bikini bottom from under a yellow beach robe.

"Hey Wheelkey, what do you think of this?" Terry was shoving the advert at him.

"Gerraway!" snarled Keyes, his hands fending off the irritating distraction aside. For by this time the girl was stepping into a pair of pink panties before easing them up those gorgeous legs.

"Stick your tongue back in your mouth and take a deco at this," urged Terry. "Everybody except the Leprechaun here, wants to try out this place tonight. What do you think?"

By this time the young thing had removed her top and was contemplating how to discreetly don her pink bra. Keyes concentrated on the place mat. "Mm," he said, absorbing a glossy photo of alluring femininity dancing under coloured lights.

"Would you look at that boyos!" squeaked Taffy, pointing.

"What? What?" repeated Wheelkey, his head swivelling back and forth like the turret of a gun.

Throwing all caution to the winds the nymph had dumped her terryrobe on the sand and for the briefest of moments was topless until her bra covered her bare essentials.

"What is it Taff?" asked Wheelkey.

"That woman there," said Taffy, pointing again.

"Where? Where?" rhymed Wheelkey.

"That girl over there dressed in the pink underwear. She was topless just a second ago, boyo." He glanced along the table at his shipmates. "Did any of you lads see her?"

"Oh aye," assented Angus.

"Me too!" confirmed other witnesses.

"Hussy!" spat the Leprechaun.

"Shit!" swore Keyes, and angrily crumpled up the place mat. His colleagues ribbed him with imaginative descriptions of the girl's ample bosoms.

"Hey!" said Wheelkey. "I should take a stroll down there and chat her up. Maybe she'd like to come to that nightclub with me."

"In that dark suit boyo?" scoffed Taffy. "She'll think that you're an undertaker on the lookout for stiffs, see you."

Don leaned over the corner of the table and stared pointedly at Wheelkey's crotch. "He wouldn't have to go that far to find a stiff I can tell you."

Wheelkey scowled back at his antagonist but he had to admit to himself that on that beach he'd stand out like a crow at a budgie jamboree.

"It's time we were getting back," announced Charlie. "It's a long walk back to the ship.

"It's only quarter after one," said Don, eying his wristwatch. "We've got plenty of time. Let's see if there are any more tourist traps. I'd like to get something for my missus."

The tariff was paid and the engineers trooped off in the general direction of their vessel. Rambling through streets of sun-bleached buildings was searing to the eye in spite of sunglasses purchased that very morning. The afternoon temperature was a balmy 72°F but the shipmates were sweating heavily in their dark suits. One after another they loosened their ties and removed their jackets to droop them over their shoulders. The heat radiating from the sidewalks felt like walking on boilertops.

It was thirsty exercise.

"*Bar Internacional*," read Wheelkey from the sign above the open doorway, the *Pinus canariensis* wooden door long since destroyed by a bunch of drunken seamen from a British tramp steamer back in the Thirties. He squinted into the gloom beyond. "What do you guys think?"

Angus shook his head dubiously. "Ah think we should be gettin' back, Wheelkey. Ah don't want tae be staggerin' intae the main restaurant steamin' drunk."

Don concurred. He sure didn't want the odour of booze following him through passenger accommodation either. The Leprechaun, sanctimonious as ever, began to spout off about the evils of drink until Taffy held a fearsome fat fist under his little pug nose.

"Ok then. I'll tell you what," Keyes suggested. "You three sit out here on the stoop and flag down the first taxi."

And with that he went inside, the other four on his heels. The same fly that investigated Gerry and his shipmates circled them then set course for the barkeeper as if to tell Luis that he had five new customers. The same ritual, this time with five glasses, took effect. The newcomers were intrigued by the reverence that Luis gave to the bottle of coke upon being extracted from the safe. Each glass was meticulously treated with twelve precious drops of pop.

Keyes picked up his glass and scrutinized its contents. A skim of Coca-Cola about twice as thick as the meniscus floated on the amber liquor. "That's the first time I've ever seen coke layered into rum."

The others were suitably impressed. Simultaneously they cautiously took a sip of this Canarian ambrosia before unanimously agreeing that it went down as smooth as Devon cream. Presently Luis was asked to replenish the glasses and the ceremony was performed again.

"This way the drink lasts longer - see you," observed Taffy, licking coke from his upper lip.

Outside the three abstainers were observing a darkhaired urchin playing with a toy car on the narrow sidewalk. A single vehicle had yet to pass by. The kid drew close enough that they could see that his toy was a taxicab.

"Here laddie," Angus said kindly. "That's a braw wee taxi ye've got there."

Of course the lad couldn't understand English but then it probably wouldn't matter if he did because he was addressed in broad Scots. However upon hearing the word, taxi, his dark brown eyes shone on his smiling dirty face. "Taxi!" he said. "Vrruum - vrruum!"

"Aye. Peep-peep yersel'," said King. "We need a real one."

The boy's countenance went blank.

"A big one," said Angus. A song popped into his mind, *El Rancho Grande*. "Grandy - grandy!"

Comprehension brightened the child's face again and he ran into a house nearby. He was soon back with a beaten up, but much larger, toy taxi.

"No - no," repeated Angus. He stretched out his arms. "A big one - a real big one. Grandy - grandy! A real big grandy!" He performed a turning motion with his hands as if spinning a car's steering wheel. "Vrruum - vrruum!"

His companions mimicked his antics and Don took a twenty-five peseta note from his wallet. The money had the desired effect. The lad rushed back to his house and was back immediately to announce, "*Un momento*."

Within minutes a taxicab rolled down the street. The kid whipped the banknote from Don's fingers and ran off.

"Hey you guys - the taxi's here!" Angus bawled into the bar.

The trio tore open a door and piled in beside the driver. A torrent of Spanish erupted from his lips in protest as he kept gesturing to the back seat. The other five engineers spewed out onto the street and fought for space in the back of the cab. The taxidriver's objection became much more vehement until a hundred-peseta note flashed before his eyes. Still muttering profanities he clashed the gears when moving into first. He needed no direction. After less than seven hours in port the outrageous reputation of the visiting liner's crew was public knowledge.

The dockside still had the appearance of an open-air mortuary when they arrived. The driver was placated with another C-note and a handful of coins, some of which were escudos and farthings. They readily changed back into uniform and went into the mess for afternoon tea.

The exaggerated welcome from the twelve-to-four a/c watch was a sign of foreboding to their relief. With his boilersuit soaked in sweat Kevin Cunningham hastily related the tribulations of trying to cool down a vessel laying stationary against a dock. Only one side of the ship's water intakes could be used effectively.

Down in the engineroom they'd lost the vacuum on the starboard main condenser. Apparently opening a cross-connection between the main circulation pumps solved their problem. Normally this situation was not a issue in port because only the ship's auxiliaries were required to fill her needs. Everything would be started up, the passengers loaded, and off she would sail. But here in Las Palmas, all units had to run as if the liner was at sea.

For instance the forward motion of the ship helped to force fresh air into the ventilators which was effectively distributed below to the various fans. This lack wasn't a problem for the powerful forced draught fans that supplied air to the boiler rooms. But the fan motors for the thermotanks were another matter. All of them were old with some more decrepit than the others. Thus, even when running full out, there was an insufficient volume of cool air to fulfil all the passengers' needs.

Now it became a case of robbing Peter to pay Paul. Upon reacting to requests for cooling air, temporary vacated cabins had their volume flows reduced or shut off completely until such times when their original occupants returned on board.

"And it's going to get bloody worse," Kevin prophesied forlornly. "Especially tonight when the passengers are tucked up in their carts."

But as it happened the four-to-eight watch passed without incident mainly because most passengers took advantage of the glorious sunny afternoon bathing the island.

The main restaurant was practically empty when Angus went in about fifteen minutes after the dinner gong. Nan was sitting at her usual table looking radiant. She tanned easily and her skin fairly glowed to a creamy gold after a day on the beach. He casually drifted to her side whilst taking his readings. Without looking directly at her he asked if she had any plans for the evening.

"I'll go ashore with a suitable escort," was her soft reply.

Angus scribbled some temperature numbers on his slates. "How would ye like tae go tae a nightclub wi' me?"

Nan's face became radiant as she smiled up at him. Cautiously his eyes sought out any party who may be interested in this exchange.

"Me and some o' the lads are gaun tae a place called La - Le somethin'." He stared up at the ornate deckhead high above his head as if it would reveal some clue to the name he was seeking. His face brightened, "*La Lechuza*!"

"The Owl," translated Nan. "Yes, I'd like that very much but won't your friends mind?"

"No - Ah dinnae think so," surmised Angus. "Cheap booze an' a guid time will keep them happy."

"All right, I'll meet you by the elevators on R Deck Square," said Nan. "What time will you be ready?"

"Ah'd better get somethin' in my stomach afore we start," Angus told her. "Let's say a few minutes afore ten o'clock."

There wasn't any problem getting a taxi at that time of night for most of the passengers were ashore sampling the delights of Las Palmas nightlife. A convoy of taxi-cabs loaded up a bunch of engineers and electricians before slowly motoring along the quay.

The Owl nightclub was in full swing when they disgorged from the taxicabs. In the red glow of a smoke-filled room there was, perhaps, about fifty people gyrating to a Spanish version of *Let's Twist Again*. The bar was packed but a vacant table presently became available for Nan and Angus near the doorway. The couple sat down whilst the rest bee-lined to the bar. Over the cacophony of drums, guitars, a saxophone and a trio of rhinestone ploughboys Angus asked Nan if she'd like a drink. With little effort he passed through the wedge that his shipmates had formed at their newly established watering hole and was soon back with a glass of Muscatel for Nan and a Cuba Libré for himself.

Never much of a dancer but rather more of a bum hugger at the Lanark Memo when the music was slow and romantic, the fast rhythm made Angus reluctant to venture onto to dance floor. However the Iberian version of the brand-new hit, *The Lion Sleeps Tonight*, was slow enough to motivate him to ask Nan if she'd like to dance.

In normal circumstances a girl might place her head on her partner's chest to savour the mood of the moment but in Angus' case it was different. He was shorter than Nan by three inches. More really since his partner wore high heeled pumps to match her yellow pantsuit. So they cruised around a minuscule section of dance floor with his head against her upper chest and his chin cushioned upon her left breast.

A sudden jolt snapped him out of his dreamy mood. They both gaped at Wheelkey who was sashaying around with a local floozie. Coal to Newcastle, he mouthed.

"What was all that about?" asked Nan when Keyes lurched off into the throng.

"He's bluidy sozzled. He's been oan the local rum a' day."

By one o'clock the club was in full swing and many revellers clustered around the bar. Angus hinted to Nan that they should start thinking about going back to the ship. He hoped to grab an hour's kip before going on watch. Nan was tired too but had to powder her nose first. She'd phone for a taxi at that time.

On her return she pointed out an attractive girl near the bar. He followed her direction and noticed a young female dressed in a summer frock. She appeared to be in her late teens or early twenties and was dabbing her eyes with a handkerchief.

"Whit aboot her?" asked Angus, facing Nan.

"Your friend Keyes propositioned her."

Angus looked at the girl again. "She looks auld enough to handle herself."

"She just turned sixteen."

"Oh!"

He could see Wheelkey milling around with the other engineers.

Angus pushed his chair away as he arose. Nan placed a hand on his sleeve. "That's not all."

He sat down again.

"See that guy standing next to the girl? The one with a black droopy moustache, dark suit, ruffled shirt and bootlace tie?"

Angus nodded. He was only a little skinny fellow with a face like it was carved from teak. "Who's he? Her pimp?"

"That's what your buddy thought," replied Nan, then took a deep breath. "Actually, he's her father!"

Her lover got to his feet. "It might be a guid idea if ye phoned for a couple mair taxis. When ye've done that go tae the front door an' gie me a shout as soon as they get here." He kissed her. "When it happens - it'll happen fast."

As Angus went over to his shipmates a trio of muscular Svengalis was cleaning their fingernails with stilettos and listening attentively to the little guy. One at a time they casually glanced over to the girl's father who was consistently stabbing a finger at Wheelkey. Keyes, on this other hand, was laughing and birling a woman around on the dance floor quite obvious to his faux pas and its impending repercussion.

Nan waved. The door closed again as she went back out.

Before Wheelkey knew what was happening four of his brawniest shipmates acquired a limb each before hoisting him into the air. With minimal maneuvering they had him on their shoulders much like they were toting a baulk of timber. Then they rushed towards the door. Initially Wheelkey had made a feeble protest believing his comrades were having some fun at his expense. Now he started to yell. His potential antagonists showed surprise as he went past.

In order to save him from bodily harm it was Wheelkey's misfortune that his fellow engineers failed to assess the impending consequence of transporting him fore and aft - or head first. Angus was at his feet acting like a tiller. The other engineers followed like a living wake. Their living battering ram's scream stopped suddenly coinciding with the clatter of their egress - *en masse.*

Someone opened a taxi's boot just as the four adversaries burst out into the street. The now somnolent Wheelkey was bundled into the trunk like a cabbage into a hippo's open maw. His saviours boarded and with a parting wave at the glowering Spaniards the taxicabs roared off into the night.

CHAPTER TWELVE

Last port-of-call

0715 Wednesday

A hint of recently fried kippers permeated the main restaurant making him nauseous. Angus felt like he'd been dragged through a hawthorn hedge backwards. The dining saloon appeared to be half empty yet the engineer knew that there some two hundred souls were seated for breakfast.

Nan was sitting at her usual spot with her sketch board. She was dressed in a pale yellow frock and looked as fresh as a morning mist caressing a meadow of buttercups. Intent on her work she didn't see the engineer's approach until he was upon her. By her side on the table lay a half-eaten croissant, a glass of pineapple juice and an untouched coffee.

"Angus! How are you this morning?"

He squinted down at her through pinhole pupils for his eyes felt like they had been sandblasted. "So - so Nan," he vaguely replied. "So - so."

"How's Mister Keyes today?"

"He's a' keyed up," punned Angus. "He says that is the first time that he's had a hangover wi' a lump oan his heid."

"He's darned lucky that he didn't get his throat slit," opined Nan.

Angus nodded in agreement. "Did ye hae a guid sleep?" And all the while he was trying to remember when he last slept for more than six hours.

"I slept like a top," she replied, her charcoal stick making sweeps across the paper. She glanced up. "The ship's foghorn woke me up at quarter-to-six. I got up and slipped into a robe then when out on deck to see what was happening. I watched the ship cast off and back away from the pier. It didn't take long before the island was a just dot on the horizon."

Angus moved behind her. She'd portrayed the great restaurant with remarkable skill. Only the diners were faint outlines. "That's smashin' Nan," he complimented her in all sincerity. "Ye should draw professionally instead o' diggin' up auld bones."

"I love palaeanthropology Angus," he was assured. "And this hobby that I have for sketching helps me in my work. I'm only sorry that I don't have enough time to paint my work. This holiday has worked wonders for me. I can sit out on deck, sunbathe on a canvas chair and draw at the same time while the pressures of my job are a thousand miles away."

"Aye - weel - as long as ye're happy." He took a swing and scribbled the reading onto his slate. "Some o' us still hae tae work though." He checked his wristwatch. "Ah need tae get back."

"Can I see you today Angus?"

He surveyed her regretfully. "Eh - no. Ah'm sorry Nan but Ah hae tae catch up oan my rest. As soon as Ah'm relieved Ah'm gaun tae hae a nice breakfast, an' put my heid doon until Ah'm called for my next watch." He brightened. "But Ah'll hae a wee chat wi' ye in here tonight."

Angus managed to almost four straight hours of blesséd sleep before he was called for his afternoon watch. It was then that he discovered that the trousers in his third and last set of whites were too big for him. Three sets of whites were usually enough to last an engineer for a trip after which they were sent ashore to be laundered and starched. But in his case, he had to be presentable at all times when in the company of passengers. Nobody told him that buying an extra set or two was a prerequisite for this job. He'd paid the valet service a quid to clean the other two sets but they weren't due back until the following day. He pulled the trousers as high as possible so the bottoms wouldn't foul his feet. He cinched his belt tight. His midriff appeared slightly bulky after he'd fastened his tunic but otherwise everything was ok.

He had a pleasant high tea consisting of delectable wafer-thin sandwiches, filled with ham, roast pork or roast beef. These were followed by scones laden with fresh butter and strawberry jam. A slab of sultana cake came next with scrumptious petit-fours to end his repast. Grabbing an assortment of fresh fruit for Jack and Gerry, he slipped down to the a/c office.

The watch changed over amiably without any concerns whatever. Looking aft from the open section of A Deck the sea was absolutely beautiful. Angus took a few extra moments to savour the balmy air and watch the boiling creamy-green wake astern carve an ever-widening vee through a cerulean sea all the way to an azure sky.

He climbed a ladder up to Boat Deck and strolled for'ard. The sun, long past its zenith, was just perfect for the lines of passengers basking on deck chairs. All was well with his world and the feeling of well-being seemed to be felt by everyone he met. Near midships Bernie and Denise Sneddon were sauntering along hand-in-hand. To the engineer and other observers they were for all the world to see, a happy loving couple. Angus carried on circumnavigating the open deck and checked in on the Highland Grill before descending to Promenade Deck aft.

The Cabin Class Smoking Room and Naiad Bar were sparsely populated, mostly men seeking refuge from their better halves. The First Class Cinema had very few patrons even though the newly released picture, *Whistle Down The Wind*, was playing. The First Class Ballroom, of course, was empty. It would come to life later during the next watch. The First Class Smoking Room, Long Gallery and Main Lounge had one passenger each.

A shop girl in the Main Shopping Centre told him that business was slow but expected it to pick up on the homeward-bound run. Continuing his routine for'ard, the other public rooms were almost as desolate. The odd steward or attendant seemed to be the only forms of life until he entered the Observation Lounge. Here the euphoria of the day returned, albeit assisted by booze.

Among the drinkers was Mo Greene. His attitude had changed over the course of the voyage and by now accepted his commission as a holiday, a paid holiday. He'd frequently detected the lovey-dovey overtures that Sneddon was paying to this wife. The scrap dealer had expressly forbidden Greene to contact him while on board so there the matter had rested. He raised his empty glass to the bartender and presently a steward came by with a tumbler of Teacher's Scotch whisky and soda on a salver.

When Angus neared birling his swinger Greene inquired about its function. The engineer explained to him about the wet and dry temperature variations and how they were related to humidity and dewpoint. "Y'know," he slurred. "You've got a pretty cushy job, haven't you?"

"Aye sir. Ah suppose Ah dae," agreed Angus. "But sooner or later somethin' will go wrang an' Ah'll hae tae get intae my boilersuit an' fix it." He smiled. "But so far Ah cannae complain. Ye just hae tae take the guid wi' the bad - right?"

Greene had to agree with that philosophy. After all, that's what he was doing. He raised his glass in acknowledgment and the engineer moved on.

His jaunt round the deck at the start of the watch had put him behind schedule so he didn't get to the main restaurant until seven-thirty. Nan wasn't at her usual spot. Maybe she'd already dined and left. Unobtrusively he glided over to starboard moving aft, passing between the great columns and passengers dining on the outboard side. Diners in the shadow of those lofty columns perceived an illusion of privacy.

Traversing the massive room near its after end a catering officer stopped him near a mirrored column just abaft of the captain's table. The fellow reported that one of the punkah louvres in the port after private dining saloon was stiff. The engineer acknowledged the complaint and said that the unit would be attended to when the restaurant was empty. Nan's voice was heard as he pencilled a large asterisk in his slate to remind him of the needed repair. The instant he peeked round the column to confirm his ears, she glanced up and saw him.

"What about that young officer there, Captain?"

Captain J. Fawcett, HSR, craned his grey head upwards to view the interloper. "Ah! Mister - eh - how are *you* tonight?"

Caught right off guard Angus blushed. "K-K-King," he stammered. "Angus King. Eh - eh - Ah'm just fine Captain."

Nan leaned over the table, the top of her red silk gown bowing open to reveal some cleavage. "This gentleman looks capable enough, Captain."

Jamie Fawcett's pale-grey eyes were drawn to a serendipitous view momentarily before coming to rest upon the face of his guest seated opposite him. The ship's master was an old buzzard with receding hair. His thin cheeks glowed more with single malt whisky than from the elements. He was reputed to be a bit of a lecher and his high rank helped serve him toward that end.

The captain hated dressing up for dinner and on other official or auspicious occasions. He preferred to wear a tired old navy-blue battledress uniform when on the bridge. He'd picked up the habit from countless voyages on company freighters. On one particular trip he'd overheard a disgruntled third mate opine that the skipper more resembled a bus driver than a ship's captain. That particular fellow was at present sailing on the Vladivostok - Aleutian Islands run on the Company's only coal burner. Even so, from then on when the term, The Bus Driver, was mentioned the deckies knew it referred to Captain Fawcett.

The Bus Driver eyed the engineer. "If you think so Miss Barrie," he beamed. "By all means take him." He squinted up at Angus. “Mister King, at the moment I’m considering a special request for which I’ll need a volunteer.”

He received a blank look in return.

“Miss Barrie received a phone call . . .” The vacant stare metamorphosed into one of curiosity. “Ship-to-shore. Her friend Miss . . .”

“Maggie MacDowell,” supplemented Nan.

“Quite. Well, Miss MacDowell will be embarking at Madeira as Miss Barrie’s guest for the remainder of the trip.”

“Excuse me Captain Fawcett,” interjected Nan. “But I think Maggie will probably need the help of two men. She told me that a fair amount of rock and lava specimens are involved.”

“Very well young lady,” the skipper eyed Angus again. “Commandeer one of your ratings for the job Mister King.”

Puzzled, the engineer panned the diners around the captain’s table. Judge Ordowich winked at him. “Ah thocht leave was cancelled for a’ the ratin’s, Captain.”

“It’s not leave Mister,” retorted Fawcett, testily. “It will be an assignment.”

At this point the engineer began to wonder how far Nan had gone to curry favour from the skipper. He was known throughout the ship to be a horny old bugger by officers and crew alike. Just then Fawcett reached for his menu and opened it.

“I don’t normally have dessert,” he said to his guests. “I try to keep temptation to a minimum.” He patted his paunch reflectively before continuing. “But tonight, the American Apple Pie with French vanilla ice cream has a certain appeal to me.”

He beamed with delight and closed the menu so that Angus could see the back. An extremely complimentary charcoal head-and-shoulders sketch of the skipper caught him as a stalwart mariner, commanding and reserved, rather than behind the wheel of a Leyland bus.

Angus caught Nan's eye and mouthed 'you fly bitch'. Nan demurely smiled. The captain noticed that the engineer was still by his side. "Are you still here Mister?" he demanded.

"Eh - sorry Captain," apologized Angus. "But Ah need tae get mair details - like whit time we'll needed an' such like."

Fawcett smiled at Nan. "Would you be kind enough to telephone the air conditioning office tomorrow morning, my dear? Just ask the switchboard and they'll put you through."

Nan returned the smile and promised that she'd call before breakfast.

"Very good my dear," the captain said kindly. He raised his bushy eyebrows at the engineer and gruffly ordered him to go about his duties. His weathered face lit up again as he addressed his guests. "Like I must do. My apologies to you all Ladies and Gentlemen but I have to be on the bridge. We'll be ringing standby shortly for our imminent arrival at Funchal."

In response the bass A tone of the ship's whistle reverberated faintly in the distance.

He was late getting back to hand to the a/c office over the job. The four-to-eight gang had already gone.

"Anything I should know about, Gus?" asked Dan, peering over Angus' shoulder as he copied the slate's data in the log.

"A' quiet oan the Western front," said Angus, closing the log book. He left the pencil in to mark the page. "Guid job."

"Huh," replied MacTaggart. "That's what you said last night. The Highland Grill was like an oven last night when I went to check."

"Weel, that's nuthin' tae dae wi' me," disputed Angus. "Ye can see by the log that the temperature was normal when Ah checked it."

"Aye - I suppose you're right," Dan replied morosely, his Ayrshire accent coming to the fore. "It wasn't your fault that some stupid bastard wedged the door open - supposedly to let cool air in."

MacAlastair chimed in. “Christ, the wee Freon compressor was pumping its heart out trying to cool down the earth’s atmosphere. We keep trying to explain to the HG manager to tell his minions to keep the bloody door shut. How can you cool down a room if it’s open to the world?”

“Guid job,” repeated Angus and left Dan and Harry postulating on what could be done to eliminate this condition.

Angus missed the standby, which was short and sweet. The ship had anchored because her draught was too much to go alongside. Naturally the theme at the engineers’ dinner table was the possible delights, wicked or otherwise, that might await them in Madeira’s capital city. Wheelkey, in spite of his soreness, was enthusiastic enough for another run ashore. Taffy, Don, Steamboat and Terry were raring to go with him. The Glaswegian asked King why he hadn’t changed into his civvies yet.

Carving into his ham steak Angus mulled over the pros and cons of a night in another exotic town. He’d failed to contact Nan privately about the task needed to be performed on the morrow. Over the past few days the other engineers acted as if they thrived on booze and lack of sleep. He guessed that they were just as weary as he was but stoically kept on going through the motions to demonstrate that they weren’t party poopers. Be that as it may Angus could feel himself falling into that trap. After all he was only twenty-one years old and a whole new world was beckoning him.

‘Shite! Why am Ah even considerin’ it?’ he thought. His first pay had just gone into his bank in Carluke. In effect he’d been borrowing from the company over the past month or so by getting subs against his paycheck. He still owned his father for lending him money to get kitted out before joining his ship. He was broke - or rather - in debt. There was no way he could go ashore.

“No,” he said finally, dissecting a roast potato. “No’ the night. Maybe the morn.”

"Aw, come on Gus," coaxed Don. "We'll have a great time. Cheap booze and cheap dollies. What else can you ask for?"

Wheelkey put his knife and fork down on his platter and stared at King shrewdly. "You're skint - aren't you?" He gestured to the others. "Remember lads. It's just his second trip. He's only had one month salary. What d'you say we all chip in and pay his way for tonight."

The shipmates were all in agreement. After all they'd been in the same boat, so to speak, during their initiation to the Merchant Navy. But Angus was too proud to accept charity and so declined their generosity. Reluctantly they arose one by one and left him mulling over his coffee.

A little later he went out onto Boat Deck. He went to the rail and peered down. A tender was alongside and people were bustling down the cruise liner's ladder to the boarding pontoon and onto the lighter. He gazed out at the island. It towered high above him, dark and sombre against a purple sky. Lights twinkled at sea level and gradually petered out some distance higher than Funchal. The city itself glittered and glimmered diamond ribbons that denoted streets climbing partway up the mountain.

For no reason whatever, hairs on the back of his neck lifted and his body shivered as if someone or something had walked over his grave. His long dead grandmother was reputed to have the second sight and his mother had often remarked that some of it had been passed down to Angus. Just as suddenly the sensation vanished but left him with foreboding. A footfall behind him drew his notice. It was Christie.

"Not going ashore, Angus?" The flare of a match lit his face up momentarily. His dark eyes gleamed behind his glasses as the flame touched his cigarette. He offered the pack to his friend.

King took one and shook his head."No, Ah'm deid tired," he said. The lie at least was partially true.

"Broke eh?" One didn't get to be a second engineer by being stupid. He reached into a pocket. "I can lend you a fiver, if you want. That's enough to get you drunk and a leg over in a bangy-taxi."

Angus thanked him but shook his head again. "Whit aboot yoursel' Bob? Are ye no' gaun ashore?"

"I've been here before," Christie replied blowing a plume of blue smoke towards the island. "Lots of wine shops and flowers and not much else. D'you fancy a game of chess?"

Angus pondered on the offer. It occurred to him that Christie was a very lonely man. But then if he had a reputation for lashing out at his juniors, what else could he expect? He was civil enough to his peers, fellow seconds, but he never socialized with them except perhaps at mealtime.

"Aye - quick game an' then Ah'll turn in."

He lost his queen in six moves.

"I don't where your mind is tonight Angus but it's certainly not on this game."

Angus made a special effort to concentrate so that even with the loss of his key piece Christie had to go all out to checkmate him.

0355 Thursday

"Good job Angus," Dave told his relief. "Been ashore?"

Angus shook his head.

Hedges looked at him curiously. "Well, I might get up in a few hours and have a look at the place. This watch isn't the greatest for sightseeing or partying either for that matter."

The watch changed over easily. Don was a bit under the weather but would soon sweat out the booze in the heat of the machinery spaces. Jack and Gerry were as sober as judges since they'd been confined to the ship. Angus was reaching into the drawer to retrieve his Twaddle when the phone rang.

"M21 needs an engineer," said Don.

"Whit for?"

"Dunno," shrugged Travers, getting to his feet. "In the meantime Gerry can get some coffee while I'm away. Jack - you watch the fort."

Angus placed a hand on his colleague's shoulder, forcing him back down onto his chair. "Ah'll get it Don. Ye smell like a bluidy wino. Archie would go bananas if a passenger reported ye. Just ye sit here an' take it easy," he advised.

"Ok thanks Gus," breathed Don, a sour fruity odour permeating the air.

"Right then," said a confident Angus, opening the door. "Ah'll go up tae yon cabin first an' fix whit's needed done then start my roonds."

"Give us a buzz if you run into problems," advised Don, sinking back on his chair.

By rights Angus was supposed to contact the steward who was in charge of the section where Cabin M21 was located. But the guy was nowhere to be seen simply because the cabin's occupant simply hadn't informed him. The engineer tapped lightly on the polished surface of the door. A moment passed and a feminine voice asked, "Who is it?"

"Air-conditioning engineer Ma'am," King replied through the panelled door.

"Just a minute."

The sound of the door being unlocked was heard before it swung open. Nan, clutching pale-green diaphanous night attire to her body, invited him in. An aroma of Chanel No. 5 hung heavily in the air.

CHAPTER THIRTEEN

Maggie MacDowell

Gerry recalls:

Mister King came back to A17 fanroom about half-an-hour after we'd dropped the hook in the Bay of Funchal. His white uniform was all rumpled, particularly his trousers, which were utterly devoid of the standard knife-sharp creases. He looked totally shagged out, reminiscent of the big grey, Nicolaus Silver, after he'd won the Grand National the previous year. Instead of its normal jaunty angle his peaked cap perched on the back of his head like an upended saucer on a clump of russet heather. He flopped down onto a chair with an exaggerated sigh.

"Where in the hell have you been?" asked Mister Travers.

Trying to appear nonchalant Mister King doffed his cap and ran his fingers through the thatch of tousled ginger. "Ye wouldnae believe me." He turned his attention to me and Jack before reaching into his trouser pocket. He removed a florin and flipped it. As it spun in midair, he said, "Call it!"

"Tails!" declared Jack.

Mister King caught the coin, slapped down on the desktop, and withdrew his hand. Mister Travers leaned forward to view the result. "Heads, it is. It looks like you won, Gerry. What did he win, Gus?"

"A wee run ashore, startin' at nine this mornin'."

Pleased and flabbergasted at the same time I said, "I thought shore leave for our lot has been banned for the rest of the trip, Mister King."

"It has," confirmed the engineer. "But in your case the order has been rescinded."

"Lucky bugger!" said Jack.

"Weel onyway," said Mister King. "Ah'll see ye on R Deck Square at nine twenty-five. Dinnae be late for the tender leaves at hauf-nine sharp."

When the watch ended I took a quick shower then went into our mess and had a nice breakfast of bacon and eggs, sausages and fried bread. Word had already got around so I had to endure a few envious looks and caustic remarks.

Mister King was chatting with a female passenger when I arrived on R Deck. He introduced me to her as Miss Barrie. The woman had a pleasant personality and her stature must have been nearly six feet in her white low heels. I guessed that she was in her late forties. Her sandy hair had been styled so that wavy curls seemed to bounce on the shoulders of her yellow cardigan. She wore a tangerine frock patterned with tiny green tendrils of some obscure plant. I can't remember the colour of her eyes for sure but I believe that they were grey or light-blue. The happy banter of engineers followed us down the ladder as we boarded the tender.

It was a beautiful morning and the sun was shining from a cloudless sky. The air temperature was in the low sixties but got higher as the day went on. The deep-blue water was fairly calm with a little swell which made the journey towards shore beneficial for some of the queasier passengers. As we approached the quay side, a buxom brunette was waving frantically while bouncing up and down with excitement.

The tender slid alongside.

When we debarked, the woman ran into Miss Barrie's arms and they hugged and laughed. "You've changed your hair!" "So have you!" and similar personal observations passed between them while Mister King and me looked on like a pair of simpletons.

Finally their exuberance diminished enough that we could be introduced to Miss Maggie MacDowell. In her mid-thirties Miss MacDowell was the epitome of the sixty-inches-high

Nelly Forbush character in Rodgers and Hammerstein's *South Pacific*. With a round mischievous face and brown eyes she fairly effervesced energy. She wore a pink blouse, faded jeans and plimsolls. A hint of Hyacinth floated from her.

Taking Miss Barrie by the hand she ran over to a 1935 MG-NB Magnette open tourer. It was a four-door car with a British racing green body and spoked wheels. She opened the front passenger door and ushered her friend into the plush leather seat. To us men she merely gestured with her head to climb into the back.

The engine gleefully burbled on start up, and slipping smoothly into second gear, we roared off leaving a dissipating plume of blue exhaust. My parting glimpse was of half-a-dozen engineers standing on the wharf looking enviously at their rapidly diminishing colleague.

We headed west out of Funchal at a great rate of knots. For a time we had the ocean on our left with almost sheer mountains of forest on our right. Miss MacDowell was a good driver shifting the gears up and down to accommodate the ever varying contours of the narrow road. We gradually left the coastline, zooming past different forms of sub tropical greenery that grew to the sky.

Before long we'd edged south again to glide into a little community called Ribeira Brava where the tank was topped up with petrol. We headed almost due north into the interior. The road sometimes followed small rivers and streams before climbing over saddlebacks that were strewn with hairpin bends and zigzag curves that scarily verged on heart-stopping ridges. On either side, precipitous mountains reared above us, their verdant slopes mysterious and forbidding. Occasionally we'd plunge down a steep slope to splash through a shallow ford, roar up the opposite bank, and climb to a new height.

A place on the northern coast called São Vicente terminated our exhilarating journey. The car stopped at a stone hut near some caves which we were told were volcanic.

We climbed out the car and stretched to ease our stiff limbs. There were ten ammunition boxes stacked along a wall of the hut. All of them except one were patterned in the usual army camouflage green. The outstanding container had a desert camouflage. Each ammo case had rope handles at either end.

Miss MacDowell turned out to be a volcanologist. She'd spent the last few weeks in the area studying and collecting rock samples. Since it was around noon hour, she opened the car's trunk and lifted out a food hamper. Mister King and me shifted the boxes into a sort of circle and using them as seats, we settled down for a picnic lunch.

"The rest of my group left by boat yesterday," announced Miss MacDowell. "It's too bad that there wasn't any room for them on board the *Queen of Dalriada* but their loss is my gain." She looked at all the stuff that lay about us. "They must have taken half the island with them," she said while chewing a ham and tomato sandwich. "This is all that is left."

After our repast she asked if we'd like to have a look inside the caves. The three of us assented and were supplied electric torches that were kept inside the bothy. Guided by Miss MacDowell we ventured into tunnels that had been formed by volcanic action some four hundred thousand years earlier.

During the thirty minute tour we were shown weird formations with weird names. Stalactites I had heard of but lava cakes and erratic blocks were beyond my ken. It seems that the latter were some kind of rock nodules which had been carried along with the molten lava during the volcanic genesis of the island. They had become stuck in narrow fissures. Our voices echoed amazement from multicoloured rock faces and across crystalline lakes that glowed eerily in torchlight. There was no doubt in our minds that those awe-inspiring sights would become an important tourist attraction in the near future.

Our eyes blinked in protest to the bright sunlight as we exited the tunnels. We loaded the heavy boxes into the car.

One was put in the hamper which was restored to the trunk. Another two boxes were stowed alongside the hamper. The trunk lid wouldn't shut so a fathom of handline was lashed to the lid and hitched to the back fender.

There appeared to be something special inside the dun ammo box so it was placed end up in the front seat between the two women. Miss MacDowell was quite unconcerned about the car's springs when she commanded us to pile the remaining boxes in the back seat. The only seating left was on top so we clambered up and perched on the boxes like a couple of gargoyles. The motor was started and we lurched off south, Mister King and me clutching on the rope handles like grim death.

And what a journey that was! Everything went passed in a blur. I felt like I was on a wild horse in some western rodeo. Those cowboys had it easy. They just had to stay aboard for ten seconds. On some acute corners we got a breather for the MG had to slow down to negotiate them. At other times we fairly flew along fighting centrifugal force on the wide bends.

Approaching a ford, our lady driver accelerated downhill to get extra momentum to scale the far side when Mister King lost his grip. With a backward somersault he rolled over the lid of the trunk to land arse-down in the cool mountain stream. I hollered at Miss MacDowell to stop. And two hundred yards up the far slope the car came to a screeching halt with clouds of dust blossoming all around.

I scrambled down and rushed back. Mister King was dazed and still sitting in the water when the women paddled in. "Are you hurt Angus?" asked Miss Barrie, her tone fraught with concern.

When we helped him to his feet, he rubbed his posterior. "Nothin' seems tae be broken," he ruefully announced. "Just my wringin' wet dignity." He sadly shook his head and said, "There's nae need tae hurry, Maggie. The ship disnae sail till bluidy midnight!"

"We have to get back in time for our afternoon watch Mister King," I reminded him.

"That's why I was hurrying," added Miss MacDowell.

"Whit for?" asked Mister King. "We're oan watch noo, aren't we? Are we no' oan ship's business?"

"That might be ok for you, Mister King," I said. "But I'm just a dogsbody and I'd like to remain on a/c if you don't mind."

"Don't worry," said Miss MacDowell. "We'll get you back before your watch begins."

"You'll have to get dried off before you catch pneumonia Angus," urged Miss Barrie.

"Aye, ye're right there, Nan." He tested his shirt and windcheater for moisture. "Just doon below is a' wet." he leered at the two women. "Would you lassies like to see me wanderin' aroond in my shirt tail?"

Miss MacDowell's face lit up at this suggestion then she said, "Angus, I've got a beach towel in the boot."

"That's bluidy marvellous!" smiled Mister King, walking towards the MG.

Miss MacDowell fumbled around in the boot before finding the towel for the engineer.

"Right you twa - back intae the car while Ah take aff my troosers an' shorts."

The women boarded the vehicle.

"Nae peekin' mind!" warned Mister King.

He kicked off his slip-on shoes and had his wet things off in a trice. He dried himself off and wrapped the towel about his waist kilt-fashion. After putting his shoes back on he climbed back up on the ammo cases and sat as kilted Scotsmen are wont to do: legs apart with the front drooped down for decorum. Had it been me, my legs would've been clamped tighter than a prim spinster's.

"Take it easy noo," said Mister King as I mounted up beside him.

The MG moved off slowly before accelerating to a reasonable speed.

"That's better Maggie!" he shouted.

Miss MacDowell was busy adjusting her centre rear view mirror slightly upwards so that her view might reveal something beyond a pair of bony knees. Looking in the same mirror, I could tell by her dilated pupils that she'd focussed in on her target.

The return journey was as hectic as the drive north. Just to break up the monotony of sheer terror, there were a couple of really alarming instances when the car suddenly veered off the road for no apparent reason other than the driver's eyes tarried too long on the centre rear view mirror rather than on the road ahead.

On the outskirts of Funchal Mister King called a halt and nipped behind some bushes to change back into his clothes which had dried during the journey.

The tender was approaching the quay side just as we drew to a complete stop. The same engineers observed our arrival through inebriated eyes. A pair of them were swaying like palm trees in a light breeze. I learned later from Mister King that they had been imbibing on free samples of bual which was customary in the various wine shops throughout the city. We quickly unloaded the car while Miss MacDowell ran over to the tender as it came alongside. She must have made some arrangement with the vessel's master for two seamen were sent to load the boxes on board.

Thanking us for our help Miss MacDowell placed a fiver in our hands, much against our wishes since we'd have gladly paid twice that amount for the experience. But she wouldn't hear of it. She vaulted back into the car and told Miss Barrie that she'd be back with her gear in time for the next tender.

Our last chore was taking the tan ammo box up the ladder to R Deck. After all the passengers had boarded the cruise liner the little ship edged forward to where a landing net would lift the other boxes into the hold. Two stewards were assigned to take the first box down to the ship's hospital. Mister King and me tailed them down the companionway to C Deck. At the time we were baffled as to why it had been sent there but the reason became apparent later on.

It happened we'd had about fifteen minutes to spare before our watch began. Since Mister King needed more time to get into uniform, he asked me to ask Mister Hedges if he'd change over the watch in his cabin. As for me I'd just enough time to grab a bite to eat before going to work.

CHAPTER FOURTEEN

The beast is released

Gerry recalls:

The ship left Madeira on Thursday at midnight and the next morning watch went by without incident. I spent that Friday, the nineteenth I think it was, darning a pair of socks and doing a bit of laundry. It was an easy day and I even got some time to do a bit of reading and play some cribbage on the Pig Deck. I'd hoped that the rest of the trip would pass just as smoothly. Some hope.

We usually had our evening meal before going on watch. Our messroom was set up for seven tables. Each room accommodated six ratings or sometimes eight at a push. We queued up at a hatchway for our grub and the peggy or cook's helper would dish it out. The fare was generally rough but if you're hungry enough you'll eat anything.

As usual, Friday night was fish and chip night. Harry, the cook, excelled himself with thick pieces of cod dipped in beer batter, made from the overspill from the taps in the Pig and Whistle's Bar. The chips weren't too bad either although I like 'em a bit crisper. The boiled peas were something else. As Tinker had mentioned earlier in the trip, few crew cooks ever took the trouble to soak dried peas first before boiling them. They believed that if they were cooked long enough they'd soften up.

Tinker was seated at the supper table along with his sidekick, Teach. Ronnie Livingstone, the engineroom greaser, Charlie Everton, the bilgediver, Jack and me made up the table for six. The old fireman was complaining about the peas. He liked them mushy so that his gums could chew them. It was at this point that Teach felt it was time for a little entertainment. He leaned over to the little gypsy and hinted, "Hey Tinker, why don't you tell the guys about the time you lost your teeth?"

And so the little gullible firemen once more related the story of how he lost his dentures. Our mess was in an uproar by the time he had finished. I can't ever remember having a more enjoyable supper. The guys were all but falling off their benches. Poor Tinker couldn't quite understand why he'd been the fount of all that mirth.

That afternoon Mister Travers spent the first hour of the watch answering the phone. I'd just come back to the a/c office from a call on C Deck. He slammed down the receiver and handed me a chit. "Nip down to our stores and pick up these tools for Mister King in M21."

I can still recall that list to this day. It was a pistol drill with chuck key, an electrical extension cord, a 5/8" diameter brick drill bit with a Stellite tip, a brick saw, two tapered steel punches, a two-pound ball pein hammer, a triangular file, a pair of cotton gloves and some cotton wipers.

I never ceased to be amazed at the difference between crew and passenger accommodations. Up for'ard on the port side of D Deck where I was berthed, the bulkheads were painted with drab green gloss. Our deck was gloss painted gloss too, a dull reddish brown. But up here on Main Deck the warm opulence of the panelled alleyways oozed money.

The scend of the sea made some of the handsome panels creak, a meek protest against the hardly noticeable yawing of the ship. Even so, I was tempted to remove my shoes and promenade gaily in my stocking soles through the rich deep pile of the royal-purple Axminster carpet.

I knocked on a stateroom door. Well, actually I kicked it lightly with my shoe because my hands were full. Miss MacDowell opened it and let me in. Miss Barrie was hovering over Mister King who was kneeling on the carpeted deck working on something inside the sandy-colored ammo case. He was stripped down to his singlet, his white tunic draped over an easy chair. Quite unbecoming for a ship's officer in the presence of passengers I might add. He was utilizing his small screwdriver to etch a line on one of two grey rocks nestling within the box. The stones were just a bit bigger than rugger balls.

"Thanks Gerry," he said, taking the pistol drill from me. "Just plug in that electrical cord ower there while Ah lock the drill bit intae the chuck."

He picked up a dark celluloid sheet that looked like an x-ray negative and held it to the light. From its information he took a reference to pencil a line on the drill's web, presumably so that the bit wouldn't go too deep. He centred the bit at one end of his scored line. It only took seconds to pierce the stone because it was very brittle. He used the brick saw to deepen the scribed mark. A hole was drilled at the other end of the line. Locating a tapered punch in each hole he alternately tapped them further into the holes with the hammer.

While he worked Miss MacDowell divulged what had happened since we'd brought this box on board. She'd come across many of these erratic blocks, as they were known, during her sojourn in the volcanic tunnels of São Vicente but these two had intrigued her. Well, one of them actually. Although identical in size the block Mister King was working on weighed more, much more than its mate. Naturally she wished to know hence Mister King's labours.

She picked up the x-ray that the engineer had been referring to and held it against an ornate table lamp. Its light revealed two roundish shadows in the middle of an elliptical shape. "The ship's medical officer was kind enough to have these rocks x-rayed for us."

Mister King peeped up from his toil and grinned knowingly at Miss Barrie. "Did ye draw anither charcoal sketch oan the back o' a menu, Nan?"

Miss Barrie smiled and shrugged, some inside joke I guess.

A minute later the stone split wide open. A pair of orbs, about the size of tangerines, lay nestled together like peas in a pod. They had a pale-blue sheen with some kind of map or chart etched on their surfaces. He hefted one the spheres in both hands before passing it up to Miss Barrie. “Let’s clear up the tools, Gerry.”

I tidied up while the ladies scrutinized the discoveries.

“My God!” exclaimed the older woman.

“What is it Nan?” asked Mister King.

“Look at this pattern on the surface of this sphere.”

The engineer examined the curious but defined lines on the miniature globe. “Dae ye think this one came frae anither planet?”

Miss Barrie shook her head. “Angus, what kind of material do you suppose this thing is made of?”

A puzzled look changed the engineer’s composure. “It’s hard tae tell if it’s metal or some kind o’ ceramic. Gerry, pass me yon file.”

“Oh, don’t mark it Angus!” she objected.

“Och, a wee scratch will no’ dae ony harm.”

Before the woman could prevent him he placed his hand under hers to brace the ball and attempted to file a tiny nick on its surface. The tool just slid off without leaving a mark. He tried again with more force. It was like trying to file oil.

He gave up.

With a sigh of relief Miss Barrie opened a book on the coffee table. She flipped through a few pages until she came to a chapter entitled Pangaea. She turned a few more pages and said. “Look at this map. You too Maggie”

The sphere’s engraving was compared to the illustration. They looked very similar.

“What do you think Maggie?” asked Miss Barrie.

“This is unbelievable!” gushed her friend. “This ball shows how Earth was supposed to look like at the end of the

Mesozoic era." Then she frowned. "But how can that be? The volcanoes on Madeira were formed four hundred thousand years ago. The Mesozoic era ended about sixty-five million years ago when the Cenozoic era began."

She hunkered down and using both hands scooped the mate from its stony nest. "I wonder if this one is the same. It could be that . . . Good Grief!"

"What?" echoed Miss Barrie and Mister King.

"This could be our moon from the time you mentioned Nan. Look, there aren't as many craters on it," replied Miss MacDowell. She turned it around. "This looks awfully like the photos taken by the Russian Luna 3 two years back in October. Y'know, that was the spacecraft that made the first-ever circumnavigation of the moon."

Her friend laid her orb down on the coffee table to study Mis MacDowell's observation.

"Weel, a' this stuff is awa' ower my heid," declared Mister King. "Dae ye mind if Ah use your bathroom tae wash my hands?" The woman he called Nan shook her head. "Ok then Gerry, wrap everythin' up here an' clean up ony stour that might hae escaped frae the box."

On his return he put his white uniform jacket back on, buttoned it up, and jammed his cap on his head at a jaunty angle. "Where's my swinger?" he asked, glancing around the stateroom. It lay on a lamp table next to an armchair. "Right," he said, picking it up. "Ah'm awa' tae dae my roonds. It's nearly time for dinner, ladies. Ah'll probably see ye in the main restaurant in a wee while."

The sphere on the table began to roll.

"Watch it!" Mister King moved smartly to catch it but he was too late. As soon as it hit the carpeted deck the orb split into two hollow hemispheres. He picked them up and gave them to Miss Barrie.

"Look at the inside of these Maggie!" she all but screeched. "These things are made from raw gold. And look how smooth the inner surfaces are. I wonder how they were held together. There aren't any dowels or anything. You're an engineer Angus," she said, holding them close so that Mister King could see them better. "How do you suppose these were locked together?"

But Mister King just stood there as if in a trance. Perhaps stunned might've been a better description for his eyes were glazed and his face, ruddy from a week of sun, was now pale and he was shivering like a dog shiting broken glass.

Concerned, Miss Barrie placed hand on his shoulder. "Are you all right Angus?"

A few seconds later he seemed to come out of it. "Ah'm a' right," he mumbled. And without another word he left the room. I picked up the tools and left in his wake.

His head felt fuzzy upon entering the Observation Lounge. About two or three dozen passengers were having pre-dinner cocktails. Angus twirled his swinger briefly and gave the thermometers a cursory glance. For some obscure reason an incident from his youth popped into his mind as he wrote his findings onto his log card.

Davie, Guy and he were standing on the steep slope of the glen where Jock's Burn had trickled through for eons. They were gazing up at Bobby Alexander who was perched at the very top of a very tall spruce tree. His arm was stretched upwards to allow his hand to explore a crow's nest. "There are fower eggs in it," he hailed down.

"Weel, bring yin o' them doon Bobby," Guy hollered at the top of his voice.

"Ah cannae," said Bobby. "If Ah put it my pocket, it'll likely get broken an' my Mammy 'ull gie me laldy!"

"Weel, can ye no' jist haud it in yer hand?" suggested Davie. "Ye jist need yin hand tae hang oan wi'."

"Too bluidy dangerous!" scoffed Bobby. "Yin slip frae this height an' Ah'm a goner!"

The three boys respectfully stepped back from the potential point of impact.

"Put it in yer mooth," ventured Angus. "It'll be safe there."

The other two sagely nodded in agreement. Bobby thought about it for a moment before popping the mottled brown egg into his mouth. Slowly and carefully he started down. About two thirds of the way down he stood on a thin dead branch that gave out under his weight. Although he only dropped a couple of feet before regaining a safe position, a bushy twig had clipped his chin. He finished his descent and bent over to allow the contents to dribble from his mouth.

"Yungks!" chortled Guy, observing the bloody half-formed crow fetus. "Och weel, there's anither craw's nest further alang the glen. Maybe its eggs will still be fresh an' ye'll hae better luck climbin' up tae that yin!"

A half digested kipper followed the unhatched bird among the carpet of pine needles. "Bugger you, Guy Grove! Ah'm gaun hame!"

The scene changed. Eleven-year-old Angus was in Maggie Turret's classroom pondering the mysteries of weather. Cold fronts, warm fronts, isobars and occlusions were drawn on something called a synoptic chart. The bane of the lad's life was mental arithmetic, a sad fact of the Eleven Plus stage in the Scottish Education System. In a twinkling, his mind was reviewing his college achievements in English, mathematics, physics and other subjects.

Another seemed-to-have-been-forgotten incident filtered into his mind. He was about eight or nine years old during that summer school break, Angus loved to travel with his father by horse and cart from Carluke to Lanark Market, a distance of five miles.

Over the years his dad had been a bit of an entrepreneur who strived to earn money for his wife and five children. He had a quarter acre plot of land on which he grew bedding plants, strawberries and other soft fruit. He fattened pigs, raised day-old-chicks to egg-laying pullets and any other enterprise that could turn a coin.

On holidays such as the Lanimers or the Orange Walk his dad's dappled grey garron was hired to lead the parades. As far as Angus was concerned Bobby was just a white carthorse about sixteen hands high. That meant that a boy his age could run under the equine belly without ducking my head too much. When not at work Bobby grazed in an old chicken pen. This grassland was completely surrounded by a wire mesh fence and was about six feet high. The chicken run had been divided into two sections at one time but now only two posts stood where the gate used to be.

What triggered this particular reminiscence was beyond the engineer's comprehension. He recalled climbing up on one of the chicken coops to wave a piece of bread at Bobby. The garron loved bread. Before long he was clambering on his back as he munched his treat. As the animal plodded away the boy hung on tightly to the mane. It wore neither bridle nor reins - and of course - no saddle. That had been great fun! He felt like Hopalong Cassidy!

But Bobby was finished for the day. He trotted toward the gateway where the posts were just wide enough to let him through. Quickly Angus lay full length along his back, keeping his legs up so that they wouldn't be crushed by the posts. Unexpectedly Bobby veered to the right after he passed through but his unwanted rider kept on going in the same direction. The lad's chest hit the springy turf and winded him. Bobby plodded back and nudged him with his soft muzzle. The glint in his eye seemed to say one can only go so far on a measly slice of bread!

By the time King got back to A17 fan room he felt mentally drained and the new watch had taken over.

"We were just about to send out a search party for you," said Dan MacTaggart. "Is everything ok?"

“Aye,” Angus replied, handing over his swinger. “Everythin’s just hunky-dory.”

In his cabin a splash of water on his face didn’t help to obliterate the weird sensations that were scooting around his brain. He headed for the mess.

Terry Baker, Peter Deery, Charlie Benson and Don Travers were already into the main entree when Angus sat at their table. “What happened Gus?” Don beamed. “Did she cross her legs before you got it out?”

“Dirty Protestant swine!” protested Deery, his prudish zeal ever on simmer.

“No, no,” replied Angus. “Ah dinnae feel weel. Ah think Ah might be comin’ doon wi’ the flu or somethin’”

Will Keyes overheard him as he sat down. “With the way you’ve been dipping your wick all trip I’ll be surprised if it isn’t a dose of something else.”

“Gentlemen, gentlemen,” censured the little Irishman. “Such a subject at the dinner table.”

Keyes grinned and picked up a menu.

The Tooth Fairy appeared at King’s back.

“Hey Gus,” announced Charlie. “Your favourite is on tonight - barrron of rrroast beef!”

Angus let the gibe fall on deaf ears and ordered a salad. Then another. And another.

This didn’t go unnoticed, particularly by Travers. “Hey Gus, what’s with the rabbit food? Are you going on a diet?”

“Shit!” swore Keyes. “He’s all skin and bone now. The only place he can lose weight is from his dick. Just cut off half a pound and graft it onto me!”

The banter continued and shortly after Deery left in disgust. Angus rose from the table too waving off enticements to go the wardroom for a beer.

Inside his cabin Angus got ready for bed. He was quite aware that the night air out on deck was about 70° Fahrenheit yet his body was shivering. He closed his porthole even though his cabin was almost fifteen degrees warmer than outside. A folded beige blanket lay at the foot of his bunk. He spread it across the red chintz canopy. Another blanket was retrieved from his wardrobe drawer. Slowly he climbed into his bunk. His teeth chattered as he cowered into a fetal position beneath the sheets. As sleep drifted over him the engineer envisioned having to report sick at the end of the morning watch. He fell into a deep slumber . . .

He was standing in a grove of trees with long needled leaves, twice as long and thick as Scotch pine. Below them grew a type of bracken that Angus had never seen before. Just beyond, tall lush grasses swept over an undulating plain. Upon it enormous trees were sporadically clumped together right to the horizon where a ridge of volcanoes vented vapour and smoke. An angry sun blazed down through a hazy yellowy-blue sky and the air felt steamy and heavy as if loaded with carbon dioxide. Every now and then a zephyr carried a whiff of burning brimstone.

The ground trembled intermittently, a portent of an uncertain future. Here and there tall cycads flaunted their attractive but toxic seed pods among their herringbone fronds. He trod on soft brown humus, a carpet of decomposing fronds. This decay combined with the pine needles emitted a pungent yet pleasing smell, reminiscent of a greenhouse. His ague had disappeared for the warm humid air felt comfortable.

Flowers, the size of dinner plates, bloomed on a verdant bush by a small lake. Angus moved closer to examine what looked like a species of magnolia. Larger than starlings, a squadron of dragonflies in iridescent greens, reds and blues darted and hovered above the lake's dun surface. The magnolia exuded an unusual aroma. Curious, Angus reached out to touch it.

His outstretched arm was covered in long reddish-brown hair. He withdrew it to examine his hand, a grey calloused palm with a stubby thumb but had four powerful fingers. Horrified he peered down at his body. Except for a leathery area on his chest it was totally covered in hair. Both hands reached up to his face. Ten talons combed their way down through hairy cheeks. "Ah'm haein' a nightmare an' Ah cannae wake up!"

A ripple on the water interrupted his thoughts. A smooth reptilian head popped up momentarily before submerging again. Warily he moved away from the lake's edge. A sizable sprig of spruce dropped on his head. What was that? He gazed up to see a gigantic lizard munching contentedly on the upper branches of a coniferous tree.

Saturday 0030

"Got any beer in your cabin, Sphere?" rhymed Maxie Harris, hopefully.

Tony Ball glanced across the table at him as he liberally spooned relish between two slices of bread in the fervent hope of enriching an otherwise tasteless cheese sandwich. He clamped the resultant concoction together with short fat fingers. "No," he said, and bit into it.

Bomber morosely stirred the dun liquid in his cup and wondered if it was supposed to be tea or coffee. "Y'know after a tough watch a fellow deserves a bottle or two."

"Hard watch?" mumbled The Sphere. "What's hard about leaning on a desk for four hours? I had to change a couple of busted gauge glasses and clean a load of crap out from under a bilge valve seat. Look at me!" he said. "I'm fading away to a shadow!"

His gesture was met with indifference because in Maxie's eyes the floater was as fat and round as a giant Victoria plum. He sighed.

The Sphere reached over to the platter of heaped sandwiches centred on the mess table between them. He selected one that had wings less poised for flight than its neighbours. Lifting its lid he extracted a slice of corned beef. He reopened his half-eaten sarnie and popped in the supplement. He took another bite and began masticating with a little more satisfaction. Then suddenly he stopped in mid-chew. "Hey! I saw Barnes taking a case of McEwan's into Gus' cabin just before I came on watch."

Maxie's eyes gleamed with anticipation. "Why don't we go to his cabin and relieve him of a bottle or six?"

The Sphere gulped down the last of his sarnie. "Don't you think he'll mind?"

"Not if we don't wake him up!"

The two engineers sneaked into King's cabin. Not wanting to awaken their shipmate by switching on a light they left the door wide open. The sealed beer case sat invitingly on the coffee table. Harris opened his penknife and stealthily cut into the cardboard. Presently the duo had their feet on the table and quaffing away in satisfaction. Angus slumbered on . . .

The reptile moved away. Angus wandered off in the opposite direction. Other strange flora came into sight. Curious insects crawled and slithered below the bushes and among their leaves. Cones, some as large as a pineapple, were scattered everywhere. Picking one up, the claw on his right forefinger nimbly scooped out the bean-sized pine nuts. He began to eat.

A hairy creature came into view. It had a sleek dark blonde - almost tawny - coat and its bare chest had the breasts of a female. It didn't look like any gorilla or orangutan Angus might have seen in a zoo. Neither did it have any of the attributes he'd saw in sketches of ancient man. No, this being was unique within itself. It walked upright and seemed to be of similar height as he since their eyes were on the same level. Yes, the eyes. There was recognition in them. No, deeper than recognition, more like love? They came face-to-face and embraced. "Vair!" the creature said.

"Who?" Angus spoke aloud.

The Sphere and Bomber glanced over to the sleeping form. They shrugged in unison and continued chug-a-lugging the pilfered brew.

"Me, you fool!" A clear resonant voice uttered from those self same Scottish lips. And then it softened. "Sheia."

"I've missed you Vair," said the presumably female of the species.

"And I missed you," said the voice, now in complete control of Angus' consciousness.

"Can you free me now?" asked Shiea.

"No, not yet, my beauty," Vair replied. "The climate is all wrong. It has changed drastically. I will seek out others of our kind for information." A deep sigh emerged from Angus' lips. "I've been garnering intelligence from this being's brain. It is a curious organ that functions quite haphazardly on a mixture of chemical and electrical impulses. Strangely enough some snippets of logic emerge from this morass of grey pulp every so often."

"Till then, my love."

"When things are right, this planet will be ours once more."

The drinking stopped in mid-sip as the interlopers' eyes met. Maxie pointed a forefinger to his temple and made circular motions. They got up simultaneously, grabbed a couple of bottles each and slunk out of the darkened cabin.

CHAPTER FIFTEEN

Ménage à quatre?

0345 Saturday

After the storekeeper had awakened him Angus was pleased to discover that his ague had gone and his dream was not even a memory. Perhaps his warm cabin and extra blankets had helped to break his fever. Stretching and yawning he got up to wash and shave. He was grateful to the Valet Service for cleaning his tropical Number Tens. He donned a fresh set that fitted him admirably.

He went into the mess to behold a motley unshaven group rigged in their patrol tunics. He noted Travers, Baker, Benson and Deery were huddled around a table. He sauntered towards them, nodding to Morgan, Currie and Eaton in passing. Black Bob Christie and John MacKay spoke in low tones at the second engineers' table.

The customary platter of curled up sarnies had its usual unappetizing appeal so he went to the fruit bowl on the buffet table at the forward end of the messroom. He came back with an apple, a pear and an orange and sat down beside Don. Getting up in the middle of the night has little inspiration for conversation whether on land or at sea. When the apple including its core had been devoured, Angus bit into the orange. Juice dribbled down his chin.

"Aren't you going to peel that first?" asked Terry.

A baritone voice hollowly replied to the negative and the orange spurted juice with his next bite.

Terry's other shipmates were casual about this exchange and just shrugged. Idiosyncrasies were just another part of sea life. The second engineers purposely made loud noises as they evacuated the mess and headed for the engineroom elevator, a hint for their juniors to follow.

Gerry recalls:

Jack and me were five minutes early reporting for duty. My head felt like Reginald Dixon's Blackpool organ had been blasting in my head all night. I'd been to the Pig and Whistle right after supper with the resolve to have just one pint. It was that time on the voyage when most of the engineroom department ratings were broke. Our standard views in morality had slipped somewhat since the chance of getting a free beer was in the offing.

Of course the queers knew this. Most of them were good stewards and money in the shape of tips flowed into their pockets or purses like a deluge. Although they weren't too fussy on how a guy looked, a brawny firm body drew them like magnets. And like steel on magnets their soft perfumed hands were allowed to wander over hairy chests and between firm muscular thighs for the price of a pint or four. If the greaser or fireman was flush, like on payday, the amorous queer got a smack across the chops for his audacity. But all the straight guys, such as me, were skint and thirsty that night.

One of them asked if was ok to fill up my pint pot. The offer was accepted immediately for I'd just spent my last shilling on an ice-cold lager that seemed to have mysteriously evaporated. My pint pot was replenished in a trice and my benefactor happily squirmed down beside me, his perfume drowning the aroma of beer.

He was a willowy delicate-faced creature with freshly-permed blonde hair. His enormous baby-blue eyes were augmented with greenish shadow and accenting mascara. A row of even, dazzling-white teeth was the focal point of his rouged powdered face. A slim manicured hand with crimson fingernails explored inside the front of my denim shirt. I felt quite embarrassed but when I gazed around the Pig Deck about eight of the catamites were plying my workmates with similar abandon.

My second pint followed the first with remarkable ease. With the draining of the third my new 'friend' was getting more adventurous. His nimble fingers were now on safari between my thighs. I seized his left wrist, hauled the foraging digits away and slapped my empty pint pot into the palm of his hand. Pouting his disappointment, he wiggled to the end of the queue that perpetually festooned the bar.

Another effeminate being slipped onto the former's seat and gregariously offered me a slug of Dewer's Scotch Whisky. Such generosity could not be refused so placing my lips to the mickey, I tilted my head back and allowed this ambrosia from the land of the haggis bashers to gurgle down my throat. Questing fingers sought something that I was reluctant to furnish. I lowered the bottle and with a sigh of contentment, wiped my lips with the back of my sleeve.

From behind me came a shriek of rage as the first queer grasped my new companion by her orange coiffed pelt. Before her victim could retaliate, I rescued my fourth pint from certain misfortune. The two fairies rolled about to-and-fro around the deck clawing and scratching one another. Their shrill cries and curses caught the attention of the drinkers.

"Catfight!" shouted a donkeyman.

The Pig Deck uproared with cheers and screeches. Emergency hoards of cash and hastily scratched IOU's became bets. I stood there grinning with a full pint of lager in one hand and a mickey in the other. As far as I was concerned the first stage of my night's entertainment was over. I made my way to my bunk before the MAs showed up. In spite of my resultant hangover I was grateful to Jack for making the effort to get me out of my bunk.

Mister Cunningham and Mister Hedges, the twelve-to-four engineers, had already been relieved. I noticed right away than Mister King seemed different. Really nothing that I could put my finger on, although he did have a faraway look in his eyes. Mister Travers warned us that it might be a busy watch because we were steaming north at a great rate of knots and into a cooler clime.

"Gus," he said. "I want to you to keep a close eye on the First Class Restaurant and Long Gallery temperatures.

As if suddenly jarred from deep thought Mister King's head slowly turned to face his colleague to politely ask, "Oh? Why is that Don?"

"I may have to shut down the Fozzie in a hurry and get the heating on before the passengers go for breakfast. With a bit of luck the weather may hold off until the eight-to-twelve watch relieves us."

"Ok - fine," he acknowledged.

Just then the phone rang. "We'll take care of that right away," confirmed Mister Travers after taking the message. "Well, it hasn't started yet. Gerry, a passenger in Cabin B15 is complaining about the heat. Nip along to B5 fan room and speed up the fans if they aren't at full speed already. Ok then," he said, picking up his flashlight and a small wheelkey. "I'm off to do my rounds."

When he left, I got up just as Mister King picked up his swinger and opened the door. "Right then Gerry, I'll walk with you as far as A Deck Square. Let's go."

We headed forward along the port corridor on A Deck. I noticed that Mister King's gait was different. The engineer normally walked with a brisk even pace. But now he sort of lurched along with a wearisome movement with slightly hunched over shoulders. The liner was quiet except for the customary creak from the woodwork, its protest against yawing and pitching in a light sea. At ten past four in the morning all the passengers were sound asleep and probably the night stewards were too. It was if we were sailing in a modern day *Mary Celeste*.

"How are you feeling this morning Mister King?" I asked.

"I'm all right," he responded, but the timbre in his voice was different. "Why do you ask?"

"Well," I hesitated. One can never be sure when talking to officers. "I thought that you took a mild stroke or heart attack in yon stateroom last watch. What happened?"

Mister King shrugged off my query. "I can recall no such thing Gerry. I've never felt better in my life." He halted at the bank and changed direction toward the nearer of the two elevators on the port side. "I'll see you later," he said as the doors slid shut.

I got back to the a/c office about ten minutes later. Jack's face was stuck in a *Tit-bits* magazine and his feet propped up on the desk. I took the chair opposite.

"Any more calls?"

Jack shook his head, riffling through the naughty rag until he reached a provocative page.

"Maybe I should nip down and get some kye," I suggested.

"A bit early I would've thought," countered Jack, his eyes focussed on a comely Joan Collins. "Why not wait until Mister Travers gets back?"

"Hey Jack, did you notice anything different about Mister King?"

Jack thought for a moment before shaking his head. "Nope, I can't say that I have." He turned over another page. "Why do you ask?"

"How about his accent?" I persisted.

"I can't say I did. Why?"

"Well, I know that he didn't say much in here at the start of the watch but I think that his burr has disappeared. I mean that there's no more rolling r's. The guttural ochs and achs have disappeared too."

"Maybe he's taking elocution lessons. All those bloody Scotchmen should, y'know."

I shrugged and left it at that.

0426

Inside the elevator the previous night's dream suddenly bloomed into his consciousness as he stabbed the up button for Sun Deck. 'I've learned all I can from your mind.'

"Who the bluidy hell are ye?" Angus loudly snapped.

'My name is Vair and I come from a place that you've never heard of.'

"Why can ye no' go back tae where ye came frae?"

'I can't go back. I can only go forward. I don't think this era is suitable for me yet. Further data is required.'

"Why did ye pick oan me?"

'You were the nearest being when my sphere opened,' was the reply.

"It was you that was inside yon wee golden ball?" Angus incredulously asked. And then with a tone heavily laced with sarcasm he added: "Huh - yesterday must've been my lucky day! Whit in the bluidy hell are ye, a genie or somethin'?"

'No. I'm an entity composed of pure energy,' answered Vair. 'My mate Sheia and I were once beings similar to you.'

Slowly Angus began to comprehend. "Dae ye mean tae tell me that was your missus in my dream an' Ah was you or you were me or whitever?"

'Yes.'

"So ye stayed in the age o' the dinosaurs an' was a' hairy like a caveman?"

'That's one way of putting it,' conceded Vair

The engineer exited the elevator on Sun Deck. Turning to his right he went out a door and went down a few steps onto Boat Deck. It was warm and muggy. He spun his swinger.

"Tell me somethin'," continued Angus. "Whit held yon two haufs o' the golden ball together? Ah didnae see dowels or anythin'."

"A force field," Vair replied aloud.

"A force field?" echoed Angus in disbelief. "Ye mean like twa magnets stickin' together?"

"Much stronger than that."

This answer was digested in his mind. "So how come your missus didnae come oot tae?"

"We cannot last in this state unprotected for too long. We have to reside in a warm body such as yours."

Just then a steward stepped out onto the landing within earshot. He took a deep breath and savoured the night air before lighting up a cigarette.

Still speaking through Angus' lips albeit in an authorive manner Vair went on. "You see, your body is less than perfect. I'll have to search the planet to find out if any others of my kind survived."

"Weel, Ah'm no' an anthro-apologist but Ah dinnae think that there's any gorilla-like creatures like ye wanderin' aboot in oor jungles."

Vair snapped back indignantly. "We were not gorillas. We were or are intelligent beings that walked upright."

"Sorry. Ah didnae want tae ruffle your feathers." Angus pondered for a moment. "Tell me, how did ye make yon wee orbs an' put all the fancy engravin' oan them? Ah mean, it must've been awfy difficult wi' totty wee thumbs."

Vair held up Angus' hands and flexed the thumbs. "Because we didn't have thumbs as long as these it was impossible to make anything at all. So we developed our minds instead."

The steward shot Angus a troubled look, heeled out his cigarette and hastily went back inside.

"That must've took a wee while," surmised Angus and nodded. At least Vair nodded in his stead.

A dull roar erupted almost directly above him and the stars directly aft of Number One Funnel were blacked out by a cloud of soot. They were blowing tubes in 2BR.

"According to your memory this release of carbon happens worldwide. I wonder how much it has affected climate?"

"Dunno," said King. "Ye'd hae tae ask some scientist."

"Obviously you don't know if there are any highly educated beings on board. I mean, apart from the two females."

"Ye've got that right. Ah'm just a flunky oan this boat."

'I'm going to leave you for a while to search for further information."

"Take your time an' if ye find anither brain tae stay in, it'll no' bother me one wee bit."

And with that Angus recorded the outside wet and dry air temperatures. 'It might get a foggy afore the end o' the watch,' he thought. The engineer always began his indoor checks on Promenade Deck where the Observation Bar and Lounge were located.

He never ceased to be fascinated by the oncoming ocean viewed from the five-foot high windows that curved around the forward end of the public room. It was especially impressive at night when the lounge was empty and the obsidian waves threw iridescent spray against the rising and dipping bows of the cruise ship. A distant blast from one of the ship's whistles heralded fog. It was an eerie sound, a sound of foreboding, particularly for the poor slumbering engineer who happened to be next on the fog standby rota. And sure enough only minutes later the bows and the well deck faded away in mist. He logged his readings and decided to have a smoke before making his way aft to the First Class Lounge.

That elegant room sat amidships on that same deck. He recalled being told that its dimensions were seventy-two by fifty-one feet and was built between three decks to give a central height of thirty feet. The panelled walls, for bulkheads seemed to be too harsh a term for such splendour, were of oak with huge ribbons of mahogany edged with Indian laurel. Although Angus never knew such exotic woods existed, around him in dado of light-maple were blends of makore, or African cherry, which further enhanced this highly polished grandeur. Great round columns of polished mahogany grew up from the Green Wilton carpet among sofas, easy chairs and ornate tables. There was even a magnificent fireplace.

He spun his swinger. A familiar tune sprang from the Steinway concert grand piano on an enormous stage at the after end of the room. A lady with her back towards him was playing it rather well so he made his way towards her. He was halfway up the steps to the proscenium when she turned and smiled. It was Nan Barrie. He moved towards her, leaned on the piano, and smiled into her eyes.

"Ye play awfy weel." Angus complimented her.

"Thank you," she smiled. "But I think that's enough for tonight. She ceased playing and closed the highly polished lid.

His hand went to hers. "Please keep oan playin'."

Her long fingers delicately rippled into Symphony No. 9 in E minor from Antonin Dvorak's 'From the New World'. Angus had never heard of the famous composer but the music was pleasant to his ears. She rippled on the ivories for a little while longer before saying that was enough for tonight.

"Are ye haein' trouble sleepin'?"

She slowly nodded her head. "I was too excited after our discovery last night. Maggie and I talked about it for hours until she fell asleep. I was still keyed up so I went for a stroll on deck." The whistle sounded again. "I came in here because that foghorn will probably keep me awake. Playing the piano helps me to relax," she added.

"Ah wish Ah could relax," said Angus.

"Why, didn't you sleep last night?"

He related his experience from the previous night. His surreal description of both the creature and its environment caught her attention. She reflected on his curious reaction just after that sphere had split into two halves. 'Was there any connection?' she wondered.

Angus didn't mention the discussion that he'd had with Vair only a short time before. He didn't think that she'd believe him. And come to think of it, he really wasn't too sure if he believed it himself. "Ah'll walk ye back tae your stateroom," he offered.

Down on Main Deck Nan softly unlocked her door and stepped into darkness. "Coming in?" she giggled.

Angus did not require a second invitation.

"I'll just turn on a table lamp," said Nan. "There's one over here somewhere. She stumbled over a low hassock. "Darn!"

"Are ye a' right?" he asked, helping her up. A light in the corridor gave him a glimpse of a table lamp so he switched it on. "Where's Maggie?"

"Sound asleep in the bedroom." Nan went to the sofa in front of a coffee table. "Please close the door Angus then come over here. I'd like to show you something."

The engineer drew to her side, sat down and draped an arm across her shoulders. "An' whit wee precious treasure dae ye hae for me," he leered.

She reached for a book on the coffee table but Angus stayed her hand and kissed her. "Ah dinnae hae much time," he whispered in her ear. "Ah've got a lot o' public rooms that still need checked oot."

"But I've got to show you something."

"Show me later," he mumbled, kissing her ear.

She put her arms around his neck and soon urgent hands were groping and fumbling and undoing buttons and zippers. Unfastening her bra he began to kiss and fondle her breasts. She responded with a gasp and their lips met. Her tongue pried into his mouth searching and exploring while seeking fingers roamed down his flat belly. They wandered at will through his pubic hair and massaged his testicles.

His fingers navigated a hairy zone too in their quest to stimulate certain sensitive areas. A hint of moisture was his reward. She in turn clutched his hardness and rubbed the tip of it against her clitoris. Both of them were still clutching and gasping when he entered her. Her legs closed like a vise about his waist and frantically they sought that ultimate sensation. Nan climaxed first and as he withdrew his penis, a jet of sperm gushed up her stomach and oozed across her tender breasts.

"I just came in for a cup of cream," announced Maggie from the bedroom doorway.

Their embrace fell apart and the lovers hastily tried to appear nonchalant. Maggie, attired in a transparent baby doll nightie, sashayed seductively over to them and stared at the sticky effluent on her room mate's belly. She drew a finger along Nan's stomach and held the glistening digit in front of King's face before licking it.

"Can I borrow your erection set?"

He glanced at Nan who shrugged. "Help yourself," she said. "I'm going for a shower."

After she went into the bathroom, Maggie gently pried his hands away from the now limp member. She fondled it back into stiffness. "What a size!" She seized it as an engineer would grip a heavy wheelkey. This was the incentive for him to go into action. He slipped off her panties and pushed his face into the dark mass of curls that hid a hidden valley. Her ecstasy was mercurial and she grasped him by the ears and held him tight against her crotch.

Angus felt his tumescence growing stronger and prouder. He moved up her stomach probing with his tongue and licking as he went. Her palm-sized breasts felt soft and tender and her nipples had swollen to the size of raspberries. Sensing that she was ready for him he entered her slowly and gently. Maggie eagerly accepted the intrusion and urged him to thrust harder and harder. Which he did. His enthusiasm was contagious and soon the gyrations of the couple were being to tax the memory on the sofa's springs.

They were still hard at it when a towel wrapped Nan returned. Upon climax, a booming voice filled the room.

"*Sheia*!"

Maggie screamed and went limp. Angus went limp too. Frightened, he pulled on his boxer shorts. Nan rushed over and looked down at her friend. Her somnolent countenance emanated the epitome of satisfaction.

"It looks like you put more into it second time around," observed Nan.

"It wasnae me," replied Angus. "It was Vair."

"Is that a Carluke word?" asked Nan.

"No," the troubled engineer vehemently denied. "Vair was in that dream that Ah telt ye aboot in the Main Lounge."

She gave him a long hard look. "Angus, are you sure that you're all right?"

"Look Nan, Ah ken it's awfy hard tae believe, but this guy Vair is for real. He was a caveman or somethin' years an' years ago when the dinosaurs were runnin' aboot the world."

The word schizophrenia popped into her consciousness and leerily she gestured to the book on the coffee table. "Angus, this is what I wanted to show you before we got carried away."

"Oh aye, whit's this then?"

She opened the book and ran a finger down the index before going to the appropriate chapter titled Mesozoic era. Rippling through further pages she stopped at a painting of the environment that was believed to have existed more than sixty million years ago. Above the picture was the legend: Maastrichtian Period 65 - 71 million years ago.

Angus pulled the book towards him and Vair said, "This picture looks remarkably similar to my home."

Astonishment bloomed on Nan's face. It was like Archie Andrews without Peter Brough. How could Angus' voice change so completely into a deep rich baritone absolutely devoid of provincialism? She nudged Maggie. "Here, Maggie! Wake up and listen to this."

Maggie remained unconscious, her face pale as death. "Maggie - wake up!"

She shook her friend with greater vigour and noticed that her flesh had cooled in spite of the cabin's warm ambience and the steamy interaction with Angus. Now she was really worried and frantically sought for a pulse. Finding none on her wrist Nan felt her girl friend's carotid artery. Nothing.

Panic began to consume her. "Help me to get her off the sofa Angus."

Maggie was placed belly down on the deck with her face turned aside. She thumped her friend's back with her clenched fist and began to deliver the Holger-Neilson method of resuscitation. Remembering his training from earning his Royal Lifesaving Society badges Angus rubbed the woman's inside legs to encourage blood circulation.

"What are you doing?" asked Vair.

"She's dead!" Nan exclaimed through her tears. "You killed her, Angus!"

"Ah didnae mean it - honest!" Angus all but screeched.

"I asked: what are you doing?" repeated Vair.

"We're tryin' tae bring her back tae life, can ye no' see?"

"Let me," said Vair.

The next thing Angus knew was that he was laying prone on the deck with a worm's eye view of himself flopped back on the sofa. With a gulp he took a deep breath and exhaled. Or rather Maggie did. King opened his eyes and stared down at her. "Whit in the hell happened?"

"I've repaired the unit. There was a minor electrical short in the nerve system in her brain," explained Vair.

Angus and Nan helped Maggie up off the carpet and back onto the sofa. She was dazed but showing a distinct sign of recovery.

"This is fuckin' unbelievable!" swore Angus. He glowered at Nan. "Dae ye believe me noo?"

Nan's mind was having difficulty trying to grasp this whole situation. The peculiar way that the engineer's voice kept changing was classic schizophrenia. How was it possible for this type of affliction to come on so suddenly? Though she didn't know too much about the illness she was pretty certain that it came to affect a person gradually. She was also certain that Maggie had been clinically dead for quite some time yet there appeared to be no signs of brain damage. Perhaps it was a bit too early to tell. Anyway, it seemed prudent that she sought medical attention. She picked up the phone.

"Who are ye gaun tae phone?"

"I'm going to get the ship's doctor up here right away."

"She's all right," said Vair.

"Maybe so but I'm calling him anyway . . ." 'I'm having a conversation with two different voices!' "Hello, switchboard? Can you put me through to the doctor please? Yes, I'll wait."

Angus started to put his uniform back on. "Weel, Ah'm no' hangin' aroond here tae get logged. Ah'd better get back tae the office."

"Angus, can you come back here after breakfast? I want to discuss the Maastrichtian Period with Vair. His experience will be invaluable."

"Weel - eh . . ."

"I'll be here," promised Vair.

He - they - left just as Nan got through to the doctor.

"What dae ye mean . . . Ah'll be there?" asked Angus as he stepped out the elevator on R Deck.

"Well, we will. We can exchange knowledge with those females. There are a lot of facts about this age that remain unknown to me."

"Did ye no' get any info when ye toured some o' the brains in this bluidy ship? "

"Yes, I did," Vair replied, adding: "One thing I discovered was that your brain is the only one on board that is a suitable medium for my being.

"Am Ah no' the lucky one?" Angus groaned sarcastically.

"I did pick up a lot about the geography and climate. You'd be amazed at the change in this world since my time."

"No' really," replied Angus. "It was runnin' aroond inside my heid a' last night."

"That's true," conceded Vair. "Anyway, I must say some of the minds were enlightening even though more than a few of them were damaged by alcohol. The others? For instance, do you know a man called Tinker?"

Angus smiled knowingly.

"That guy's scary," opined Vair, adding: "He reminds me of the tiny little creatures that did mischievous things to my kind and other creatures. Some of them had wings. Maybe that Tinker fellow is an offshoot from one of them."

"Dae ye mean fairies an' pixies an' such like?" Angus squeaked incredulously. "Ah thought they were just bluidy figments o' imagination."

Vair shrugged Angus' shoulders before going on. "Some of the unskilled people aboard this vessel were a great source of information. Due to reading, I suppose. We'll have a look at the book storehouse that you call a library in the near future."

"Ah'll try an' fit it in wi' my schedule," was the response.

"It'll fit," Vair assured him. "Particularly since I'm the one who's running the schedule!"

"Weel, Ah've still got a job tae dae," said Angus and shoved open the First Class Restaurant doors.

Gerry recalls:

It was nearly five o'clock when a sweaty Mister Travers barged into the a/c office, his face red with effort. "Has Mister King come back from his rounds yet?" he wheezed for he was quite out of breath.

Jack glumly shook his head.

"Oh shite!" cursed the engineer. "The Fozzie's crapped out again. Gerry, you'll have to give me a hand to get it going again."

Reluctantly I grabbed a wheelkey and followed him out the door. He nipped into the nearest pantry and scooted down a series of ladders through other pantries. Reaching the main galley, he headed for a set of stairs that took him to the working alleyway on C Deck. From there he descended another ladder which led to the port mezzanine in the Main Generator room. The roar in the MGR was deafening and the whole place was hotter and muggier than a Turkish bath.

The Foster Wheeler was basically a refrigerating plant that was cooled by steam. Yeah, I know, even though it's been explained to me two or three different times I still have trouble grasping the theory and I was never quite sure on whether the engineers were pulling my leg or not.

As most people know, water boils at 212° Fahrenheit or 100° Centigrade at sea level. The higher one goes, the lower the boiling point. That is why it is impossible to cook an egg by boiling it on a mountaintop because the low atmospheric pressure corresponds with a lower boiling temperature. A condenser emulates that effect.

Anyway, I've been told by different engineers that the principle behind the system is the same as a regular air conditioner except that steam was the medium instead of Freon. The only trouble was enormous energy was required to maintain the vacuum that is needed to allow the exchange of heat. In this case four enormous air ejectors were available for that purpose but usually one was sufficient to maintain ambient room temperatures.

Copper tubes inside the condenser carried freshwater that exchanged its heat from the cooler condensate created by vacuum. This water was pumped up to cooling chambers that were linked to the First Class Restaurant, Main Lounge, and Long Gallery airconditioning systems. From the upper deck, great fans blasted air into those chambers where countless sprays of cooled water charged the flow of air. A heat exchange took place again when the moisture carried naturally by the humid air became dew under the blast of these sprays and the result was a lovely cool breeze delivered to the public rooms. A series of baffles prevented water from leaving the chamber through the duct work. The now-heated water was returned to the system, strained and filtered, and the cycle resumed. If the outside air temperature rose and the public rooms became busier, another giant air ejector was brought on line to overcome the added burden.

I hated working down in the MGR. It was noisy enough with four turbogenerators running but when a large air ejector was put on line, it sounded like hell on Earth. Perhaps hate isn't the right word 'Fear' was probably more apt and when all four nozzles went on line they sounded like express trains driven by banshees that scared me absolutely shitless. The thought of superheated steam suddenly escaping does have a bowel loosening effect.

Anyway I opened and closed valves under Mister Travers' direction and we got the bloody thing up and running again. When we got back to the a/c office there was still no sign of Mister King. After a quick coffee Mister Travers went down below again to complete his rounds.

A call came in. A passenger was complaining of the cold. Then another. And another. Rather than answer individual calls Jack and me decided to turn on the heat for all the cabins. Naturally we started with the First Class. We ran the length and breadth of the whole damned ship putting steam on the thermotanks. Jack met Mister Travers near the Verandah Grill a/c fan room and he in turn helped to ease our burden.

It must have been just after seven when all three of us were back in the a/c office panting like asthmatics. Mister MacAdam, our boss, was sitting at the desk chomping at the bit. "Whaur hae ye a' been?" he roared. "Ma phone wakened me up oot a braw dream jist afore sunup. Whit in the bluidy hell is gaun oan?" he blazed. Or words to that effect, for his brogue was even worse than Mister King's.

And speak of the devil, who should come squelching in right on cue with his shoes soaking wet?

"Whaur hae ye been?" the HSE repeated. "Ah didnae ken that we had a paddlin' pool oan board."

"The First Class Restaurant is flooded, Archie!" exclaimed Mister King. "Ah've been searchin' a' ower but Ah cannae find a broken pipe anywhere."

The HSE shook his head in exasperation. "That's because there's nae watter pipes in the bluidy place." He paused momentarily. "Did Ah no' hear a whistle blawin' durin' the nicht?"

Mister King nodded. "Aye, there was a foggy for a wee while. It only lasted for aboot thirty minutes."

"An' then this cauld spell come oan."

Everybody nodded in agreement.

"Tell me," continued the HSE. "Is the Fozzie still runnin'?"

Mister Travers and me nodded.

"How mony nozzles are switched oan?"

"Two."

Mister MacAdam placed his hands together. His fingertips formed a peak, tent fashion, and he glowered up at Mister Travers. "We jist came oot o' a warm fogbank intae cauld weather," he began. "The Fozzie is blastin' freezin' cauld air intae the best public rooms oan this damned boat. Whit dae ye suppose has happened tae the dewpoint?"

Mister Travers pondered on these facts before answering. "I think that it might cause a bit of dampness."

"A bit o' dampness?" echoed the HSE. "It bluidy well rained in there, man! Noo, get yer arse doon intae the main jenny room an' shut doon the Fozzie afore ye they stert ca'in' ye Noah!" He scowled at the rest of us. "Get some heat intae these rooms an' see if we cannae dry them oot a bit. I'll need tae gang an' see the Chief Steward an' try an' baffle him wi' science. Bullshittin' oor ain chief isnae gaun tae be sae easy."

He left the fan room bemoaning the ordeals and misfortunes that a Hotel Service Engineer had to carry.

CHAPTER SIXTEEN

Fly me to the moon

0930 Saturday

His fellow engineers had come to accept Angus' new diet so he endured breakfast without any snide remarks. Even though Vair had his mind under control, he couldn't stop him from salivating as Wheelkey stacked bite-sized pieces of sausage, ham, and bacon onto his fork before dipping the concoction into his runny egg. The Glaswegian's face was aglow with ecstasy as his jaws chewed with exaggerated relish. King's usual plate of porridge should've brought a sunny highlight to the meal after eating lettuce and some other unidentified curly greens but Vair wouldn't let him add extra salt and the rich cream was a definite no-no.

When he'd completed his dubious repast Angus was reluctant to visit Nan in her stateroom. This was blatantly asking for trouble. He suggested phoning to set up a date with her out on Boat Deck. Vair asked him what a phone was and upon learning the instrument's use remarked, "How quaint. We're going to see her now."

Angus rapped on the door of M21 just as Hodgekin was sighted making a beeline for him. "Oh God!" he groaned. "Ah telt ye this'd be a problem. Noo Ah'm in deep shite."

But the fourth mate just walked right by him as if he was invisible, because thanks to Vair, the engineer might well have been. The door opened and Maggie peered up at him, her face bright and perky. "Come in, come in," she welcomed him brightly.

Nan had three open books spread out on the coffeetable. "I didn't bring much material with me on this trip," she said apologetically. “I am on holiday after all. Maggie’s got a fair amount of literature but I’m afraid most of them are on geology and volcanology. Anyway, let’s get started.”

She patted the sofa. “Sit down here beside me for I’ve got a lot of questions to ask you.”

“And I you,” replied Vair, pleasantly. Leafing through the first book randomly he had Angus stop at certain pages to study some paintings and charcoal sketches of certain creatures that lived during the Maastrichtian stage which signified the end of the Cretaceous period.

Nan pointed to a mosasaur asked Vair what was the name that his people gave to this type of animal.

“We didn’t name them,” replied Vair. “We didn’t have to, for images of what one saw could be reflected in another’s mind, quite irrespective of distance. Thus . . .”

Angus’ eyes focussed directly into Nan’s. Instantly her mind saw an enormous living creature dragging its crocodile-like body towards her. It had a head like a dolphin with rows of savage teeth. The ugly creature unhinged its jaw in the manner of a snake and hissed threateningly. The strange beast had wide paddles instead front legs. Its back legs were almost nonexistent. Its powerful tail turned its body and the thing slid off into a murky shallow sea.

“Now you know that the painting is quite wrong and the colours don’t even come close.”

The palaeanthropologist placed her hand to her breast and said, “God! That was much too real for comfort.”

“That’s twice I’ve heard that word in as many minutes.”

“What word?” asked Maggie, assuming a place on the other side of Angus.

“God,” replied Vair. “What does it mean?”

“We humans believe that He is the Supreme Being,” said Maggie. “He created the Heavens and the Earth.”

“Supreme Being?” probed Vair. “Do you expect a response when you call His name like that?”

"Weel actually," Angus dryly interjected. "Invokin' The Almighty like that is mair likely tae be answered wi' a bluidy great bolt o' lightnin'!"

"Has anyone seen this being?"

"Not as far as I know," replied Nan.

"Then how do you know this god's gender?"

This question from Vair brought a series of shrugs.

"And you say everyone on Earth pays tribute to this god?"

Nan pondered on this query for a moment before answering. "Yes, and to the Son of God as well but there are many different religions on Earth and each of them has their own name for God."

"The sun of god?" repeated Vair. "Do you humans pray to the sun?"

"No," replied Nan. "Son - as in male offspring. Although the Ancients did consider the sun was a deity. They built great edifices like pyramids and enormous solar clocks like Stonehenge to worship and measure the seasons too."

"Then they were smarter than you are now," announced Vair. "The sun gave you life and keeps you alive with heat and light. And not just for you, but for every living creature on this planet."

Maggie's eyes widened. "Are you telling us that the sun actually is a god?" She went on. "Scientists have determined that the sun's energy is mainly nuclear fusion or in other words, a star."

"That is true," allowed Vair. "But in the beginning the solar wind brought heat, light, electric, magnetic, chemical and other forces together to create life which then evolved into myriad kinds of species."

"But we believe that we have souls that are everlasting after we pass from this life," Nan said passionately.

"That is true also." Vair nodded Angus' head in agreement, adding: "After death your soul or life force once again joins the solar wind and continues onwards to its point of origin where the eight universes converge and where The Ultimate Power waits. So you see, the sun is not a deity but a messenger, an angel if you wish, of The Ultimate Power."

"Whit universe are we in?"

"The nineth."

"Huh? Ah thocht ye said that there were just eight universes," said King.

"There are," replied Vair. "The nineth just began to form only about four and a half billion of your years ago. As did universes ten through to sixteen." Vair went on. "You see when the first universe was complete, it doubled. Those two doubled also when they reached completion. The whole of Space is a geometric progression. Do you understand?"

"No," said Angus shaking his head. "Ah havenae a clue. Whit aboot you lassies?"

"It is difficult to grasp," conceded Nan.

"Getting back tae the sun bein' an angel or whitever," interposed Angus. "Whit aboot the stars? Are a' the stars in the heavens messengers tae?"

"But of course," replied Vair. "They herald The Ultimate Power's glory at night. Prayer is quite unnecessary and just a complete waste of breath."

"What about the concept of good and evil?" asked Nan.

"There wasn't any evil before Man showed up," was the succinct response. "But that problem will be resolved in the fullness of time." Vair stated cryptically. "So you see, in the not too distant future there won't be any need for religion whatsoever."

"Aye, mayhaps ye're right," chimed in Angus. "My faither used tae say that mair folk have been killed in the name o' religion than a' the wars put together."

"What is war?"

Recalling World War II when German bombers attacked the shipyards in Clydebank Nan gave Vair first hand experience of the evil and horror of war. "We humans have been plagued by kings, popes, religious freaks, incompetent politicians and other madmen for thousands of years. There always seems be some idiot who covets what his neighbour has. And not only that, war and conquest is inevitably followed by the misery of pestilence and famine."

"Enough of this talk of conflict and deities," Vair said firmly. "All that will have to stop. It's quite obvious that you humans have absolutely no concept of the real force that brought the universe into existence."

"I suppose you're right," conceded Maggie. "I've always been out of my depth as far as religion is concerned anyway."

"Will you answer some questions for us?" asked Nan.

"If I can."

"If you and your people lived here on Earth about sixty-five million years ago, how come we haven't come across any traces of your people in our studies? I mean, as far as I know we palaeanthropologists haven't found any bones or tools or any other clues of your existence."

"As efficiency decreases by a certain amount, all of the organs in our bodies renew themselves from time to time. In effect we can live forever. We are immune to all diseases. If an accident happens such as the loss of a limb, it is replenished in a surprisingly short time."

"What if a large animal like that mosasaur decides to have you for lunch?" asked Nan.

"That one did," said Vair. "But as you witnessed we have certain methods to prevent that from happening. We use a force field to protect us too."

"Would this force field be powerful enough to prevent a boulder or a tree falling on you and crushing you to pulp?" insisted Maggie.

Angus smiled and Vair said, "Probably."

"What about reproduction?" asked Nan.

"Each one of us has a mate," replied Vair. "But eternal life isn't necessarily an incentive to increase our number although that may change once I discover what is happening to your climate."

"What about our climate?" asked Maggie.

"Has the Earth been warming up lately?"

Maggie thought about that for a moment. "Well, I believe that we had a mini ice age about four hundred years ago. But the last big one was about eleven thousand years ago." She went on. "Then again some of my colleagues think that if a few volcanoes erupted at the same time their dust entering the atmosphere would insulate us from the sun's heat and thus cause an ice age. But we believe that is unlikely to happen. Still, one never knows."

Vair nodded Angus' head. "What about the increase of carbon and methane in the atmosphere?"

"What about them?" asked Nan.

"Don't you think the constant addition of their particles to the atmosphere will have an insulating effect too and trap the sun's heat?"

"You mean like a greenhouse?"

"What's a greenhouse?"

"Ah used tae work in greenhooses leafin' an' pickin' tomatoes," interjected Angus.

Vair visualized his host's teenage experience. "Oh yes - a space that is enclosed by a transparent substance to trap sunlight for heat-loving flora."

"Gless," supplemented the engineer.

"Quite," said Vair. "Anyway, what I wish to learn is how much and how often these and other gases are introduced to our atmosphere."

Nan and Maggie glumly looked at each other. "We haven't a clue Vair," said the cute volcanologist. "It's not a science we are familiar with. But on some days the smog gets that bad a person can't see one's hand in front of their face."

She idly flipped through the pages of a tome and stopped suddenly as an idea came to mind. With a spring in her step she moved across the cabin to a small leather trunk. Maggie opened the lid and searched through some books until she found the one she wanted. She riffled hurriedly through the publication and stopped at a particular page.

Excited she proffered the book to her friend. Before perusing the pencilled sketch in front of her Nan glanced at the book's title: Legends and Folklore from all over the World. She shrugged noncommittally before showing the picture to Angus.

"This is a good likeness of Blox," said Vair, looking at the two women.

"Who's Blox?" asked Maggie.

"Xaan's mate," replied Vair. He read the title on the cover. "This means that one of your kind must have saw one of mine. Where does this information come from?"

This revelation caused Maggie to smile. "Sasquatch!"

"Bigfoot!" beamed Nan.

"Size seven," said Angus, lifting his left foot.

"What does this mean?" asked Vair.

"There have been sightings of creatures similar to Angus' description of you all over the world," replied Nan. "In the Himalaya Mountains they are called Yeti or Abominable Snowmen. If true, it means that your kind was walking the Earth millions of years before Man's fore-bearers crawled out of the ocean."

Angus yawned. "Noo that ye ken where your relatives are, maybe Ah can get some sleep." He peered blearily at his wristwatch. "Holy smoke!" he exclaimed. "Ah've got less than three hours until Ah'm called for watch." He got up and headed towards the door. "Sorry to run ladies but Ah'm deid tired. Ah'll see ye later."

Thanks for all your help," said Vair. "Now I've got a few things to check out while Angus is sleeping."

The door closed leaving the elated women in an animated discussion.

2055 Saturday

"I see that you're still on the rabbit food kick Gus," observed Wheelkey, carving a chunk from a pink one-and-a-half inch thick filet mignon. He popped the delectable morsel into his mouth and a rivulet of bovine plasma dribbled down his chin as he masticated it with relish.

Enviously Angus watched him dab the wayward juice with a monogrammed PL linen napkin but Vair forced him to ignore the jibe so he herded a couple of shallots onto a lettuce leaf instead. Morosely he stuffed the vegetation into his mouth and began chewing the cud. He was utterly exhausted. Sleep had been a rare commodity ever since they'd left Funchal. His fork skewered an aesthetically carved morsel of raw carrot and was instantly crunched to oblivion by enthusiastic molars. It was bad enough that this entity was controlling his brain but a strict diet on fodder was just too bloody much. And it was beginning to have noticeable repercussions too.

Across the mess Pete Eaton looked up from his consommé Mikado with a disdainful sniff. With a distorted face he called over to Angus' table to ask, "Who's shit?"

Wheelkey gulped down another chunk of bloody meat before riposting, "It's yours if you want it, Steamboat." Then a whiff of faeces sneaked up his nostrils. Slowly his head craned the far reaches of the mess room.

"Is Bomber in here?"

"No," replied Baker. "He just relieved me. Five minutes late I might add," he added with chagrin.

Wheelkey focussed on Angus' plate of herbage. "Hey Gus, are you trying to upstage Bomber?"

Maxie Harris had a less-than desirable reputation of fuelling his innards with certain foods to create extremely odorous flatulence. With an off-the-wall sense of humour he would stalk his prey until they were trapped in a confined space, such as in an elevator. The more victims, the merrier, was his opinion. The weekly Emergency Drills had been a constant source of amusement for him.

On the previous trip Jake White, a Canadian marine engineer, had supposedly terminated Bomber's main purpose in life. Now it seemed that Angus was about to usurp Maxie's quest for infamy.

Conversation at the table became subdued. In fact the whole mess room was quieter that usual. Only the occasional clatter of cutlery on dinnerware broke what seemed to be a brooding silence. Overindulging on free samples of Madeira wine was a major reason. In the Leprechaun's case it was a hangover from the previous watch when Christie had caught him keeping the engineroom ratings from their duties by preaching long winded sermons.

The Tooth Fairy gracefully laid a plate of strawberry shortcake adorned with a scoop of French vanilla ice cream in front of Keyes. "Ta sweetheart," he flirted.

He reached for his dessert spoon and asked, "Do you want to make up a fourth at darts after dinner, Gus?"

"No thanks," was Vair's hollow reply. "I'm dragging my backside as it is."

"More like lifting it," jibed Wheelkey.

Angus shot him a look. "Ah've only had aboot fower hours sleep since Madeira." He wiped his lips with the linen serviette and got up. "I'm aff tae my bunk."

2145

He had been asleep for about two hours when the dream began. Or was it a dream?

"How would you like to be the first human being to circumnavigate the moon?"

"Mmm?" murmured Angus turning over.

"I'll take that as a yes," said Vair. "Hang onto your hat."

He was hurtling up to the deckhead then effortlessly passing through it. The engineer couldn't feel the cool night air as he continued to rush toward the eternal stars. Below the *Dalriada* steamed steadily north, its dim luminescent wake marred by soot because Larry Treen was blowing tubes in 3BR. Rising higher he could discern faint auras of light, perhaps coming from cities in Portugal or Spain.

The shadowed moon, black and mysterious, drew closer by the second and presently it was passing on his right. At the apogee of the flight Angus could observe how much the back of the moon differed from the side that he had been accustomed to seeing for most of his young life. It drew closer and closer and passed once more on his right side. Beyond them loomed a gibbous earth with two darkened continents, Europe and Africa, partially spotted with fairy lights. He and twilight were about to descend on Brazil.

Even though it was dark a kind of fluorescence was emitted from a series of rivers playing hide and seek among endless canopies of various shades of green. Their intermittent appearances showed that their waters were destined to swell a much larger waterway, the mighty Amazon River. Down, down, down, he went to an area a bit east of an enormous mountain range called the Andes.

He, they, was in a jungle glade not unlike the one in his previous dream. Was that just last night? Angus knew that the equatorial heat should've been oppressive yet, to him, he had the sensation that it felt just right. Curious bird calls, monkey squabbles and other bizarre noises filled his ears - or would've done if he had any in this mad dream. They glided through some broad-leafed growth and came upon a narrow stretch of phosphorescent water that was partially blanketed by some kind of duckweed. Vague colours could be distinguished in this peculiar light.

Hunkered by the river edge was a humanoid shape. Long reddish hair covered most of its body. If last night's dream was anything to go by, this creature was a compadre of Vair. Before they - he - could move closer the duckweed suddenly rippled open in front of this being and a massive snake sank its teeth into a hairy arm. Almost instantly the great coils of an anaconda enveloped the hairy creature's trunk like gaily coloured truck tyres. Apparently unperturbed the victim arose easily and looked the serpent right in the eyes. The cruel slits glazed over and the tensed coils went limp before slipping to the jungle floor like a massive strand of mottled-green spaghetti.

They moved nearer and merged with the creature's life force. 'Boy, talk about three men in a tub!' thought Angus.

"Who's your friend, Vair?"

"Just a human I came across the other day," was Vair's succinct reply. "How have you been, Leia?"

"I've been very well, thank you," replied the creature called Leia. "This environment is quite ideal for Xaan and me. It's a pity that some of those humans are beginning to encroach on our paradise. More and more of them cut down thousands of trees every season. We are going to have to do something about those incompetents before long. What happened to your body Vair? You and Sheia dropped out of our sensor range just before the series of cataclysms that separated the land."

"Our bodies are probably down somewhere near the earth's upper mantle I should imagine," explained Vair. "We just had time to encapsulate our essence in golden spheres before our tectonic plate dipped under the adjacent one. This human released me less than two days ago. I decided to leave Sheia where she was until I could establish how much the earth's atmospheric conditions have changed during our suspended animation. You and Xaan were fortunate to live in this area."

"Yes," agreed Leia. "But we can't reach our mates." She pointed to the north. "Gron, my mate is with Blox, Xaan's mate. They live near the end of the world's axis, in a land of ice and snow. They wander through a region of forest and mountain that is freezing cold for nearly three seasons."

“Excuse me,” interrupted Angus. “But how many of ye were oan this planet back then?”

“Ten,” replied Leia. “Five males and five females.

“What about Gaia and Thall?” asked Vair.

“They live among a land of giant mountains that are covered in ice for most of the year. They had two young ones but their intelligence never developed properly so they just wander hither and thither like automatons.”

“And Jal and Kaar?”

“Who knows?” Leia shrugged. “We lost contact with them soon after you. They were at the other end of the earth’s axis.”

“The South Pole,” Angus informed him.

“That’s what the humans call it,” supplemented Vair. “A continent of ice and snow. We appear to be scattered all over the globe.”

In real time the out-of-body experience had only lasted a few minutes so far . . .

1245 Sunday

Maxie was sprawled out on his easy chair draining the last pot of what was once a tray of beer that had been ordered before dinner. He belched. Directly opposite, The Sphere contemplated the half-empty pint mug in his fist and hiccupped.

“I could go another beer,” stated Harris. “D’you have any in your cabin?”

A round head slewed slowly from side to side as if interacting with the slight roll of the ship. “No.”

“Hmm.” Maxie peered down into his mug as if he expected that somehow the container would replenish itself. With that wishful thought he placed his beer glass on the coffeetable. His face brightened.

“Gus!” he said brightly.

“Wuh - where?” asked The Sphere, pulling himself up to glance towards the door.

"He hasn't touched that case of beer since we delved into it the other night." Harris eased himself up from the chair. "Let's go and ask him for a couple of bottles."

"I dunno," The Sphere replied, dubiously. "That guy's gone a bit strange lately. I know that's normal on tankers but even then it usually takes a couple or three trips before they turn into Christies."

"Maybe he's still awake," speculated Maxie. He arose and opened his door. "C'mon let's nip along and jar him."

The Sphere trooped along in his wake.

Maxie rapped on King's door none too lightly and banged it wide open. The cabin was in total darkness so he switched on the light.

"Hey Gus!" he yelled, and shook the somnolent form beneath the covers. "Have you got any spare beer?"

No answer.

"Hey Gus!" Harris shouted even louder. He shook Angus' shoulder urgently. "Wake up!"

"What's all the bloody racket about?" roared Bob Christie, who happened to be passing. He shoved past Tony's rotund shape and entered the cabin. He eased one of King's eyes open. The pupil was rolled back. The second checked for a pulse rate but couldn't find one. He turned around. "You!" he pointed at The Sphere. "Call the doctor. Tell 'im that he'll have a case in the hospital shortly."

The little fat man scurried off. He jabbed Harris in the chest. "You! Unlash that stretcher along the alleyway and bring it here." Maxie began to edge by him. "On second thoughts, never mind. It'll probably be a bugger trying to get round all those tight corners in our accommodation, far less that damned elevator."

"What are you going to do Sec?"

Black Bob leaned over his friend's bunk and scooped his body up into a fireman's lift. "Gerroutoff my way!" he snarled. Harris jumped back with certain alacrity and stumbled over his original quest: Angus' case of beer. By the time he'd snapped open a bottle, Christie was long gone.

"When did you last contact the rest of them?" asked Vair.

"I communicate with Xaan all the time," replied Leia. "We sometimes meet physically every once in a while but telepathic communication with the others is extremely rare. I believe their environment becomes more and more detrimental to their faculties with the passing eons. They may have lost their powers."

The anaconda stirred and peered around as if orienting itself. Gradually the creature's body straightened out then it slipped back into the clouded water.

"Ah thocht that ye had killed the beast," said Angus.

"We only destroy evil or prevent it from happening," replied Vair.

"Weel, yon beastie looked awfy evil tae me."

"It's a part of nature," said Leia. "The snake hunts to live."

"If ye say so," replied Angus, unconvinced.

"What are you going to do Vair?" asked Leia.

"I need more information about this planet's environs."

"How are you going to do that?" asked Leia.

"My friend Angus here will assist," replied Vair. "But I'll have to get him back to his body first. I don't know how long it will survive without its essence."

"Holy smoke!" exclaimed Angus. "Dae ye mean tae say that Ah could wake up deid in the mornin'?"

"I'll contact you later Leia," said Vair.

They were soaring around the moon again when Angus asked, "How come ye're takin' the long way?"

"I like to gaze upon the earth's only satellite," replied Vair. "Besides, it was the only way to navigate accurately back in the old days." He went on. "The continents were drifting apart at different rates. The only thing that was consistent was the moon so we used it as a GPS."

"Whit's a GPS?"

"A global positioning system," replied Vair. "I have no doubt that you humans will be using something similar in years to come."

"If ye say so," said Angus as they flashed down past a BOAC VC10 passenger airliner.

"Are these aircraft common on earth?" asked Vair.

"No' yet," replied Angus. "But they're quickly startin' tae kill the passenger ship industry." He went on. "These planes can cross the Atlantic Ocean in six or seven hours whereas our fast liners take aboot five days."

"That plane emits a lot of carbon gases," observed Vair. "Multiply that a few million times into the next century and it'll make a big difference to the earth's climate."

"In whit way?"

"You'll find out," Vair said cryptically. "Ah! We're here."

But the bunk was empty. Bomber Harris was chug-a-lugging on a bottle of lager when they descended into the cabin. "Where in the hell am Ah?" queried Angus upon observing the empty bunk.

Just then The Sphere peeped round the chintz curtain. "Have you left any for me?"

Maxie extracted a bottle from the case and lobbed it over. Ball caught it deftly.

"That's my bluidy beer!" screeched Angus' mind.

"How's Gus?"

The Sphere shrugged and reached for an opener. "Dunno," he said. "They're all running about like chickens with their heads cut off down in the Sick Bay."

Referring to King's memory Vair transported them down to the hospital location.

The ship's medical officer had found a faint pulse the engineer's carotid artery but couldn't figure out why his patient was unconsciousness. Nurse Highman had provided a possible reason. On the previous voyage the young fellow had been viciously struck on the head. She had parted his hair to show the doctor the scar. Is it possible, she had asked, if a minuscule amount of blood has leaked and built up pressure inside the patient's scull? The x-ray machine was positioned over the lesion and a picture was taken.

Roentgen rays were buzzing into Angus' cranium when he sat up. "What is going on?" Vair asked.

The doctor and the nurse tried to restrain him but they were too late. The engineer perched on the edge of the Gurney and took in the surroundings. "Why am I here?"

"You were at Death's door," replied the doctor. He brandished the stethoscope dangling from his neck. "Your blood pressure was almost zilch and your pulse was about three beats per minute. Now lie down. I want to take more x-rays of your head."

Angus slid off the Gurney and with his head shaking in refusal said in Vair's voice, "I'm all right, honestly. I feel as fit as a fiddle." He energetically performed knee bends a few times to prove his point.

The doctor remained unconvinced. "Stand still. I want to check your heart again."

The cold diaphragm planed across his bare chest before transferring to the engineer's back. The physician hauled off his stethoscope and stuffed it into the wide pocket of his lab coat. "Damned if I know," he swore with frustration. "Your heart and lungs are normal."

"Then can I get back to my bunk?" asked Vair. "I'm back on watch in less than two hours."

"Oh - all right," conceded the doctor. "But I want you back here when surgery opens."

"Thanks doctor," replied Vair, placing his hand on the examining room door handle.

"Ah-hum," said Nurse Highman, clearing her throat. "Do you plan walking all the way up to the engineers' quarters dressed like that?"

Angus gawked down at his skivvies and contemplated his attire or the lack of it. "Can ye lend me a blanket?" Of course Vair had no such inhibitions.

With a giggle the nurse lifted a folded beige blanket from a shelf and handed it him.

"Thanks," grunted Angus and went out where a worried Christie was waiting for him.

Relief cast a smile on his normally dour countenance. "What happened Angus?"

"Ah dinnae ken, Bob," replied Angus.

"You were probably hitting the sauce too hard," concluded Christie. "All those free wine samples in Madeira would rot anybody's guts."

"Aye - maybe ye're right Bob," acknowledged Angus, stepping over the high coaming into the working alleyway.

The glossy red paint felt cold on his bare feet. When they reached the engineroom entrance Angus once again stepped over a coaming onto the treaded steel catwalk that led down either to the engineroom or to the elevator which went to their accommodation.

"Yeow!" yelled Angus and leapt back into the working alleyway.

"What's the matter?" asked Christie, pressing the elevator's call button.

"Those floorplates are red hot!" exclaimed Angus.

"What do you expect?" replied Christie. "The HP and LP turbines are directly below."

Angus waited for the second to open the lift doors before scooting along the catwalk on tippy-toe. "Whew!" he exhaled, his feet now in contact with the brown linoleum of the elevator floor. "That's better!"

His companion slid the doors shut with a crash and pressed the UP button. A thought entered his mind. He turned and smiled. "Hey Angus, have you ever seen that picture, *Cat on a Hot Tin Roof*?"

“Very funny Bob,” was the sardonic reply.

The young man padded through the blue carpeted passageway of the engineers’ quarters, up the companionway and swept into his cabin. He stopped so abruptly at the sight of Harris and Ball swigging his beer that Christie ran into him, kicking his Achilles heel.

“Aow!” yelped Angus. Hopping around on one foot he cursed the pain, the pilferers and the world in general. “Get oot o’ here ye pair o’ thieves ye!” he howled.

Christie stepped aside to let the culprits scramble past. Peace descended on the cabin and Angus flopped into an easy chair to nurse his ankle. The second sat on the opposite seat and gawked at the injury. “No blood,” he observed. “I’m really sorry I kicked you.”

When the belated apology failed to act as a balm, Christie went to the sink and ran cold water through a wash towel. He squeezed the excess from it and gave to his shipmate. Gingerly the cloth was wrapped around the purple contusion. It was then he noticed that grime, grease and grit marred the sole of his foot. Another torrent of oaths escaped from his lips and he got to his feet. Cautiously he applied some of his weight on the affected foot. Seizing a towel and his flip-flops he told Christie that a shower was in order. Seeing that his friend was beginning to overcome his difficulty the second said that he’d leave him to it and went to his own cabin.

The warm shower relaxed Angus. He had just snuggled in between the sheets when Vair asked, “I’m going to seek out my fellows to find out what became of them. Would you like to come?”

“No thank ye verry much,” emphasized the engineer in his normal brogue. “Ah’ll talk tae ye when ye get back. An’ if ye dinnae get back that’ll be just fine tae.”

Back in the hospital Nurse Highman showed the developed picture of Angus’ cranium. “I’m sorry Doctor, but I only managed to get one snap of that patient’s head before he sat up. I think that there something wrong with the x-ray machine."

The Medical Officer held the negative up to the light. The picture was a dazzling white. "Mmm," he said. "We'd better tell all our staff to make the radiology room off limits until make port. We'll have to get it checked out. We may have a slight radium leak."

CHAPTER SEVENTEEN

Last night at sea

1245 Sunday

The Highland Grill was in full swing celebrating the final night at sea. Champagne flowed like water and the passengers were making the most of it. Bernie was cavorting with a tipsy Denise around the tiny dance floor. They were being jostled back and forth as revellers tried to get the most out of the saxophone player's cool rendition of *Blueberry Hill*.

'It's about time I got Mo to earn his keep,' reflected Bernie, as his wife snuggled into his shoulder. 'Another glass of vino into Denise and she'll go out like a light.'

The music stopped and he half-carried her back to their table. He ordered another bottle of French champagne. Half a glass was enough to initiate Bernie's scheme. Placing his wife's arm over his left shoulder and his right arm around her waist they vacated the nightclub and made their staggering way forward along the starboard side of Boat Deck.

Just a few feet forward of the Highland Grill and a deck above, Angus was snuggled comfortably into his blanket. He had dropped off to sleep shortly after returning from a long soothing shower.

"There's evil afoot," said Vair, sensing Bernie Sneddon's malevolent intention from the deck below.

"Oh, no-o!" moaned Angus. "Ye've got tae let me get some bluidy sleep!

It only took a few seconds of perusal in that vile brain to reveal the complete plan. "Don't worry about it," said Vair. "I'll sort it out."

"That's right hunky-dory wi' me," murmured the drowsy engineer. "Just leave me in peace."

Vair waited until the Sneddons reached their stateroom on Sun Deck forward. Five seconds inside Bernie's mind revealed his dastardly plan. Denise was stripped to her underwear and helped into a nightdress. Her husband threw back the covers on one of the single beds, tucked her in and left, locking the suite's door.

He scanned the Observation Lounge from its entrance, his eyes seeking out Mo Greene among the host of celebrating inebriates. A young woman tottered against him laughing. She planted a toy hat on his head and tooted a kazoo. Streamers were strewn everywhere and balloons were being drunkenly hand-batted back and forth. Spotting Mo at the bar he wove his way through the liquor powered throng.

"There's a woman over there looking for you," Bernie said to the drunk seated next to Greene. The fellow blearily tried to follow the unsteady digit.

"Y'mean that blonde piece with the big boobs?"

"Yeah, that's her."

The guy slipped off the barstool and set off on a zigzag course to the buxom female. Bernie laid the key of his suite on the vacant stool. Bernie and Mo's eyes met and the key was slipped into the latter's jacket pocket.

Vair penetrated the drunken torpor of Denise's mind. She sat up and woozily reached into the top drawer of the night table between the pair of single beds. She turned on the night light before fumbling for a hi-lighter yellow marker and the envelope containing the travel insurance contract. She turned to the page entailing the double indemnity clause, circled it, and collapsed on top of her bed.

Not long after Mo crept into the stateroom. Silently he crossed over to the bedroom and went inside. Denise lay on her back softly snoring. From Bernie's bed he retrieved a fluffy pillow when his eye happened to fall on the hi-lit clause in the insurance policy. It seemed to jump up at him from the bright penumbra of the bedside lamp. He placed the pillow aside and began to read.

"The bastard!" he cursed in a whisper. "The lying bastard! He said that she was only worth thirty grand to him dead. And all the time he knew that he was going to get one hundred and twenty-five thousand quid." Mo could feel his blood pressure rising in anger. "And the rotten get just offered me a miserable ten per cent."

Greene conveniently forgot about the cost of the free cruise plus his spending money. He flipped onto the next page. "Holy shit - double indemnity! Quarter of a million quid!" By now his wrath was getting out of control. "Cool it Mo," he said to himself. He recalled the anger control sessions in stir. The prison psychoanalyst thought that his coaching had cured Greene of his fiery temperament but instead his patient had found that revenge served cold was much more satisfying. He drew a few deep breaths and slowly he calmed down. "I'm going to get at least half out of that cheapskate or he goes over the wall." He gazed down at the woman. "No point bumping her off until the contract is resolved."

He left the stateroom, locked the door, and headed back to the Observation Lounge. In the elevator he searched his pockets and found a pen stub. On a ten-shilling note he printed seven words: MEET ME AT BACK OF BOAT NOW! He wrapped the key holder in the banknote.

The lounge was even busier than before and he had to squeeze through the crowd to reach the bar. Sliding alongside Sneddon, he ordered a scotch on the rocks. The drink was served after a few minutes. Bernie watched him pay before knocking the drink back in one swallow. He caught Green's eye hoping for some kind of acknowledgment that the deed had been done. Instead the would-be murderer glanced meaningfully at his left hand which was resting on the bar top. Bernie looked down and the hand lifted revealing the ten shilling note and key holder. His own hand concealed the banknote instantly. When Greene left, he waited momentarily before reading the message. He downed his drink and made his way aft.

Greene was standing by the jackstaff at the extreme stern of the ship. Above his head the Blue Duster fluttered anxiously if it was trying to take wing over the turbulent monochromic wake. Nervously he rapped the ship's rail with his fingers. He pushed up the left cuff of his jacket and turned the face of his wristwatch to the nearest light, a glimmering lamp standard about four yards away. Just after two o'clock.

Bernie came clumping along B Deck towards him. "Is she dead?"

Greene countered this question with a single phrase. "Double indemnity." Had it been light enough, he would saw Sneddon's face turn pale immediately. "I want half."

"Ok" replied Bernie, too readily. "Did you kill my wife?"

Mo's eyes squinted up at him. 'This bastard's too bloody glib for my tastes,' he thought angrily, but aloud answered: "Yes."

"Good," responded a smiling Sneddon. He handed Mo a thick envelope before turning away.

Greene gaped at it and asked, "What in the hell is this?"

"Twelve and a half thousand pounds," replied Sneddon. "Our contract is paid in full."

"But you just agreed to half - one hundred and twenty-five thousand quid!"

Casually Bernie replied, "That was before I knew that Denise dead."

Instead of enlightening him that his wife was only dead drunk, Mo saw red and before either of them knew what was happening, his muscular hands had encircled Bernie's neck. The victim responded by grabbing his assailant's wrists but with little effect. He emulated his antagonist's grip with little effect because Mo practically had no neck but what he did have was solid muscle. They grappled and pushed until the small of Bernie's back was hard up against the ship's teak handrail. Mo tried to push him overboard but it was almost impossible because of the height difference between them.

Eddie Buchanan nipped out on the arse end for a quick puff. The sounds he heard were the wash of the ship passing through the water at twenty knots, the wind thrumming through the shrouds, the flapping Blue Ensign, and - what was that? He peered further aft and in the feeble light saw what looked like two passengers wrestling.

Mo's thumbs were relentlessly crushing his opponent's Adam's apple. He felt his leg come against one of the huge bollards which was used to secure the vessel's hawsers when in port. Gradually he managed to get one foot on top of it - then the other. Now he could get the purchase necessary to heave Sneddon into the sea. With a mighty thrust he did just that but Bernie had managed to secure a tight grip of Greene's collar and tie. Down, down, down, they both toppled into the violent wake.

"Christ!" swore Eddie, tossing his cigarette butt aside. He rushed to the point where the two went over and peered down into the boiling wake. Nothing. Only the gush of swirling energy marked their passing. Buchanan scooted for'ard, taking the steps to A Deck two at a time.

He barged into the a/c room startling the occupants, Kevin Cunningham and Marty Wilton. Dave Hedges was out doing his rounds.

"What's up Eddie?" asked Marty. Cunningham was on the phone.

Clinging to the desk for support Eddie wheezed out, "Man overboard."

"No shite?" replied Marty just as the engineer hung up.

"Try and calm down Eddie," soothed Kevin, offering the rating one of his Senior Service cigarettes. "And tell us what happened."

Buchanan took the smoke and leaned towards the engineer as he reached out with his Zippo lighter. He sucked in the smoke and went into a spasm of coughing. Kevin took a drag of his own cigarette and exhaled easily. “They’re not that strong,” he chided.

Gradually Eddie’s convulsions settled and he related his experience.

“Christ!” exclaimed Cunningham and reached for the phone. “Hello Rona? Get me the bridge please.”

The ship came about and steamed up her wake, slowing down as she went. The *Dally* got back up to full revs after it was determined that the entry point had been reached and passed without result. Radio signals went out to vessels in the vicinity to look out for two men in the water. If one or both men had survived the turbulence of the liner’s wake then there was a good chance of being picked up. Maritime traffic would gradually become heavier as the cruise liner steamed into the busy English Channel.

Captain Fawcett, after having extracted himself from a warm comfortable bunk and an even warmer and more comfortable blonde, ordered that the passengers be tallied to find out who was missing. It would be a difficult task he well knew because half of his cargo was living it up in the various bars throughout the ship while the other half would be lying dead drunk in their cabins, quite unable to answer their stewards’ queries. It was hoped that the Radar would continue to operate perfectly and thus avoid collisions with freighters, tankers, icebergs, whatever . . .

0340 Sunday

It seemed as if he’d only closed his eyes for a moment when Jeffries, the twelve-to-four storekeeper switched on his cabin light to waken him for his watch. “It’s time to go on watch, Mister King.”

“Aye - ok. Thanks Harry.”

His cabin felt a bit cooler. A quick wash and shave refreshed him and he dressed into his number ones. The doeskin jacket and trousers felt much warmer and definitely much more comfortable than his whites.

Bob Christie glanced up at him as he entered the mess. “You’re looking much better now Mister King.”

MacKay, the senior second-of-the-watch, placed his cup of coffee and dabbed his lips. “Ah, Mister King, welcome back to the world of the living. Mister Christie here tells me that you were chappin’ on Auld Nick’s gate.” There was a hint of humour in his lilt for he hailed from the so-called Realm of Fife.

The junior’s neck flushed. “Thank ye Mister MacKay. But it wisnae a’ that bad. It looked worse than it was.”

“Aye,” agreed MacKay. “That Portugee red biddy will do that to a man. You should stick to the *uisge beatha*, Mister.”

“Aye Mister MacKay,” acknowledged Angus, and moved forward to join Terry, Don, and Charlie.

“What’s this we’ve hearing about you, Gus?” asked Don.

“Och, it’s bugger a’!” countered Angus, while considering the two questionable sandwiches stalking each other on the dinner plate in the middle of the table. “Bob Christie got a bit anxious because Ah was in a real deep sleep.”

“Is that right?” asked Terry.

Wheelkey, seated across the mess with Steamboat and Taffy, overheard the three juniors. As usual, his envy of King’s physical attribute inspired a comment. “Hey Gus, just admit that you got a hardon that lasted too long and kept the blood away from your brain.”

“Piss aff!” hissed King, just as a steward came to the table with a platter of fresh sandwiches. Perceiving that the fellow was about to turn away Angus urged, “No, no, no’ *you*. Just put them doon there, if ye please.”

The steward switched plates and rambled away. A flurry of hands grabbed this newly made provender.

"Ooh!" Don squeaked with delight. "Ham and cheese!" and reached for the Branston Pickle.

Having finished their repast the boiler room engineers rose from their table, ready to go below. Wheelkey stepped over to where the juniors sat. Angus was just about to sink his teeth into his fourth sandwich. "Here," he said. "I thought that you were on a rabbit-food diet."

A couple of lettuce leaves, the remnants of a tomato salad, languished in a pool of vinaigrette at the bottom of a porcelain bowl. Angus rescued them from drowning and mounted them as a third layer to his ham and cheese. Slapping on the lid of white bread, he chomped into his sandwich. "Satisfied - Wilberforce?" he mumbled.

Keyes' face darkened at hearing that label bandied aloud in company. He wrongly believed that very few of his fellow engineers were aware of his hated given name. He shrugged it off before trooping out with his companions. Angus proceeded to munch away, extremely pleased that Vair was roaming the world at large and not curbing his yen for meat.

The reliefs were intrigued with the excitement that had developed during the previous watch. It was weird that no one had mentioned it in the engineers' mess. Eddie Buchanan was pissed off because he now had to report to the bridge and be interrogated by Hodgkin. Angus mentally commiserated with him for he had run afoul with the fourth mate on occasion.

In terse phrases the a/c log book painfully related the busy time the twelve-to-four watch had. Unstable breezes had caused public room and cabin temperatures to fluctuate. In particular, the Highland Grill had been a bit of a nuisance until it closed during the previous hour. Inebriated passengers were complaining that their cabins were either too hot or too cold. Eddie and Marty couldn't escape from their duties quick enough when Gerry and Jack relieved them.

After listening to Dave's woes Angus went out on the after deck to take the dry and wet temperatures of outside air. The night sky was an inverted bowl of blackness pierced with needlepoints of silver. The sea sweeping past below him carried low undulating ridges of shadow which blossomed into dark yellow froth when they hit the wake. In the glimmer of a ship's light the thermometers divulged their readings, 68/67° Fahrenheit. Quite comfortable, he thought, and then he started to shiver.

"For pity's sake, let's get back inside out of the cold," admonished Vair.

"Ah kinda hoped that ye'd buggered aff for guid."

"I've still got a few things for you to do first," he was told.

"Och - bluidy likely," scowled Angus. "Like whit?"

"Where do humans store their knowledge if not in their minds?"

The engineer considered for a moment before answering. "In great libraries an' museums, Ah suppose."

"On board this vessel?"

"Och, no-o," drawled Angus. "A' yon literature are stored in grand buildin's in great big cities like London, Paris, New York - an' maybe Glesga." He mentioned the latter as an afterthought. He opened a door and stepped over the coaming. "There's fower libraries oan board this ship that Ah ken o'." He went on to clarify those book sanctuaries while walking for'ard. "First, Second an' Tourist Classes have a' got one each. An' so dae we - the engineers Ah mean. Ah would imagine that the deckies have got one tae but Ah wouldnae hae a clue o' where it might be. Ah would think that the First Class Library has got the best stock o' books. We'll be gaun in there later durin' the course o' my roonds."

"We're going there now."

"Weel, there's a whole lot o' public rooms that are mair important tae check than the library."

"Not anymore."

When the engineer reached the first pantry some force impelled him to ascend the stairs and out onto the port passageway on Main Deck. He set a course for the First Class Travel Bureau and the four passenger lifts and entered the port inboard elevator and thumbed the up button.

At that time in the morning the elegant shopping arcade on Prom Deck was completely desolated. Nearby was the First Class Library. The room was so enormous it reminded Angus of the great hall in Kirkton House, an imposing edifice in his home town of Carluke. The odds that the library's one hundred square yard area met that of Kirkton Hall's were moot. The reading room's ceiling of twelve feet six inches was comparable with many large houses in Britain. The instant he stepped onto the Wilton carpet, its deep pile of mixed grey, slate-blue and brown bestowed a restful feeling of sanctuary.

The bulkheads (how could such magnificent walls panelled in golden leather pigskin be called mere bulkheads?) strangled sound before it reached the delicate cochleas of the rich and famous. The characteristic creaking normally heard in other parts of the vessel met doom at this library's portals. Here in a soothing atmosphere of tranquillity surrounded by pastel hues of cream and brown, a person might while the hours away in the congenial company of thousands of books. As well as being aesthetic accompaniments soft velvet curtains could suffocate any sound might elude the pigskin bulkheads.

Luxurious settees and easy chairs, sheathed in grey and brown leather to match the carpet, were abundant so that a reader might feel at ease. Tables too abounded, including one with an expansive leather top upon which were tidily arrayed newspapers, magazines and other journals. The librarian's table was vacant, no doubt slumbering in her bunk.

A medley of alcoves embraced the bookcases, each rendering its own light, each supplemented by concealed trough lighting on the deckhead. Angus ignored the fiction and poetry sections and sought out the non-fiction category. Not knowing exactly what Vair was seeking he reached up to a bookshelf, raised the glass panel which disappeared into the upper partition of the shelf and took down a tome.

Problems of the Future by Samuel Laing read Angus surveying its spine. “Weel, it’s a start,” he sighed. He placed the book on a nearby table and pulled up a chair. He opened the cover and leafed through to the prologue. “Oh God!” he muttered. “It’s one o’ yon books wi’ fine print.”

He rested his finger on the first line and began to read.

“Turn the page,” ordered Vair.

Angus shrugged and turned the page.

“Again.”

“Again.”

“Again.”

Presently Angus came to the tome’s end and closed the cover, the edition seemingly read in less than a minute. It was returned to its shelf and another book took its place. And another, and another, and another. Before long, every nonfiction book had been scrutinized. The newspapers and journals received short shrift. ‘Just as weel,” he thought for his fingers were hurting like hell.

“You know,” concluded Vair. “A lot of your so-called peaceful religions are extremely vicious: war, conquest, various forms of murder including genocide, theft, pederasty, torture, child abuse, just to name a few. In fact they’ve broken every commandment in their holy books.” Vair shook Angus’ head sorrowfully. “Where’s the next library?”

“The engineers’ wardroom - next deck up,” replied Angus. “But there’s no’ much in it.”

“Lead on.”

Hamish Emsworth was the ship’s boilermaker, a job that entailed inspecting the innards of boilers on a regular basis. In port he would liaison with contractors who did the repairs necessary to keep the boilers in good running order. Emsworth was a soft-spoken Aberdonian whose duties at sea entailed watchkeeping in 2 BR, usually on the eight-to-twelve. On this particular night the engineer had trouble sleeping for he was worried about his imminent examination for his second's ticket in Southampton.

Along with the mishmash of comic books that abounded in the engineers' library there was a goodly supply of first rate novels. But Hamish had shunned them and had chosen instead a tome from 1914: John Tod's and W. C. McGibbon's *Marine Engineers' Board Of Trade Examinations*. The moment Angus entered the wardroom irritation marred his face. His eyes squinted up from his study as he watched this a/c wallah ripple through the pages of the sparse collection of nonfiction books. Before long he became aware of a presence peering over his shoulder. "What do *you* want?"

A booming commanding voice said. "I want to read your book."

Emsworth's seldom use of foul language had been noted by fellow Scots. Glaswegians, in particular, thought that he talked a bit too posh for their liking. But on this early morning the boilermaker showed that he could be just as abrasive as the best of them. "No - bugger off!" he vehemently snapped.

Fingers of steel grasped his left shoulder. Hamish tried to get up but he was firmly anchored to his easy chair.

"I want to look at your book."

Painfully he held the tome up to the clutching digits which released instantly. Tender massage gradually allowed blood to flow back into the arteries that served his shoulder. Above his head he could hear pages riffling and before long the book fell back into his lap. "Couldn't find what you were looking for - eh?" he said, watching Angus head for the wardroom door.

The a/c engineer opened the door and glanced back. Again the hollow voice spoke. "Actually there was some information in that book that was useful to me."

"Huh!" Emsworth grunted in disbelief. "Nobody but nobody could read a book that fast.

"I did."

The boilermaker scoffed in disbelief. He opened the book randomly and began reading aloud. "*Which burns faster, Newcastle coal or Welsh coal? Which is the flaming coal? Which makes more smoke?*"

"That is Question Number 180 in *Elementary Questions with Answers Including Notes and Verbals. Answer. Newcastle and Scotch coal burn much faster than Welsh, but do not give out such an intense local heat. With Welsh coal there is little or no flame, and very little smoke.*"

Emsworth's jaw dropped for his junior's response came back verbatim. Not only that, Vair recommenced unasked: "*Note. - Smoke in the funnel consists principally of the nitrogen liberated from the air during combustion, carbon in fine particles, carbonic acid, carbonic oxide, and steam which is formed from the hydrogen during the progress of combustion. Coal is composed of carbon, hydrogen, sulphur, oxygen, nitrogen, and ash; the first being the principal supporter of combustion in the furnaces of a boiler. Welsh coal contains about 85 to 90 per cent. carbon, 4 to 5 per cent hydrogen, .75 to 1.5 per cent. sulphur, 1 to 2 per cent.nitrogen and oxygen, 3 to 5 per cent. ash, etc.; Newcastle and Scotch coal having a smaller percentage of carbon and a larger percentage of oxygen, nitrogen, and ash. If the two words, NO CASH, be taken as a convenient reminder of the component parts, each letter being the initial of the various substances of which coal is composed. Air is composed of two elements - oxygen and nitrogen, the former being required to support combustion, and in so doing it parts with the nitrogen. The relative weights are 23 of oxygen and 77 of nitrogen. In practice, 24 lbs. of air are required to 1 lb. of fuel for perfect combustion. Water $H2O$ = 8 of oxygen and 1 of hydrogen by weight.See also Note to Question 33.*

"Do you wish me to quote that note too?" Angus' strange accent-free voice had Emsworth completely dumfounded. Frantically he thumbed back the pages seeking Question 33.

"It's on Page 29," Vair said helpfully and began quoting: *Note. - As before explained 24 lbs. or 300 cubic feet of air is required in practice for each lb. of coal burned, this forms what is commonly known as carbonic-acid gas (CO2) or perfect combustion, when a less quantity of air is admitted carbonic-oxide gas (CO) is formed, which is imperfect combustion. 1 lb. of carbonic-acid gas gives out roughly three times the heat obtained from 1 lb. of carbonic-oxide gas. Should, however, carbonic-oxide gas be formed in the furnace and combustion chamber, when it reaches the top of the funnel it will combine with a further supply of air and form carbonic-acid gas and burst into flame providing the temperature of the unburnt gases is high enough, so causing a great loss of heat, not to mention injury to funnel plating.*

Leaving Emsworth absolutely astounded in that a second tripper should be well-versed in coal combustion. Probably the only coal burner the second tripper had ever seen would've been an old paddle steamer puffing on the Clyde. Closing the door behind him Angus asked Vair if he wanted to go to the Cabin Class Library.

Vair shook Angus' head. "No," he replied. "What you, we, just quoted to your friend was what I needed all in a nutshell."

"Ah dinnae understand."

"Where do you suppose all those gases go after they leave your funnels?"

"Dissipates intae the atmosphere, Ah suppose."

"True," conceded Vair. "But they don't just vanish. They mingle in the stratosphere and disrupt the ozone layer."

"Whit's the ozone layer?" asked Angus.

"It protects life on earth from some of the harmful light rays emitted from your sun."

Angus was none the wiser. He had come to accept that any knowledge gleaned from his brain travelled along a one-way street. Vair told him bugger all. Exasperated he asked, "How does this affect me?"

"Imagine all that smoke and gases leaving your funnels multiplied by thousand upon thousand of ships, factories, and those millions of machines you call automobiles. Add on the estimated world population growth, what do you suppose the earth's climate would be like in - say - sixty of your years."

Angus hadn't the faintest idea but just said, "Ah guess there will be an awfy lot o' smoggy days. There's nothin' Ah can dae aboot it anyway. Besides, Ah'll probably be deid by then."

"No, you won't," prophesied Vair.

CHAPTER EIGHTEEN

Beached!

Gerry recalls:

It was around six thirty when Mister King, Jack, and I were enjoying our morning kye and discussing the weird murder/suicide from the previous evening when Mister Travers walked in. “Hey Gerry,” he said. “We’ll be passing your home island in a little while. Why don’t you go out on deck and take a gander?”

“It’s aboot time Ah took a swing,” said Mister King, wielding his Twaddle. “Ah’ll come oot oan deck wi’ ye.”

So we sauntered aft and went out onto the open section of A Deck. The early morning twilight allowed us to view the darkened coast lurking on the southwest corner of Guernsey. The stalwart lighthouse on Gull Rock winked coyly at us every now and then, its salutary beam swept across the ocean like a burnished scythe to warn unsuspecting vessels to shun those perilous environs. Although it was cool out of deck, mid-forties as I recall, it appeared reasonably comfortable to me even though I was simply dressed in my long sleeved denim shirt and jeans. Mister King’s doeskin uniform was much more compatible in that situation yet he was shivering like a cat shitting a lemon sole skeleton backwards. And his voice with its deep cavernous resonance became even more sinister yet curiously remained dignified.

“Gerry, in a few moments I’ll need you to do something for me.” He said it in that odd booming voice.

“What’s that Mister King?” I asked with a sinking feeling.

Just then Miss Barrie with a pink cotton dressing gown over her night apparel and carrying a leather shoulder bag, ghosted down the companionway from Main Deck. Her eyes were distant as if she was sleepwalking. She proffered the satchel to me. I took it by the strap and its unexpected weight almost caused me to drop it onto the deck. Then without a word the woman ascended the ladder and disappeared.

"Where are we now Gerry?" Mister King asked in proper Queen's English.

I squinted at the shadowed island. About three miles from us Pleinmont Point was on our starboard beam. As the ship continued to steam steadily north the coastline gradually fell away. Guernsey is roughly shaped like a right-angled triangle, its hypotenuse facing the Atlantic Ocean. Even so faint lights could be discerned on the darkened shore. Cottages along the coastal road of Rocquaine Bay were stirring from slumber.

The upended flowerpot called the Maritime Museum at Fort Grey was still in darkness as was the nearby hotel and hamlet of L'Erée. Sarnian lamps were yawning on ready to face a new day. Frequently those lights were blanked out by the ominous shadows of Nipple Rock, Black Rock and Haute Canée. And somewhere in between, numerous half-hidden rocks foamed like mad dogs eagerly waiting to sink their granite teeth into some trusting vessel.

Mister King nodded when I told him that Perelle Bay and Vazon Bay probably lay directly abeam out there in the gloom. We were approaching Cobo Bay when Mister King's eyes glazed over much in the same manner as Miss Barrie's had a little earlier.

Down in the engineroom a peculiar situation was beginning to develop. On the port side of the shaft tunnel just aft of Number 13 watertight door, Terry Baker was pumping up the liner's fire sprinkler. It was a long boring task. The reservoir for the sprinkler system was an upright cylindrical tank which was half full of water. The upper half of this large vessel was charged with compressed air. In the event of a sprinkler being activated somewhere aboard ship, the compressed air would maintain a steady supply of water to quench any fire.

Over a period of time tiny leaks in the network tended to cause a pressure drop. Nowadays sensors automatically maintain the water pressure in sprinkler systems. But forty-odd years ago the most junior engineer-of-the-watch, namely the floater, had the tedious duty to run that dinky rinky-dink air compressor until the pressure was back to standard. Much to Terry's chagrin, The Leprechaun was nowhere to be found. So he waited impatiently in the dimly lit tunnel listening to the monotonous drone of the port drive shaft and the rattling clatter of the old piston pump. "I'm going to strangle that little get," he thought aloud.

On the starboard side of the tunnel just by the ballast pump that serviced the Cabin Class Swimming Pool Peter Deery, aka The Leprechaun, was preaching hellfire and sin to a couple of ratings, a sermon demanding repentance from the pitfalls of drink and fallen women. Ronnie Livingstone was a bit nervous about being absent from his duties in the engineroom, especially when that mad second engineer Christie was on the rampage. But then he was always like that. But this Deery guy was an officer so if anyone was going to be in trouble it would be him. Still, one could never tell for sure where Christie was concerned . . .

Alec Russell, the donkeyman who looked after the CO2 refrigeration room, was a man dedicated to cooling brine. If he'd hadn't have left his post to take a piss he'd never run into this little fart. Now he had to stand here and take all this guff. If the walking second happened by and noticed that the brine room was empty Russell would be demoted to work with Tinker. Meanwhile this little bastard was making more noise that the bloody propeller shaft.

On the engineroom manoeuvring platform Black Bob Christie's chagrin was a bit stronger than Terry's. In fact he was flaming mad after coming across a puddle of lubricating oil on the top step of the platform's starboard ladder. For safety's sake another person might have wiped it up and forgotten about the matter. But not Black Bob he stormed back and forth across the starting platform bawling and screaming for the culprit's guts.

Deep down aft in the tiller flat Les Dolan was pouring himself a cup of coffee from the little percolator that had mysteriously emigrated from a pantry on B Deck. He had just finished polishing the brass work on the Sperry-Rand servos. Now those gauges, valves and pipes gleamed just like the rest of the steering gear's equipment. The incessant noise from the servos and the main hydraulic pumps didn't bother him. Neither did the hunting of the great rams that turned the 140-ton rudder nor the constant rumbling of the twin propellers just outside of the 3/4" thick hull.

Les sprawled out on a bench, his back against the white painted hull and took a sip. Suddenly his eyes went glassy and he sat up, his spine ramrod stiff. He laid the cup down on the bench, rose to his feet, and with a zombie-like gait lurched reluctantly to the main switches for the servomotors. With two snap thunks he isolated the units.

Up front in the darkened wheelhouse the quartermaster was jolted from a mundane exercise. "The helm's not answering Mister Llewellyn."

The second mate peeked up from the shielded radar monitor. "Ok Briers, change over to the port telemotor. I'll call down to the tiller flat."

He moved to a bank of phones mounted on the after bulkhead and picked up the solitary receiver. He flipped a switch and an orange glow announced Steering Ge - the last two letters had been scratched out since time immemorial. He pressed the buzzer and waited . . .

In Number Three Stokehold two firemen/trimmers were arguing about religion again. The two shipmates had imbibed heavily at the Pig and Whistle during the previous evening and were a bit worse for wear with only a few hours of kip.

Pat Faughnan and Sean Riordan were fast friends since they both met at the Seamen's Pool in Liverpool. Normally religion, colour, and creed make little difference to any ship's crew members, the philosophy being that they were all in the same boat together. Pat and Sean's case was different since the former's family came from Eire and therefore Church of Rome. The latter's family however was steeped in the Orange lore of the six counties of Northern Ireland. The recent years both families had immigrated to the capital of Ireland: Liverpool so that Sean and Pat had grown up as Scousers.

"Jeezus Chree-ist!"

Pat had overhead his buddy take The Lord's Name in vain and set about to put him straight. The fact that Sean had burned the back of his hand for not paying attention when checking the fires was insufficient reason for such blasphemy. And so unnoticed by Keyes, 3BR's watchkeeper the two went at it hammer and tongs albeit verbally.

Dolon slid in the steel pin that linked the main hydraulic units to the ship's great wheel that manually substituted for the servos and consequently overrode the wheelhouse helm. Ignoring the binnacle directly in front of him Les stared ahead as if he could see through nineteen watertight bulkheads and the vessel's steel bow. Suddenly he spun the wheel hard to starboard and behind him the great rams heaved against the rudder post yoke in obedience.

Gerry recalls:

Quite suddenly the ship veered hard to starboard. We couldn't see it from where we were standing but directly ahead was Saline Bay and a plethora of granite outcrops lay between us and the shore. Living in the Parish of Castel, I'd come to know these waters very well. My Dad and me spent many weekends fishing around this area looking for ormers. The waters were treacherous with undercurrents and razor-sharp rocks.

"We're changing course!" Briers yelled unnecessarily for the second mate had to brace his body to overcome the sudden veering of the ship.

At the very front of the wheelhouse a bridge boy slithered down the freshly scrubbed deck to knock over a pail of water which drenched his shipmate who was soogying by the starboard side.

"Stop both engines!"

Both boys leapt to their feet and swung the telegraph handles to STOP.

"Double ring full astern!" ordered Llewellyn and reaching for a phone said, "I'm going to call the Captain."

Just then Captain Fawcett barged barefooted into the wheelhouse with one arm tucked in the sleeve of his bus driver's jacket, the residue streaming aft like a brass-buttoned banner. He wore striped pyjama bottoms. "What in the bloody hell is going on?"

Llewellyn turned from his view of the bows and the impending disaster that lay beyond and reported to his skipper.

"A few minutes after we lost our steering the rudder went hard over to starboard all by itself. I've rung down double full astern on the telegraphs but so far they haven't acknowledged. Neither the tiller flat nor the engineroom will pick up the phone."

The captain padded over to the wheelhouse windows and stared out, his fingers unconsciously rapping a wooden message for help on the varnished teak sill. Just below the horizon a parsimonious sun was debating on whether or not it should impart a few of its benevolent rays on the Bailiwick of Guernsey.

In the engineroom Christie heard a clatter of steel directly below him. He stopped his bellowing and leaned over the handrail. Nothing. Exasperated he spun on heel and stared across the width of the platform, his back to the starboard ladder. The ship's intense swerve impelled him to step back down onto the top tread of the ladder - and the puddle of oil. Failing to grab the handrail in time, the vindictive second tumbled head over heels down the steps - all twelve of them - to lay at the bottom quite unconscious with a broken leg and collarbone.

The clatter of steel that Christie heard had been Charlie Everton dropping his two-gallon fanny of kye on the floorplates, a signal to his shipmate Ronnie that it was time for smoko. When Livingston didn't show up the rating heaved his husky frame up the port ladder to serve the engineers. Just as he reached the starting platform both telegraphs began to clamour, their green indicator needles swinging to FULL ASTERN. To emphasize their urgency the needles swept back and forth across the telegraph faces before coming to a jolting halt on FULL ASTERN.

On ships at sea double ringing engineroom telegraphs are an unspoken but drastic communiqué from the bridge that they have screwed up and have to back away from imminent danger as soon as possible - preferably before the vessel runs into something solid.

Charlie was in sole command of the engineroom and as a lowly bilgediver he hadn't the faintest idea on what to do. However he recalled an incident when sitting in the back of his grandfather's car when the old chap keeled over at the wheel. His dad had simply leaned over from the front passenger seat and turned off the ignition. The vehicle safety rolled to a stop and Grandfather was whisked off to the hospital. So, thought Charlie, that's what I must do - turn off the ignition.

But steamships don't have an ignition switch so Charlie's eyes panned around the myriad gauges, valve wheels, rev counters and other curious items which have proven to be helpful to ships' engineers over the years. His hazel-brown eyes came to rest on the boiler room telegraph. FULL, it urgently announced. He ambled over to it and placed a grimy hand on the burnished handle. Now, thought Charlie, if I swing this thingummy over to STOP that should tell the engineers in 2 BR and 3 BR to extinguish some fires. He knew from previous voyages that only one fire was required on every boiler when the ship was stopped or travelling at dead slow. But then, Charlie considered, the engines might not stop fast enough to keep the bridge happy.

A mere step to his right awaited a certain meticulously polished lever. Directly behind this revered handle a brass plate, also agleam from the habitual attributes of Brasso and elbow grease, told one who might care to read the poignant red-lettered notice: **Warning! Do not activate this lever!**

If the main engines' lubrication tank levels became too low, a limit switch would trigger off loud bells, klaxons and flashing red lights to inform the engineer on watch that irrefutable disaster would visit his engineroom unless he corrected those levels promptly. If one was too slow to react, a safety mechanism instantly closed the main steam stop valves thus immobilizing the engines. It was hoped by the ship's designers that such a desperate action would prevent damage to critical turbine and gear transmission bearings.

This then was the lever Charlie was totally focussed on. With a savage shove he threw it over and all hell broke loose!

In the upper regions of the engineroom were two large steam valves termed the bulkhead or main stops. These valves were the main shutoff from the boiler manifold lines to the engineroom. When opened, as they always were at sea, these valves delivered superheated steam to the main engine manoeuvring valves directly below. Since it took quite some time to manually close those valves, some means had to be adopted so steam could be cut quickly thus prevent engine damage. The automatic isolation mechanisms did just that. They shut off the main steam supply in a trice.

The minute hand of the ship's clock was clawing its weary way toward the final hour of the watch when stokehold engineers could blearily look forward to a few hours of zizz. After the bridge wallahs, Taffy Morgan and Will Keyes were among the first ship's officers to find out that there might be trouble afloat. When the ship veered, the sudden change in boiler gauge glass levels should have warned them because C and D steam drums filled up with feed water while A and E steam drums had emptied. When the vessel's heading steadied all levels went back to normal - until Charlie Everton closed the bulkhead stops.

In 3BR a hubbub of angry voices made Keyes think that not all was well in his steaming fiefdom. He sauntered towards the source of disturbance. "All right, break it up there and get back to work!"

Still up tight Pat stood his ground to ask, "Mister Keyes do you believe in our Saviour, the Lord Jesus Christ?"

At that instant, right out of the blue, the boiler steam had nowhere to go except up through the boiler safety valves. B3 boiler's relief valve just happened to be set a couple of pounds per square-inch lower so with a whoosh it lifted first.

"*Not right now*!" bellowed Wheelkey and made a beeline for the control console. "Shut off all those God damned fires right now!"

Within seconds another eleven whooshes followed suit and a cacophony sounding like twelve express trains roared up both funnels into the growing dawn . . .

Not many passengers were awakened by the cacophony although the most sober were preparing for breakfast or already in the restaurants. But a big boobed blonde with a bubble-cut was startled from her beauty slumber. She jumped out of bed and hurried forward to complain.

In the Main Generator Room John MacKay was chatting with Dick Currie, the MGR watchkeeper. The sudden buildup of steam pressure was seeking further means of escape other than the boilers' relief valves. It cleverly found out that turbogenerators could spin faster if their governors were overridden. Light bulbs beamed a radiance rarely seen by the denizens who haunted the machinery spaces. Up on the mezzanine above the runaway turbogenerators Artie Berwick was scooting back and forth in front of the main switchboard throwing in electrical breakers almost as fast as they were tripping out.

Down in the tunnel the drone of the revolving shafts lessened noticeably. Terry shut down the sprinkler pumps made tracks for the engineroom. The Leprechaun, totally ignorant of the slowing tempo from the propeller shafts, was warming up to the seven deadly sins. The first, Lust, had piqued the interest of the ratings. In spite of this the donkeyman, a creature of habit, always kept an attuned ear to his beloved CO2 compressors. They perked up and caught a fleeting change of rhythm that persuaded him to walk away.

Terry reached the engineroom platform at the same time as the walking second. Both engine telegraphs were belatedly answered and their incessant clamour stilled. But momentum was still moving the ship ahead at a disturbing rate of knots.

Saline Bay was drawing closer and closer. Captain Fawcett fretted as he grasped the wheelhouse windowsill like reins that could haul his vessel back from certain disaster. Malky

Galbraith, the bosun, showed up with four seamen. All four of them were sent away as messengers to the after docking bridge, the chief engineer, the engineroom and the tiller flat. Using his binoculars he could see the concrete observation post on Grande Rocques over on his port bow. It had been built when the Germans occupied the Channel Islands during WWII.

On his right a massive outcrop of rock formed a causeway that separated Saline Bay from Cobo Bay. But directly between him and the beach numerous rock shoals waited and he knew that colliding with any one of them might cause his command to founder. There, less than a cable ahead, surf was exploding into spume. Perceptibly the bows edged away from that rock. It was if the ship was steering by itself!

MacKay chased Terry up to reset the triggers so that the bulkhead stops could be reopened. In the meantime Charlie was directed to close the ahead manoeuvring on the starboard while the second closed port valve. Then the two men opened the astern master valves and waited until the main stops were open. By the time Terry had returned to the platform the twelve-to-four engineers who were the standby watch were on the scene ready to take over the wheels.

When the astern turbines eventually received steam to stop the propellers before going in reverse, their greed for power emptied the boilers. Once again engineers and firemen were madly dashing around their respective stokeholds flashing up fires trying to keep up with this new demand for steam.

It is widely accepted that the Scottish engineer James Watt invented the steam engine. This is a fallacy. Mister Watt actually improved the process. The ancient steam engines exhausted to atmosphere much like the railway engines before the age of diesel. He adapted the vacuum in a condenser to return the steam to its original state - distilled water which was pumped back to the boiler, completing the circuit.

Engineers term this the closed feed system. Certain engineers term it a vicious bloody circle.

Long before Sir Isaac Newton munched on his gravity-fallen pippin he came up with his famous Third Law of Motion: *for every action there is an equal and opposite reaction*. This profound dictum was proven to be so true when it occurred to Terry that the Weir's turbo-feed pumps were no longer delivering water to the boilers for they had cut out when the main stops had closed in great haste. He scrambled down the starboard ladder to get them going again.

For a moment he debated on whether to help the stricken Christie or strive towards his objective. Not a good idea, he reasoned briefly. If he revived the second before starting the feed pumps, Black Bob would ream him out so thoroughly that he'd need stern gland packing for his backside to dump normal sized turds. Instead he stepped over the unconscious engineer and went about his duties.

Topside, the ship's whistles blasted out mournful warnings in bass A to warn any vessels that might crazy enough to be cruising between the reefs and skerries that were part of the Sarnian seascape.

Llewellyn stared myopically at the prop shaft telltales. The rpm had dropped to zero. "Both engines stopped, Captain." The indicators dipped into the red. "She's going astern now."

The master grunted. Through his binoculars it seemed that he could reach out and rap on the door of the *Wayside Cheer Tavern* although it was still about a couple of miles away. The bows went to port to miss another rock before continuing on its previous course.

"Both engines are now going full astern Captain," announced the second mate.

"We're fucking still moving ahead," muttered Fawcett. "God, I hope we can stop before . . ."

"Jamie baby!"

Gerry recalls:

Off on the starboard quarter I could clearly see that we were rapidly approaching the body of rocks that separate Saline Bay from Cobo Bay. It is nearly a mile long. Seaweed and shellfish clinging below the tide line told me that the flood was about to begin. I realized that within the next few minutes the ship would come to rest in the sand - or rocks.

The blasts from the ship's foghorns were deafening. House lights on shore were flickering on, as residents were jarred from their beds. Whitewashed cottages were ghostly shapes emerging from the loom of land.

"It's time," said Vair.

"Gerry, open up that bag please." Angus asked.

The rating stooped and unbuckled the straps.

"Take out the golden ball that looks like the moon."

Gerry complied and stood up. He held the sphere out and stared into King's eyes in askance.

With a lackadaisical gesture Vair commanded, "Chuck it over the side." Over it went and plopped into the lazy surf. "Now the other one."

Again Gerry crouched down and withdrew the other orb. As soon as he picked it up it separated so that a golden cup rested in each hand.

Vair spoke. "Gerry, when the time is right you will retrieve both spheres and bring them to Mister King. Until then, you will forget what has happened to them."

"Ah dinnae want them," protested Angus.

"You have no option," replied Vair. "All that has occurred will be forgotten by you and all the other humans concerned. Now place the two halves together and drop the ball over the side of the ship."

The golden orb plunged into the bay with hardly a splash.

In horror Fawcett craned his head back in time to see a scantily-dressed buxom blonde flounce across his wheelhouse towards him. The second mate's eyes all but popped out of their sockets as did the pair of bridge boys. Malky had been at sea for nigh on thirty years and there wasn't much he hadn't witnessed. He just rubbed his grizzled chin and grinned, his brown eyes savouring a picture that somehow buoyed a pivotal circumstance. It was titillating to observe that this delightful intrusion wore a singular garment - a pyjama top which matched the skipper's bottoms.

"Susie, you shouldn't be here!" Hurriedly the captain stepped aft to usher this creature from his bridge. She in turn thought his open arms were an inducement for an embrace and leapt toward him accordingly.

The ship struck.

Down in the tiller flat Les disengaged the manual steering link. As he restarted the servo motors he could hear somebody clattering down the steep circular ladder that led from the Pig and Whistle. Back at his bench and was mildly irritated to find that his coffee was now tepid. He tossed it the bilge and reached for the percolator. A seaman materialized at the bottom of the ladder with hands on his knees and gasping like a calliope.

"What's up?" Les innocently asked, picking up an empty mug. "Want some coffee?"

The unexpected momentum doubled the blonde's weight and over went the bus driver with his giggling ladylove on top, his long legs askew on the deck.

"Shit!" grinned Briers. "She's not wearing knickers!"

Still tittering Susie rolled off her four-barred paramour onto the deck, her straddled legs allowing all personnel to see the promised land. The skipper sprang immediately to his feet and peered out. The ship was well and truly stuck on the shore of Saline Bay.

In utter frailty he whispered: "Stop engines!"

Up on Prom Deck old Judge Ordowich was supervising his Life Boys as they ran around picking early bird passengers off the deck and helping them into deck chairs. Some of his lads were administering first aid to the injured.

Gerry recalls:

I must have blacked out because the next thing I can remember was me laying on the deck with Mister King bending over me. He helped me to my feet.

"What happened?" I asked.

"We've run up oan tae the beach," he said.

But of course we hadn't because there was almost a mile stretch of water between us and the white sands loved by holidaymakers during the summer months. Just as well it wasn't summer I thought. For then it would've been broad daylight and throngs of spectators would've been laughing and cheering at our misfortune. As it was, the *Guernsey Press* hadn't such a field day since the islanders got hammered on seven thousand casks of Algerian wine back in 1937 when the French ship *Briseis* became beached.

Anyway the racket had stopped and a faint breeze whispering from the shore conveyed a whiff of land. It is the same odour land folk smell when they near the sea. The following tide floated us off and the hull proved to be sound for there weren't any leaks. But the skipper wasn't taking his ship anywhere. Threading his command backwards through those insidious outcrops of granite was too hazardous.

A couple of Southampton tugs showed up next day but they were leery about manoeuvring in those waters too. In the end a Royal Navy demolition team opened up a safe channel using plastic explosive.

CHAPTER NINETEEN

Guernsey, Channel Islands

Sunday, January 21st, 2022

Gerry put his hand up to his right ear. "They're coming in."

Angus continued to gaze blankly ahead of him while the other three turned and looked expectantly out to sea. On the horizon a four-funnelled cruise ship was sailing due south. Jake sadly shook his head.

"Yeah, the old days of steam are long gone," he commented.

"Diesel too," added the ex-chief. "I never thought I'd see the day when I'd see smokeless stacks."

"But they're not really funnels, are they Chief?" said Gerry.

"No, they're wind rotors," replied Jake. "They spin like hell in the wind and churn out electricity. They're probably made of that new stuff as well. Y'know, the alloy that has made selenium practically obsolete? Their blades capture sunlight and convert it into electrical energy also."

"And yet," Jessica interjected softly. "There is something romantic about them too. I can remember seeing pictures of four funnelled ships in history books. Probably the Titanic is the most famous."

"Maybe you're right Jessica," agreed Jake. "The old Cunarders such as the *Aquitania*, *Mauritania* or even the *Lusitania*, were beautiful vessels even though they were coal burners."

"That's right Chief," concurred Gerry. "I've noticed barge carriers and container ships using that same material for sails, rigged like those on the old Chinese junks. So it seems to me that the romance of sail is making a comeback too. Ghost ships really for instead of a crew a computer operates the sails electrically. Yeah," he sighed. "I suppose it's all for the better. I mean, since pollution has been reduced drastically over the past couple of years, most people seem to be happier and healthier."

"Except maybe the Arabs," riposted Jake, slyly.

Gerry grinned and waved his copy of the *Guernsey Press*. "According to the commodities column in this broadsheet you can trade a barrel of sweet crude for a litre of spring water."

"Well, them oil companies have been screwing us for years. It's about time the shoe was on the other foot."

A whispering purr hauled his eyes skyward. An airship had just unmoored from its mast at St. Sampson and was heading due west. Most of its skin surfaces were coated with solar cells that supplied electrical power to the aircraft's six props.

Gerry read off the name of the carrier: Tranquil Moments International Travel."Y'know, that company is part of this story."

"In what way?" asked Jake.

"Well, about six months after we'd run aground there was a case in the paper about one of our female passengers being investigated for insurance fraud. I can't remember all the facts but - wait a minute." He picked up his newspaper and pulled up its archive section. Slowly and methodically his bony finger caressed the smooth screen. "Ah, here we are," he said at last.

"Denise Sneddon was initially charged with hiring a crook called Mo Greene to bump off her husband. Greene and - he referred to the article - Bernard Sneddon disappeared off the arse end on the night before we hit the island." His rheumy eyes gazed toward the receding airship. "Yeah, it's all beginning to come back now. When I relieved . . . What's his name? It's the same name as the Scotch whisky with the black and white terriers on the label . . ."

"Buchanan?" Jessica supplemented, recalling her sojourn as bartender.

"Yeah, that's it. Eddie Buchanan! How about that? Now there's a name from the past," Gerry was pleased with himself. "Anyhow, Eddie witnessed the tail end of the fight. Greene had the passenger right over the ship's rail but Sneddon hung on to him like a leech and dragged the other guy with him. Right down into the wake, they went. Eddie came rushing back to the a/c office and told the engineer - *his* name escapes me though. He telephoned the bridge and the ship came about. She steamed right up her track but both those guys were goners."

He tapped the newspaper. "According to this, Sneddon had been insured for a hundred and twenty-five grand and when double indemnity kicked in, the insurance company went to the cops. They discovered that Bernie Sneddon's business was on the verge of going tits up. Oops! Sorry Missus K.

"Further investigation showed that he'd used his credit card to buy a ticket for that cruise but his missus had already bought him one at a discount because she had been a manager at the Tranquil Moments Travel Agency. So the cops put two and two together and figured out that Greene had been hired by the husband to kill his wife because her insurance policy carried double indemnity on the event of her 'accidental' death too. I don't suppose anyone will ever find out why they killed each other."

Gerry took another slug of beer. "So the long and short of it is, Denise Sneddon used the insurance money to buy out the two brothers who owned the travel agency. I bet they're kicking themselves now though. That's if they're still alive. She turned that company right around and jumped right in with the airships when the oil crisis peaked."

"She must be worth millions now," surmised White.

"Yeah, all of that and then some," agreed Gerry, stroking the grey stubble on his chin. "She must be in her mid-seventies now." His old face broke into a lecherous grin. "I wouldn't mind snapping up a young thing like that!"

"Once a sailor - always a sailor," smiled Jessica.

By this time Eric had beached his craft. The young man picked up a hefty net bag and made his way towards the tavern. Gerry watched his grandson with pride as he stepped purposefully through the sand. "As soon as Eric gets here we'll nip over to the hotel lounge where it's cooler. He'll be feeling kind of hungry after all that exercise."

Gerry was absolutely correct. The lounge was cool. Freshwater continually circulated through pipes from the bottom of Saline Bay to the hotel's a/c system kept the whole establishment and annexed buildings at an ambient 23° Centigrade. The room hadn't changed much since the old *Dally* had beached all those years ago. A dozen or so patrons were scattered about the quiet room.

Its theme was still Ye Olde English décor: blackened beams on whitewashed walls and ceiling. The tables and chairs were ornately carved and varnished with dark lacquer. Other furniture consisted of padded benches beneath the windows while steel legged stools fortified the bar. The solid oak bar counter was edged with green vinyl armrests, and of course, it had a brass foot rail. Behind the array of liquor and wine bottles was a large mirror which was typical of any bar that Gerry had imbibed in over the past sixty-odd years.

Jake assisted Jessica to roll Angus across the black and red wall-to-wall carpet. A waiter gestured toward an empty table and stood by to take their orders. Their drinks arrived just as Eric entered the room.

"Would you like your usual, lad?" Gerry asked.

The heavy bag hit the table's centre with a thud. "No thanks Papa Gerry, I've got a date over at Torteval. I don't want to get stopped for drink driving."

"Sensible lad. How's about a snack?" Gerry caught the waiter's eye.

Eric pulled a chair from another table and sat down opposite Angus. "I'll have a Mowbray pie, a couple of pickled eggs and a glass of Irn Bru."

Gerry reached for the satchel and opened it. He reached in and took out a sphere which was about the same diameter as a cricket ball. Its surface was cobalt-blue and not a trace of marine life clung to it. The old man hefted the ball before placing it on a pad of paper napkins to prevent it from rolling across the polished varnished tabletop. He extracted a second sphere and set it down beside its mate.

"Now what?" he breathed to himself.

"So then, how did you know the spheres were in Saline Bay, Papa Gerry?" asked Eric as he munched enthusiastically on a pickled egg.

"I don't know," admitted Gerry. He picked his pint pot and stared into the foam as if seeking an answer. "I should know but I don't. Something happened on the day that we ran up on the beach. I can remember the ship swerving and barrelling toward this hotel. I can even remember us juddering to a sudden halt but for about five or ten minutes in between, my mind is a complete blank."

Curiously Jake leaned forward and touched one of the mysterious spheres. "So why did pick this particular day to activate the search?"

"I don't bloody well know that either!" retorted Gerry. "Sorry Chief! All I know is that all last week I started to get restless in my sleep. The same dream was repeating itself time and again for the next four days but it was gone each time I woke up. The only thing I was sure of was that Saline Bay was vaguely somewhere in it. So I figured that it must have had something to do with the old *Dally*."

He watched his grandson brush away the last few crumbs of pork pie from his lips. "At sunup this morning I asked Eric to dive for me. I don't know how or what he was seeking but I could point out the search area with accuracy. When the lad asked me what he was supposed to be looking for, I just told him that he'd know when he found them."

Gerry stared at the spheres and shook his head. "I think that they're made of gold and don't ask me how I know."

Jessica and Jake looked at each other in askance. What now? They wondered. Eric pushed his plate away and got up. He reached into a pocket and withdrew his wallet.

"I'll get that Eric," said Gerry. "We'll square up later."

His grandson shrugged and with a slight wave of his hand left the lounge. The three of them eyed the spheres. Angus stared off into space. The waiter arrived with two more pints and a dry martini. Outside there was a disturbance and a dog started barking. The trio turned to witness the disturbance.

Silently a sphere opened, its halves lay agape on the paper napkins. Angus blinked and reached for Jake's beer.

"No alcohol!"

The hollow command issued from King's lips like steam ejecting from a ship's whistle. Six pairs of eyes incredulously fell upon the paraplegic.

"Ah havenae had a beer since Ah fell doon yon cliff!" protested Angus.

"No alcohol!" repeated the deep firm voice. "It's poisonous to us."

"There he goes again!" exclaimed Gerry. "It's happening again just like happened sixty years ago."

Vair flexed his host's limbs. "Quite a bit of repair and rejuvenating is required here." He made Angus grin. "No matter, I'll have you up and running about in one or two of your weeks. Is today's weather typical of this place?"

Jake, being a visitor, shrugged. "I don't know about here but January in Canada's is supposed to be cold. Right now it's a balmy 22° Centigrade."

"Canada?" Vair recalled the name from his library research via Angus six decades ago. "Oh yes, the land of ice and snow in North America."

Jake scoffed.

"Not any more. We haven't had snow for the past five or six years."

Jessica, although puzzled with the change in her husband's voice, was overjoyed at the miracle of his sudden recovery. She placed her arms around Angus and hugged him. Her kiss triggered a similar response. The other sphere opened silently.

"Vair, it's been so long!" The tone was throaty, sensual and filled with passion.

"Too long!" groaned Vair.

Jake and Gerry sat open mouthed watching the couple smooching and groping at one another.

"Holy shit, Chief!" exclaimed Gerry. "They're going to have their jollies right here in front of us!"

"Yeah," gloated Jake. "Reminds of the days when we'd go to a sex show in Piraeus or one of them other foreign ports. This one's a freebie though."

Presently Angus disengaged and gently pushed his wife back. Filled with misgiving Vair's deep voice said, "We'll have to wait a little while longer Sheia until I get this body back into perfect health. We don't want to ruin it beyond repair." He tenderly touched her left breast. "Angus did well to choose your host body but then he was preprogrammed by me to do so."

"An' we thocht it was love at first sight."

"It was as far as I'm concerned," smiled Jessica and stooped to kiss his brow. Her voice changed abruptly as a frustrated Sheia commanded that Angus should rest.

"Gerry, would you wheel Angus out to the front door while I get the car?"

"Certainly Missus King," said Gerry. Finishing his pint he painfully got to his feet."

Jake arose too. "I'll give you a hand."

"Here - what about those spheres?"

"They belong to you now, Gerry," said Vair.

By the time they'd reached the front vestibule Jessica had her hatchback reversed and up against the front steps. The car was fueled by hydrogen and fabricated from Sunstel, an alloy that captured light rays and converted them directly into electricity. Distilled water was the electrolyte that released the hydrogen ions from the oxygen ions which in turn were compressed into separate tanks until ready to be introduced to the gas turbine engine. Pressing a button caused the hatched back of the car to flip down whereupon it became a hydraulic lift. Angus was wheeled onto the ramp and was soon safely embarked in the vehicle.

Jake kissed Jessica on the right cheek.

"I've made a reservation for dinner on Wednesday evening at the Old Government House Hotel. I'd like you and Angus to come - you too, Gerry." He scratched his beard. "I don't understand it though but I'm sure glad that my old shipmate seems to be on the mend. We'll enjoy talking about old times."

With a cheery wave Jessica sped away. They didn't have far to go. The pair lived in a two-bedroom bungalow on Route de La Passee just off Portinfer Road on a property about eight metres wide by forty metres long. A stone wall surrounded the perimeter. A profusion of small bedding plants grew along the dyke's top, a typical Sarnian arrangement. Here Portulaca vied with Tagete, Mesembryanthemum and Pinks.

Once the tiny front garden was a pristine lawn perfectly groomed by Angus but water shortage saw the end of that. Instead a host of perennials such as Heuchera, Achillea and Foxglove did well under dry conditions. Xeranthemum, Aster and Celosia re-seeded year after year. It was just as well, since Angus was no longer able potter around in the garden any more. Jessica was lost as far as horticulture was concerned.

She parked the car and wheeled her husband through scrolled wrought-iron gate, along the flagstone path to the front door of their abode. Angus shakily got to his feet, opened the door and would've fell flat on his face had she not caught him.

"Take it easy," chided Vair. "I told you it'll take a week or two of recuperation before you're fit."

Jessica helped him back into his wheelchair. "Why does your voice keep changing, Dear?"

"Because some kind o' creature is rattlin' aboot inside my bluidy heid," retorted a cantankerous Angus. "He began hauntin' me back in 1962 while Ah was oan my second trip tae sea. Ah'd forgotten a' aboot it." He calmed down right after his tirade. "Sorry hen, it isnae *your* fault."

In the small living room she eased him into his favourite chair. A thought struck him. "Dae ye no' feel a wee bit strange tae?"

"What do you mean?"

"Weel, your voice changed tae back in the pub."

"Did it?"

"Aye, it did."

"Angus," Vair mentally began. "Sheia and I will be leaving you for a little while. We're going to seek out our fellows in other parts of the world."

"Aye fine," said Angus aloud. "Take a' the time ye need. A hundred years would suit us just dandy."

"What?" asked Jessica.

Sensing that Vair had left and presumably Sheia too, Angus recounted the story that had been locked in his subconscious for the past sixty years. When he had finished, Jessica reflected on their life together. He spent all his leaves in Hamilton to be with her.

One week before the anniversary of their first date he'd proposed. After a shipmate had mentioned to him about the *Wayside Cheer Hotel* on the Island of Guernsey, they had decided to spend their honeymoon there.

When their holiday was over Angus was invited to Pict House and offered the Chief Engineer's position on their flagship, *Queen Mhairi*. Upon acceptance, he pulled a few strings and managed to get Jessica a bartender's job in one of the cruise ship's many saloons and lounges. When mandatory retirement came a couple of years later, they decided to visit Guernsey again with the intention of living there permanently.

By good fortune Angus noticed Gerry working on a motor launch that was taking them to the island of Alderney. Renouf had retired some years earlier but still worked a couple of times a week on the launches that took visitors to Herm and Sark as well as Alderney.

Later on that day they sojourned in Gerry's local, *Harbour Lights*, located on the South Esplanade in St. Peter Port. They reminisced the old days when they served together on various ships. Jessica showed delight at some of their funnier escapes.

"How long will you be staying on the island, Mister King," Gerry had asked.

Angus glanced at his wife before answering. "Weel Gerry," he began. "We've thinkin' o' buyin' a wee but an' ben here. Jessica and me just love the peace an' solitude o' this island."

Gerry sadly shook his head. "Only people born on the island can buy property here, Mister King." His eyes brightened. "But I know where you can lease a nice little cottage for a reasonable price."

And so they had settled for that little piece of paradise.

It was getting dark for the winter night was closing in fast.

"What would you like for supper, Angus?"

"Just some soup, hen," replied Angus. "At least Ah'll be able tae feed mysel' efter a' these months. Ah dinnae ken how Ah would've managed if it wasnae for ye."

"That's all right, Dear . . . Listen, I've got a couple of minute steaks in the fridge. Would you like me to cook them up for you?"

"No thanks," replied her husband. "Ah dinnae think that Ah'm able tae handle a fork an' knife yet. Ah ken that ye could cut it up for me but Ah want tae feed mysel' for a change." A grin of satisfaction lit up his face then he frowned. "Besides, yon Vair is just liable tae come back just as soon as your steaks were steamin' oan the plates and then he'll want me tae chew the cud oan lettuce an' the like."

"My dear Angus, surely that's a small price to pay for getting your health back?"

"Aye maybe," Angus admitted grudging. "But Ah like my meat an' my beer."

His spouse eyed her watch. "Do you think they'll come back?"

"Oh aye, sure as the sun rises the morn." He contemplated for a moment. "They could be back right noo for a' we ken. Ye see - ye dinnae ken for sure until ye find yoursel' daein' somethin' that ye dinnae want tae dae."

The meal passed uneventfully and afterwards they sat out on the back verandah to savour the warm evening and its gentle starlight dancing on the ocean waves. Shortly after ten they went to bed.

She was striding through savannah-like grasslands. The thick ochre stalks reared about a metre above her head. A giant shadow gliding over caused her to squat and cringe. She looked up at the fierce flying reptile. The creature was a pterosaur, not that she'd ever heard of the name. It flew on to dive down on some hapless creature.

She waited until the sounds of death subsided and the familiar whines, buzzes and clicks of arm-length insects heralded all was safe. She felt peckish. Those large wheat-like ears would fill the bill. Seizing a stem, she bent towards her and doing so noticed that her arm was covered with tawny hair. Her hand was almost jet black with five talons for fingers. Examining the rest of her body, she discovered that it too was covered with similar hair, except for her chest. It was bare not unlike her patent black pumps. Her breasts were full -

palm sized - as Angus was fond of saying and her hard ebon nipples could've been used as doorstops.

Jessica screamed and sat up in bed. Angus cuddled her, mouthing soft cooing sounds and she awoke from her nightmare. "It's a' right hen," he whispered. "They're back. Ah saw ye as Sheia through Vair's eyes."

She could see his wan smile in the gloom. "When it happened tae me sixty years ago Ah nearly shit in my bunk!" He sighed. "Ok Vair whit big plans hae ye got for us?"

"We won't bother you for the rest of the night," was his answer. "Sheia and I have much to discuss."

"Then whit?"

"Then you'll know," Vair replied simply.

Angus relishing his porridge when his wife's mobile rang as they were having breakfast. "It's Jake," she said and listened. "He wants to know if we can make if for dinner tonight in the *Governor's Restaurant*."

"Sure," said Angus.

"Yes, seven thirty is fine Jake," said Jessica. "We'll see you then. Goodbye."

She hung up.

They found Jake and Gerry in deep conversation at St. Anne's Place just outside the Old Government House Hotel. Both men helped their shipmate from the car. A hotel employee rushed down the red carpeted stairs leading from the front door to receive the car keys from Jessica. As he drove away Angus, sans wheelchair, was helped up through the lofty archway to the front door.

Here the Scot disengaged himself from his assistants and ably took his wife's arm to walk unconstrained albeit shakily to the Brasserie. Asked by a servant if they preferred to dine *al fresco*, they were led out to a walled garden where could enjoy a view overlooking St. Peter Port harbour from exquisite surroundings. In previous years this dining area was open only during the summer months. Now, one could breakfast, lunch and dine practically all year round. The servant ticked Jake's name off a reservation list, tucked four menus under his arm and led the way to their table. Only two or three other diners were in the garden. After distributing the menus, he filled their water glasses and left.

Gerry felt quite out of place in this posh French-style restaurant. He donned his specs and studied the array of dishes available. Most of them were written in French which isn't any bother to most Sarnians who were fluent in English and French as well as the Channel Island patois. The prices were daunting to say the least. He removed his glasses and glanced across the table at Angus. Was it his imagination or did his old shipmate look perceptibly younger?

"Who wants to split a shattered brand with me?" asked Jake.

Gerry peered back at the menu to see what the chief was talking about. He donned his spectacles again then took them off. He repeated the procedure once more and discovered that his myopia had subtly been remedied. He observed Mister King smiling knowingly. "Chateaubriand, Mister White?"

"That's what I said Gerry," was the breezy return. "Shattered brand, that's what I'll have, my man," he said as the waiter drew to his side.

"No' for me," replied Angus, reluctantly. "Ah'll just settle for a caesar salad."

"Waldorf for me please," request Jessica.

"I guess that leaves me to share your steak Chief," said Gerry.

The sommelier glided up with his wine list. After studying it for a few minutes Jake ordered a magnum of Billecart-Salmon 2011.

While they waited, a group of men trooped into the floral dining area until most of the tables were filled. While most were attired in expensive suits, some hadn't a clue as to style and fashion. Obviously money played a big part in dressing mutton up as lamb. They came in all shapes and sizes and were stern faced, their cold eyes ever watchful on the outlook for discord. A drone of soft dialogue gradually filled the ambience of the room as the men drifted toward tables in pairs, trios and combos.

"The arms dealers," muttered Gerry. "Their convention is supposed to end tomorrow."

"There is evil in this room," announced Vair.

His powerful voice immediately caught Jake and Gerry's attention. "Oh shit!" swore the latter, knowing full well that trouble was in the offing.

The waiter arrived pushing a trolley that carried the Chateaubriand in all its glory. It positively bathed in a deep silver platter of gravy attended by scrumptious roast potatoes, mushrooms and vegetables. The tender meat was halved, placed on oven warmed plates with accompanying spuds and veg. before being placed reverently in front of Gerry and Jake. Angus salivated then seethed as Jessica's and his salad appeared from the lower shelf of the trolley.

A short time later the dealers in death were munching away to the accompaniment of bargaining for rocket launchers, tanks, missiles and all manner of weapons designed to reduce the world population by violence.

Near their table a sallow fellow with black oily hair and a pencil moustache stood up. He wore a sharkskin jacket and tight jeans. With a smirk on his lean face he dipped a spoon into a bowl of Malosol black caviar and flicked it across two tables to hit a massive baldheaded guy in an Armani suit. Surprised, his small beady eyes peered down at the gooey mess on his lapel and burst into tears.

Burly toughs fell to the floor laughing but couldn't get to their feet again. Instead they crawled toward something stable such as a chair or a table leg to draw their bodies erect. One guy hauled on a table cloth and was rewarded with a cascade of food laded dishes. This happenstance ended in another flood of tears. Some companions were pointing and giggling at the unfortunate. One laughed so hard that a blossom of urine stained the front of his trousers.

One enterprising thug began to pick his nose. After some industrious mining he withdrew his finger to examine the result of his labours upon which he enthusiastically munched with great gusto. Two tables over, one suave chap with a ragged four-inch scar down his left cheek began to bawl for his long-dead mommy.

The disgusting odour of faeces emitting from an obese guy prompted the three shipmates and Jessica to hastily vacate the room. Out on the street Jake sucked in great volumes of warm night air and asked: "What in the hell happened in there?"

"Dunno," replied Gerry.

Angus and Jessica said nothing.

The fresh air made Jake feel a lot better. "Well, at least we had time to enjoy our steak, eh Gerry?"

"Yeah Chief," agreed Renouf. "But I hope that I don't puke it back up though. What are we going to do about the bill?"

"Don't worry about that," replied White. "I'll drop by in the morning and square up with them."

The parking attendant received a generous tip when he brought Jessica's car back to the front of the hotel. They all piled in and she drove them home.

Back in their cottage over a cup of tea Vair and Sheia told their hosts about their findings. "Angus, you'll remember we met Leia in the country you call Brazil?"

Angus' face winced with trepidation. The nightmare from sixty years suddenly flashed through his mind. "Aye, noo that ye mention it," he recalled. "An' Ah mind tae that ye came close tae killin' me because ye nearly didnae get my soul back intae my body in time."

"Yes, that was a close call, wasn't it?" Vair replied offhandedly. "Well anyway, she and Xaan are still there. Gron and Blox are still roving about the Canadian wilderness and Thall and Jal still wander around the mountain range you know as the Himalayas. The thing is, their offspring, male and a female, have a condition similar to the human autism. Since the affliction cannot be remedied, Sheia and I have decided to occupy their bodies."

"Sounds guid tae me," replied Angus. "Ah'll appreciate bein' my ain man again an' Ah'm sure Jessica doesnae need any o' yer hassle either."

"It's not quite as simple as that," smiled Sheia. "From time to time we would still like to enjoy sex and well, you see, because of our unusual situation it would seem to be kind of incestuous, if you get our drift."

"Aye, that's plain enough a' right," admitted Angus. "Ye want tae use oor bodies tae get your nooky." His eyes met Jessica's. "Ah dinnae suppose we've got anither option?"

"I'm afraid not," said Vair.

"Weel, Ah'm no' gettin' any younger," noted King. "How dae Ah ken that ye'll no' get ower anxious an' hae me die o' a heart attack while oan the job?"

"That won't happen," he was assured. "Now that is settled, we can get on with straightening out the problems of this sad world."

"Like eh . . . Whit dae ye hae in mind?" Angus reluctantly enquired except he really didn't wish to know the answer.

"Well, first we have to stop your people killing each other. Next, we have to make sure everyone has the same rights to live. Only then can the human race work together and arrest damage being done to this planet.

"Here," protested Angus. "Ah thocht that ye said that ye liked it warm."

"I do," replied Vair. "But I don't want to live in a desert eight thousand miles in diameter."

Angus pulled a face.

"Aye weel, ye've got that right. When dae ye plan tae start oan a' these miracles?"

"We've already started," said Sheia.

"Oh aye? When?"

"Last night," replied Vair. "Those arms dealers won't be selling any munitions ever again."

"Why did ye dae that?"

"It wasn't entirely me. Sheia helped too." Vair explained: "To all intents and purposes the minds of those villains have been cranked back to childhood. Mentally they are now eighteen-months-old. The passage of time will cause their minds to redevelop properly."

"Some o' these guys were in their sixties an' seventies," guessed Angus. "They'll probably be deid an' buried afore their minds mature. An' whit aboot a' the younger ones? They'll probably be in their fifties an' start sellin' guns an' rockets again."

"No they won't," Vair assured him. "They've all been programmed to abhor violence and any merchandise that causes savagery and destruction."

Sheia chimed in. "Our confederates will split up. Each will police a section of the continents."

"That's a gey big job," mused Angus. "If no' impossible," he added. "Ah mean, ye'll hae tae infiltrate everybody's heid tae see if they're dangerous or no'. There's aboot nine billion folk oan this planet, ye ken."

"It's simpler than you think Angus," replied Vair. "Take those arms dealers, for instance. Sheia and I now know their contacts; who they purchased the weapons from and whom they sold them to. In one direction we'll get to the manufacturers and in the other we'll get the warmongers, drug dealers, extremists, fanatics, murderers and all the other sordid human sewage."

"Are ye gaun tae bump them a' aff?"

"I told you that we do not kill Angus. All of those people will become adult toddlers. After that we'll examine the various midguided religious groups that stifle free thinking, abuse their offspring, make their women to be subservient, and cause misery and unhappiness among their parishioners."

"Ye ken somethin'?" uttered Angus. "Ye dinnae want tae throw the bairn oot wi' the bathwater. A lot o' folk get their faith frae religion."

"Faith?" echoed Vair. "Faith comes from deep within - not from praying to graven images and obscure deities. That is just wishful thinking. If people had faith and trust in themselves and each other, we wouldn't have this onerous burden of returning this world to the pristine condition it once was before you humans arrived.

"Weel, ye've got one hellova task in front o' ye," speculated Angus. "Ah wish ye a' the best. Ah only hope Ah live tae see it. So eh, when are ye leavin'?"

"Oh, you and Jessica will live to see a better world all right," Vair guaranteed him. "And we're leaving now. Goodbye."

"Goodbye," said Sheia.

CHAPTER TWENTY

Gerry

Friday, July 24th, 2022

God, it's hot! It's 42° Centigrade in the shade, according to my *Guernsey Press*. The breeze coming in from the harbour helps though. I stopped here at the *Ship and Crown* on the North Esplanade for a quick pint and a Scotch egg to tide me over until suppertime. The pub is starting to get busy though so I won't hang around for too much longer.

I bumped into Mister and Missus King just the other day. They were window shopping in High Street. Boy, have they ever changed since that day we recovered those spheres. The years have fallen away from them. So much so that man and wife appear to be in their mid-twenties. During our chat Mister King revealed that he was going to become a father. His wife blushed and admitted that she was three months pregnant. I still have trouble trying to grasp that he is an octogenarian just like me. It's just as well all banking is done electronically these days. I wonder what they'd say if he went into the OAP office to pick up his pension cheque. He had the nerve to mention that he felt fit enough to go back to sea but Missus K. put the kibosh on that idea.

Mind you I feel a spring in my step myself these days. None of the arthritic aches and pains that bothered me for the last dozen or so years have returned. My cancer has completely disappeared. Not in remission - gone! My doctor can't explain it. Neither can I, but one doesn't look a gift horse in the mouth.

I keep getting this strange feeling that Mister King had something to with those gun runners going ga-ga that night in the Brasserie at the Old Government House Hotel but I can't put my finger on it. Pediatricians, shrinks, and other brain experts still haven't figured out the cause which has been dubbed the Sarnian Syndrome. Cases have been springing up all over the world. Curiously it only happens to certain people.

Case in point happened in just the other week. When the communist government in China collapsed some time back we figured the world could have a bit of peace for a while. No such luck. They started flexing their muscles again not only on the Russian border but towards Taiwan, Korea and Japan. The Yanks, the Brits and the French, in fact the whole of NATO were talking about settling there hash once and for all. Y'see over the past few years the hawks in their respective governments have gradually outnumbered the doves.

But a strange thing happened to all the hawks and the military chiefs-of-staff. The whole bunch of them was hit by the Sarnian Syndrome. It's said that politicians act like a bunch of kids when debating. Well, last Friday it really took effect the world over. Senators, lords, house representatives, MP's and other legistrators were all running around crapping their drawers, puking, salivating down their shirts, picking their noses, bawling for their mothers and other childish mannerisms right on global TV. Maybe with the top brass out of commission all the soldiers can come home to their wives and families.

And that's just scratching the surface regarding unusual events. Violent crime statistics have dropped dramatically. In the last three months handguns have become a rarity since their prices have quadrupled and ammunition for them is almost non existent. Law enforcement officers have noticed that heroin and cocaine pipelines are drying up. Chemists known to be employed by the Russian and Sicilian mafias have somehow been inflicted with a similar version of Toddlers' Trisomy. Grown men have been found babbling while wandering helplessly in the various jungles of the world. Some have been recognised as important members of the most active drug cartels before this condition wreaked havoc on their ruthless minds. Boffins are completely baffled since nothing has ever shown up in the ultra MRI's or any other modern diagnostic apparatus.

This place is getting too busy for my liking. I believe that there is a bus due to take me to my home in Vale.

There's nothing like a couple of fried kippers and buttered bread followed by a cup of tea. Murder on the old cholesterol, of course, but who cares at my age? I fend for myself now that my missus has been gone these past fifteen years. But it's not so bad. I have a pair of daughters who take turns to drop by at least once a week. They clean my little place, make my bed, do my laundry and other small comforts that need done in my dotage. They nag me too at times but I know that's just because they worry about me.

It looks nice out tonight. I think I'll take a stroll out to the old German observation post at Grandes Rocques for a bit of exercise. It was built during the Second World War, y'know - just like about a hundred others when the Wehrmacht invaded the island. The concrete emplacement is about a kilometre beyond my local.

I think that one of the most beautiful sights in Guernsey is watching the sun set into the Atlantic Ocean. Dusk is quite lengthy in these latitudes and tonight the air temperature is very comfortable after that stinking hot day. Long rolling swells, their crests tinted with blood and gold, seem to go on forever. Over there a seabird, a gannet probably, rides on a zephyr's coattails.

A hint of cigarette smoke assails my nostrils. It's about time that filthy habit was wiped from the face of the earth. I quit about thirty-five years ago and never missed it. Maybe that blight hitting the gun runners and druggies will hit the tobacco manufacturers. I wonder what's happening now in this big wide world of ours?

Y'know, this newspaper is really something else. I keep it all rolled up in the back pocket of my jeans. When I want to read it, it just smooths itself out like magic and there's not a wrinkle on it anywhere. I can read it plainly right now and it's almost dark. I never cease to be amazed with this kind of technology. Less than thirty years ago I'd have to go looking for a lamp post or some other source of light just to read my paper.

I suppose I'm addicted to world affairs. Hardly a minute goes by when something astounding is taking place on the other side of the globe. All them satellites speeding around up there I guess. Look at this for instance: The Sarnian Syndrome has struck again. At the annual NRA meeting in Denver, Colorado - why does the Media alway use acronyms? - Oh, here it's here. The National Rifle Association. Let's start again: At the annual NRA meeting in Denver, Colorado, the executive as well as the current president became victims of the Sarnian Syndrome. The lengthy article is filled with verbiage that say nobody has a clue of what going on. Why they keep referring to the Legionnaires' disease from over forty years ago is beyond me.

Here's another snippet: The same affliction has struck a camp of religious fanatics in the Lybian Desert. And yet another: In San Quentin, California, about sixty five percent of the convicts are reported to have this malady. This truly is amazing when one considers that this disease could strike inside a high security prison. Well, that's enough for one night. I'm going home for some kip.

Wait a minute, what's this here? Rome, Italy: Tomorrow, cardinals from all over the world will enter the Sistine Chapel to elect a new pope after the recent death of Pope Felix V . . .

Pict Line

Pict Line

www.ingramcontent.com/pod-product-compliance
Lightning Source LLC
Chambersburg PA
CBHW030819310726
48980CB00006B/551/J
9780981344706